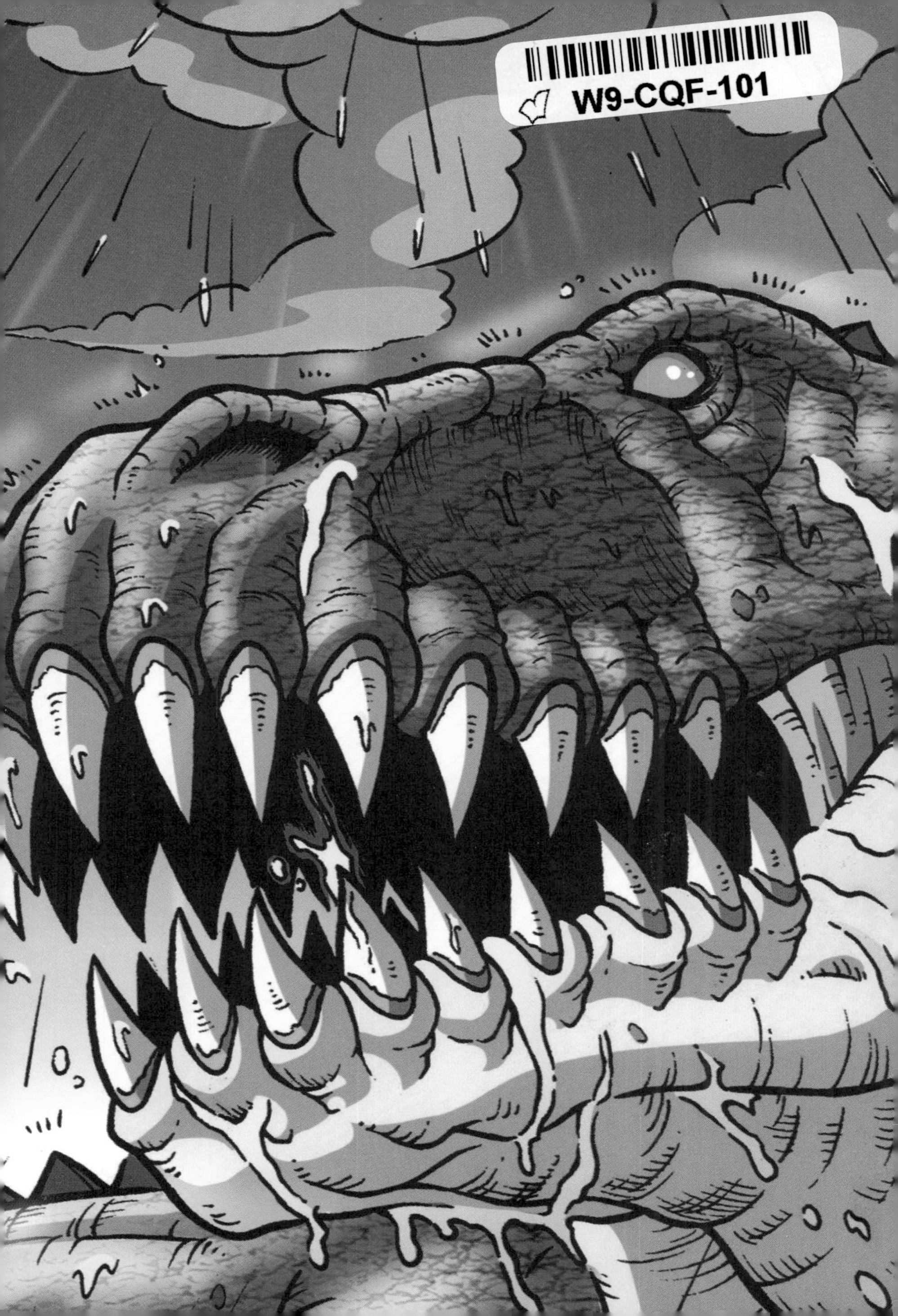

# #7 CRETACEOUS CRAZINESS

PAPERCUT*Z*

# DINOSAUR EXPLORERS

## #7 CRETACEOUS CRAZINESS


Original Chinese edition published in Malaysia in 2013 by
KADOKAWA GEMPAK STARZ SDN. BHD., Malaysia.
English translation rights in United States arranged with KADOKAWA GEMPAK STARZ SDN. BHD., Malaysia
www.gempakstarz.com



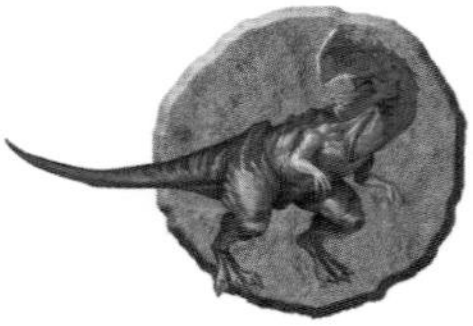

**SLAIUM & ALBBIE** — Story
**AIR TEAM** — Art
**REDCODE & SAMU** — Cover Illustration
**MAX** — Cover Color
**EVA, MAX, FUNFUN** — Interior Color
**KENNY CHUA & KIAONG** — Art Direction
**ROUSANG** — Original Design
**BALICAT & MVCTAR AVRELIVS** — Translation
**MARK McNABB** — Editor & Production
**ROSS BAUER** — Original Editor
**JEFF WHITMAN** — Managing Editor
**JIM SALICRUP**
Editor-in-Chief

Papercutz books may be purchased for business or promotional use.
For information on bulk purchase please contact Macmillan
Corporate and Premium Sales Department at (800) 221-7945 x5442

ISBN HC: 978-1-5458-0547-3
ISBN PB: 978-1-5458-0548-0

Printed in Malaysia by Ultimate Print Sdn Bhd.
September 2020

Distributed by Macmillan
First Papercutz Printing

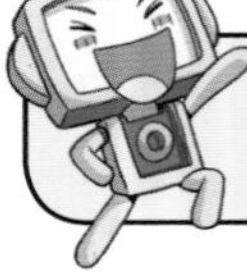

DINOSAUR EXPLORERS Reading Guide
And Lesson Planner available at:
http://papercutz.com/educator-resources-papercutz

# DINOSAUR EXPLORERS

## #7 CRETACEOUS CRAZINESS


**SLAIUM**
**& ALBBIE**
Writers

**AIR TEAM**
Art


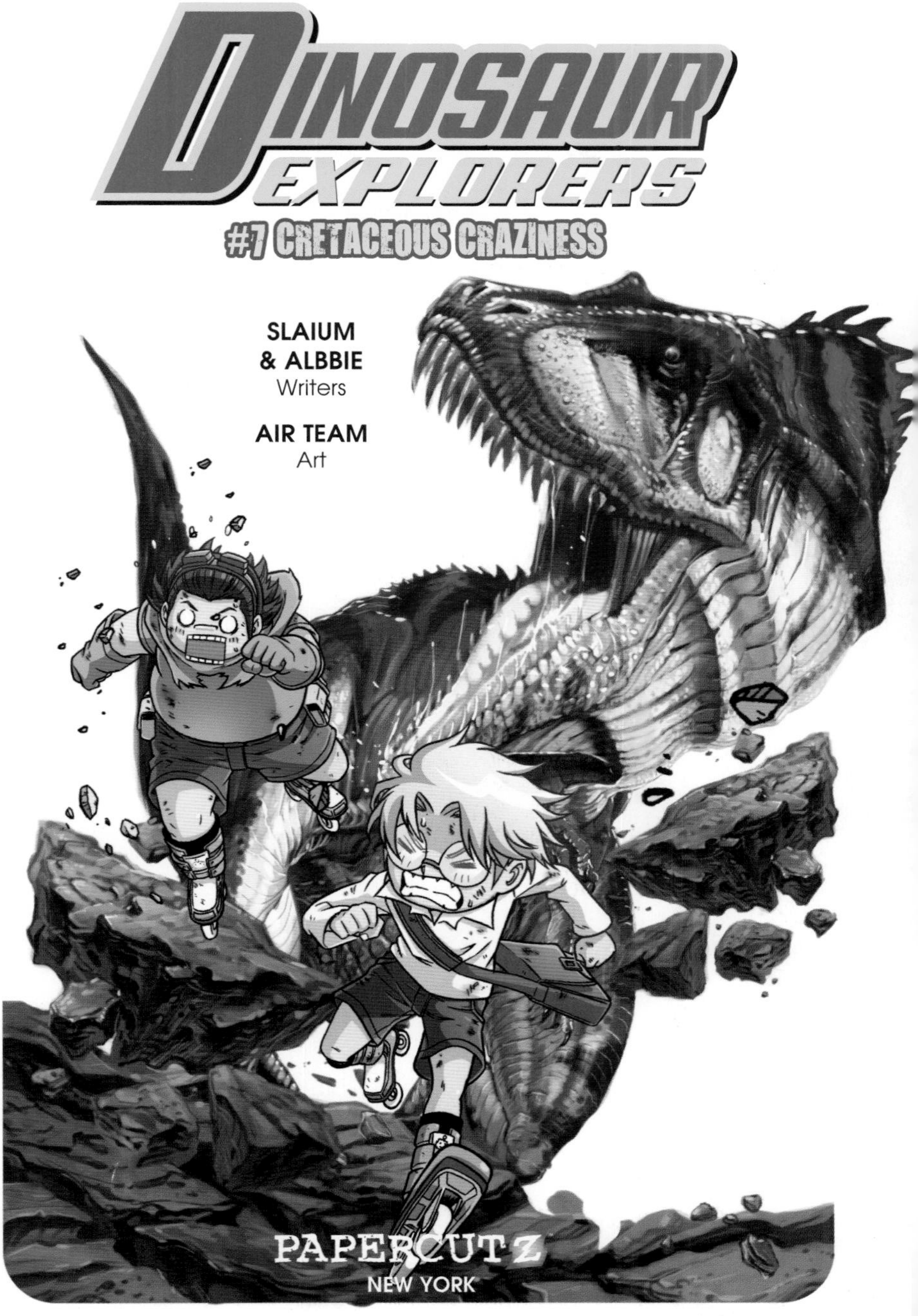


PAPERCUTZ
NEW YORK

# FOREWORD

Our planet is more than 4.5 billion years old, but we have only been around for 2 million! What strange creatures inhabited the Earth before we did?

While the DINOSAUR EXPLORERS series does refer to dinosaurs, the first two books in this series focused on where they came from—and the creatures even dinosaurs would call prehistoric! This series contains as much fun as scientific information and you will see how our planet was transformed from a dry, barren ball of space rock into the haven it is today. See how the Earth's surface and seas formed, how single-celled microorganisms became complex multi-celled creatures, how bones evolved, and how we are not descended from monkeys, but fish!

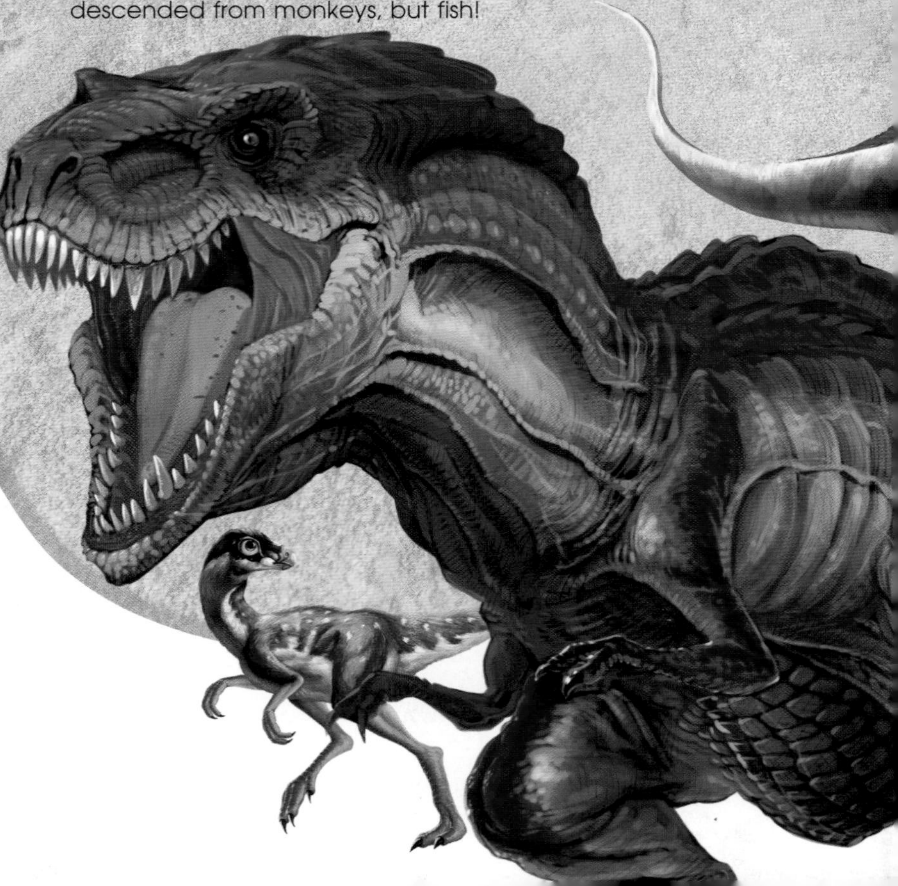

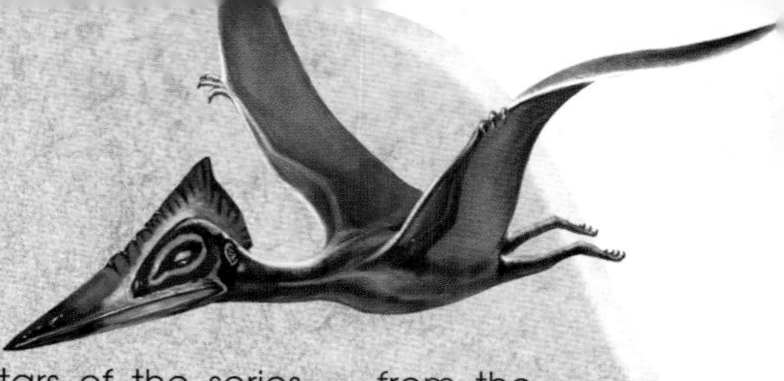

Oh, yes, dinosaurs are the stars of the series — from the magnificent pterosaurs, to the terrifying Tyrannosaurus rex, to the seafaring Icthhyosaurs; all mighty beasts of fact and legend.

Of course, we've taken artistiic license to also mix in fictional human characters to guide us through the centuries, and in this volume our heroes come face-to-face with "Cretaceou Craziness."

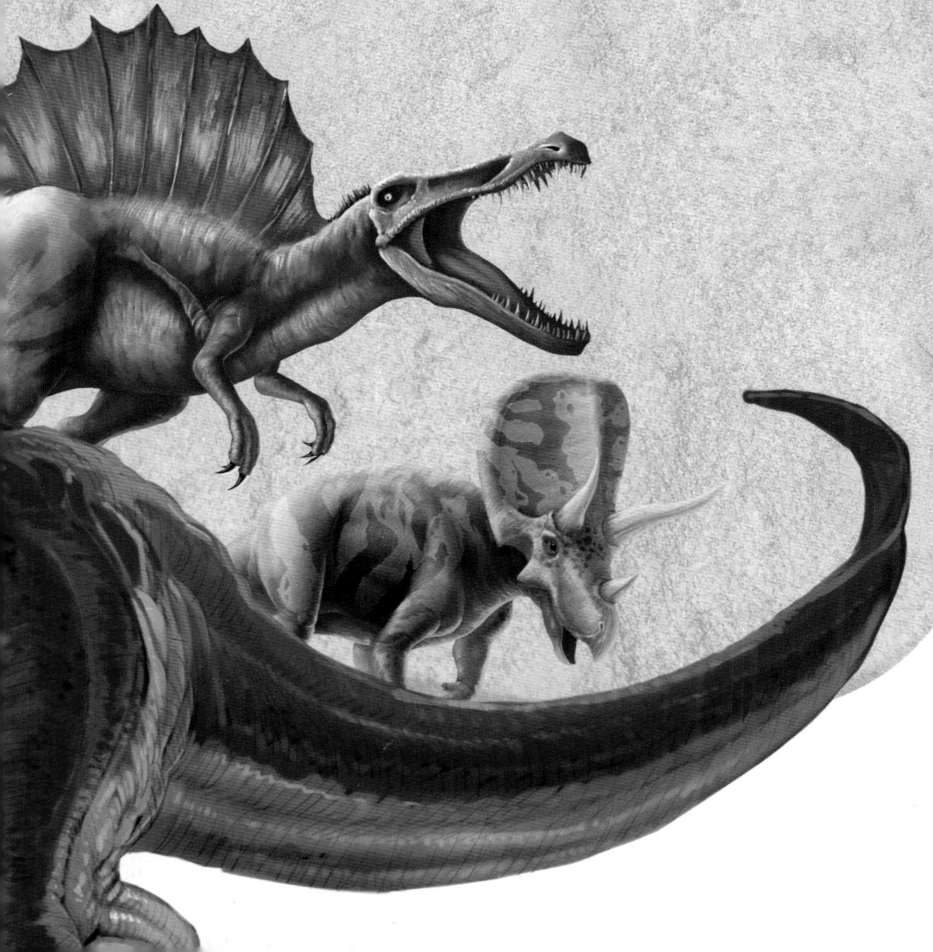

# HOW THE EARTH WAS FORMED

We know the Earth is the third planet in the solar system, the densest planet, and so far, the only one capable of supporting life (although new evidence is emerging that Mars may also be able to support various forms of life). But how did that happen?

## 2 Formation of the Earth

As the Earth formed, its gravity grew stronger. Heavier molecules and atoms fell inward to the Earth's core, while lighter elements formed around it. The massive pressures from the external material heated up the Earth's interior to the point where it was all liquid (except for the core, which was under so much pressure it could not liquify). These settled down into the Earth's 3 layers: the crust, mantle, and core.

While we cannot say for sure just when these dust clouds solidified to form the Earth, nor when they came into being in the first place, we can tell that it took place more than 4.5 billion years ago.

### The Sun's formation

Way, way back, there was a patch of space filled with cosmic dust and gases. Slowly, gravity (and a few nearby exploding stars) forced some of this dust and gases together into clumps—the gases formed into a massive, pressurized ball of heat which became the Sun, while the dust settled into planets, the Earth being one of them.

## 6 The Earth today

Even now, our Earth changes with time; its tectonic plates still move about on the lava bed of the mantle, pushing and pulling continents in all directions.

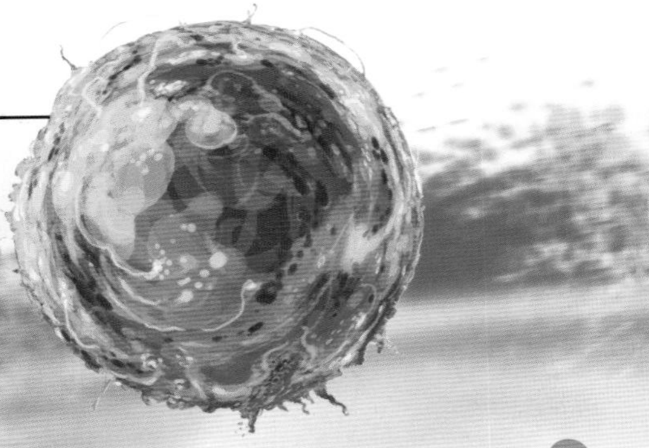

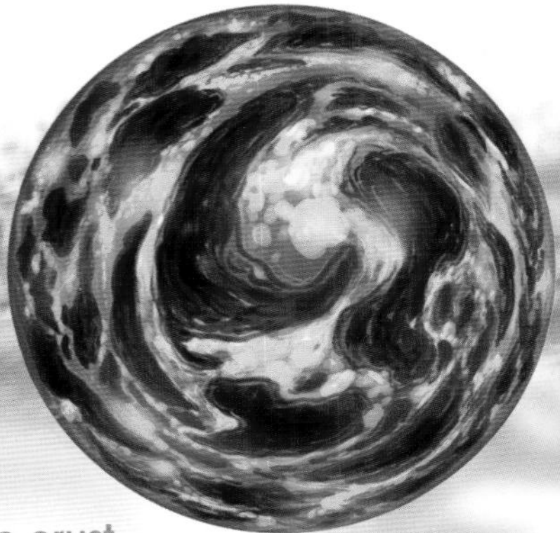

## 3 The crust

The crust was created around 4 billion years ago, as cooled, solid rock floating on the molten lithosphere merged. Even today, as the continental plates shift away from and against each other, some of this rock and molten material might still change place.

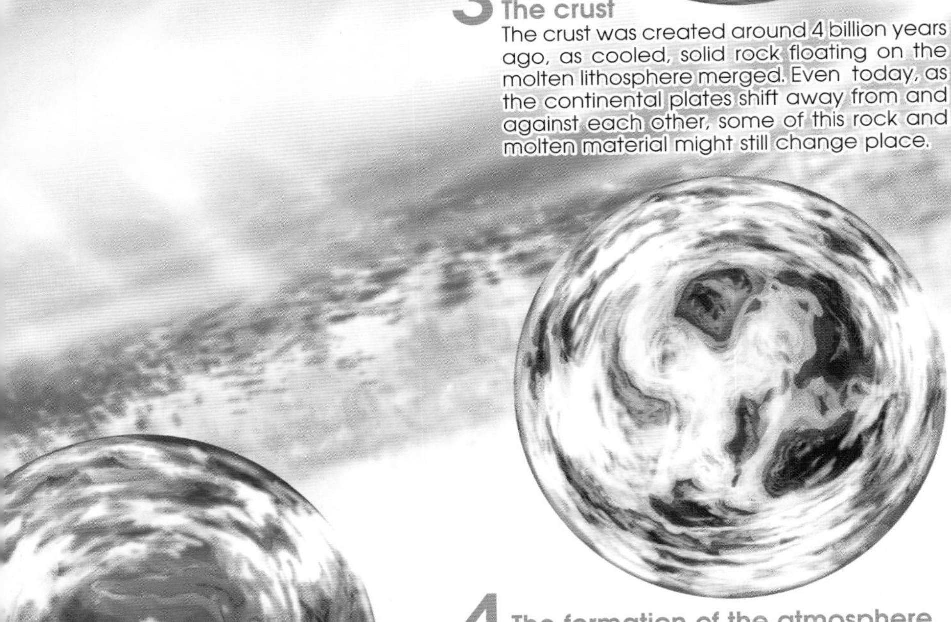

## 4 The formation of the atmosphere

After our crust solidified, volcanic gases formed our atmosphere. The cooling surface allowed the formation of water vapor and bodies of water.

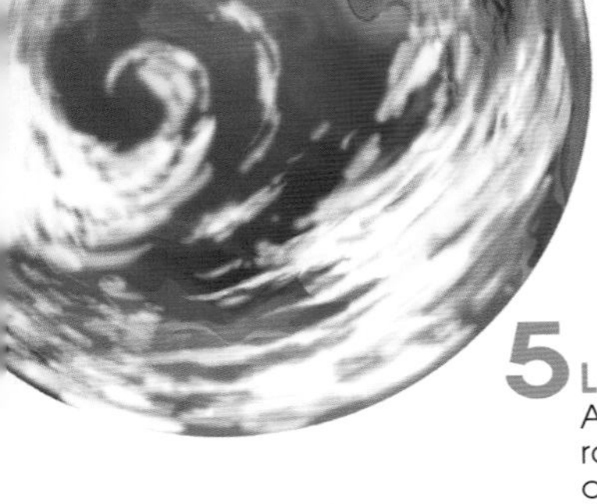

## 5 Land forms

Around 3.5 billion years ago, several land masses rose above the global ocean, giving rise to the continents we know today.

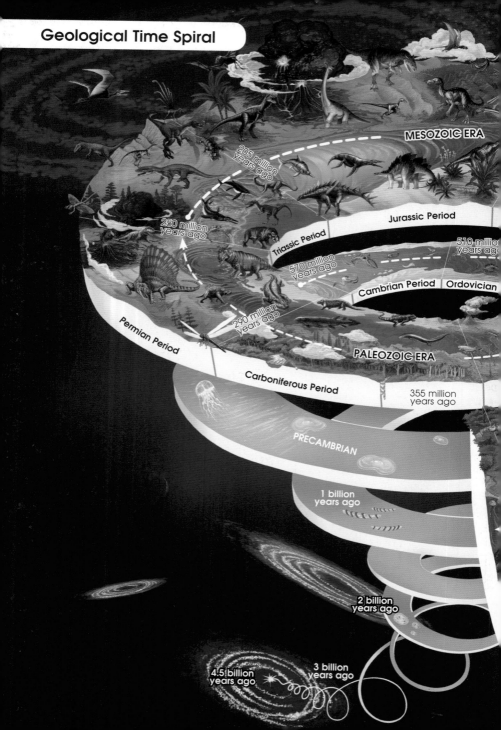

# Geological Time Spiral

**MESOZOIC ERA**

205 million years ago

250 million years ago

Jurassic Period

Triassic Period

570 million years ago

510 million years ago

Cambrian Period | Ordovician

290 million years ago

Permian Period

**PALEOZOIC ERA**

Carboniferous Period

355 million years ago

**PRECAMBRIAN**

1 billion years ago

2 billion years ago

4.5 billion years ago

3 billion years ago

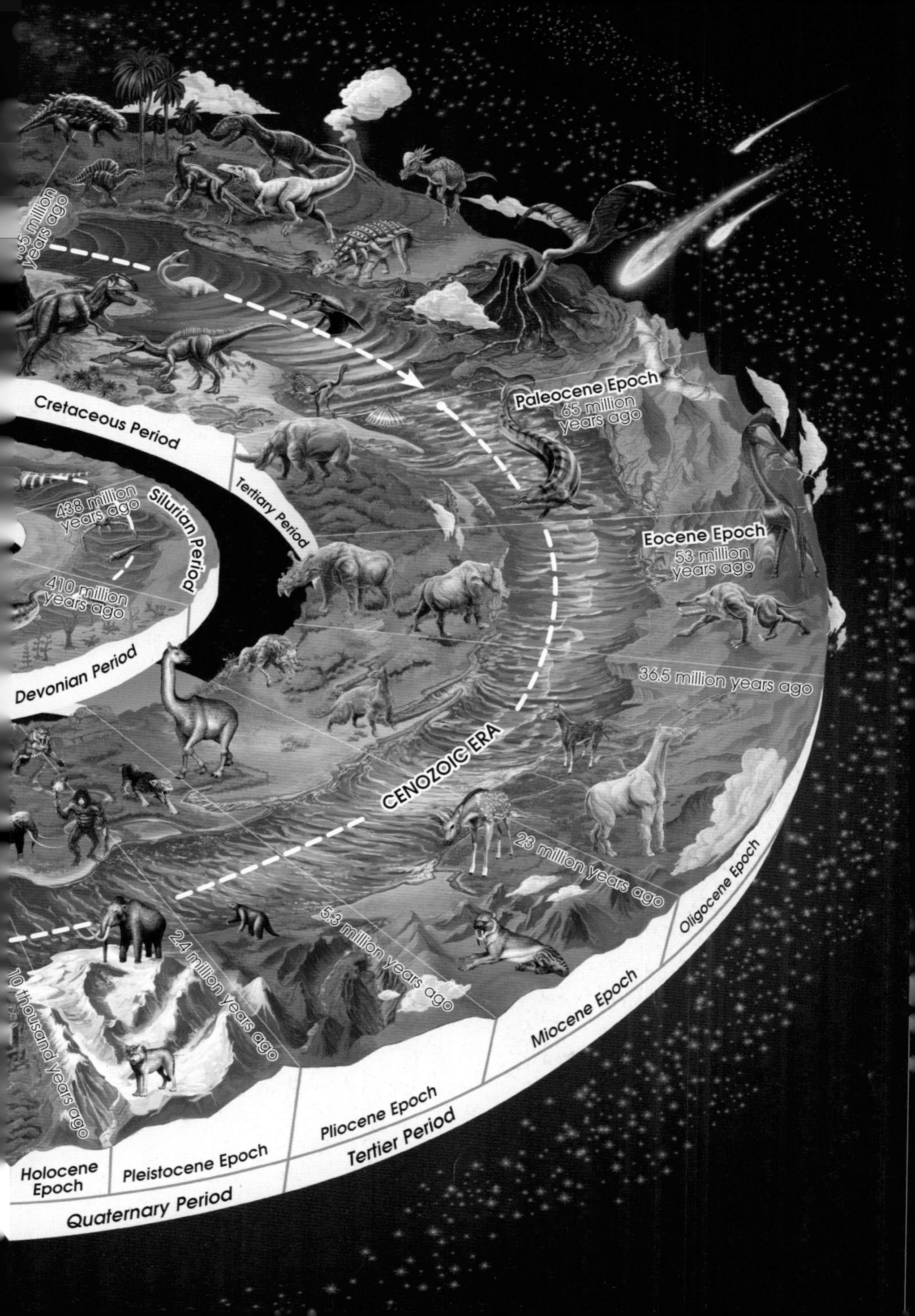
Cretaceous Period
Tertiary Period
Paleocene Epoch
65 million years ago
438 million years ago
Silurian Period
Eocene Epoch
53 million years ago
410 million years ago
Devonian Period
36.5 million years ago
CENOZOIC ERA
23 million years ago
Oligocene Epoch
5.3 million years ago
2.4 million years ago
Miocene Epoch
10 thousand years ago
Pliocene Epoch
Tertier Period
Holocene Epoch
Pleistocene Epoch
Quaternary Period

# GEOLOGIC TIME SCALE

| Eon | Era | Period | Epoch / Subdivision |
|---|---|---|---|
| Phanerozoic | Cenozoic | Quaternary | Holocene |
| | | | Pleistocene |
| | | Tertiary | Pliocene |
| | | | Miocene |
| | | | Oligocene |
| | | | Eocene |
| | | | Palaeocene |
| | Mesozoic | Cretaceous | Late, Middle, Early |
| | | Jurassic | Late, Middle, Early |
| | | Triassic | Late, Middle, Early |
| | Paleozoic | Permian | Late, Middle, Early |
| | | Carboniferous | Late, Middle, Early |
| | | Devonian | Late, Middle, Early |
| | | Silurian | Late, Middle, Early |
| | | Ordovician | Late, Middle, Early |
| | | Cambrian | Late, Middle, Early |
| Proterozoic | Proterozoic | Sinian | |
| Archaean | Archaeozoic | | |

Evolution of Major Life-Forms

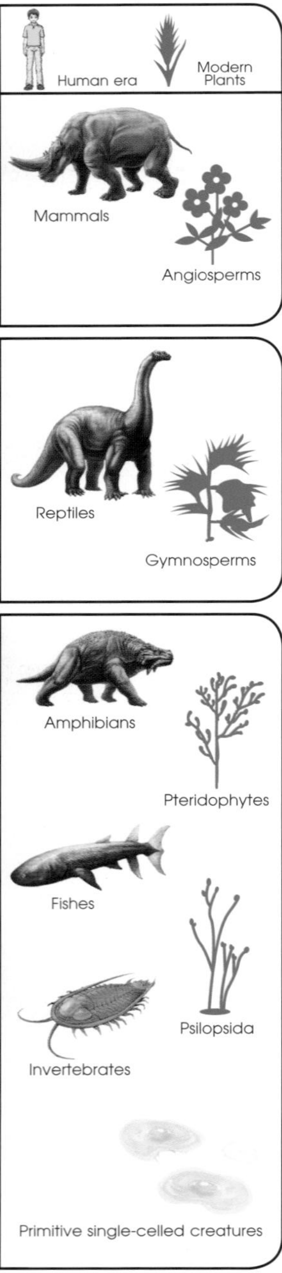

Human era
Modern Plants
Mammals
Angiosperms
Reptiles
Gymnosperms
Amphibians
Pteridophytes
Fishes
Psilopsida
Invertebrates
Primitive single-celled creatures


Years Ago
Present
10 thousand
2.4 million
5.3 million
23 million
36.5 million
53 million
65 million
135 million
205 million
250 million
290 million
355 million
410 million
438 million
510 million
570 million
800 million
2.5 billion
4 billion

# CONTENTS

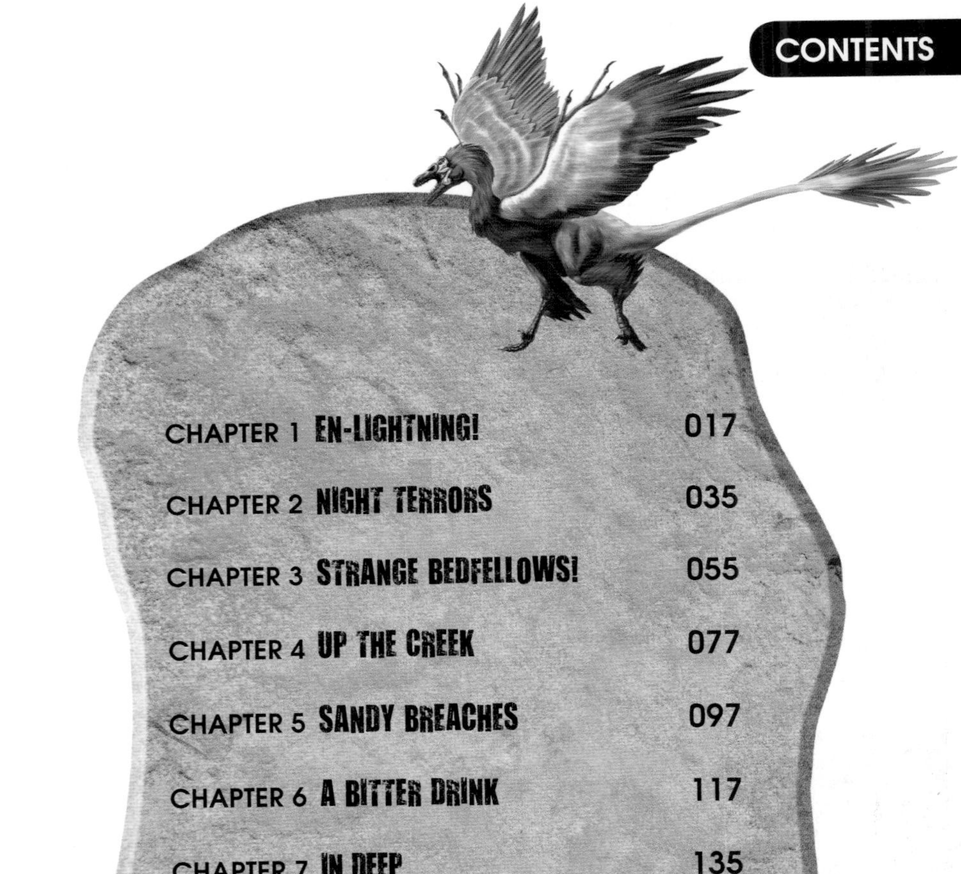



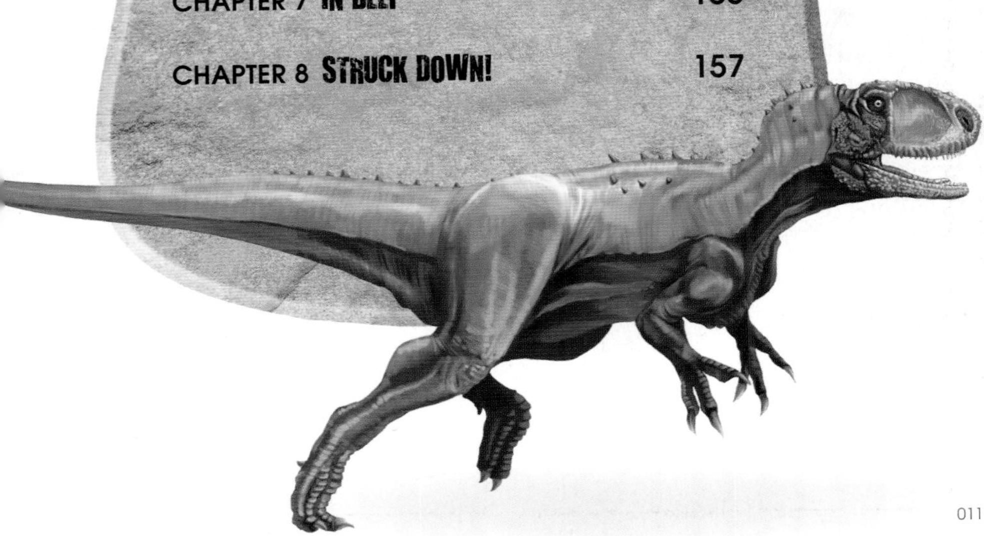

# Cast

**Sean** (Age 13)
- Smart, calm, and a good analyst.
- Very articulate, but under-performs on rare occasions.
- Uses scientific knowledge and theory in thought and speech.

**Stone** (Age 15)
- Has tremendous strength, appetite, and size.
- A boy of few words but honest and reliable.
- An expert in repairs and maintenance.

**STARZ**
- A tiny robot invented by the doctor, nicknamed Lil S.
- Multifunctional; able to scan, analyze, record, take images, communicate, and more.
- Able to change its form and appearance. It is a mobile supercomputer that can store huge amounts of information.

**Rain** (Age 13)
- Curious, plays to win, but sometimes misses the big picture.
- Brave, persevering, never gives up.
- Individualistic and loves to play the hero.

**Dr. Da Vinci** (Age 60)
- A professor at the National Scientific Research Institute.
- A genius inventor.
- Highly knowledgeable, loves adventure, but lazy by nature.

**Diana** (Age 30)
- Research-based Administrator, the Doctor's helpful assistant.
- A mature, beautiful, and capable lady.
- Good at problem solving.

**Emily** (Age 13)
- Smart, responsible, and adaptive.
- Calm under pressure, slightly vain.
- Computer savvy.

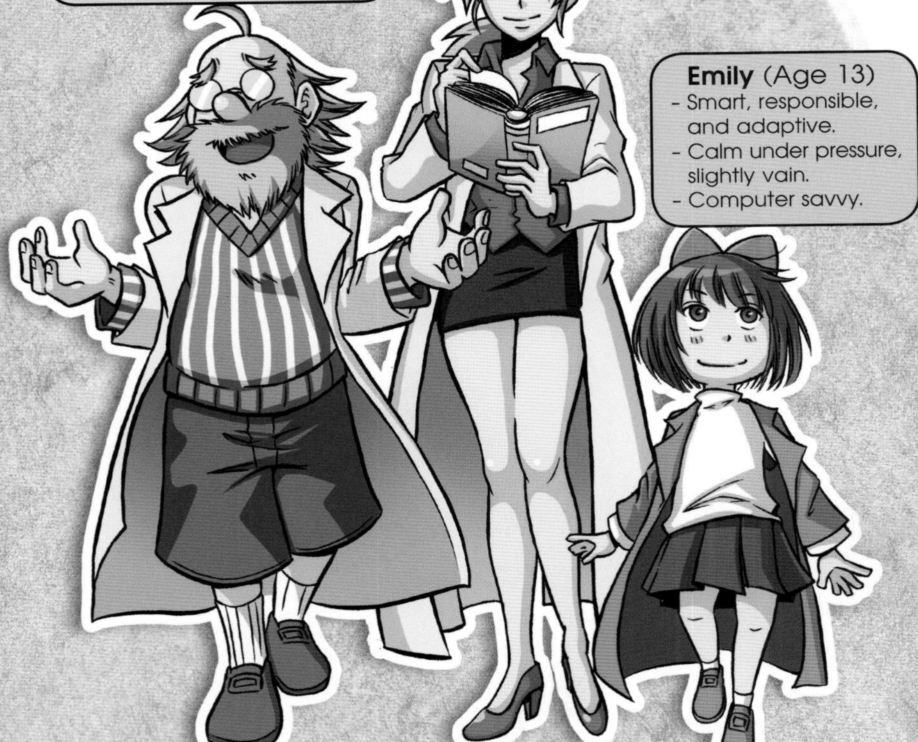

**Particle Transmitter**
- One of Dr. Da Vinci's most important inventions.
- Able to teleport the team to any period of time and space to execute their missions.
- Able to send urgently needed items to the team at any time.

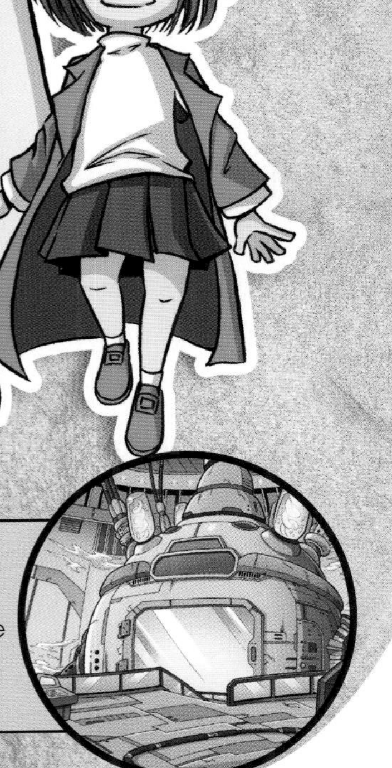

# PREVIOUSLY...

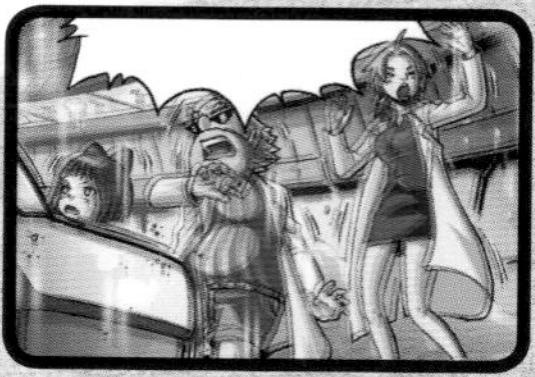

A massive earthquake sends the Dinosaur Explorers team millions of years into the past! Emerging in the Cambrian, they manage to jump away in time (literally!) to avoid sinister Silurian sea life, but find that their Particle Transmitter only allows them small jumps several million years at a time- and they're over 500 million years in the past!

Cambrian

Ordovician

Silurian

Devonian

Carboniferous

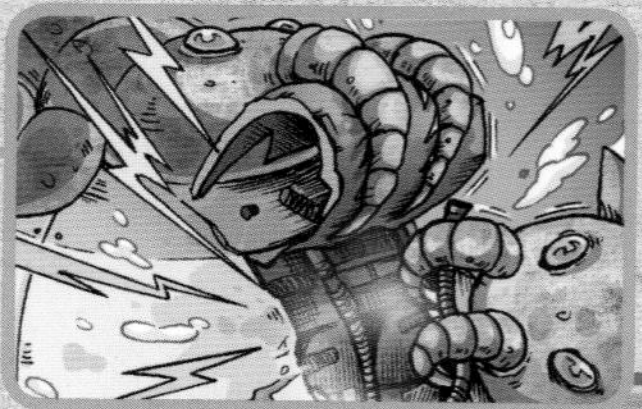

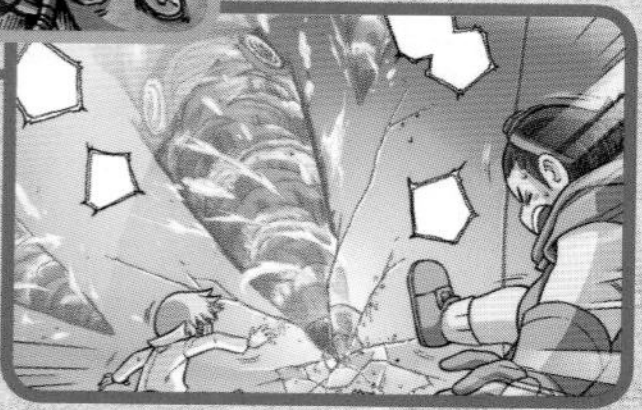

The Silurian sees their anxiety and despair results in in-fighting; Rain's behaviour angers Emily, who decides to set out with the Dinosaur Explorers to prove herself — and prove herself she does! Facing everything from giant squids to sand-burrowing sea scorpions with will and wherewithal!

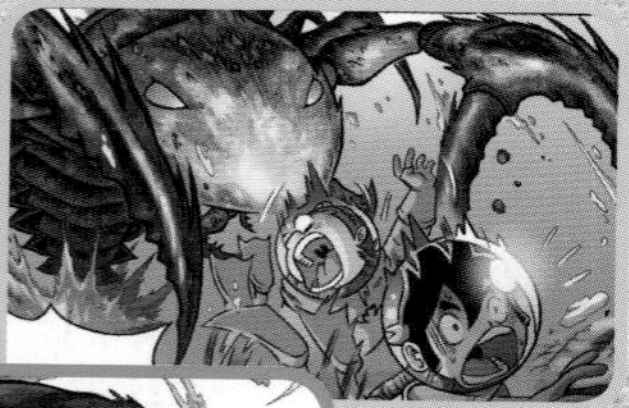

Unfortunately,the team manages to step away from the Silurian, only to end up facing the Devonian's major maulers, the Icthyostega and Placodermi! Only a labload of luck and some fried fish enable a clean get away.

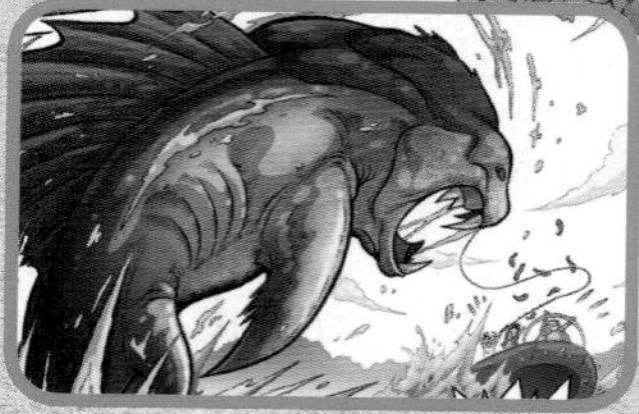

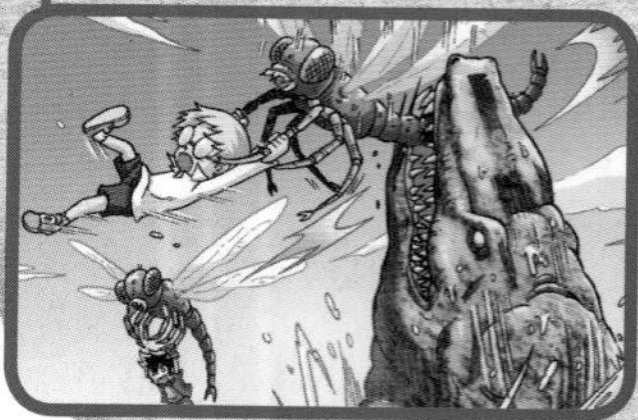

Things reach a crisis point in the Carboniferous when the team nearly becomes finger food for super-sized bugs! Battling giant spiders and huge dragonflies, our heroes struggle to escape.

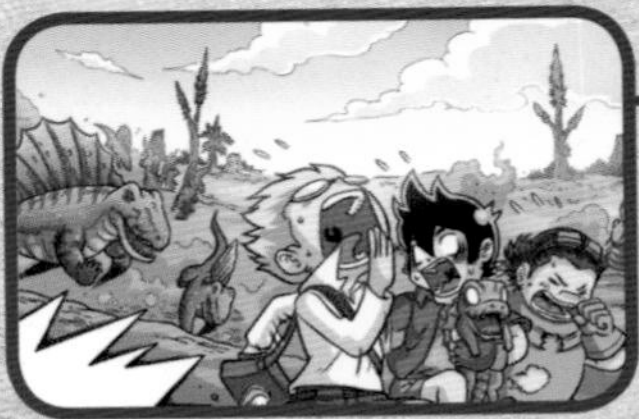

In the Permian, they're stuck with the proto-reptile great grandparents of the dinosaurs! Things get complicated when the team's forced to babysit! Thankfully, our heroes get the job done in time to jump... to the Triassic!

- Permian
- Triassic
- Jurassic
- Cretaceous
- Tertiary
- Quaternary

...where they face their greatest challenge yet — themselves! Tensions cause tempers to rise once again, but thankfully, they patch things up before they have to patch themselves up, eluding some of history's earliest predators!

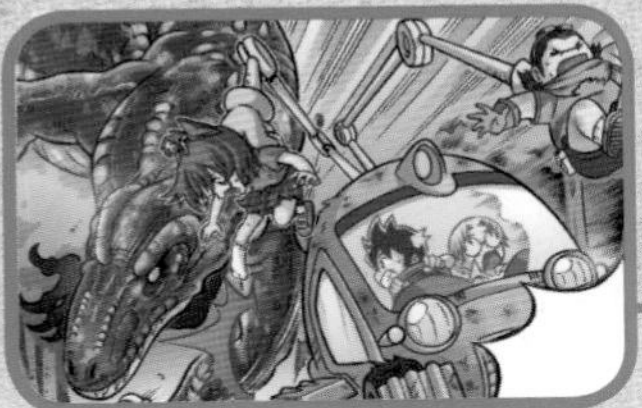

Its was a case of Sean out, Diana in during the Jurassic! Keeping a childhood promise sees their Jurassic jaunt begin well – right before it all goes wrong, forcing Dinosaur Explorers to desperately defend their lab against uninvited guests!

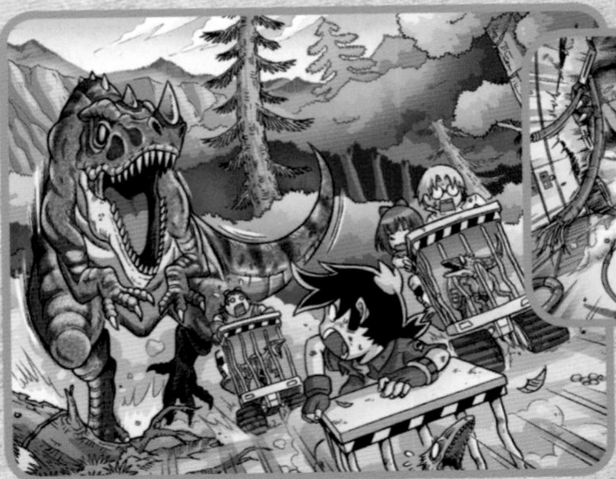

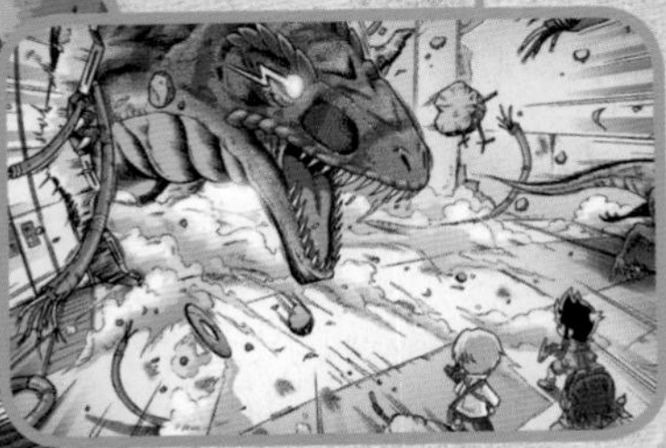

A friendly game turned into a savage cage match when the lab ran out of power for the first time, and some big bullies had the Dinosaur Explorers on the run! No time for wits or strength – only love can get them out of this situation!

*The size of this graphic novel's critters are exaggerated, and do not really represent the true sizes of the creatures. Hey, it makes for a more visually exciting story!

CHAPTER 1

# EN-LIGHTNING!

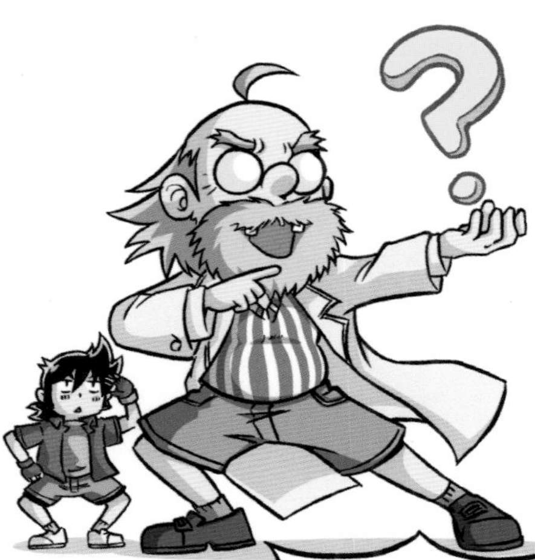

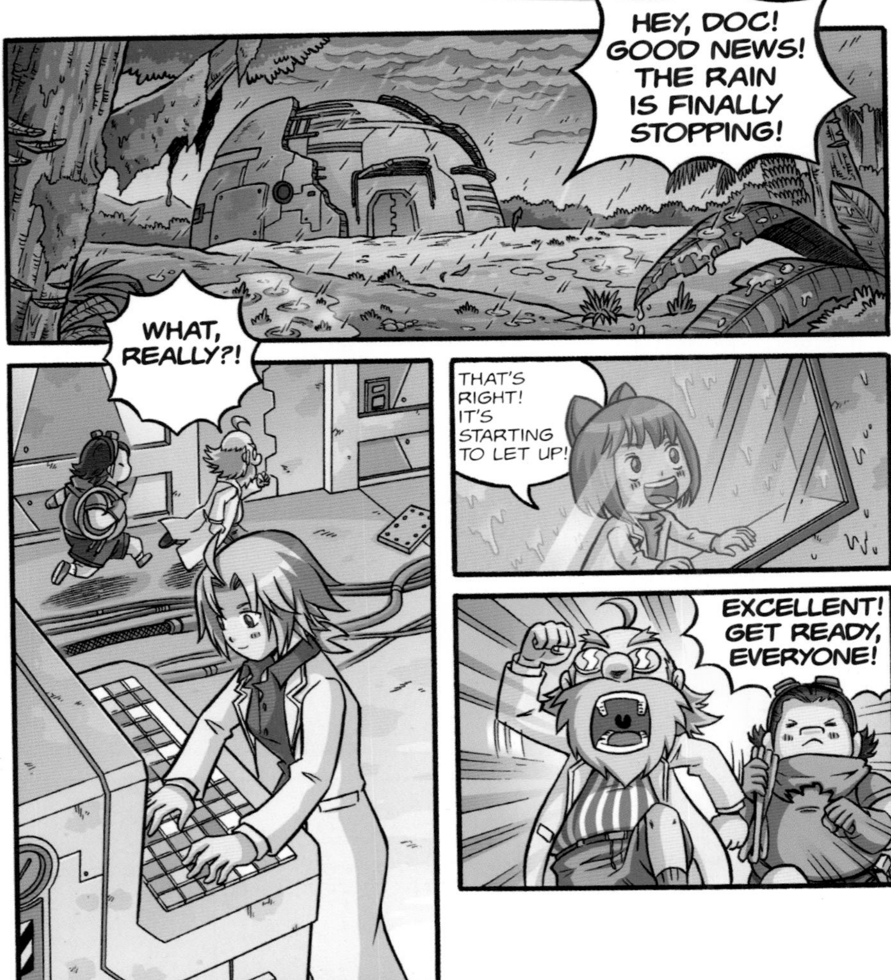
HEY, DOC! GOOD NEWS! THE RAIN IS FINALLY STOPPING!
WHAT, REALLY?!
THAT'S RIGHT! IT'S STARTING TO LET UP!
EXCELLENT! GET READY, EVERYONE!

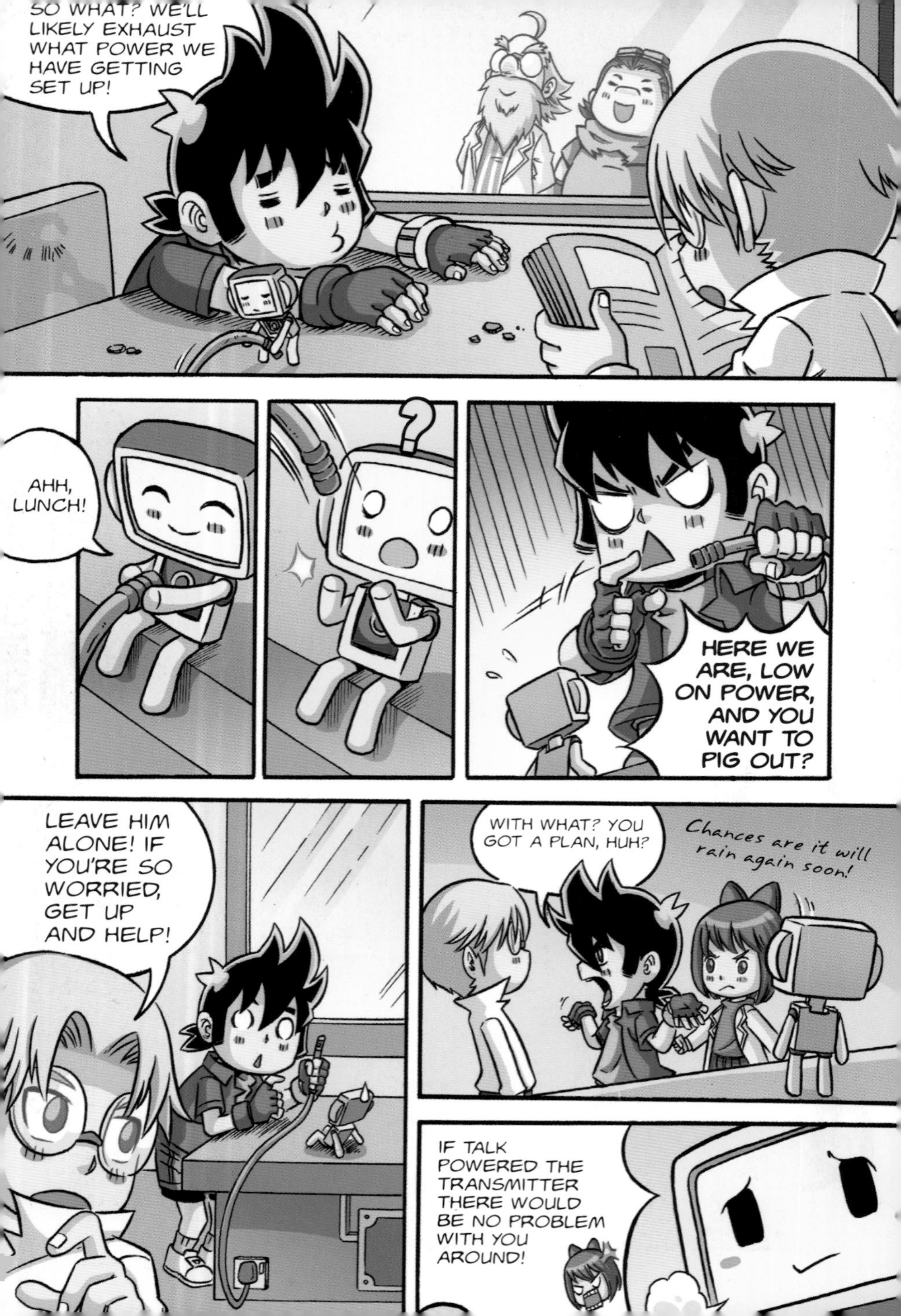

SO WHAT? WE'LL LIKELY EXHAUST WHAT POWER WE HAVE GETTING SET UP!
AHH, LUNCH!
?
HERE WE ARE, LOW ON POWER, AND YOU WANT TO PIG OUT?
LEAVE HIM ALONE! IF YOU'RE SO WORRIED, GET UP AND HELP!
WITH WHAT? YOU GOT A PLAN, HUH?
Chances are it will rain again soon!
IF TALK POWERED THE TRANSMITTER THERE WOULD BE NO PROBLEM WITH YOU AROUND!

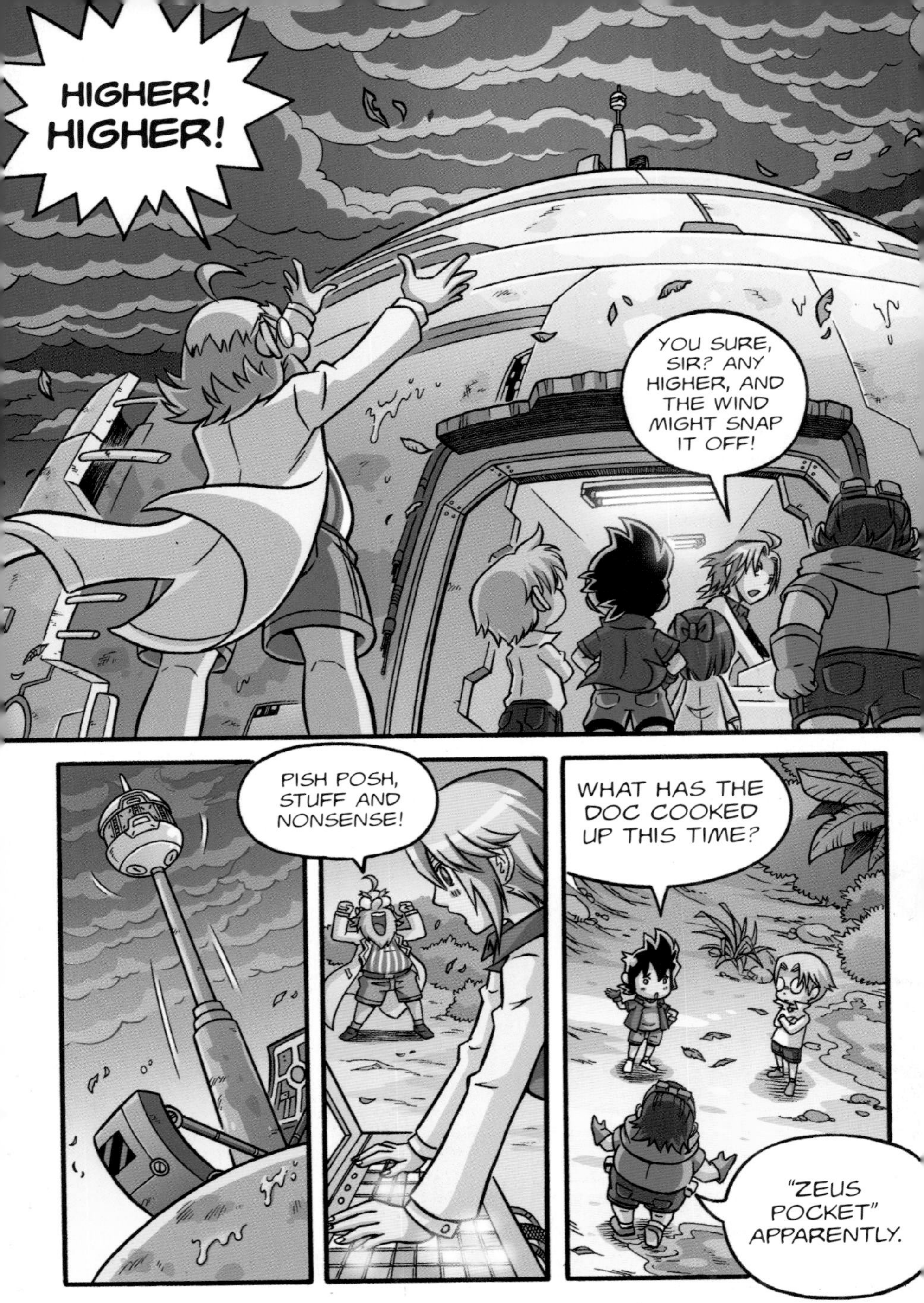
HIGHER! HIGHER!
YOU SURE, SIR? ANY HIGHER, AND THE WIND MIGHT SNAP IT OFF!
PISH POSH, STUFF AND NONSENSE!
WHAT HAS THE DOC COOKED UP THIS TIME?
"ZEUS POCKET" APPARENTLY.

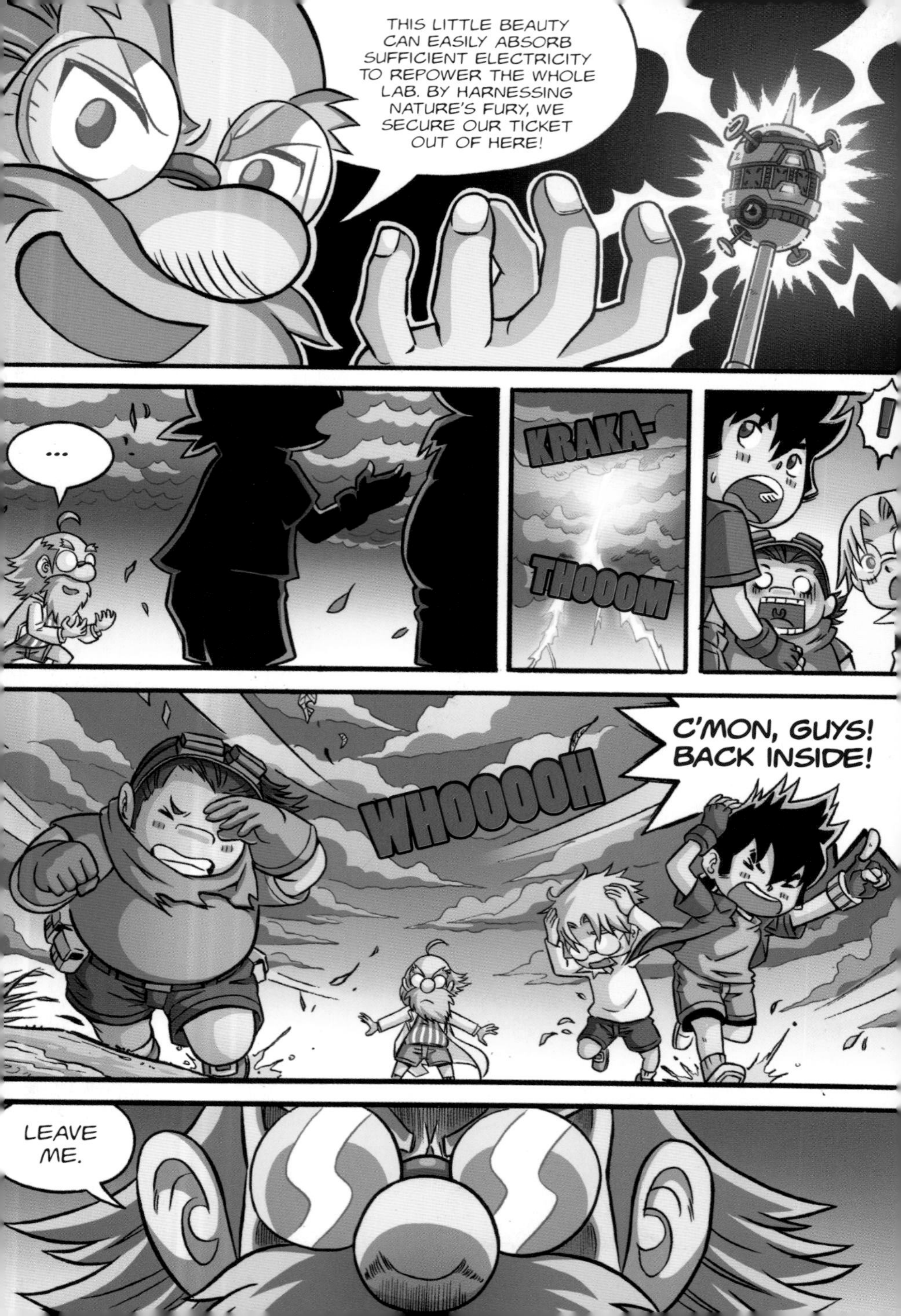
THIS LITTLE BEAUTY CAN EASILY ABSORB SUFFICIENT ELECTRICITY TO REPOWER THE WHOLE LAB. BY HARNESSING NATURE'S FURY, WE SECURE OUR TICKET OUT OF HERE!
...
KRAKA-
THOOOM
!
C'MON, GUYS! BACK INSIDE!
WHOOOOH
LEAVE ME.

I ALONE WILL BEAR WITNESS TO THIS MOMENT OF SHEER GENIUS!

BUT, DOC!

IT'S TOO DANGEROUS, SIR!

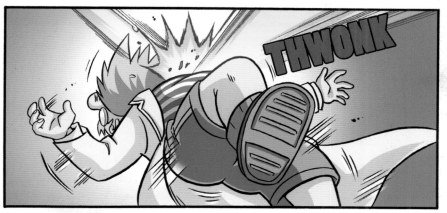

THWONK

What?!

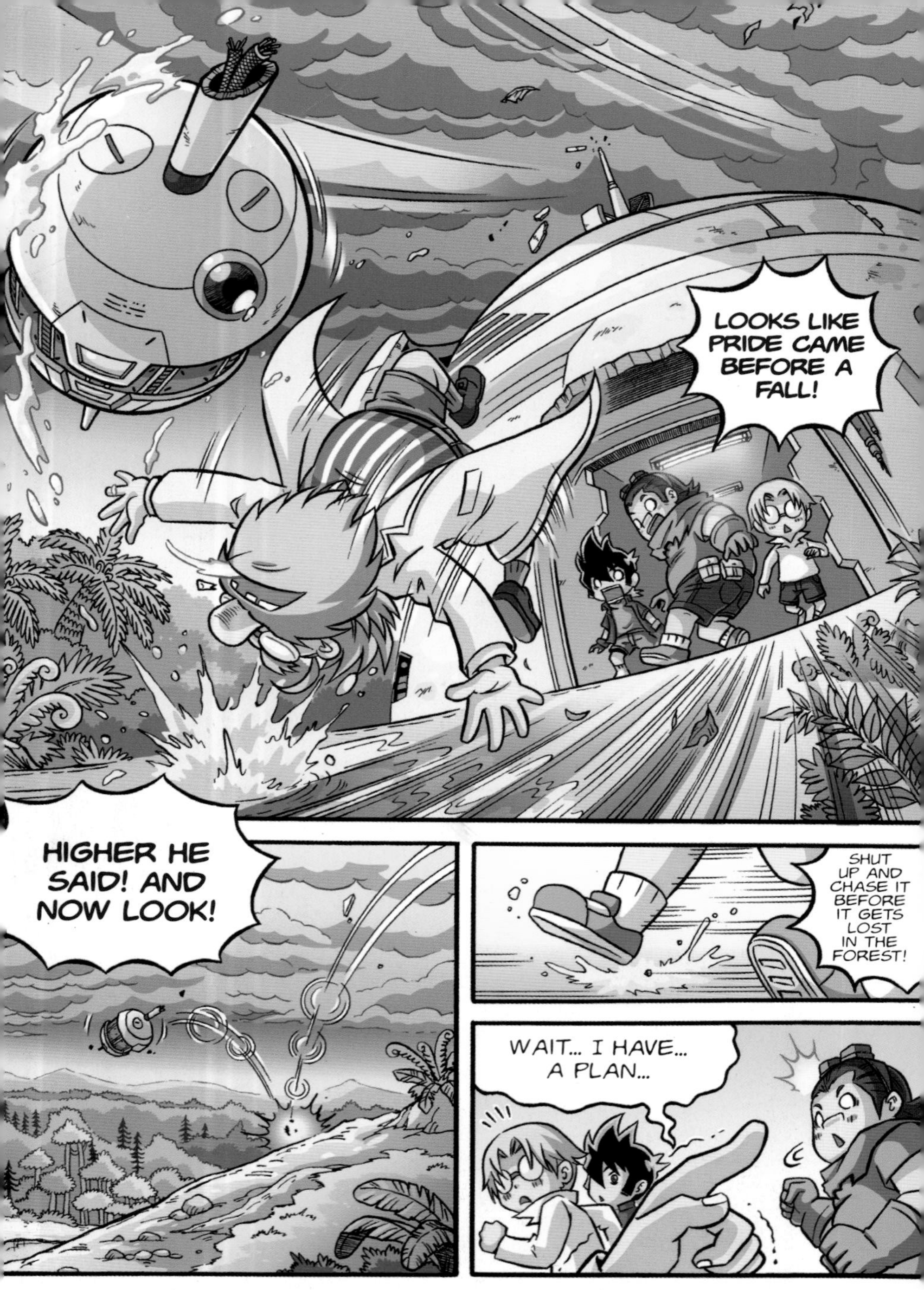
LOOKS LIKE PRIDE CAME BEFORE A FALL!
HIGHER HE SAID! AND NOW LOOK!
SHUT UP AND CHASE IT BEFORE IT GETS LOST IN THE FOREST!
WAIT... I HAVE... A PLAN...

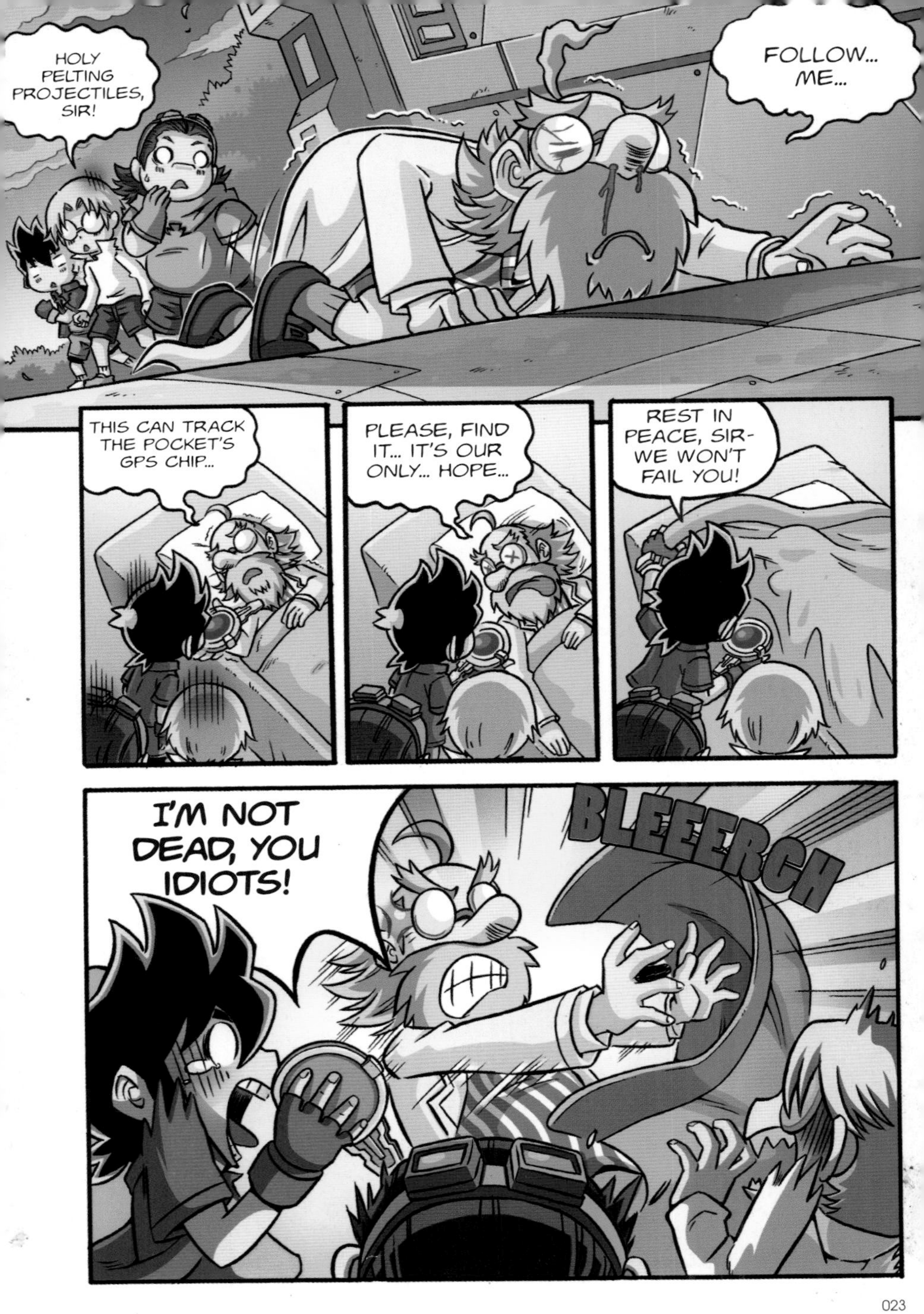
HOLY PELTING PROJECTILES, SIR!
FOLLOW... ME...
THIS CAN TRACK THE POCKET'S GPS CHIP...
PLEASE, FIND IT... IT'S OUR ONLY... HOPE...
REST IN PEACE, SIR- WE WON'T FAIL YOU!
I'M NOT DEAD, YOU IDIOTS!
BLEEERCH

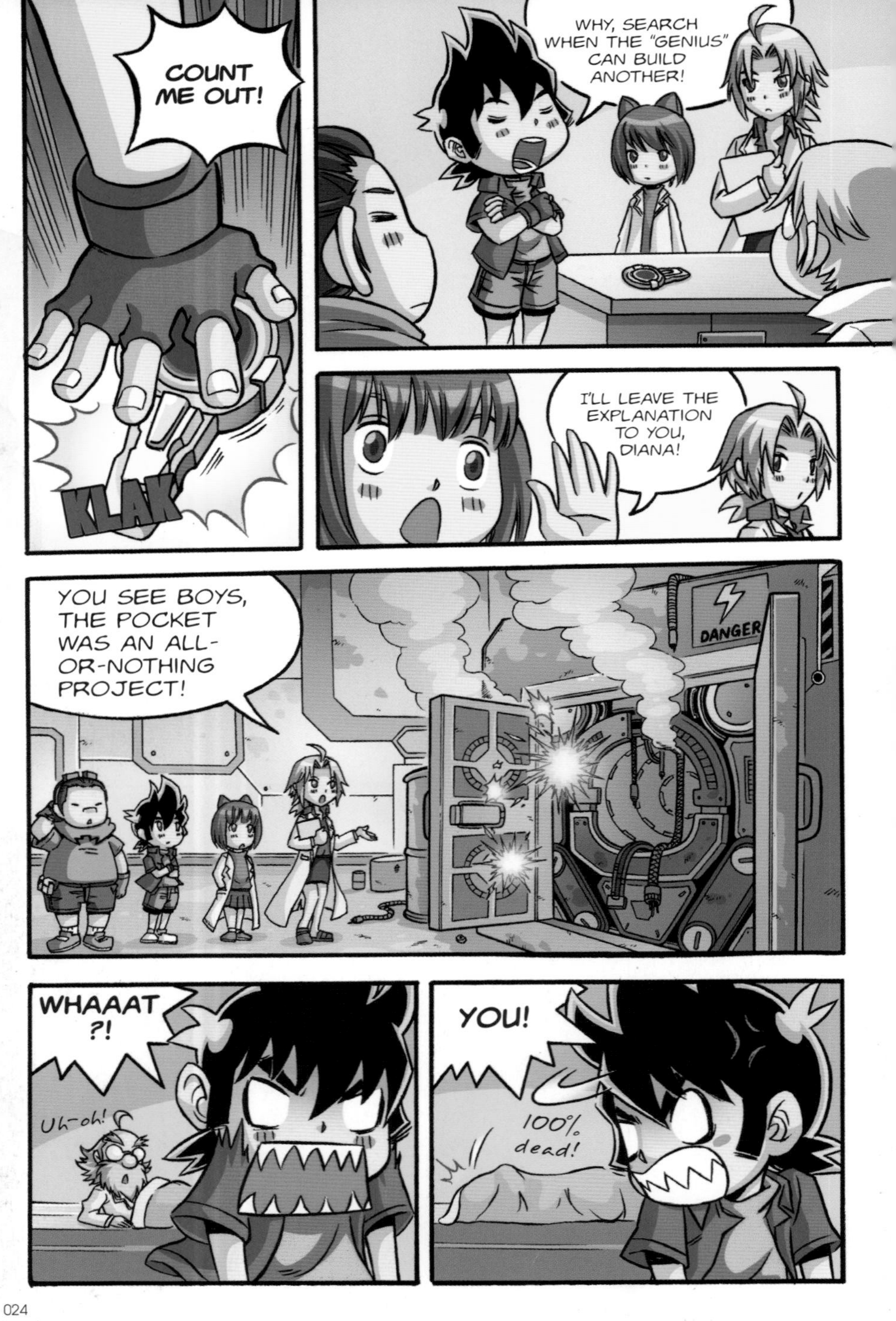
COUNT ME OUT!
KLAK
WHY, SEARCH WHEN THE "GENIUS" CAN BUILD ANOTHER!
I'LL LEAVE THE EXPLANATION TO YOU, DIANA!
YOU SEE BOYS, THE POCKET WAS AN ALL-OR-NOTHING PROJECT!
DANGER
WHAAAT ?!
Uh-oh!
YOU!
100% dead!

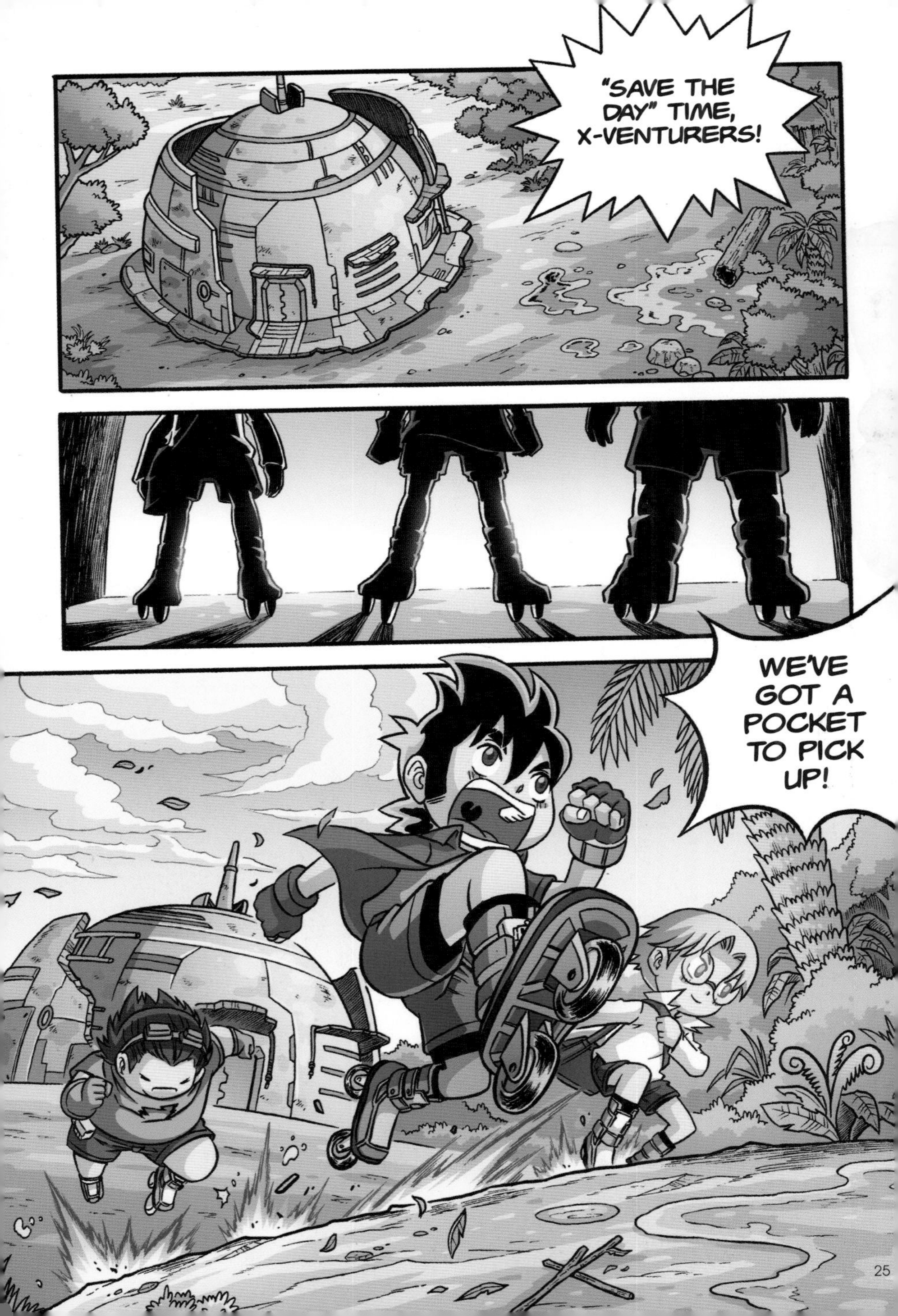
"SAVE THE DAY" TIME, X-VENTURERS!
WE'VE GOT A POCKET TO PICK UP!

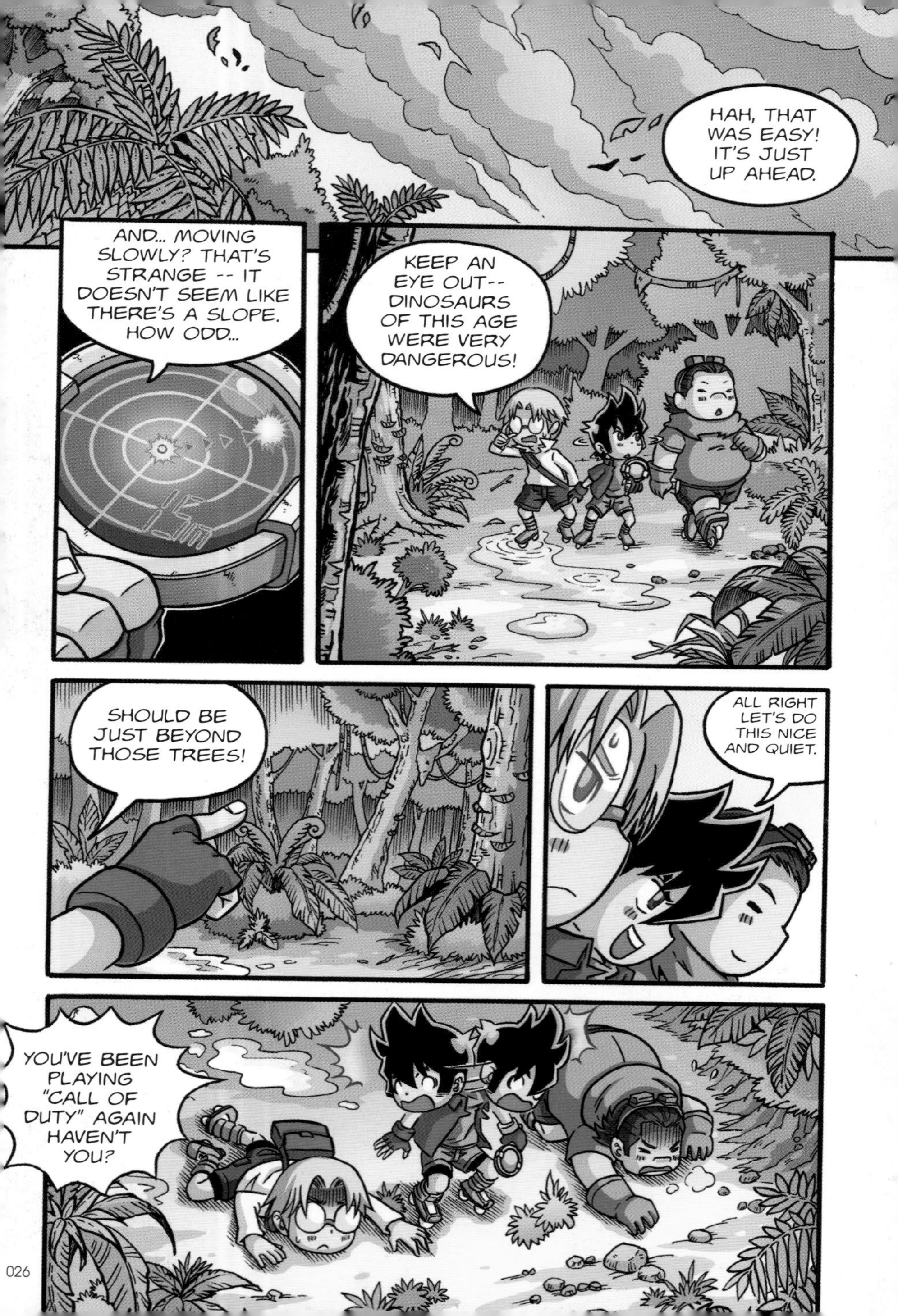
HAH, THAT WAS EASY! IT'S JUST UP AHEAD.
AND... MOVING SLOWLY? THAT'S STRANGE -- IT DOESN'T SEEM LIKE THERE'S A SLOPE. HOW ODD...
KEEP AN EYE OUT-- DINOSAURS OF THIS AGE WERE VERY DANGEROUS!
SHOULD BE JUST BEYOND THOSE TREES!
ALL RIGHT LET'S DO THIS NICE AND QUIET.
YOU'VE BEEN PLAYING "CALL OF DUTY" AGAIN HAVEN'T YOU?

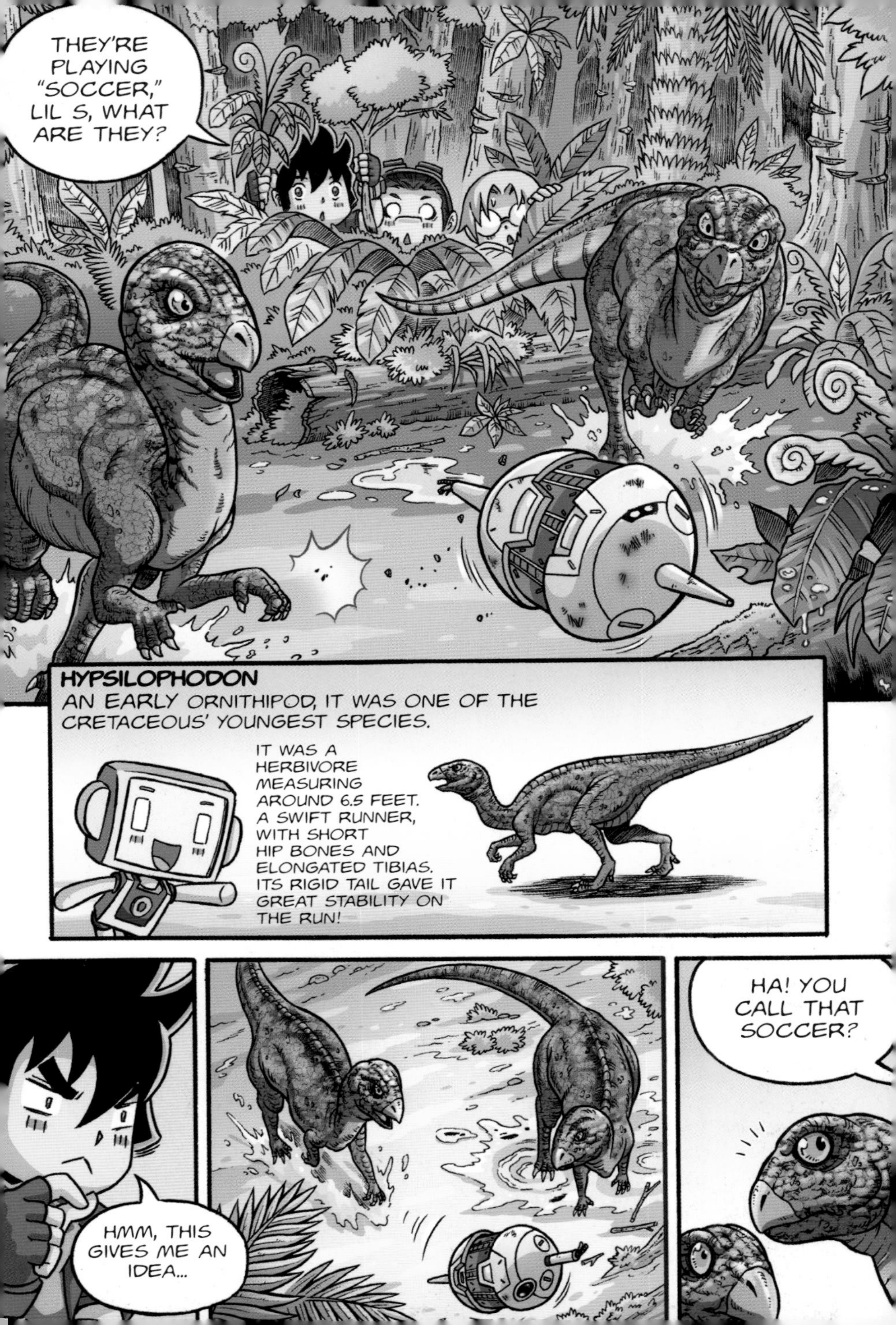
THEY'RE PLAYING "SOCCER," LIL S, WHAT ARE THEY?
HYPSILOPHODON
AN EARLY ORNITHIPOD, IT WAS ONE OF THE CRETACEOUS' YOUNGEST SPECIES.
IT WAS A HERBIVORE MEASURING AROUND 6.5 FEET. A SWIFT RUNNER, WITH SHORT HIP BONES AND ELONGATED TIBIAS. ITS RIGID TAIL GAVE IT GREAT STABILITY ON THE RUN!
HMM, THIS GIVES ME AN IDEA...
HA! YOU CALL THAT SOCCER?

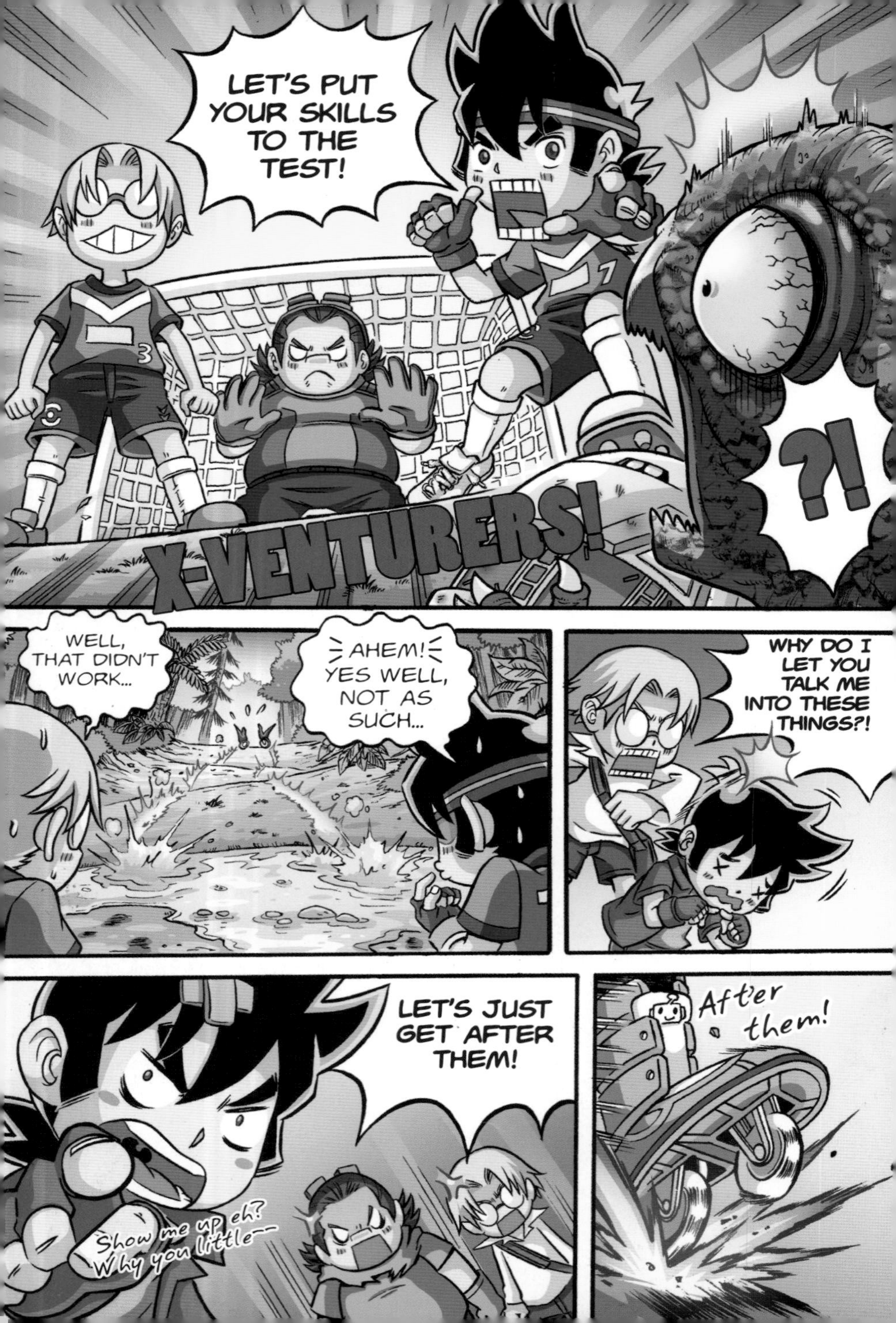
LET'S PUT YOUR SKILLS TO THE TEST!
X-VENTURERS!
?!
WELL, THAT DIDN'T WORK...
AHEM! YES WELL, NOT AS SUCH...
WHY DO I LET YOU TALK ME INTO THESE THINGS?!
LET'S JUST GET AFTER THEM!
Show me up eh? Why you little--
After them!

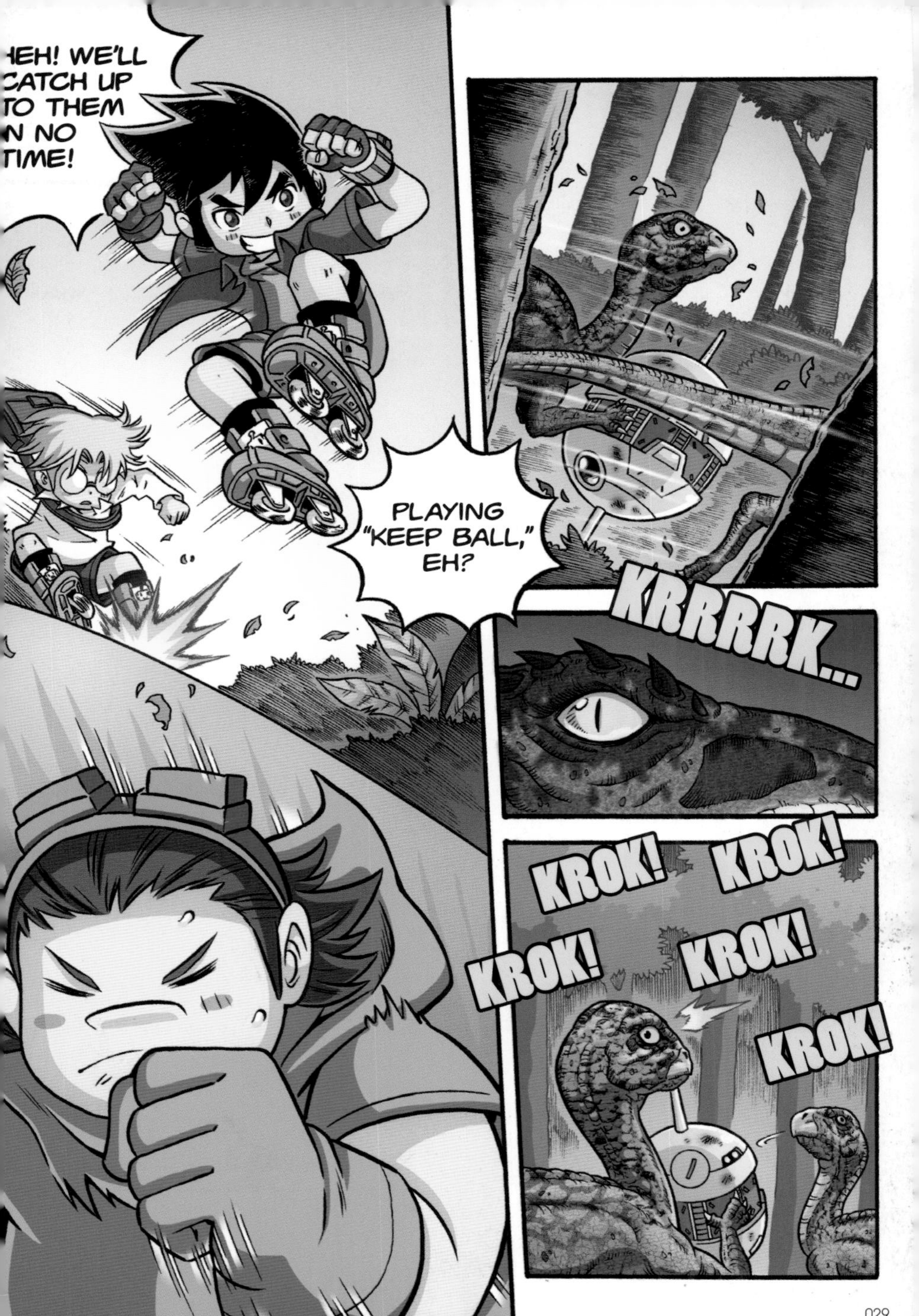
HEH! WE'LL CATCH UP TO THEM IN NO TIME!
PLAYING "KEEP BALL," EH?
KRRRRRK...
KROK! KROK!
KROK! KROK!
KROK!

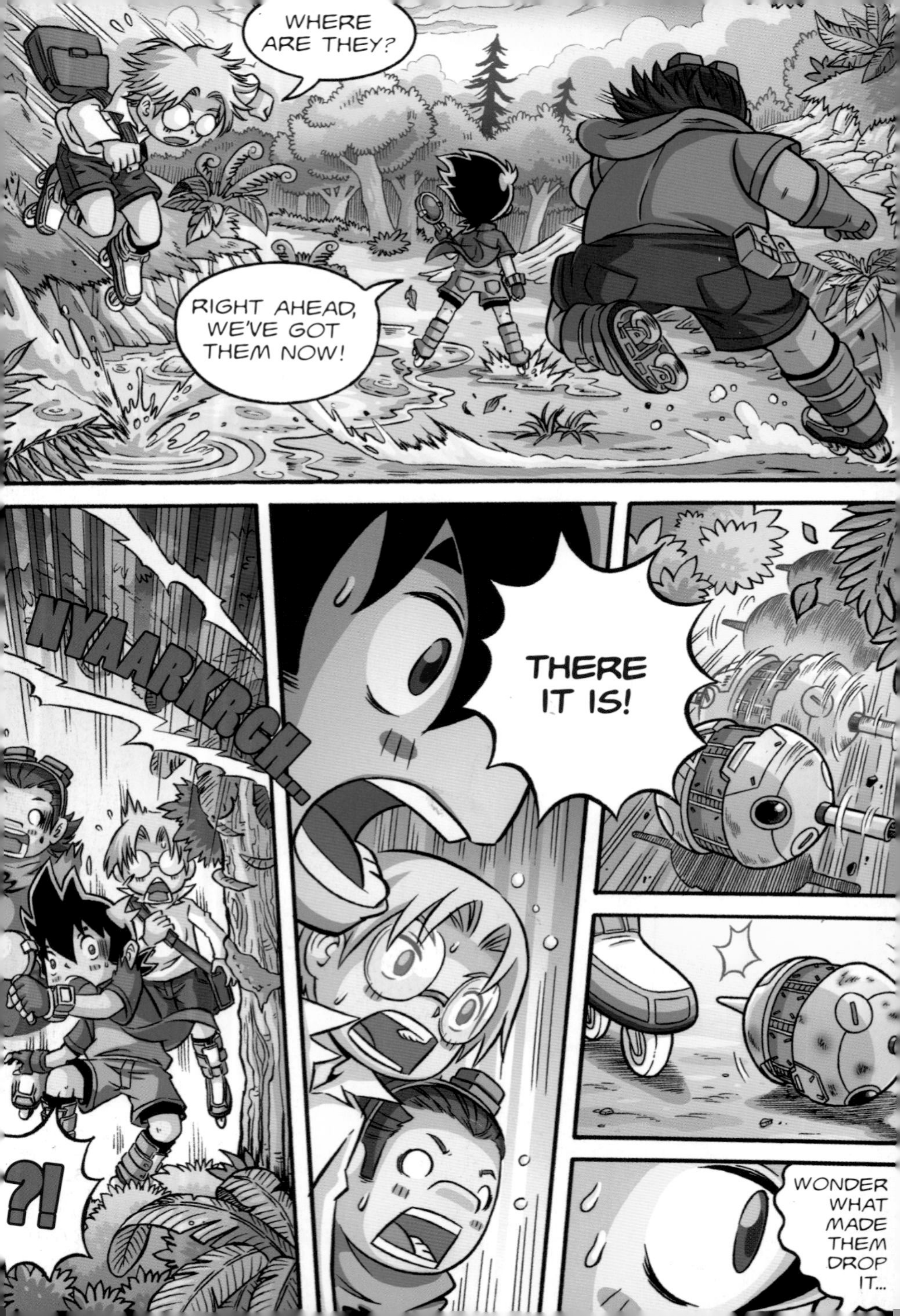
WHERE ARE THEY?
RIGHT AHEAD, WE'VE GOT THEM NOW!
NYAARKKRCH...
?!
THERE IT IS!
WONDER WHAT MADE THEM DROP IT...

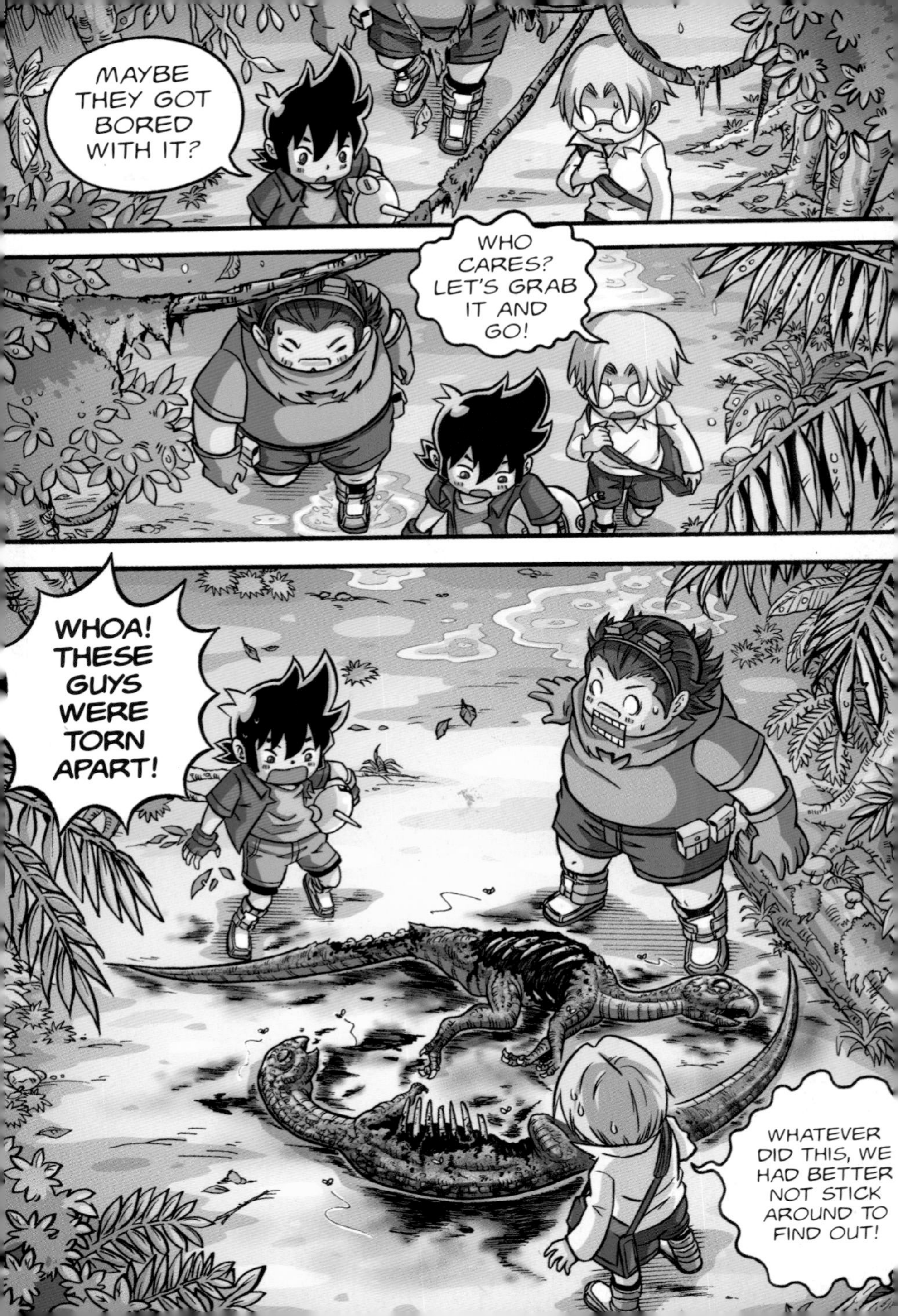
MAYBE THEY GOT BORED WITH IT?
WHO CARES? LET'S GRAB IT AND GO!
WHOA! THESE GUYS WERE TORN APART!
WHATEVER DID THIS, WE HAD BETTER NOT STICK AROUND TO FIND OUT!

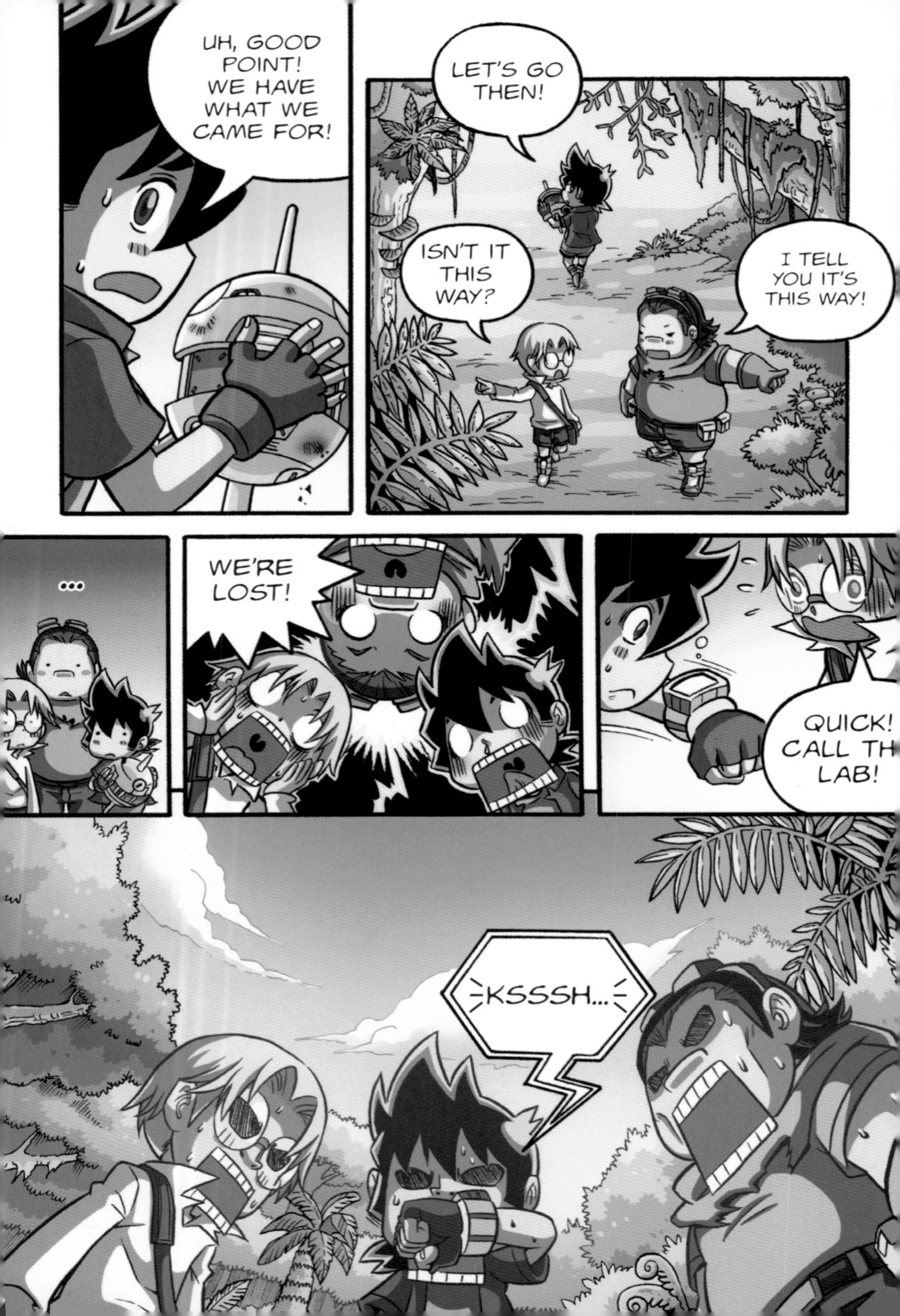
UH, GOOD POINT! WE HAVE WHAT WE CAME FOR!
LET'S GO THEN!
ISN'T IT THIS WAY?
I TELL YOU IT'S THIS WAY!
...
WE'RE LOST!
QUICK! CALL TH LAB!
KSSSH...

## CONTINENTS OF THE CRETACEOUS

During the Cretaceous, rising sea levels helped break the supercontinent Pangaea into two halves; Laurentia in the north, and Gondwana to the south. Tectonic movements that began way back then would, in time, move the continents to where they are now. The Atlantic Ocean separated North and South America (North America was still attached to Eurasia via a land bridge) and Africa was expanding, while the continent of Antarctica was almost where it is today. The Indian subcontinent had began moving northwards.

North America
Eurasia
Africa
South America
Indian Subcontinent
Antarctica
Oceania

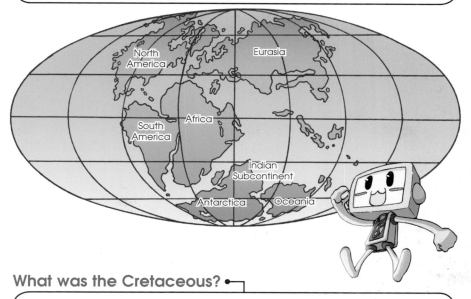

## What was the Cretaceous?

The Cretaceous was the last period of the Mesozoic era, and lasted from 145 (some say 135) to 65 million years ago. Mammals were still a footnote compared to the reptillian overlords that dominated the land, sea, and air.

## What plants were around during the Cretaceous?

The early Cretaceous saw a great increase in plant life, with angiosperms joining the dominant gymnosperms. After bees evolved in the late Cretaceous, gymnosperms became the dominant form of plantlife.

# How did dinosaurs reproduce?

Most dinosaurs laid eggs, according to fossil records. But just as some modern reptiles give birth, so too could have dinosaurs such as Apatosaurus. According to some paleontologists who have examined its pelvic bones, Apatosaurus might have given birth in a similar way to large mammals such as elephants.
That said, nothing conclusive has been proven so far.

## How dinosaurs lay eggs

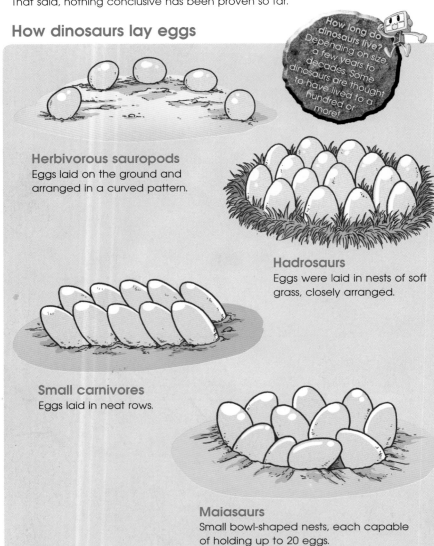

How long do dinosaurs live? Depending on size, a few years to decades. Some dinosaurs are thought to have lived to a hundred or more!

**Herbivorous sauropods**
Eggs laid on the ground and arranged in a curved pattern.

**Hadrosaurs**
Eggs were laid in nests of soft grass, closely arranged.

**Small carnivores**
Eggs laid in neat rows.

**Maiasaurs**
Small bowl-shaped nests, each capable of holding up to 20 eggs.

CHAPTER 2
# NIGHT TERRORS

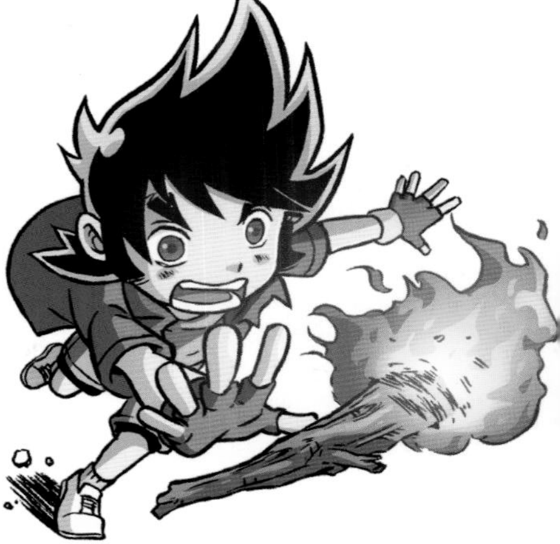

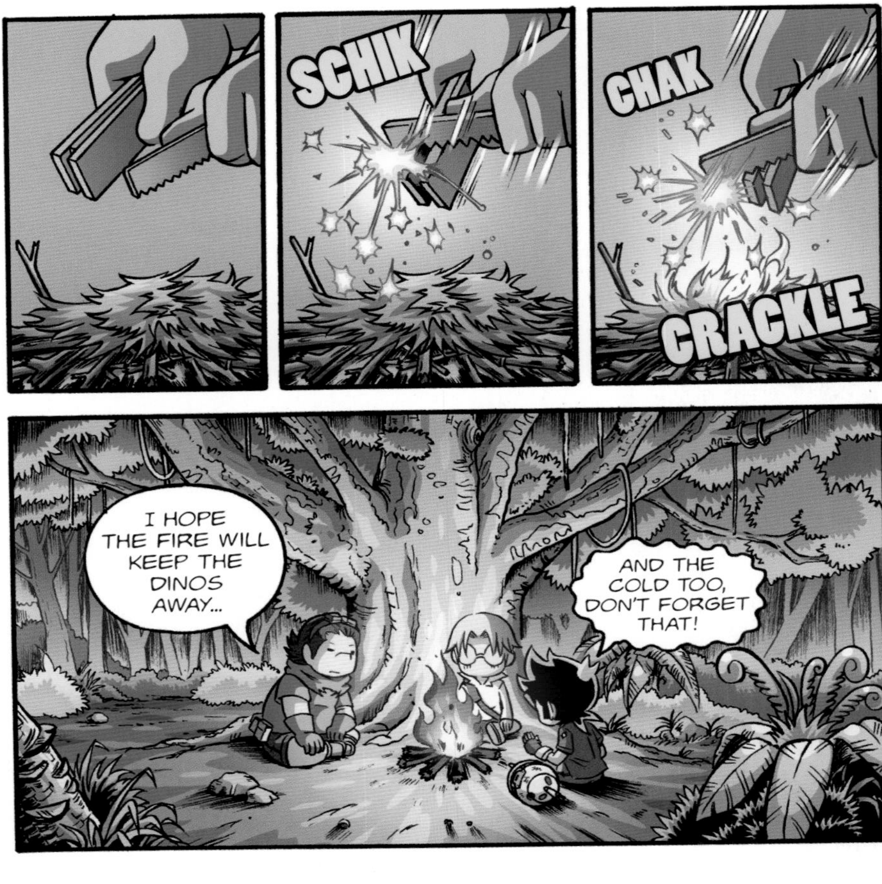
SCHIK
CHAK
CRACKLE
I HOPE THE FIRE WILL KEEP THE DINOS AWAY...
AND THE COLD TOO, DON'T FORGET THAT!

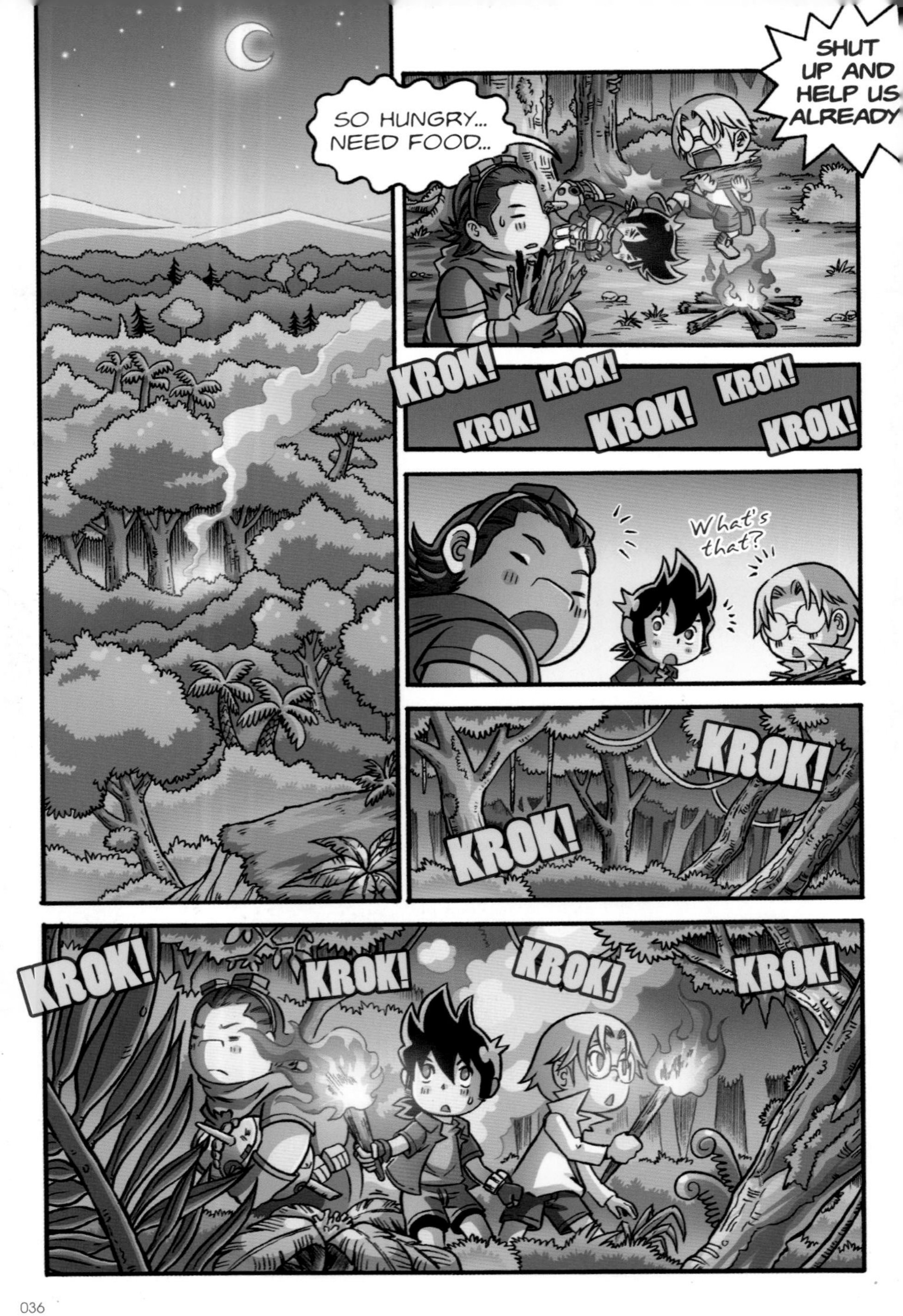
SO HUNGRY... NEED FOOD...
SHUT UP AND HELP US ALREADY
KROK! KROK! KROK! KROK! KROK! KROK!
What's that?
KROK! KROK!
KROK! KROK! KROK! KROK!

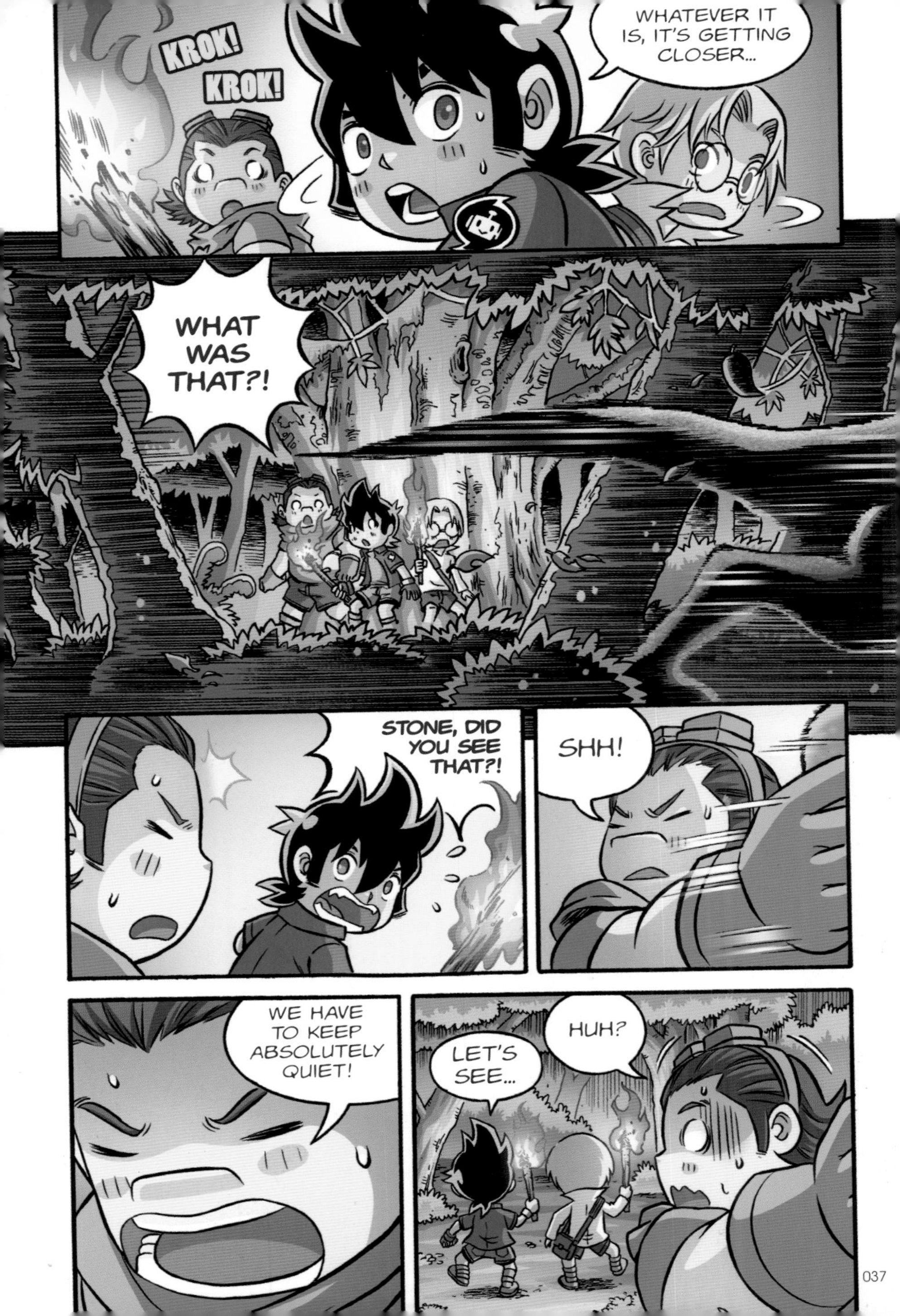
KROK!
KROK!
WHATEVER IT IS, IT'S GETTING CLOSER...
WHAT WAS THAT?!
STONE, DID YOU SEE THAT?!
SHH!
WE HAVE TO KEEP ABSOLUTELY QUIET!
LET'S SEE...
HUH?

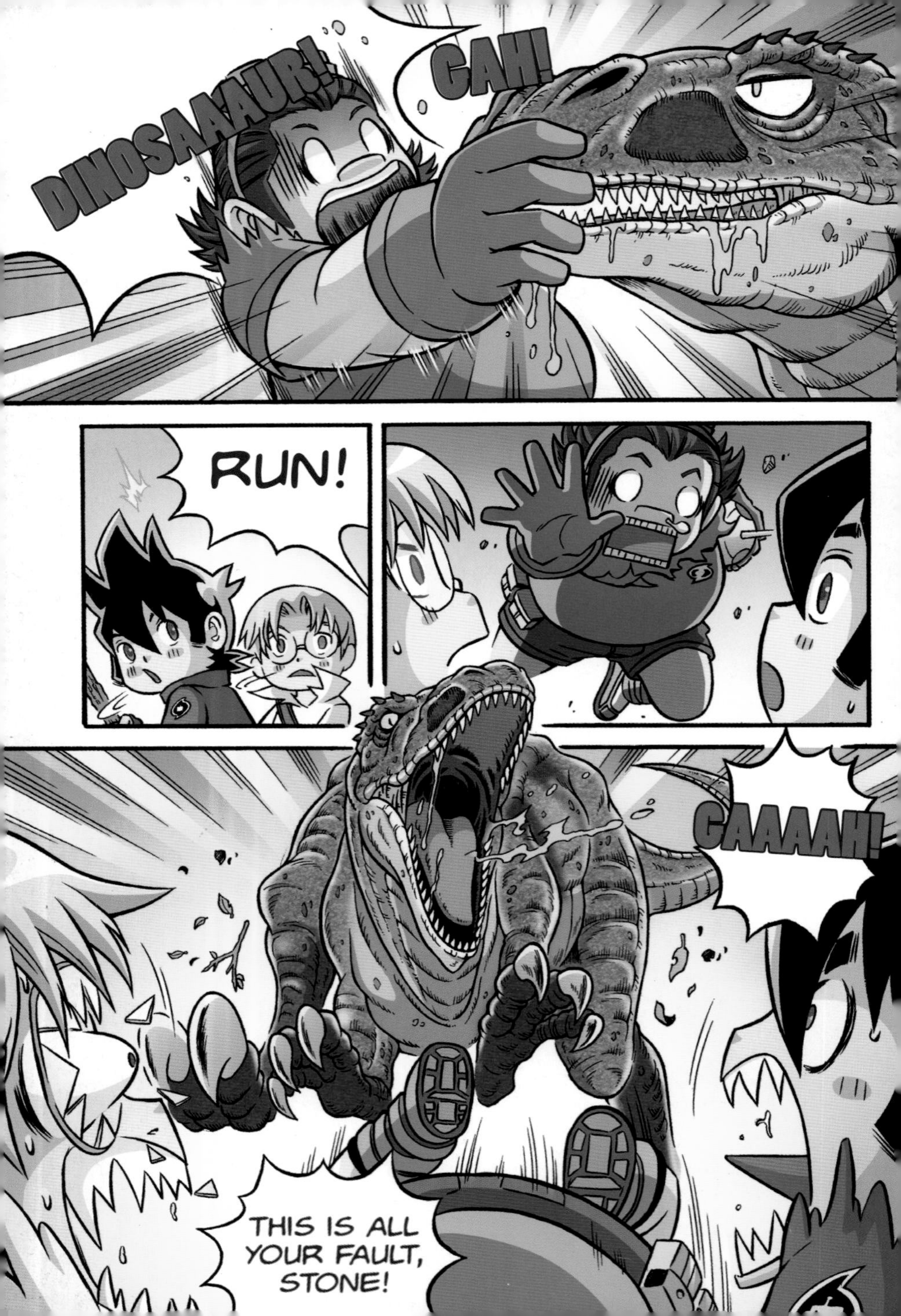
DINOSAAAUR!!
GAH!
RUN!
GAAAAH!
THIS IS ALL YOUR FAULT, STONE!

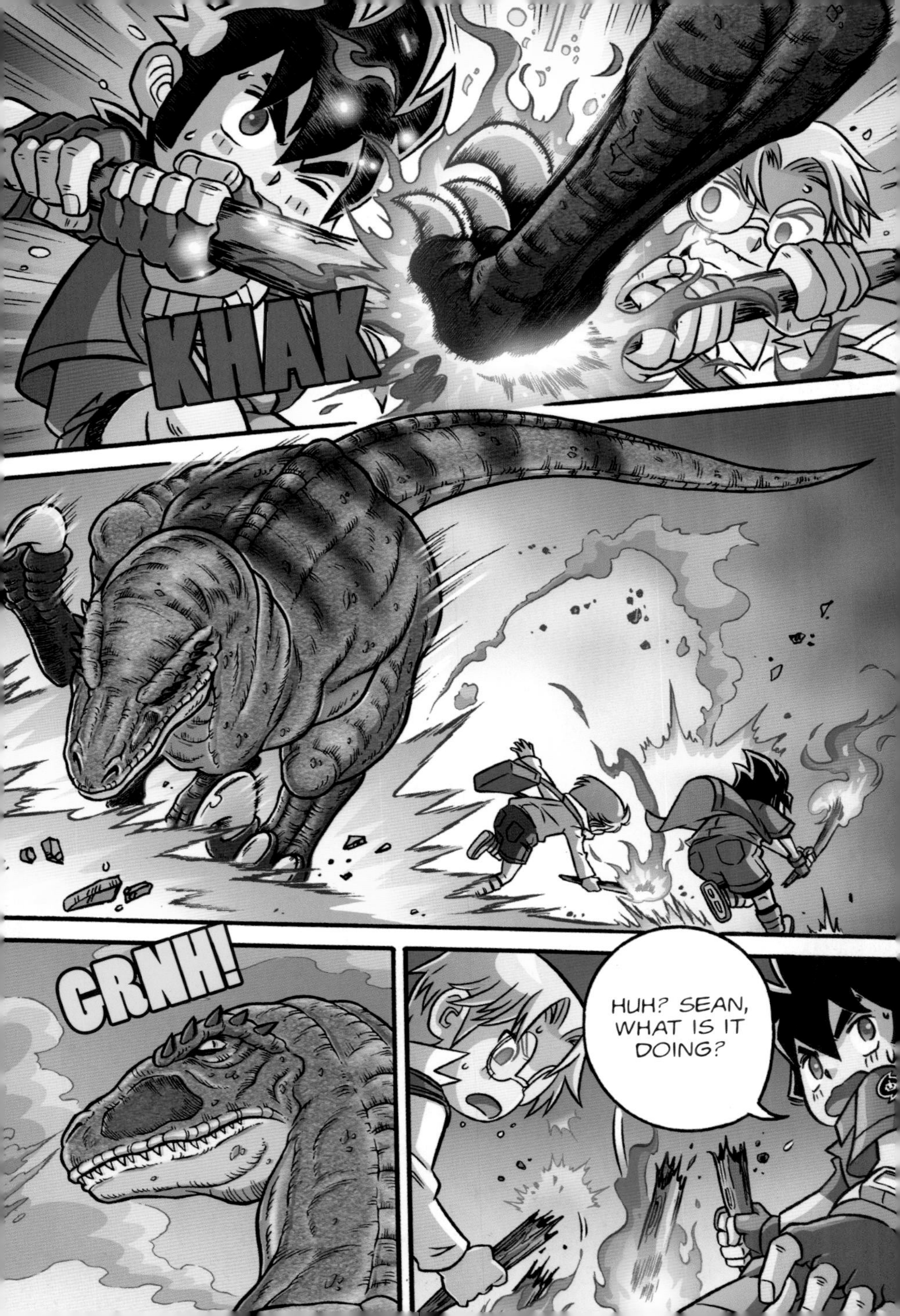

KHAK
CRNH!
HUH? SEAN, WHAT IS IT DOING?

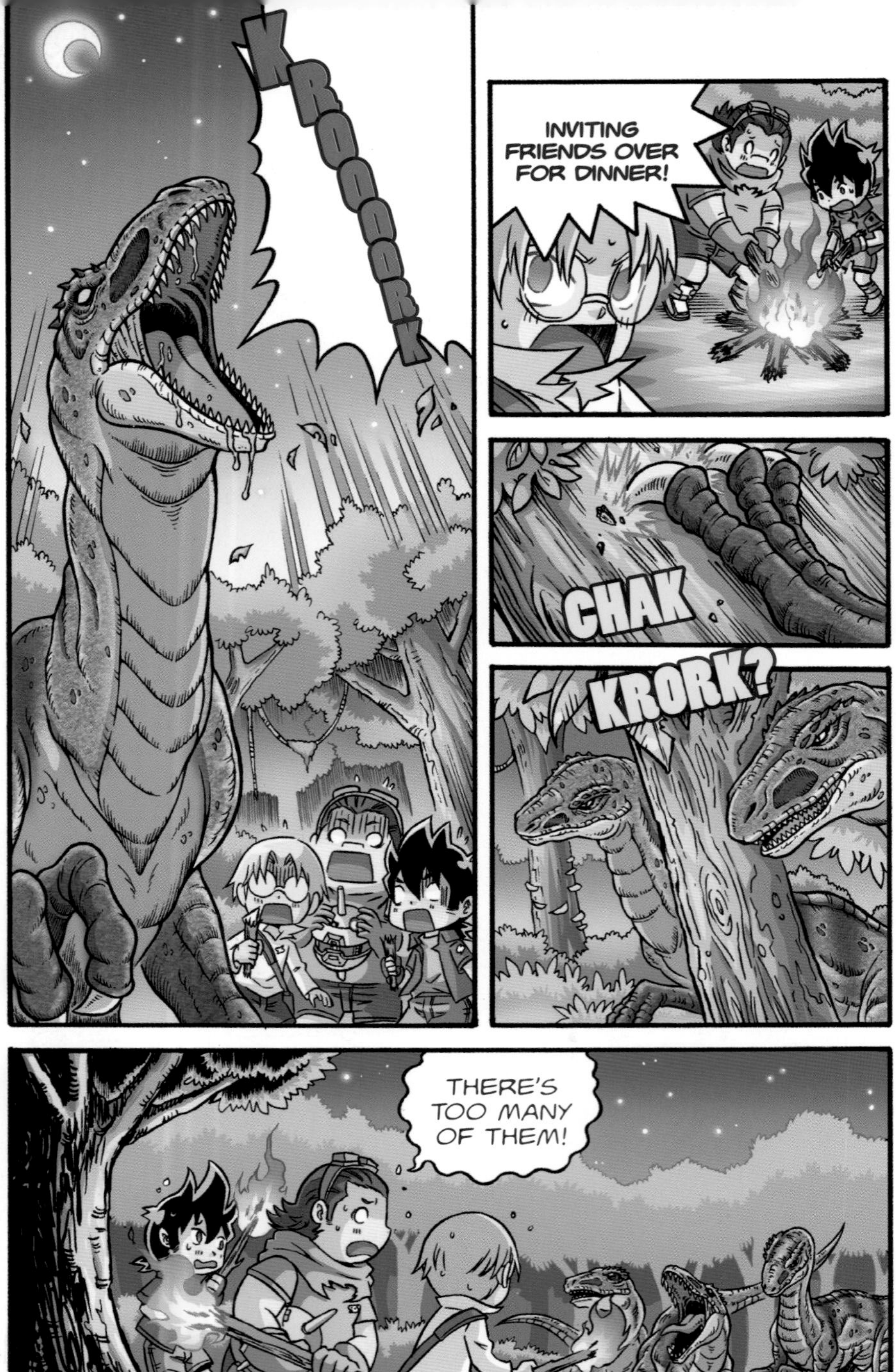
KROOOOORK
INVITING FRIENDS OVER FOR DINNER!
CHAK
KRORK?
THERE'S TOO MANY OF THEM!

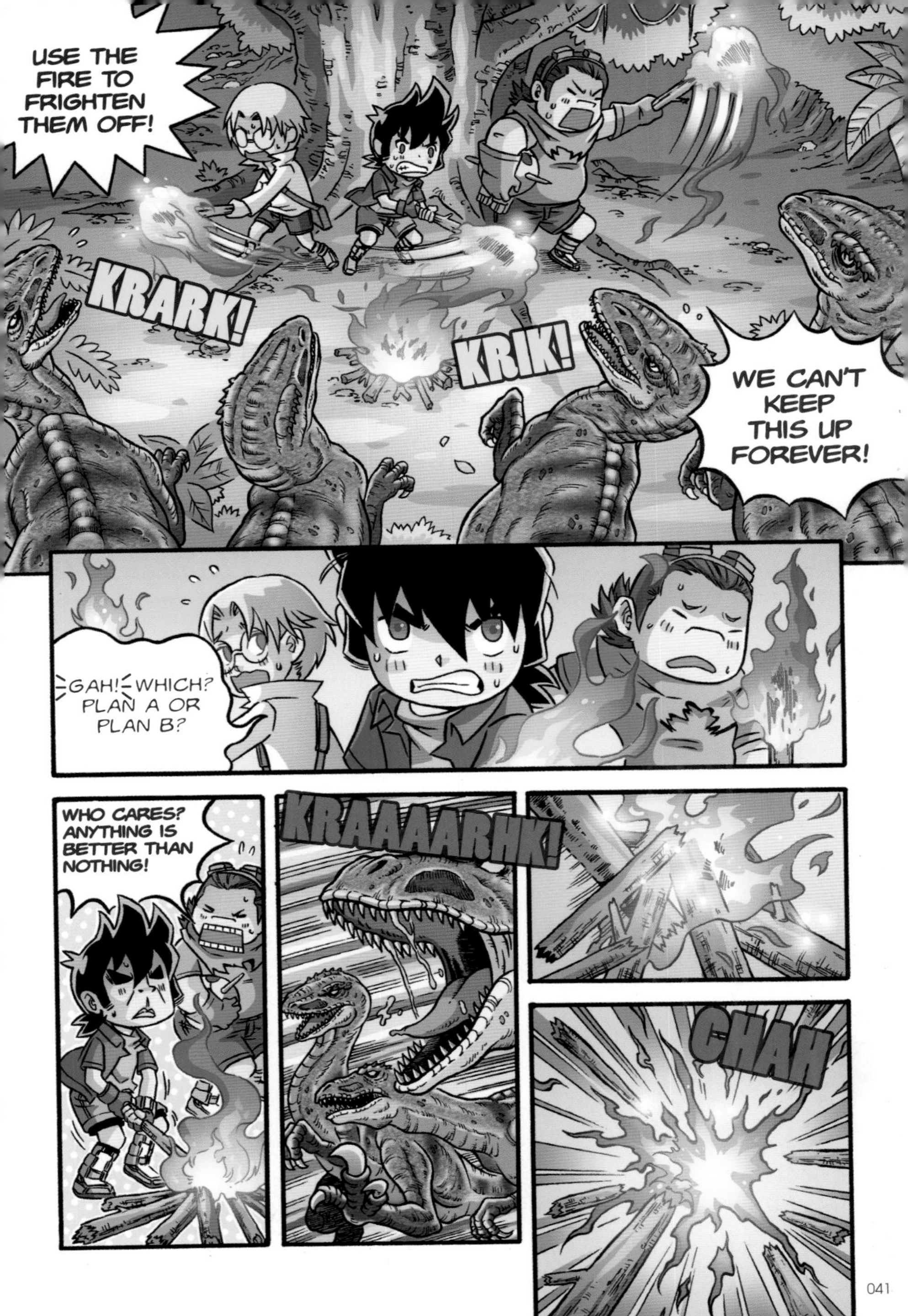
USE THE FIRE TO FRIGHTEN THEM OFF!
KRARK!
KRIK!
WE CAN'T KEEP THIS UP FOREVER!
GAH! WHICH? PLAN A OR PLAN B?
WHO CARES? ANYTHING IS BETTER THAN NOTHING!
KRAAAAARHK!
CHAH

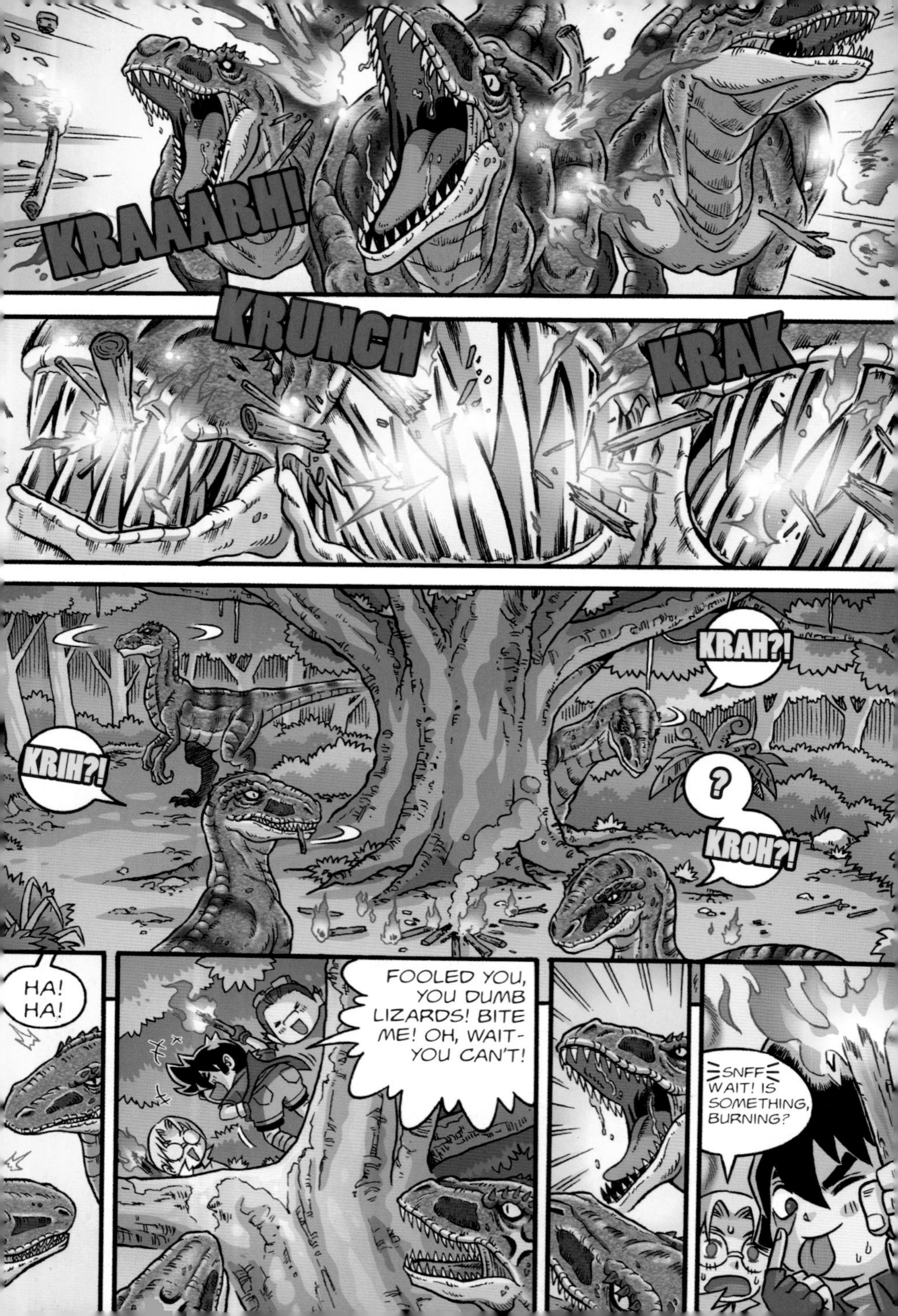
KRAAARH!
KRUNCH
KRAK
KRAH?!
KRIH?!
?
KROH?!
HA! HA!
FOOLED YOU, YOU DUMB LIZARDS! BITE ME! OH, WAIT- YOU CAN'T!
SNFF
WAIT! IS SOMETHING, BURNING?

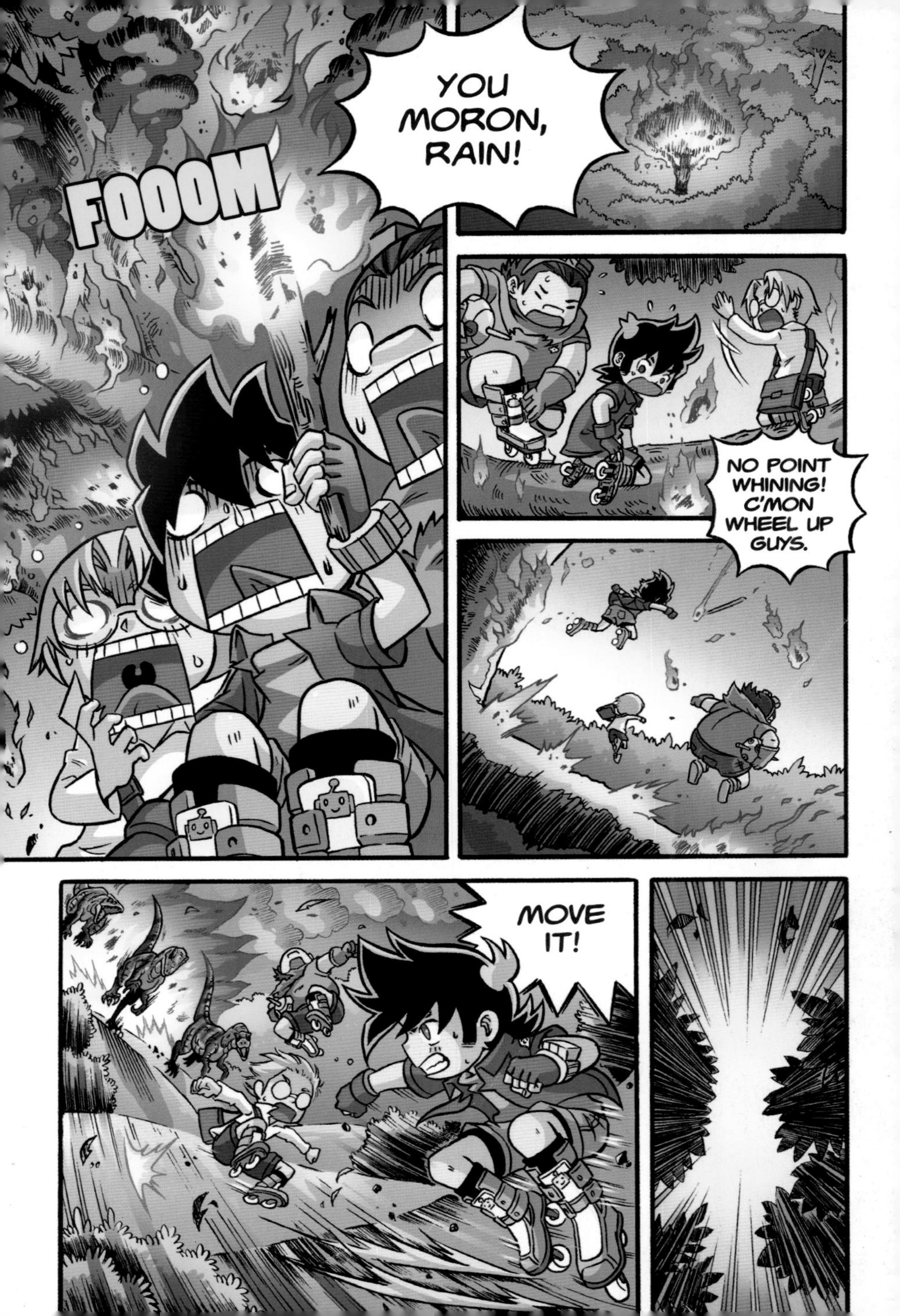
FOOOM
YOU MORON, RAIN!
NO POINT WHINING! C'MON WHEEL UP GUYS.
MOVE IT!

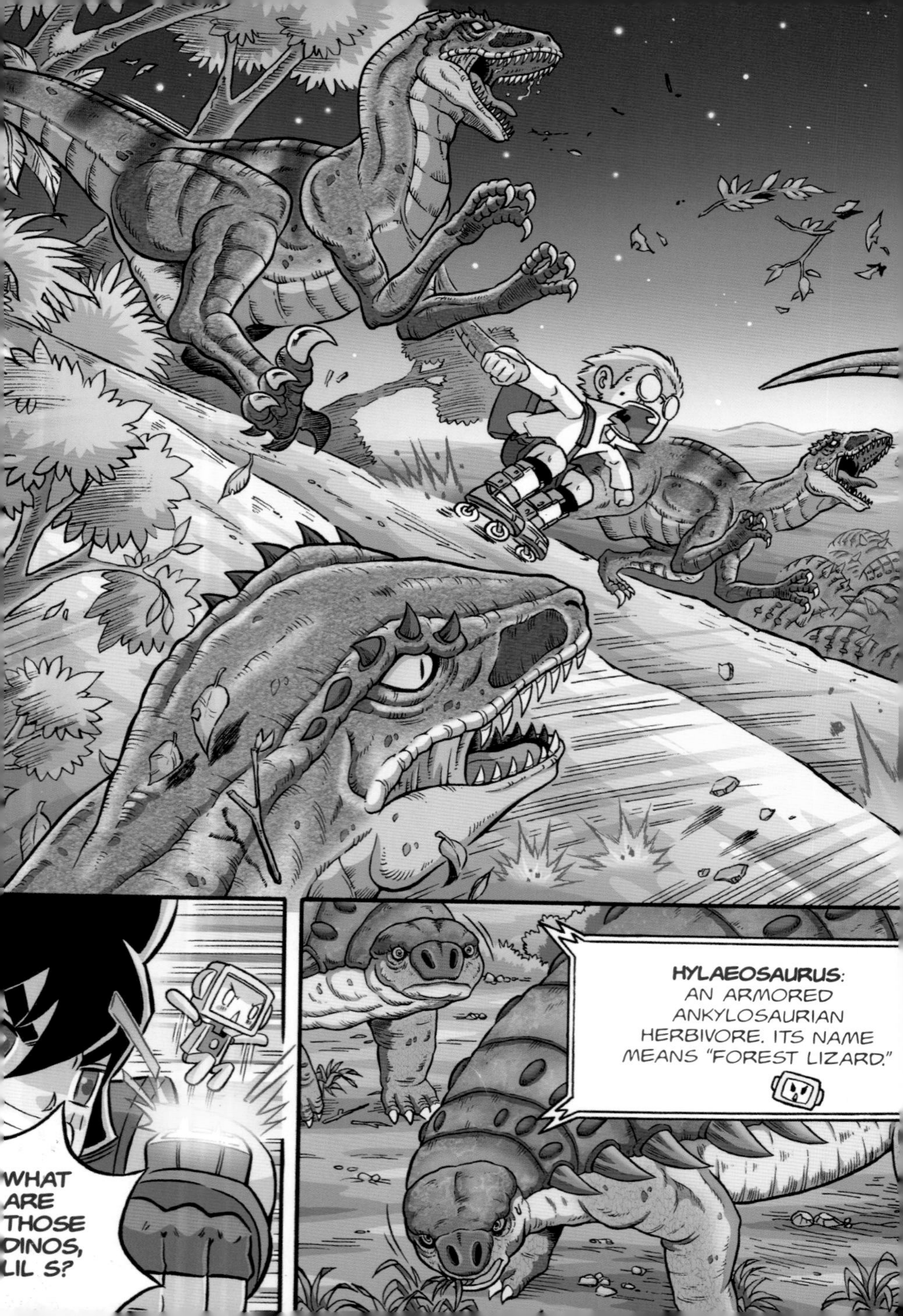
WHAT ARE THOSE DINOS, LIL S?
HYLAEOSAURUS: AN ARMORED ANKYLOSAURIAN HERBIVORE. ITS NAME MEANS "FOREST LIZARD."

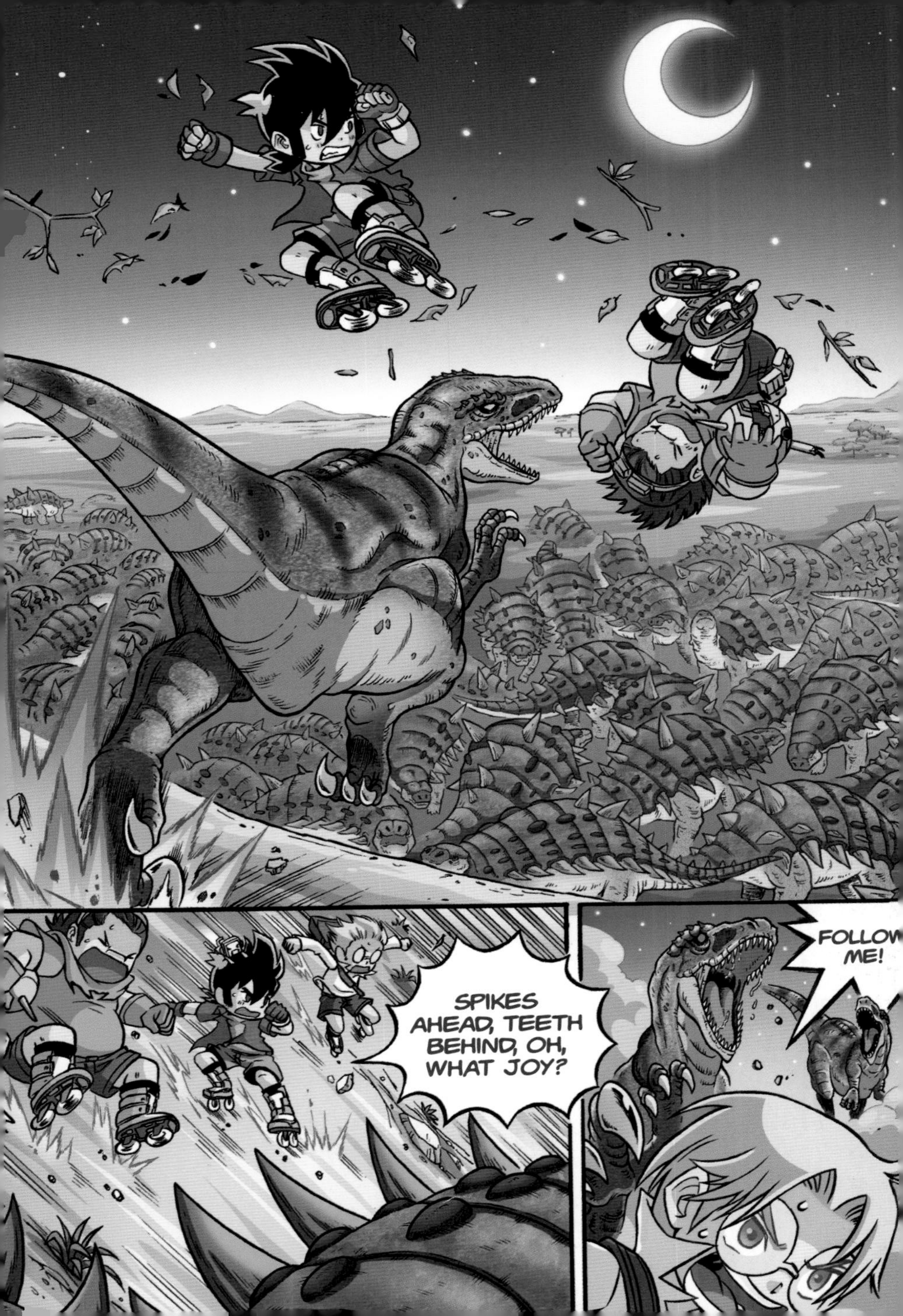
SPIKES AHEAD, TEETH BEHIND, OH, WHAT JOY?
FOLLOW ME!

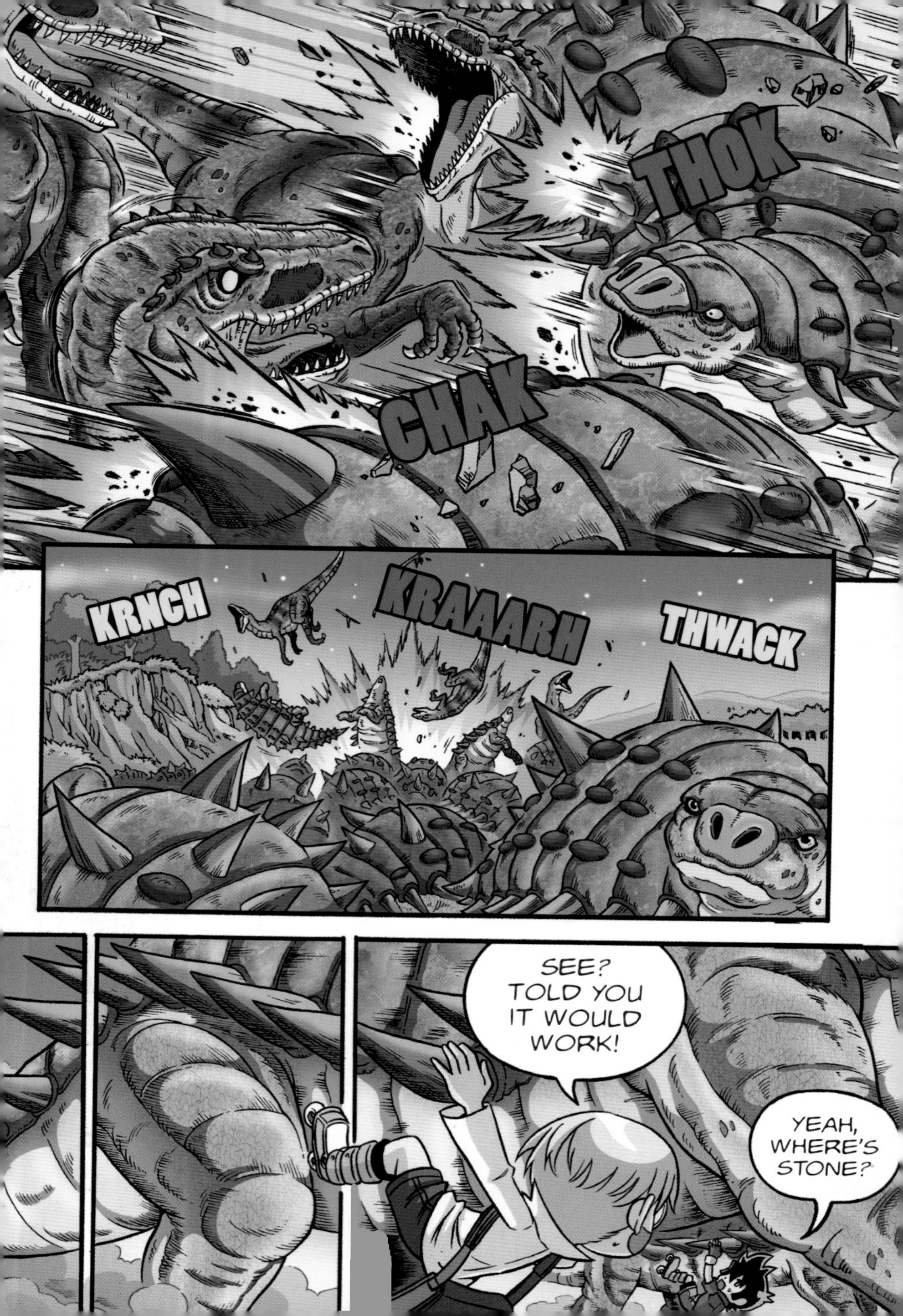
THOK
CHAK
KRNCH
KRAAARH
THWACK
SEE? TOLD YOU IT WOULD WORK!
YEAH, WHERE'S STONE?

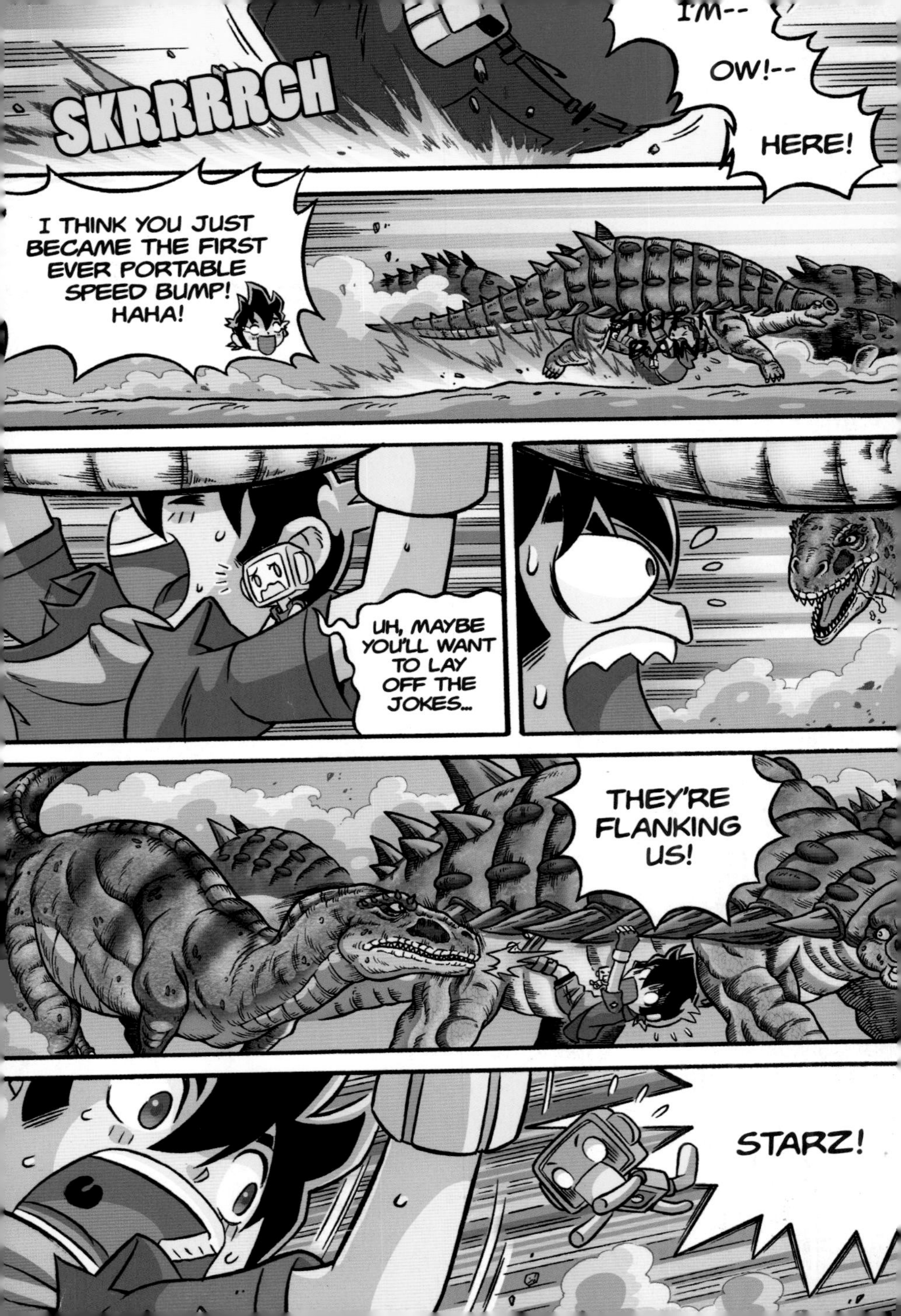
SKRRRRCH
I'M--
OW!--
HERE!
I THINK YOU JUST BECAME THE FIRST EVER PORTABLE SPEED BUMP! HAHA!
UH, MAYBE YOU'LL WANT TO LAY OFF THE JOKES...
THEY'RE FLANKING US!
STARZ!

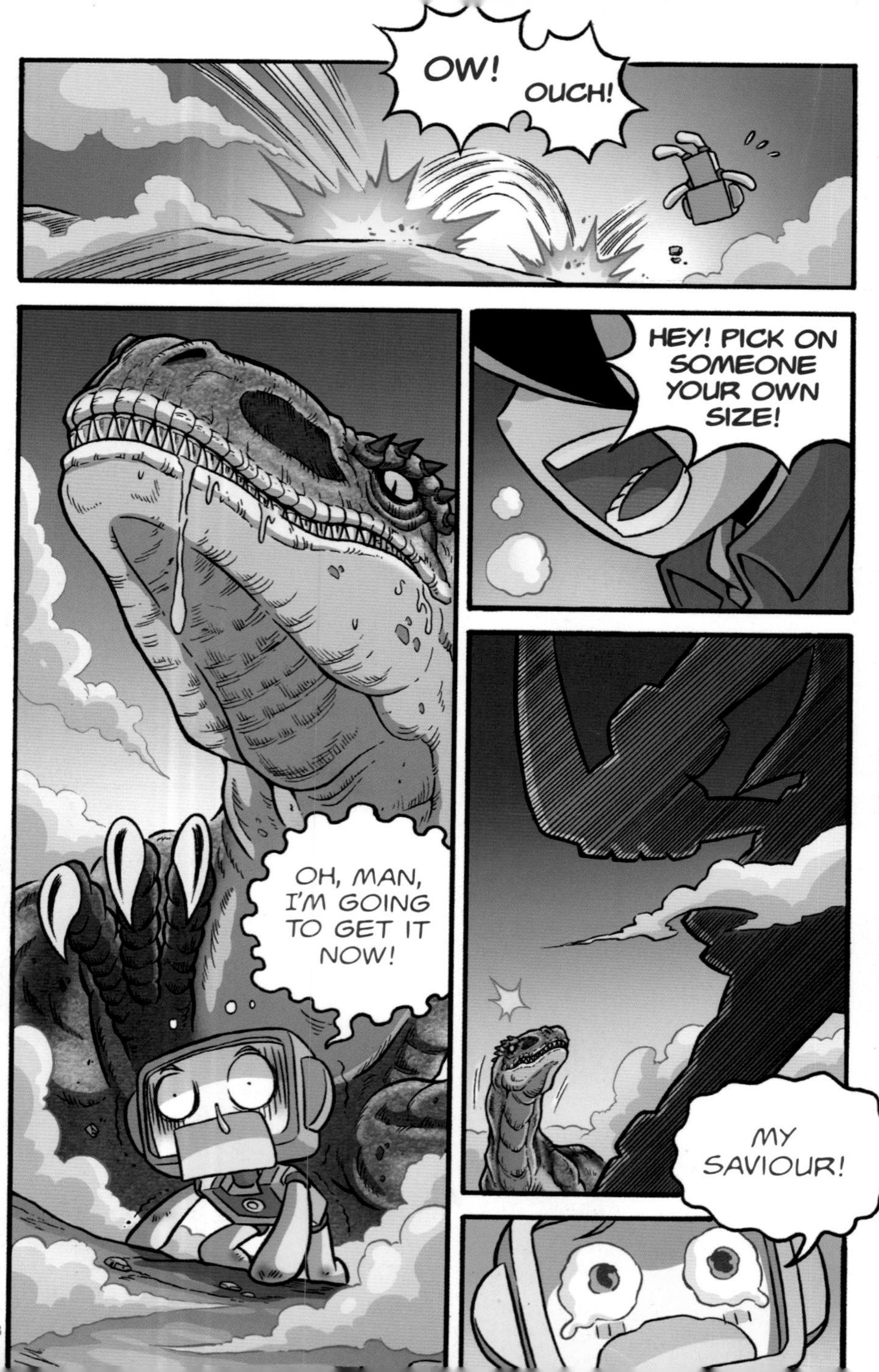
OW!
OUCH!
HEY! PICK ON SOMEONE YOUR OWN SIZE!
OH, MAN, I'M GOING TO GET IT NOW!
MY SAVIOUR!

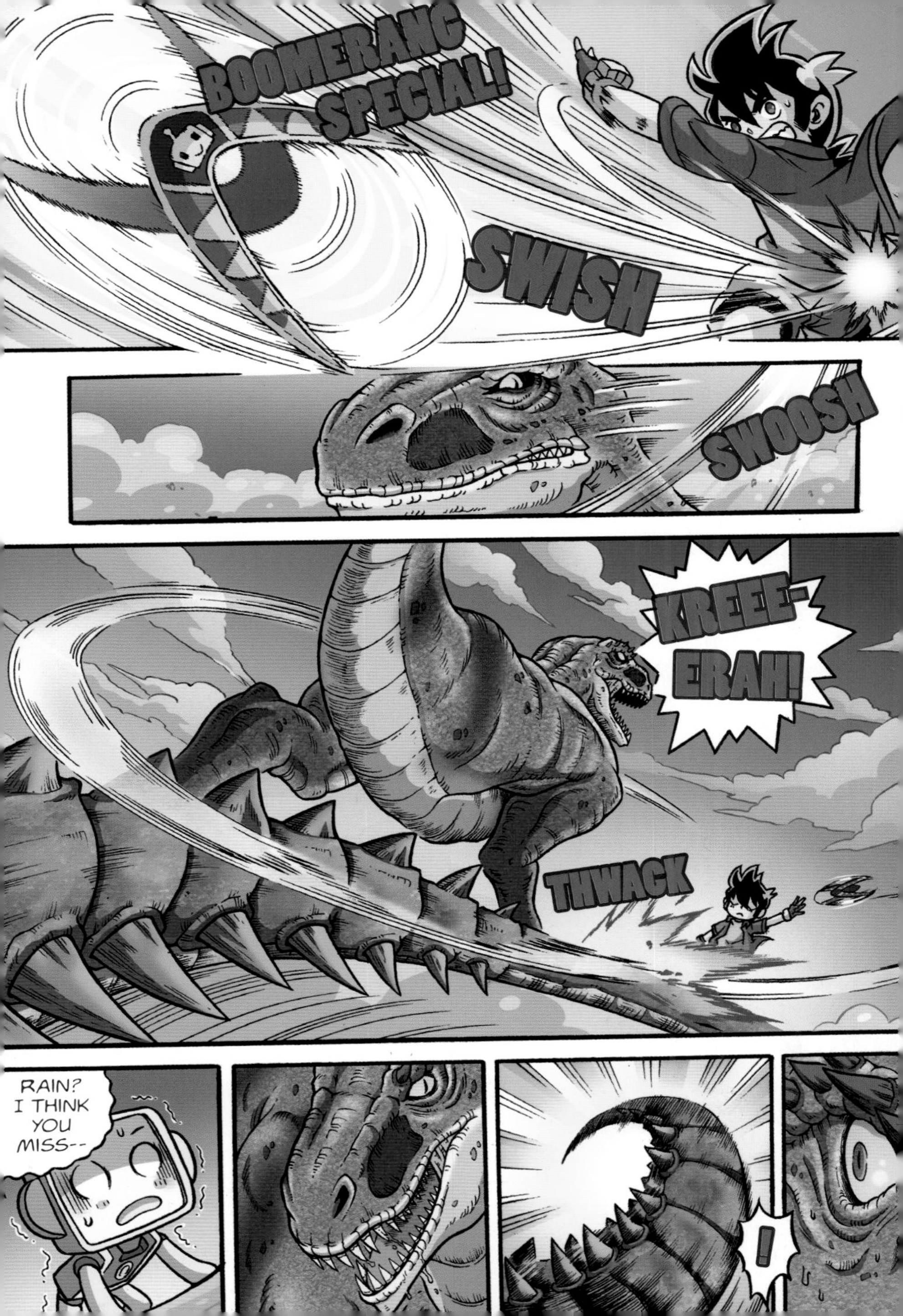
BOOMERANG SPECIAL!
SWISH
SWOOSH
KREEE-ERAH!
THWACK
RAIN? I THINK YOU MISS--
!

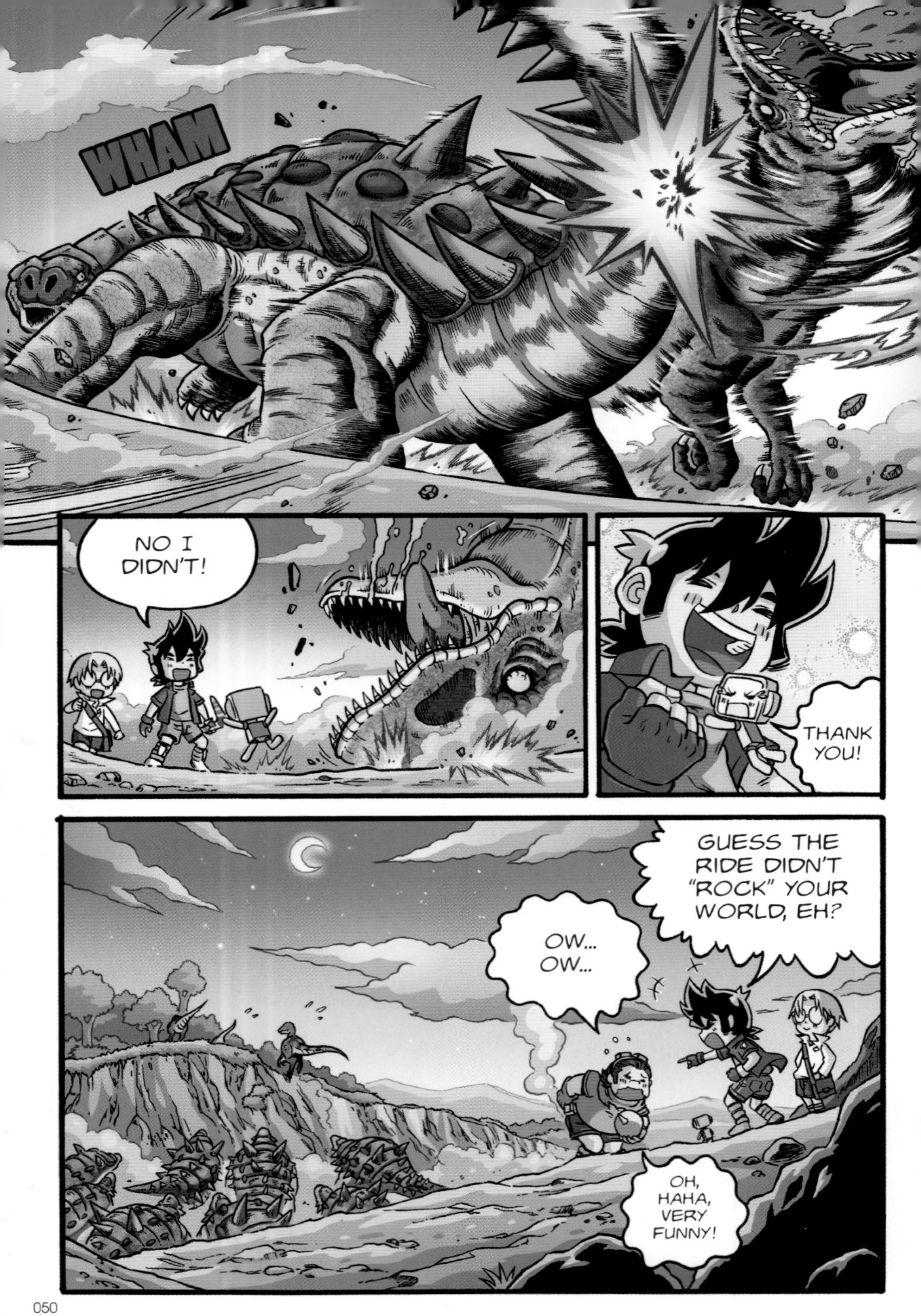
WHAM
NO I DIDN'T!
THANK YOU!
GUESS THE RIDE DIDN'T "ROCK" YOUR WORLD, EH?
OW... OW...
OH, HAHA, VERY FUNNY!

# Dinosaur senses

How did dinosaurs perceive their world? How was their sense of smell and sight? Or hearing? Even now, research into dinosaur senses are ongoing, as new fossils are discovered and knowledge of dinosaur biology increases.

## Sight

Herbivorous dinosaurs had their eyes on the sides of their heads allowing them to survey their surroundings for prey, while their predators had forward-facing eyes to help them focus and judge distances better. The omnivorous Troodon has massive eyes for its head size, implying excellent vision.

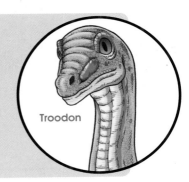
Troodon

## Smell and taste

Dinosaurs might have had noses, but it is thought that they might also have breathed by "tasting" the air with their tongues as snakes do. It is believed that they used their sense of smell to find food and/or avoid predators. The Iguanodon was thought to have had an excellent sense of smell.

Iguanodon

## Hearing

Mammals can hear high frequencies due to 3 special ossicle bones in their ears. Dinosaur ear bones were relatively large and it was believed that like crocodiles, dinosaurs were able to hear sounds at much lower frequencies than mammals. Hadrosaurs often had huge head crests that served as vocal amplifiers, which seems to indicate that their sense of hearing was well-developed.

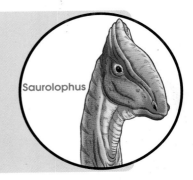
Saurolophus

# How intelligent were dinosaurs?

Scientists measure a species' intelligence according to its Encephalization Quotient (EQ; it is a brain size to body ratio), and studies have shown that the efficacy of this method applies just as much to ancient dinosaurs as it does to modern animals. Dinosaurs with high EQ also had adaptations that would have let them carry out complex actions, as well as run faster, hunt smarter, and elude enemies better.

# How is EQ calculated?

By examining the size of the brain and body, then comparing it to that of similar-sized creatures; a calculation of brain-to-body ratio is formulated.

# Who is smarter? — herbivores or carnivores?

Studies indicate that carnivores and omnivores had higher EQs than herbivores. For example, the omnivorous Troodon and carnivorous Deinonychus have EQs slightly higher than 5 (humans have an EQ of 7 or so), while the Tyrannosaurus only had 2.5, but even that was much higher than the average herbivore EQ of between 0.2 and 0.9.

## Mammal EQs

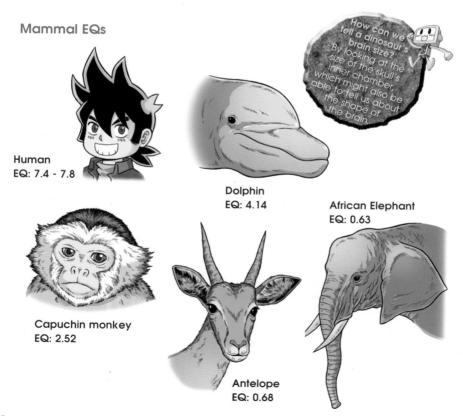

How can we tell a dinosaur's brain size? By looking at the size of the skull's inner chamber, which might also be able to tell us about the shape of the brain.

Human
EQ: 7.4 - 7.8

Dolphin
EQ: 4.14

African Elephant
EQ: 0.63

Capuchin monkey
EQ: 2.52

Antelope
EQ: 0.68

# Herbivore EQs

### Hadrosaurs, Corythosaurus (Ornithopods)
**EQ: 0.85 -1.5**
They had the highest EQs, but avoided predators through strength and speed rather than outthinking them.

### Ceratopsids
**EQ: 0.7 - 0.9**
Ceratopsids were much more formidable defensively compared to the club-tailed, armored ankylosaurs and the plated, spike-tailed stegosaurs, due to their long horns and bony neck "frills."

### Ankylosaurus, Stegosaurus
**EQ: 0.52 - 0.56**
Defensively, vertical back plates and spiked body armor provided protection against attack, while powerful spiked/ clubbed tails supplied offensive clout.

### Apatosaurus, Diplodocus (large sauropods)
**EQ: 0.2 - 0.35**
Slow to move and react like elephants, they relied on their massive size to intimidate predators.

# CAPTURING THE CRETACEOUS!

## Hypsilophodon

**Scientific name:** Hypsilophodon
**Size:** 6.56 feet
**Diet:** Herbivore
**Habitat:** Forests
**Discovered:** Mainland Europe, Great Britain
**Period:** Early Cretaceous

Hypsilophodon was named for its teeth (its name is Greek for "high-ridged tooth"). A diminutive bipedal ornithopod, it stood at waist height for the average human, and had a head the size of a human fist. It was built for speed, with short hips, long tibias, a sturdy, lightweight frame, and a tail adapted to maintain balance. Its cheeks also had pouches in which it must have stored food.

# CAPTURING THE CRETACEOUS!

## Hylaeosaurus

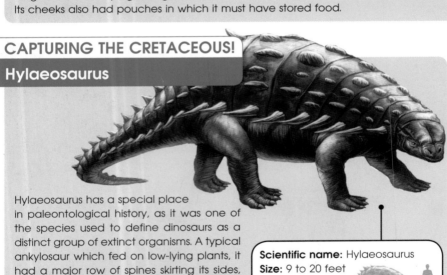

Hylaeosaurus has a special place in paleontological history, as it was one of the species used to define dinosaurs as a distinct group of extinct organisms. A typical ankylosaur which fed on low-lying plants, it had a major row of spines skirting its sides, with an additional row emerging from bony ridges from the waist down its heavy tail. The most complete Hylaeosaurus fossil known can be found in London's Museum of Natural History.

**Scientific name:** Hylaeosaurus
**Size:** 9 to 20 feet
**Diet:** Herbivore
**Habitat:** Forests
**Discovered:** Britain, France
**Period:** Early Cretaceous

CHAPTER 3

# STRANGE BEDFELLOWS!

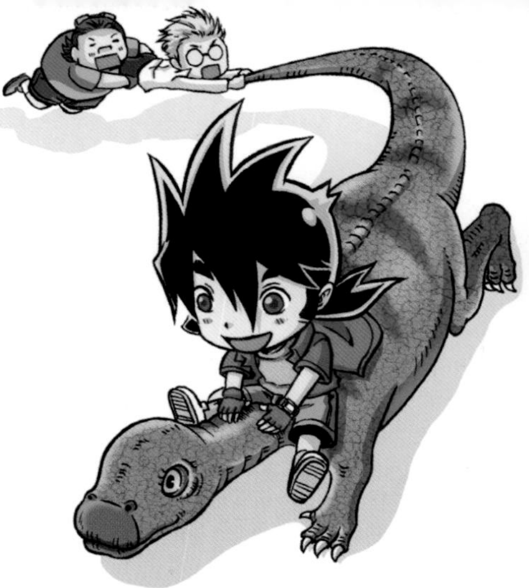

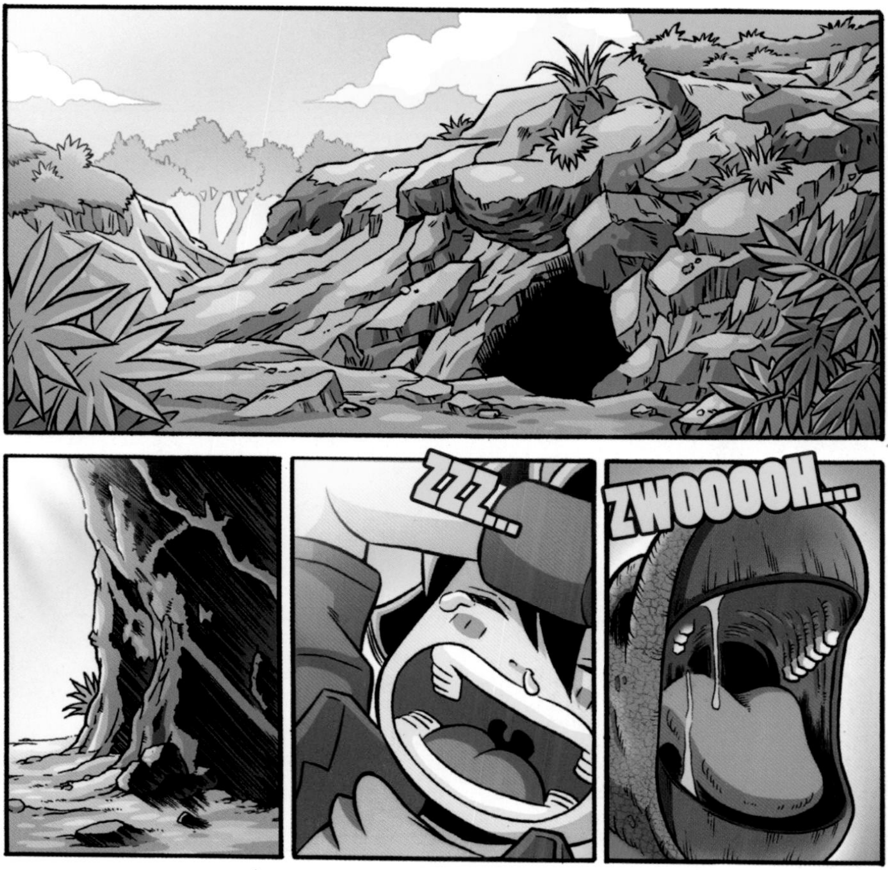
ZZZ...
ZWOOOOH...

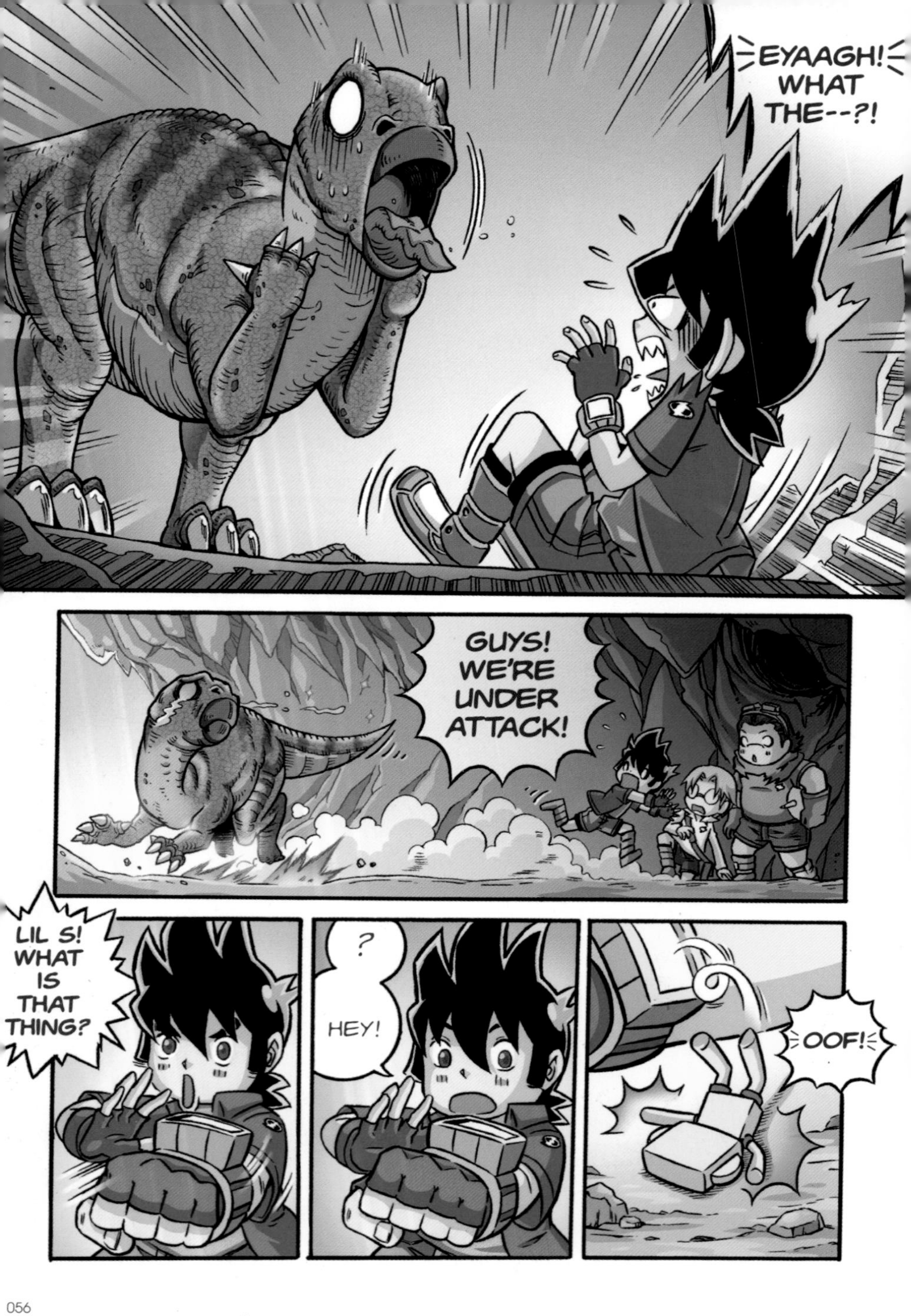
EYAAGH! WHAT THE--?!
GUYS! WE'RE UNDER ATTACK!
LIL S! WHAT IS THAT THING?
?
HEY!
OOF!

NOW WHAT IS IT?!

SORRY, I WAS SLEEPY!

YOU'RE A ROBOT! YOU DON'T NEED SLEEP!

SCANNING

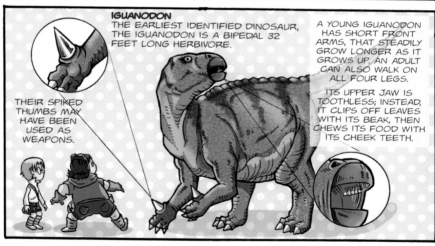

**IGUANODON**

THE EARLIEST IDENTIFIED DINOSAUR, THE IGUANODON IS A BIPEDAL 32 FEET LONG HERBIVORE.

THEIR SPIKED THUMBS MAY HAVE BEEN USED AS WEAPONS.

A YOUNG IGUANODON HAS SHORT FRONT ARMS, THAT STEADILY GROW LONGER AS IT GROWS UP. AN ADULT CAN ALSO WALK ON ALL FOUR LEGS.

ITS UPPER JAW IS TOOTHLESS; INSTEAD, IT CLIPS OFF LEAVES WITH ITS BEAK, THEN CHEWS ITS FOOD WITH ITS CHEEK TEETH.

AWW, SO IT'S JUST A BABY!

C'MON DONNIE, GIDDY UP!

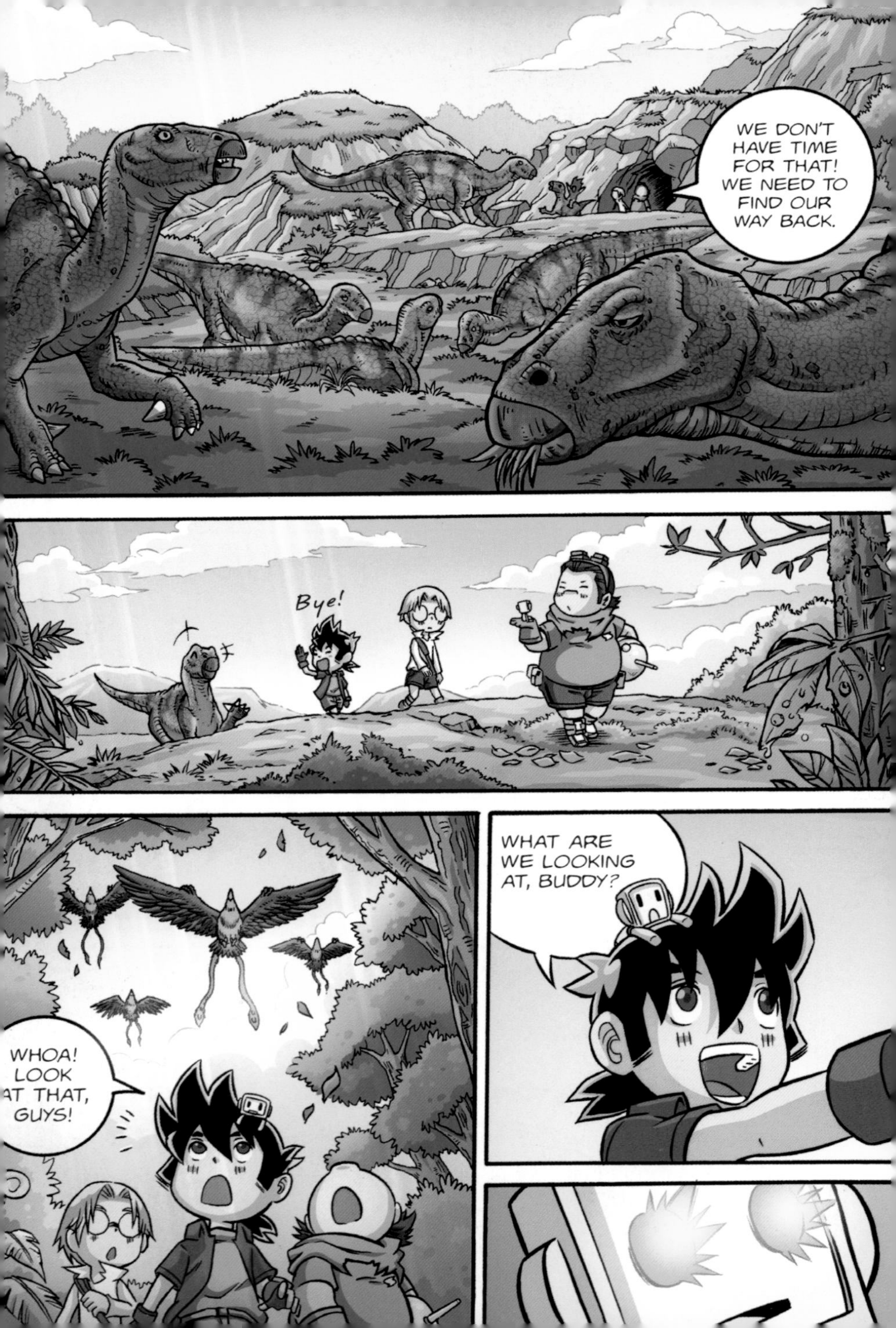
WE DON'T HAVE TIME FOR THAT! WE NEED TO FIND OUR WAY BACK.
Bye!
WHOA! LOOK AT THAT, GUYS!
WHAT ARE WE LOOKING AT, BUDDY?

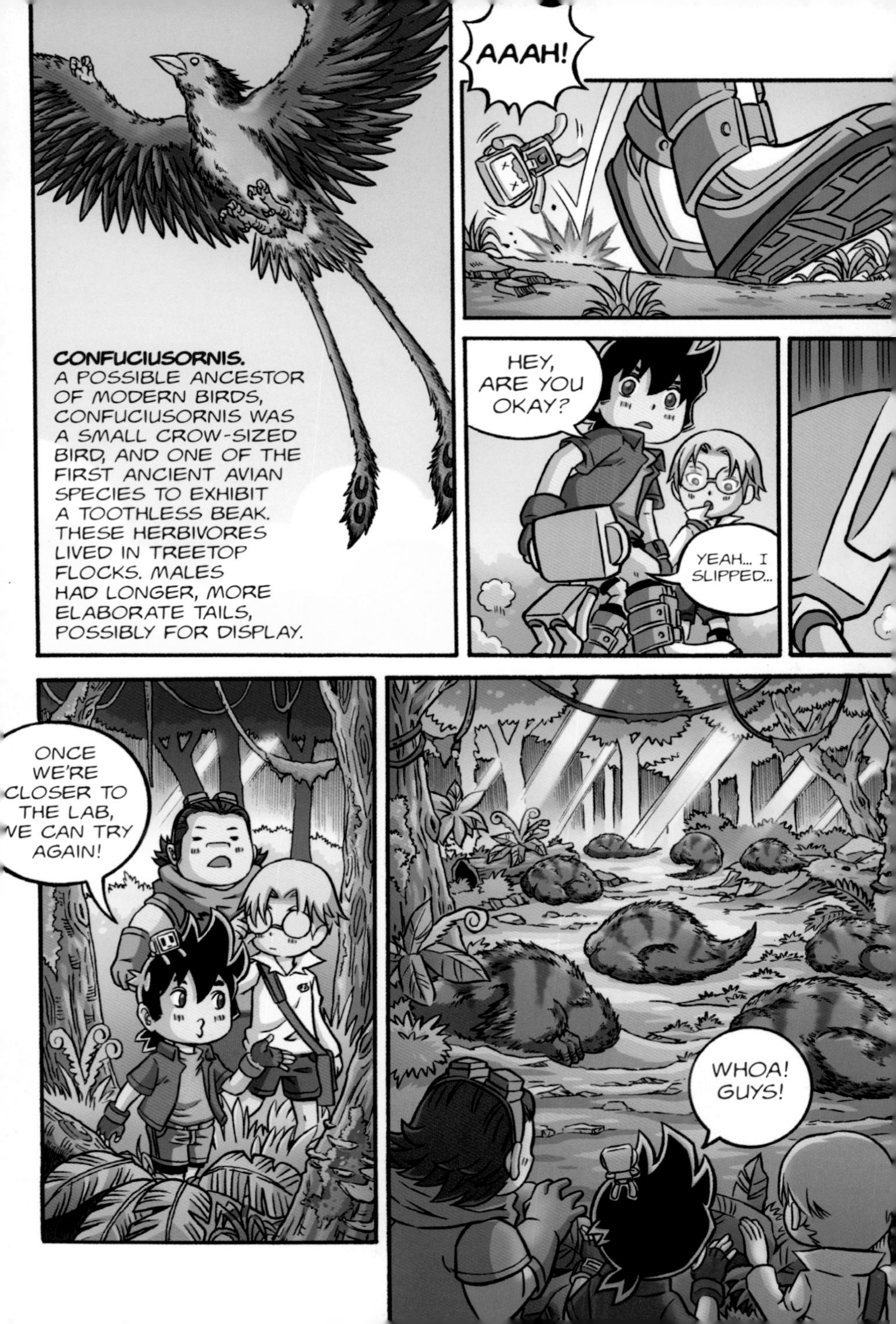
CONFUCIUSORNIS.
A POSSIBLE ANCESTOR OF MODERN BIRDS, CONFUCIUSORNIS WAS A SMALL CROW-SIZED BIRD, AND ONE OF THE FIRST ANCIENT AVIAN SPECIES TO EXHIBIT A TOOTHLESS BEAK. THESE HERBIVORES LIVED IN TREETOP FLOCKS. MALES HAD LONGER, MORE ELABORATE TAILS, POSSIBLY FOR DISPLAY.
AAAH!
HEY, ARE YOU OKAY?
YEAH... I SLIPPED...
ONCE WE'RE CLOSER TO THE LAB, WE CAN TRY AGAIN!
WHOA! GUYS!

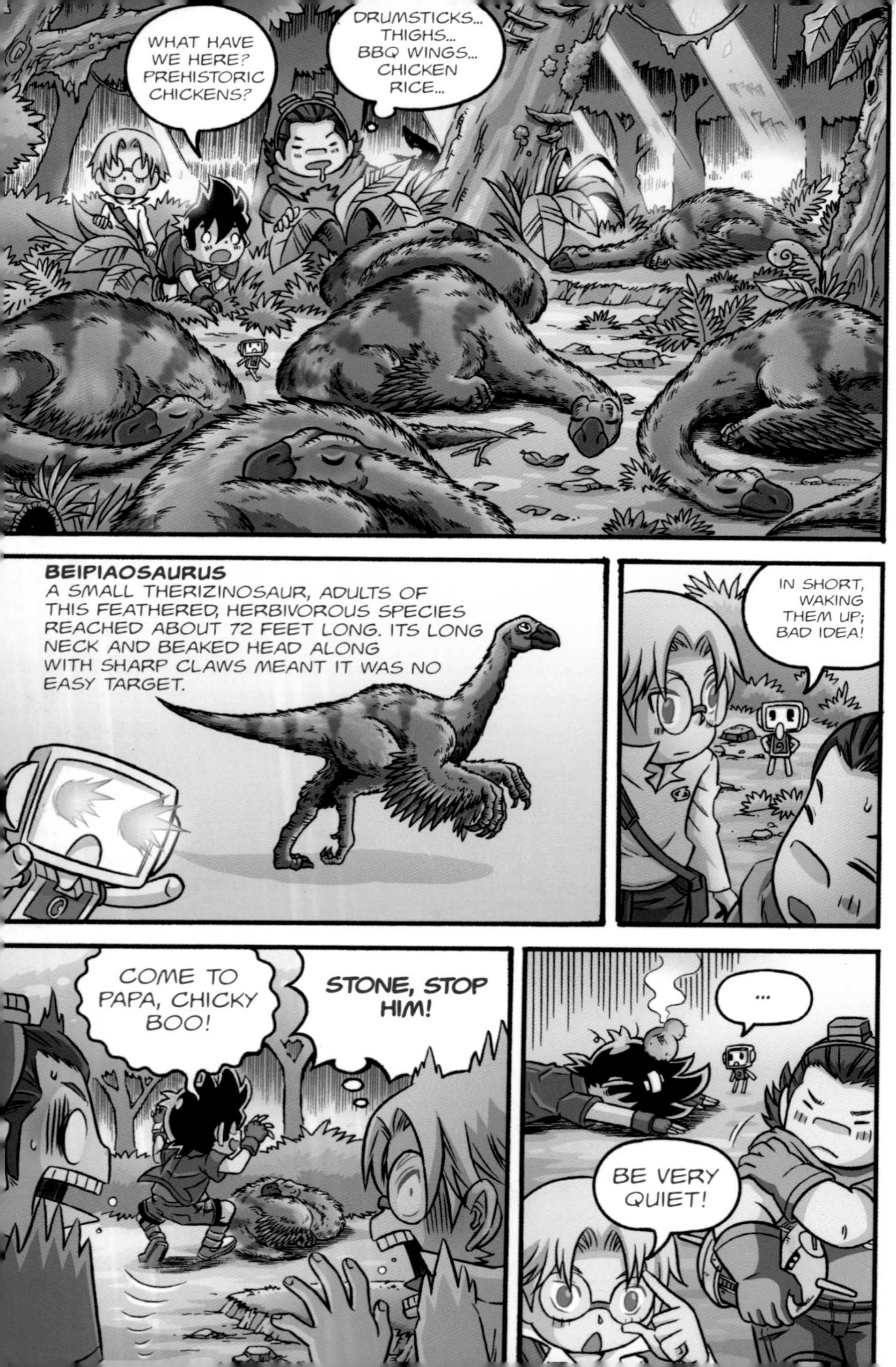
WHAT HAVE WE HERE? PREHISTORIC CHICKENS?
DRUMSTICKS... THIGHS... BBQ WINGS... CHICKEN RICE...
BEIPIAOSAURUS
A SMALL THERIZINOSAUR, ADULTS OF THIS FEATHERED, HERBIVOROUS SPECIES REACHED ABOUT 72 FEET LONG. ITS LONG NECK AND BEAKED HEAD ALONG WITH SHARP CLAWS MEANT IT WAS NO EASY TARGET.
IN SHORT, WAKING THEM UP; BAD IDEA!
COME TO PAPA, CHICKY BOO!
STONE, STOP HIM!
...
BE VERY QUIET!

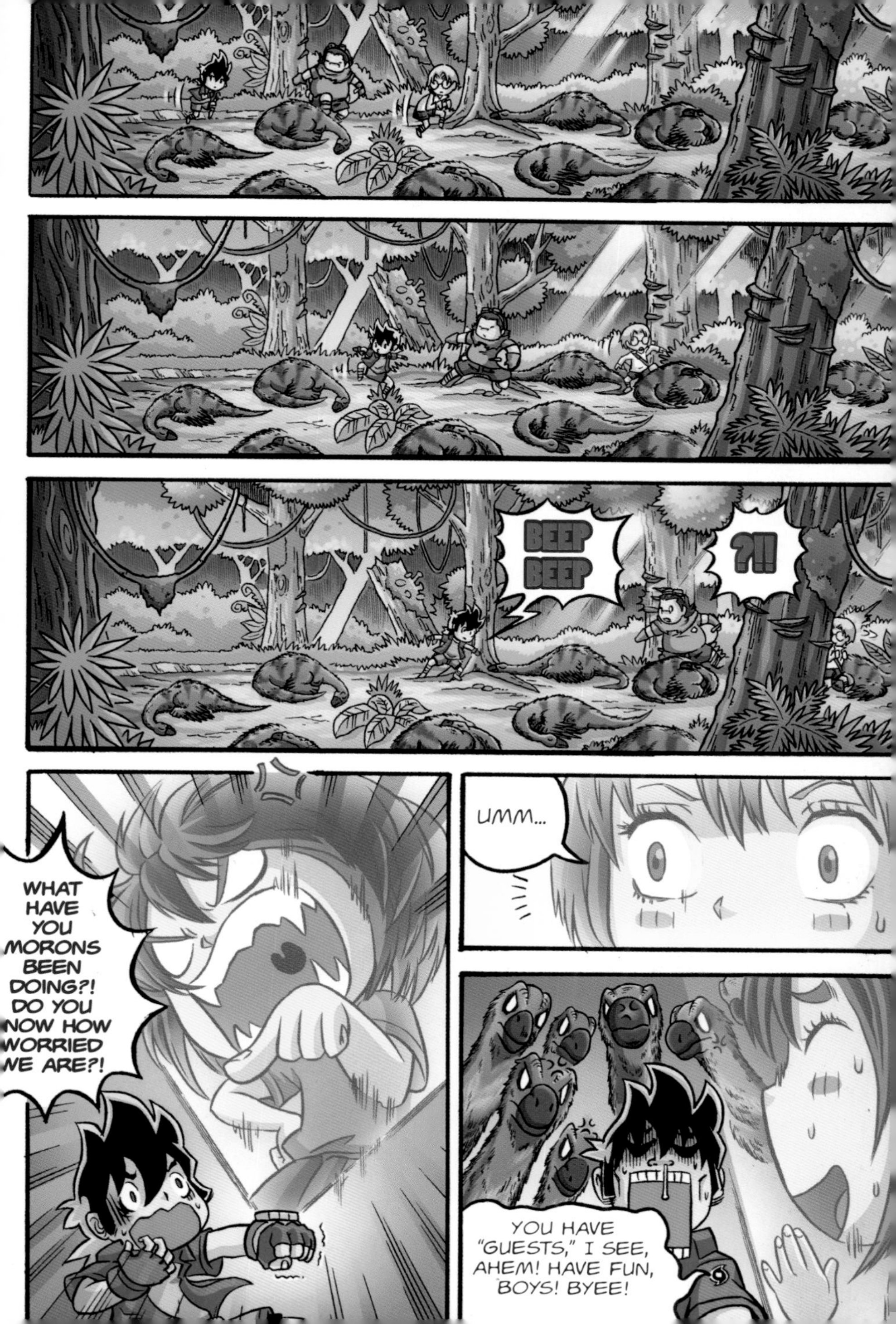
BEEP BEEP
?!!
WHAT HAVE YOU MORONS BEEN DOING?! DO YOU NOW HOW WORRIED NE ARE?!
UMM...
YOU HAVE "GUESTS," I SEE, AHEM! HAVE FUN, BOYS! BYEE!

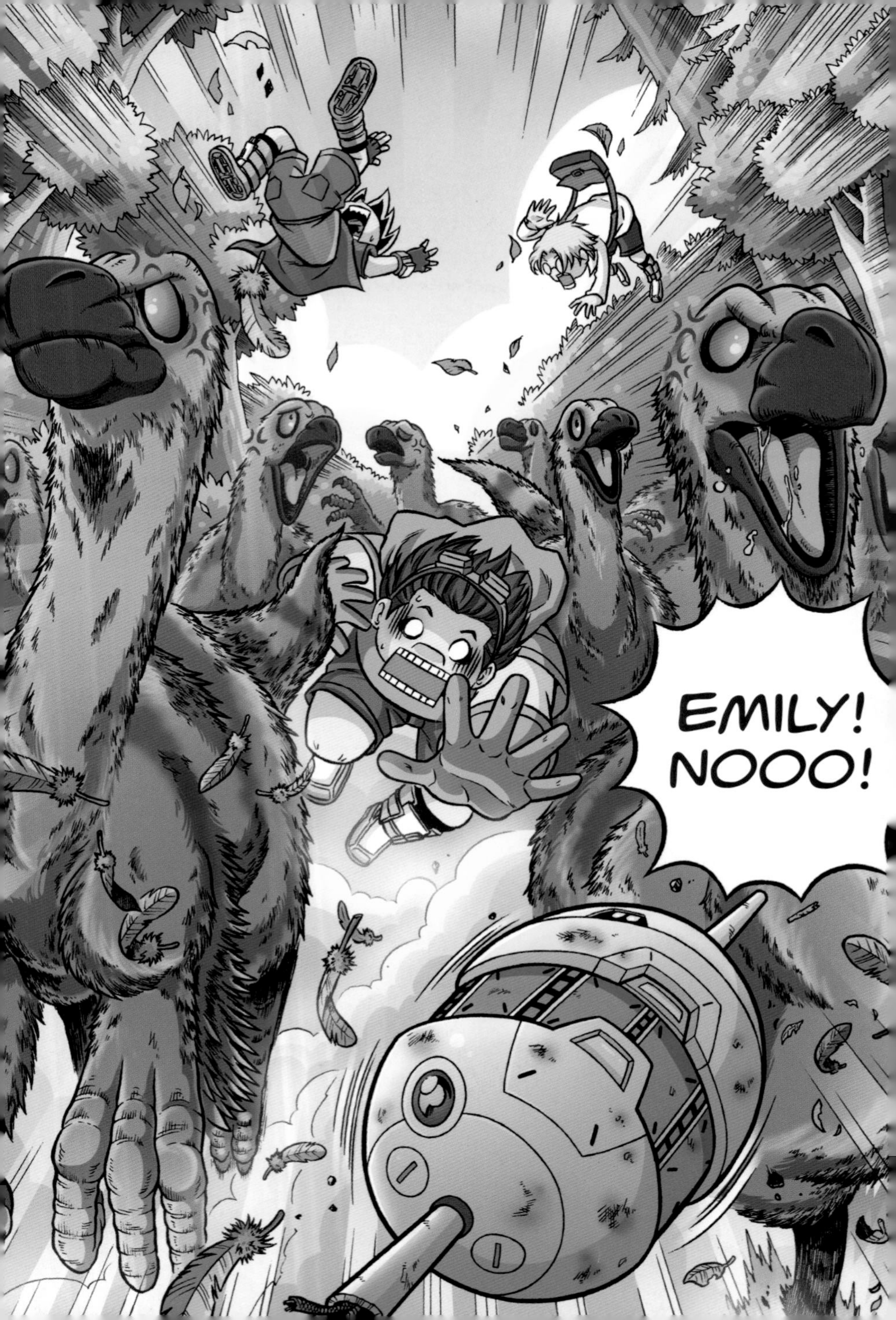
EMILY! NOOO!

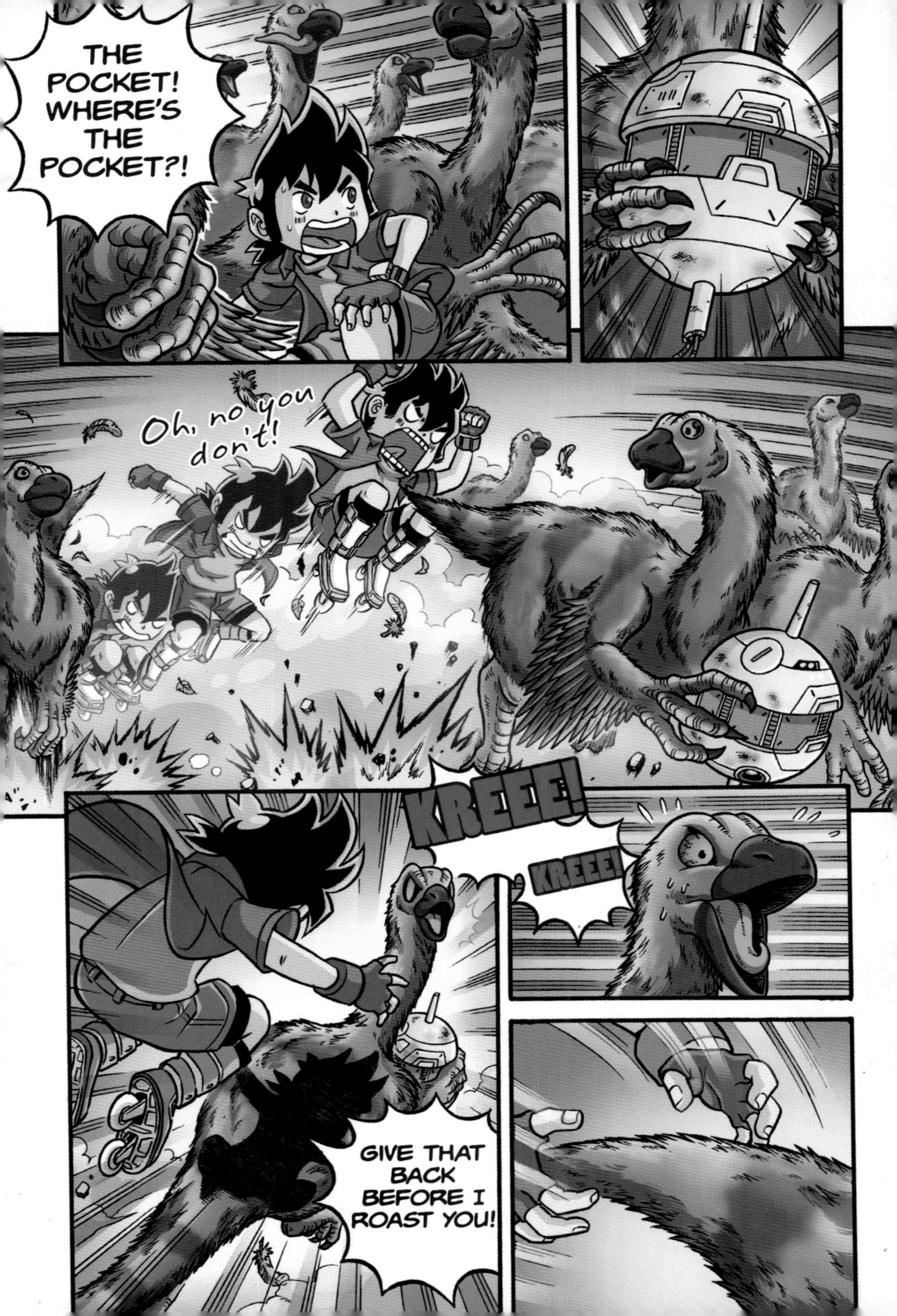
THE POCKET! WHERE'S THE POCKET?!
Oh, no you don't!
KREEE!
KREEE!
GIVE THAT BACK BEFORE I ROAST YOU!

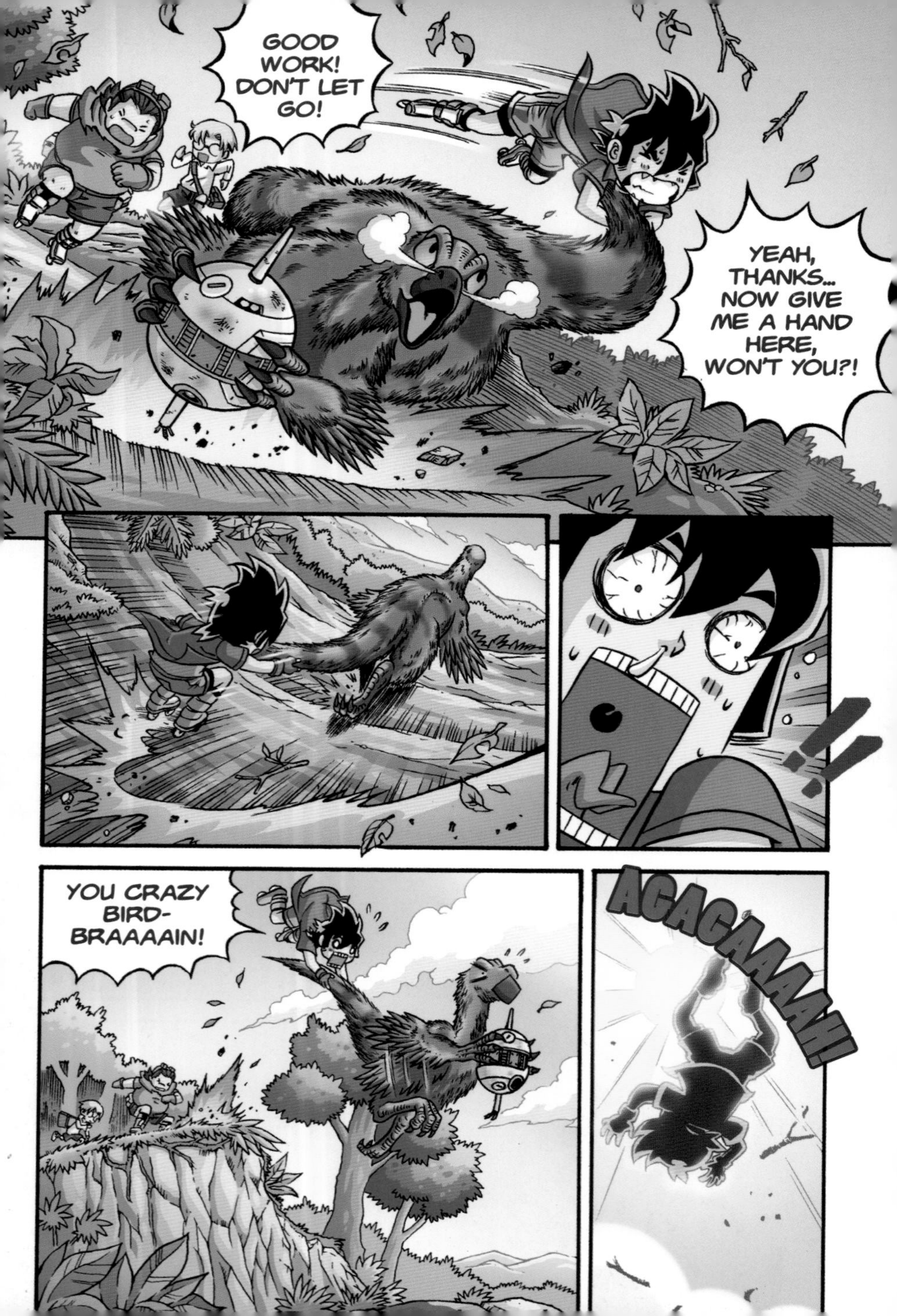
GOOD WORK! DON'T LET GO!
YEAH, THANKS... NOW GIVE ME A HAND HERE, WON'T YOU?!
!!
YOU CRAZY BIRD-BRAAAAIN!
AGAGAAAAAH!

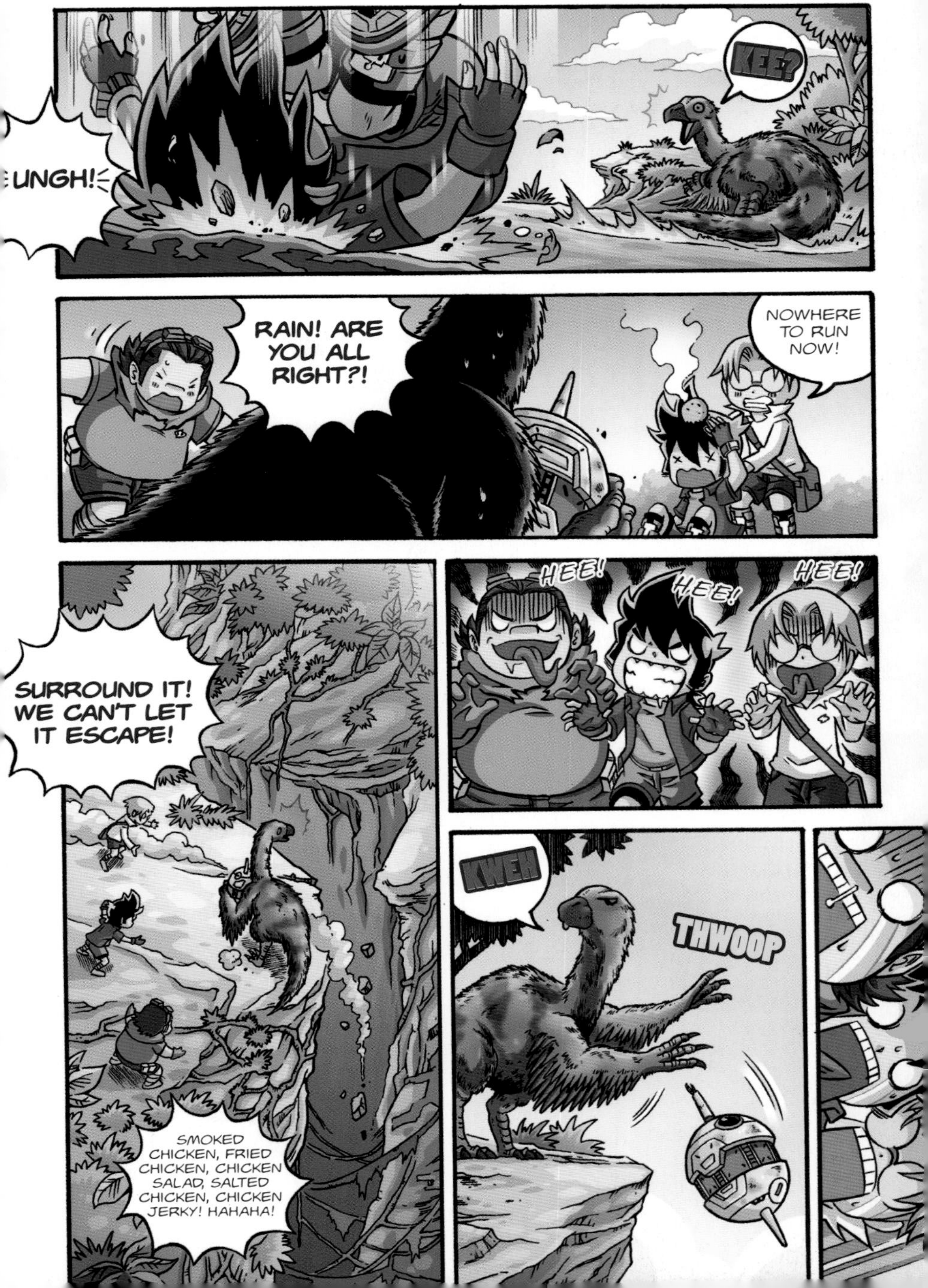
UNGH!
KEE?
RAIN! ARE YOU ALL RIGHT?!
NOWHERE TO RUN NOW!
SURROUND IT! WE CAN'T LET IT ESCAPE!
SMOKED CHICKEN, FRIED CHICKEN, CHICKEN SALAD, SALTED CHICKEN, CHICKEN JERKY! HAHAHA!
HEE!
HEE!
HEE!
KWEH
THWOOP

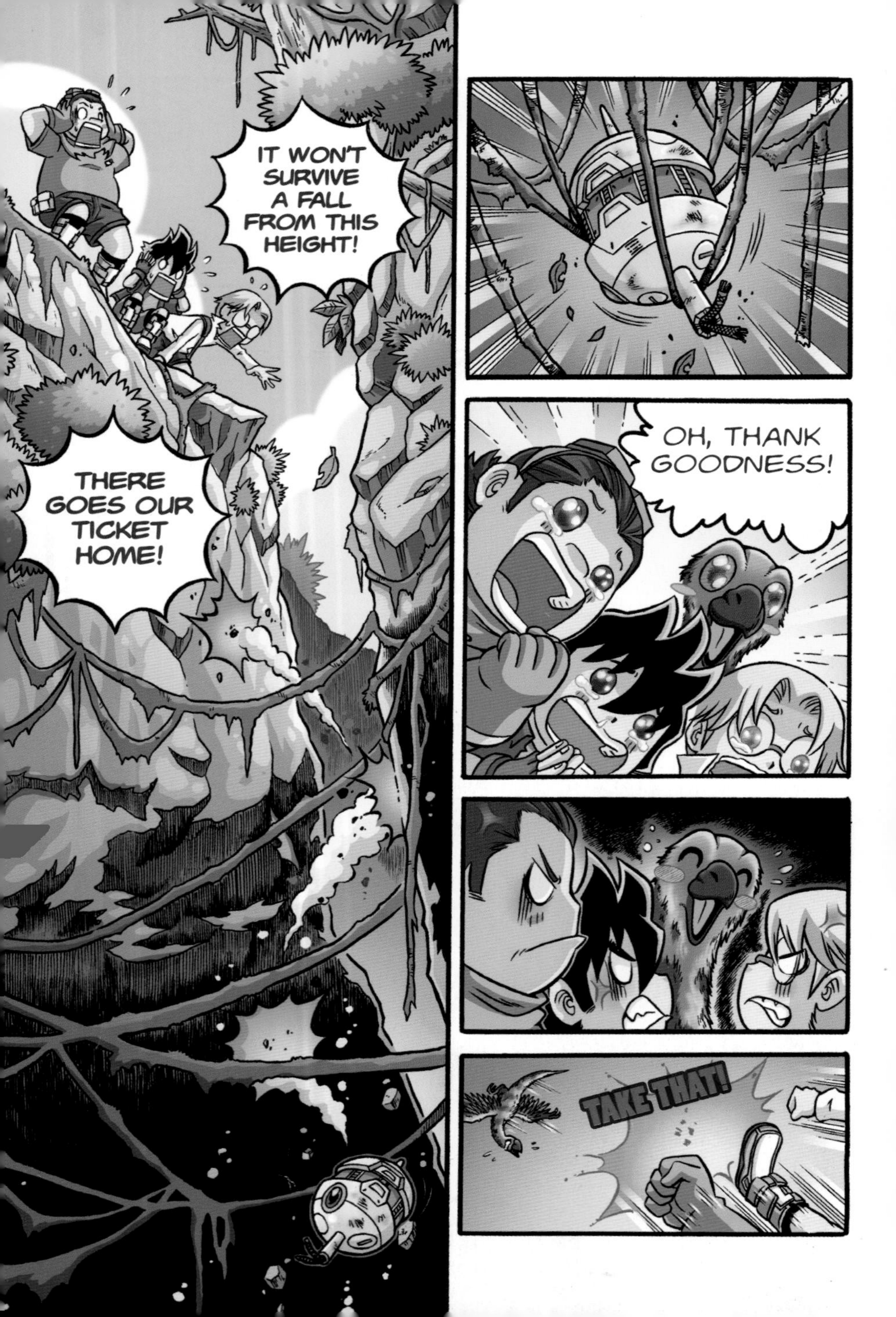
IT WON'T SURVIVE A FALL FROM THIS HEIGHT!
THERE GOES OUR TICKET HOME!
OH, THANK GOODNESS!
TAKE THAT!

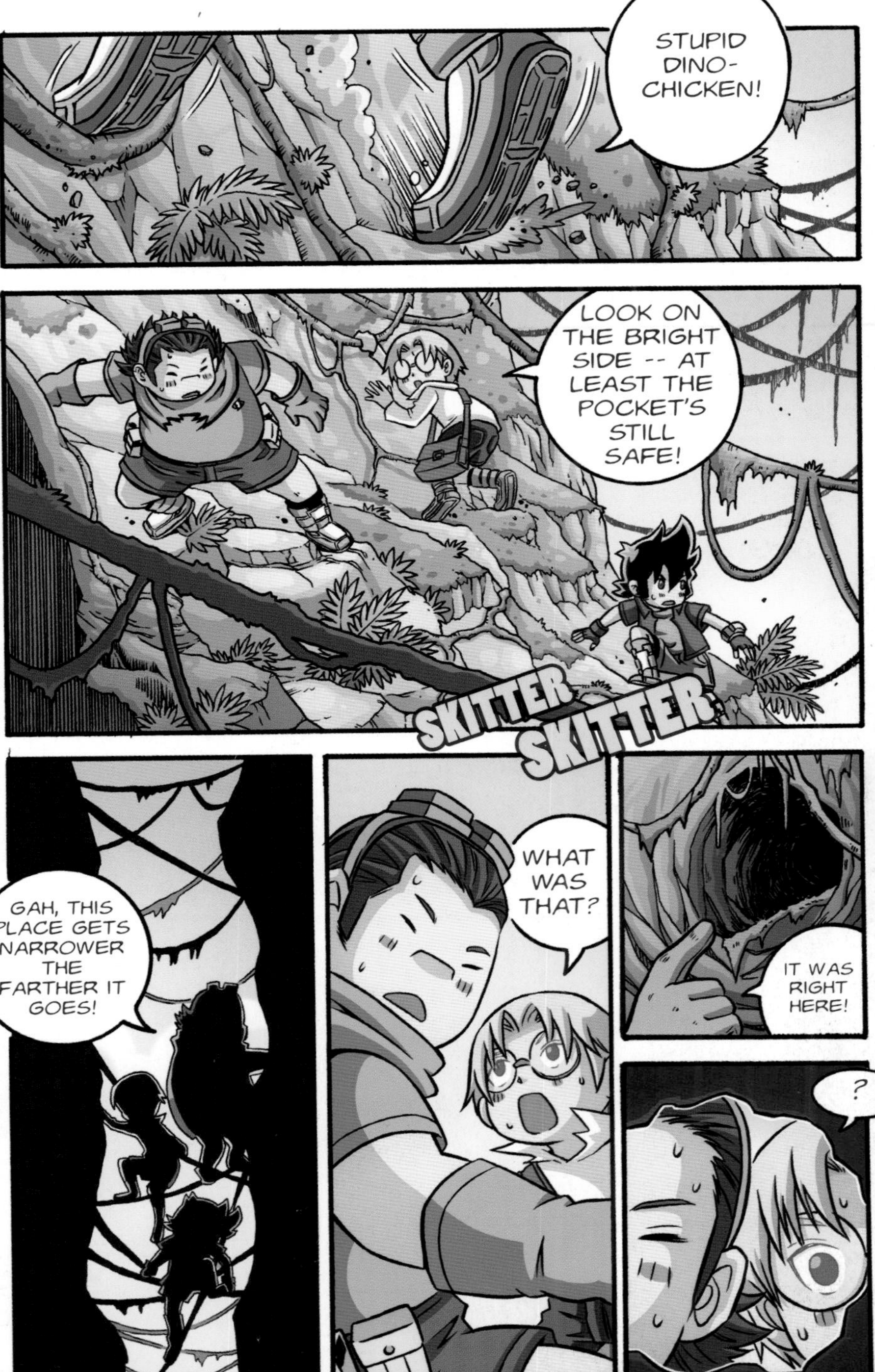
STUPID DINO-CHICKEN!
LOOK ON THE BRIGHT SIDE -- AT LEAST THE POCKET'S STILL SAFE!
SKITTER SKITTER
GAH, THIS PLACE GETS NARROWER THE FARTHER IT GOES!
WHAT WAS THAT?
IT WAS RIGHT HERE!
?

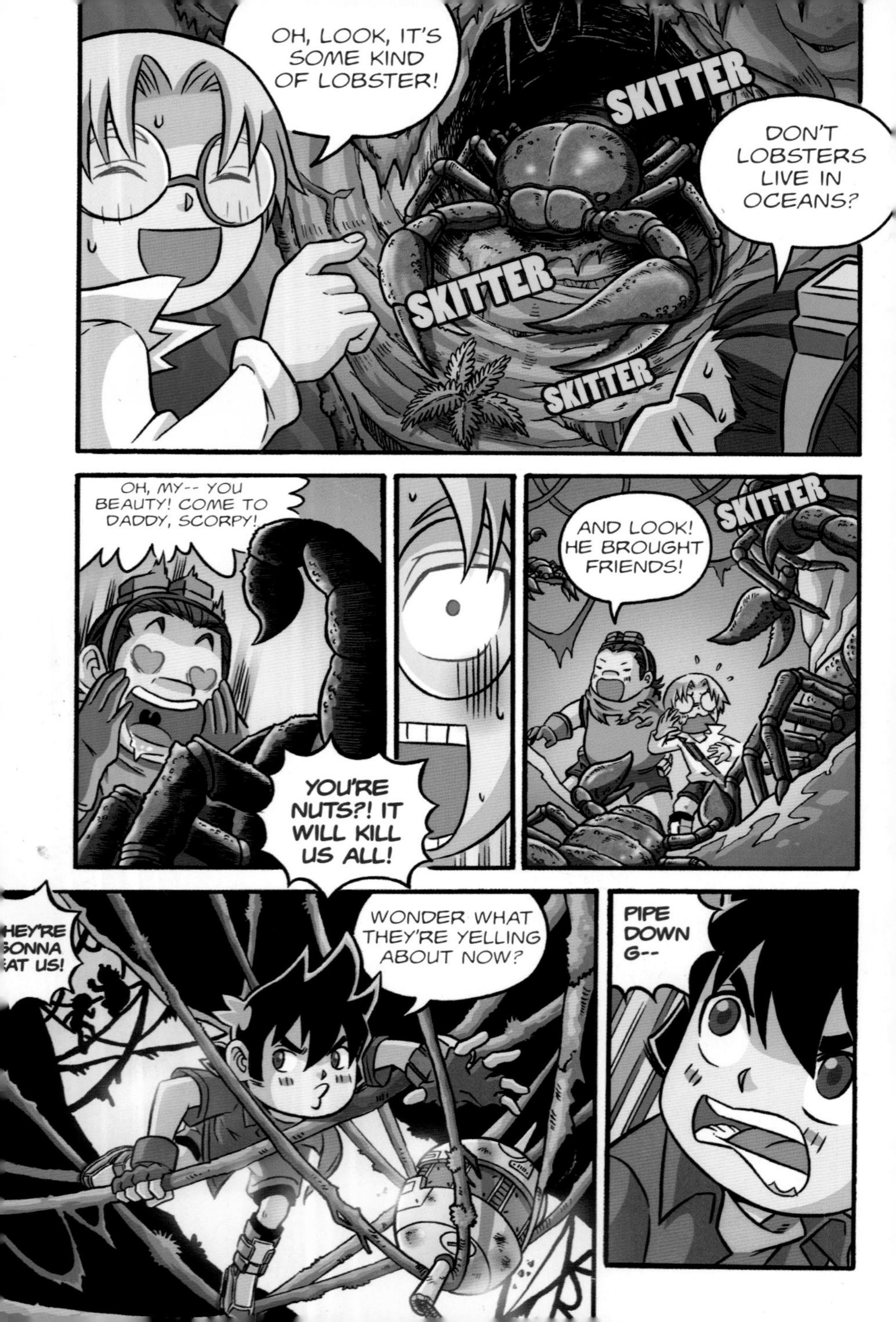

OH, LOOK, IT'S SOME KIND OF LOBSTER!
SKITTER
DON'T LOBSTERS LIVE IN OCEANS?
SKITTER
SKITTER
OH, MY-- YOU BEAUTY! COME TO DADDY, SCORPY!
YOU'RE NUTS?! IT WILL KILL US ALL!
SKITTER
AND LOOK! HE BROUGHT FRIENDS!
HEY'RE GONNA EAT US!
WONDER WHAT THEY'RE YELLING ABOUT NOW?
PIPE DOWN G--

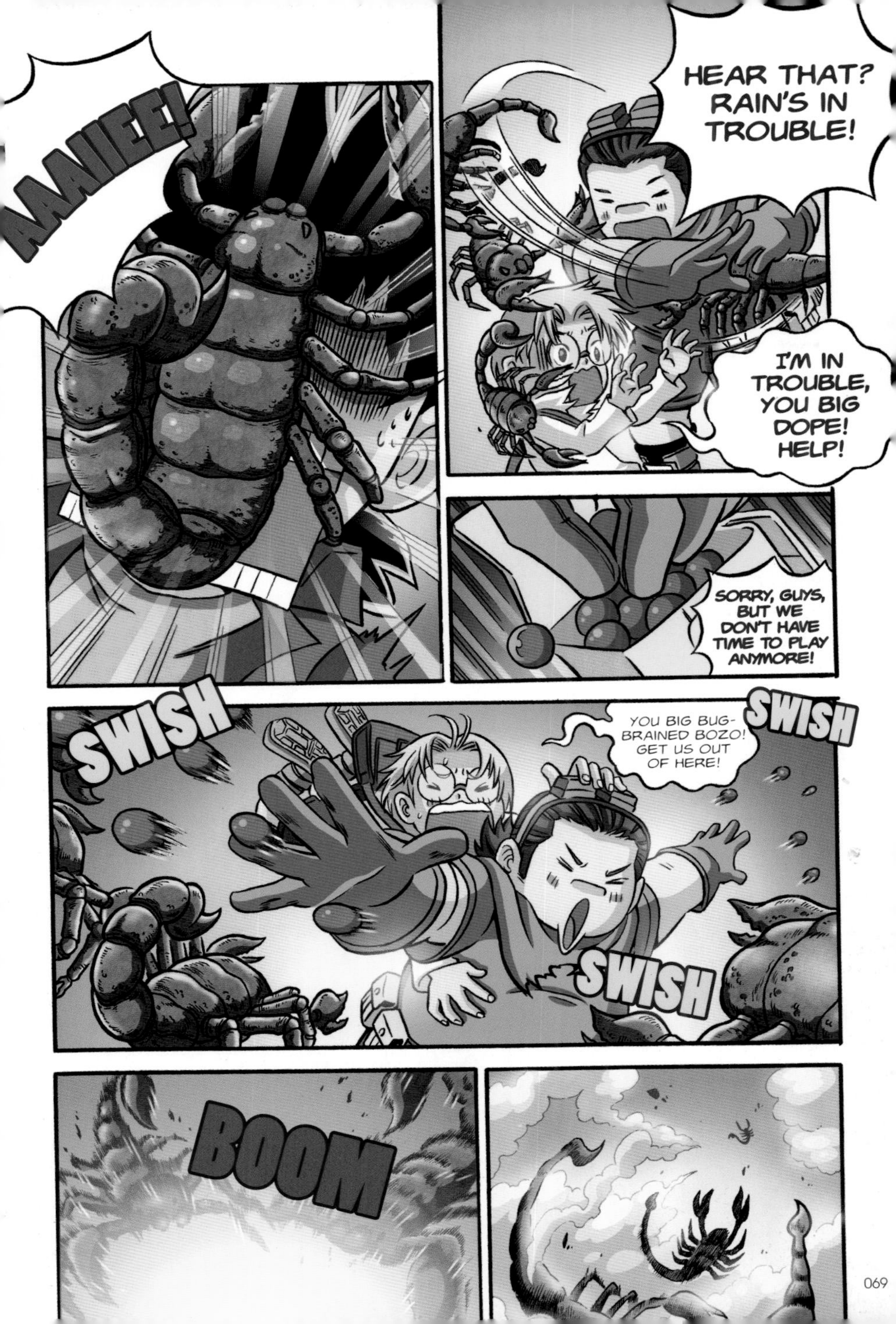
AAAIIEEE!
HEAR THAT? RAIN'S IN TROUBLE!
I'M IN TROUBLE, YOU BIG DOPE! HELP!
SORRY, GUYS, BUT WE DON'T HAVE TIME TO PLAY ANYMORE!
SWISH
YOU BIG BUG-BRAINED BOZO! GET US OUT OF HERE!
SWISH
SWISH
BOOM

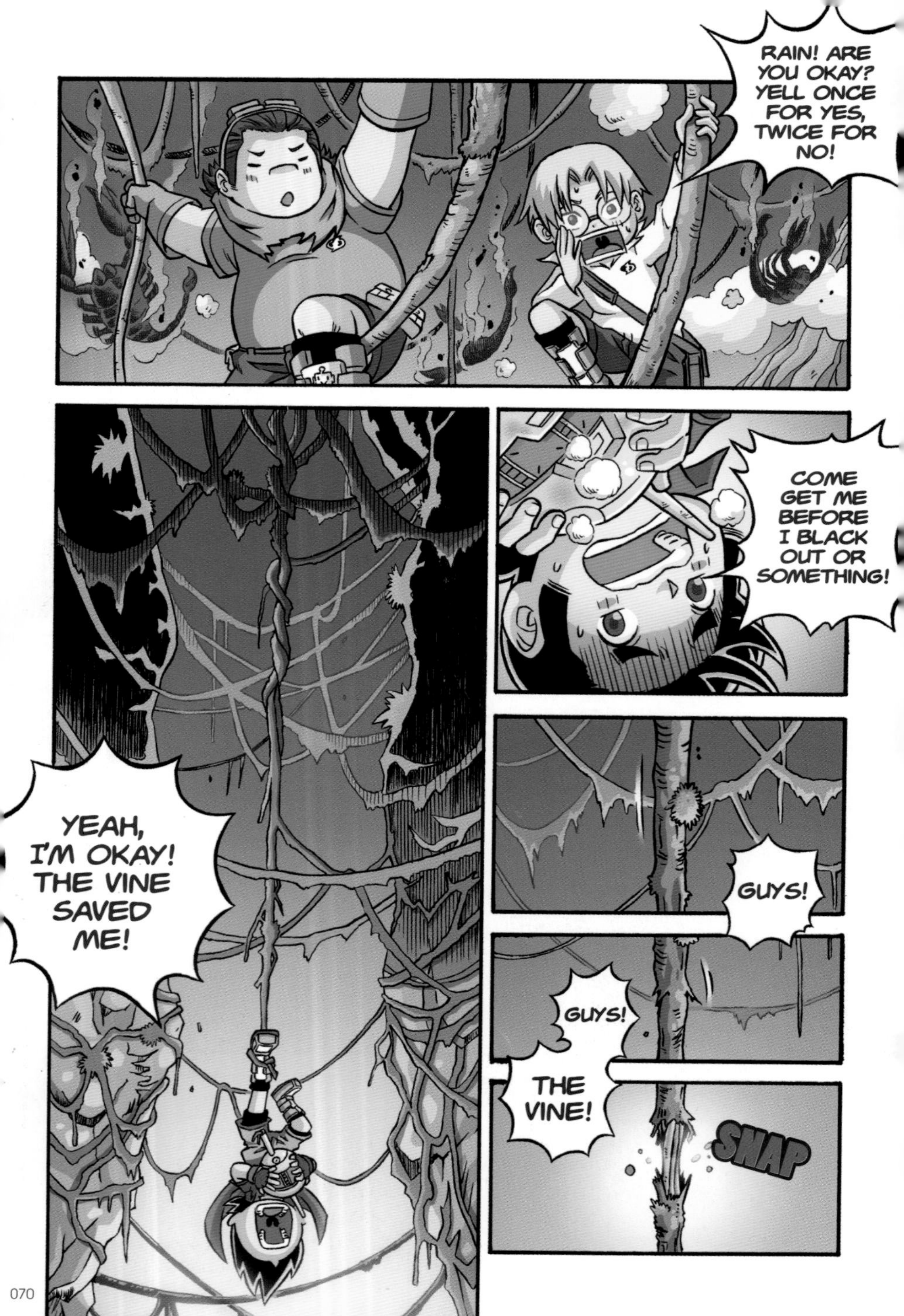
RAIN! ARE YOU OKAY? YELL ONCE FOR YES, TWICE FOR NO!
YEAH, I'M OKAY! THE VINE SAVED ME!
COME GET ME BEFORE I BLACK OUT OR SOMETHING!
GUYS!
GUYS!
THE VINE!
SNAP

## CAPTURING THE CRETACEOUS!

# Iguanodon

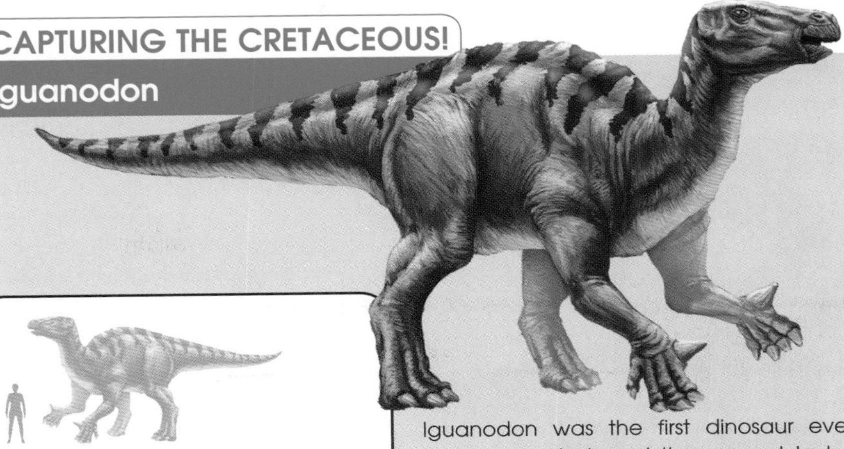

**Scientific name:** Iguanodon
**Size:** 30 feet
**Diet:** Herbivore
**Habitat:** Forests
**Discovered:** Europe, North Africa, East Asia
**Period:** Early Cretaceous

Iguanodon was the first dinosaur ever to be recorded, and the second to be named after Megalosaurus. This large herbivore normally walked on all fours, but could switch to two as needed. Its two front limbs doubled as hands and feet when necessary. It also had a distinctive "thumb spike" which may have been used in self defence.

## CAPTURING THE CRETACEOUS!

# Ouranosaurus

Meaning "brave lizard" in Greek, Ouranosaurus had a "sail" across its back, similar to those of the Spinosaurus and Dimetrodon. This sail would have worked to regulate its temperature, and unlike the sails of the others, might have also contained fatty deposits, like a camel's humps.

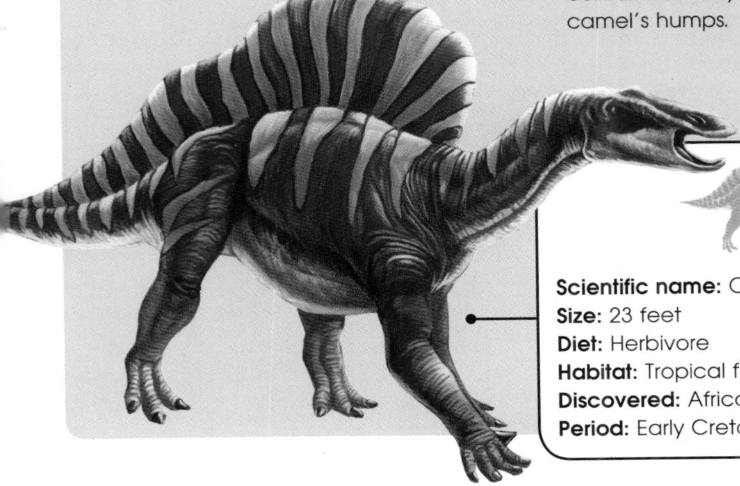

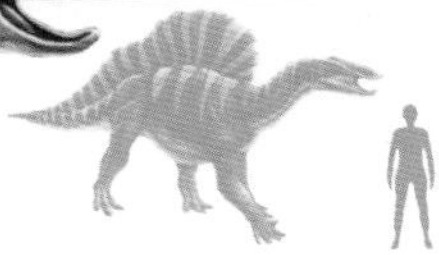

**Scientific name:** Ouranosaurus
**Size:** 23 feet
**Diet:** Herbivore
**Habitat:** Tropical flatlands and forests
**Discovered:** Africa
**Period:** Early Cretaceous

# CAPTURING THE CRETACEOUS!

## Dilong Paradoxus

Dilong was an ancestor of the T-Rex, though how far removed it was is still debated. There have been traces of feathers found around its jaw and tail; which may have helped it maintain body temperature. Its discovery informed paleontologists that tyrannosaurs actually started out small and feathered, gradually shedding them as they grew in size. It also conclusively proves that birds and avetheropods- dinosaurs that have birdlike features were linked.

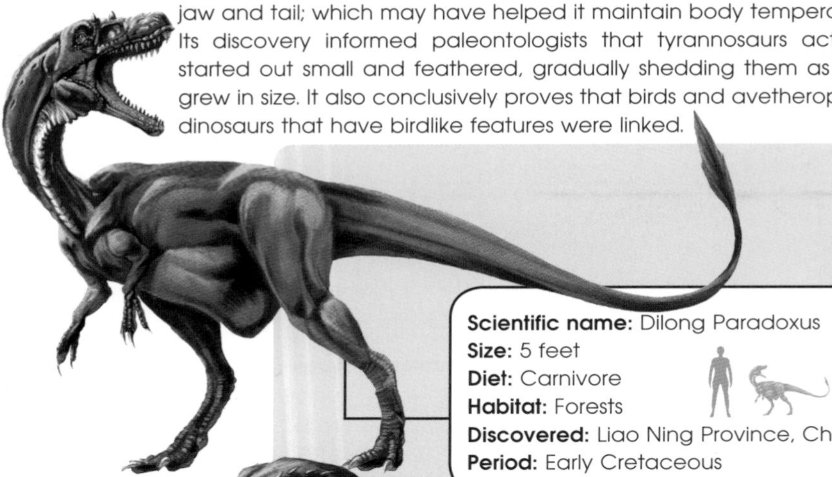

**Scientific name:** Dilong Paradoxus
**Size:** 5 feet
**Diet:** Carnivore
**Habitat:** Forests
**Discovered:** Liao Ning Province, China
**Period:** Early Cretaceous

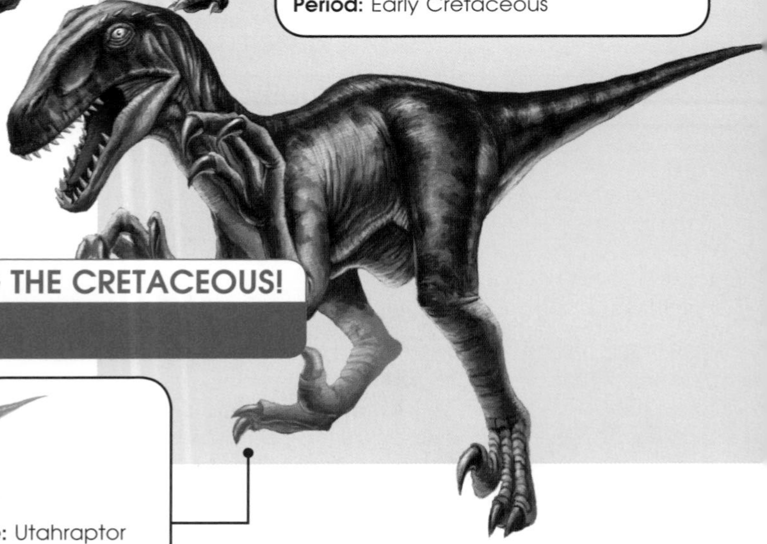

# CAPTURING THE CRETACEOUS!

## Utahraptor

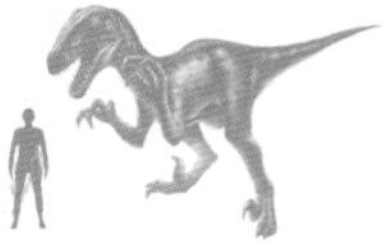

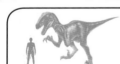

**Scientific name:** Utahraptor
**Size:** 16.5 to 23 feet
**Diet:** Carnivore
**Habitat:** Forests and flatlands
**Discovered:** Utah,
United States
**Period:** Early Cretaceous

Named after the American state where it was found, Utahraptor is notable due to both its size (largest member of family Dromaesauridae) and its relatively large brain, twice that of Deinonychus. This could mean that it was one of the smartest dinosaur to have ever lived.

## CAPTURING THE CRETACEOUS!

### Confuciusornis

Confuciusornis was the oldest known bird to have had a beak. It was discovered in China's Liaoning Province. As a result of a near-complete skeleton and well preserved fossilized feathers, Confuciusornis is the most well-known bird of the Mesozoic. Compared to Archaeopteryx, Confuciusornis had more advanced features, it was toothless like modern birds and the musculature of its chest area meant it could actually fly.

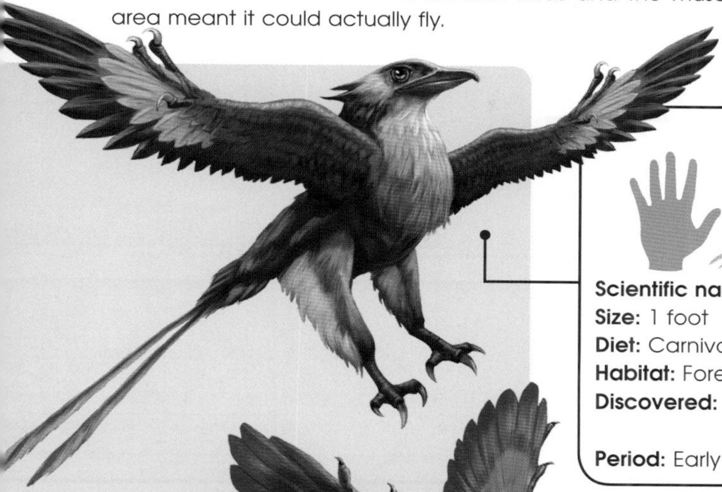

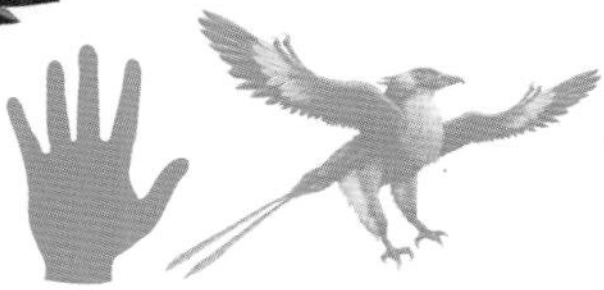

**Scientific name:** Confuciusornis
**Size:** 1 foot
**Diet:** Carnivore
**Habitat:** Forests
**Discovered:** Liaoning Province, China
**Period:** Early Cretaceous

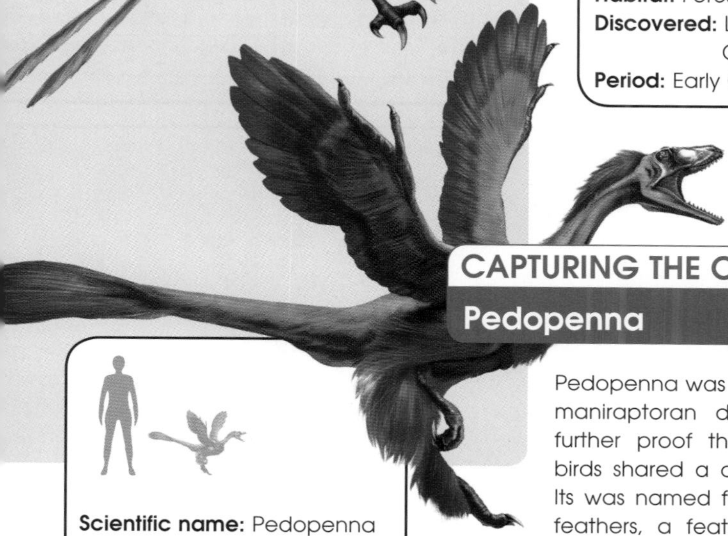

## CAPTURING THE CRETACEOUS!

### Pedopenna

**Scientific name:** Pedopenna
**Size:** (maybe) around 3 feet
**Diet:** Carnivore
**Habitat:** Forests
**Discovered:** China
**Period:** Late Jurassic - Early Cretaceous

Pedopenna was a small, feathered maniraptoran dinosaur, and yet further proof that dinosaurs and birds shared a common ancestor. Its was named for its pennaceous feathers, a feature usually found only in modern birds. Its feathers were well developed, sometimes reaching 2.17 inches. Its leg feathers were rounded and symmetrical.

# CRETACEOUS CONFRONTATION!

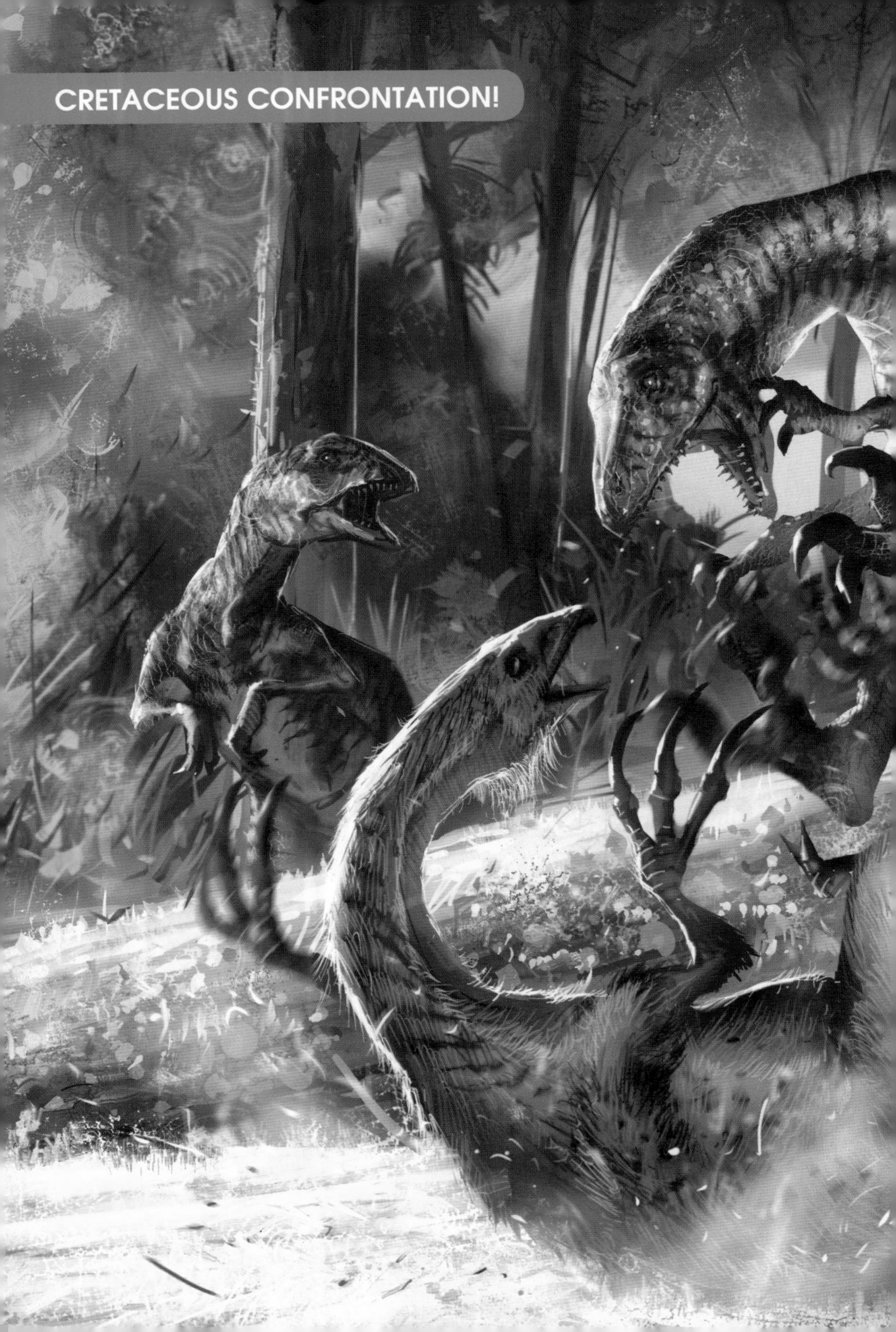

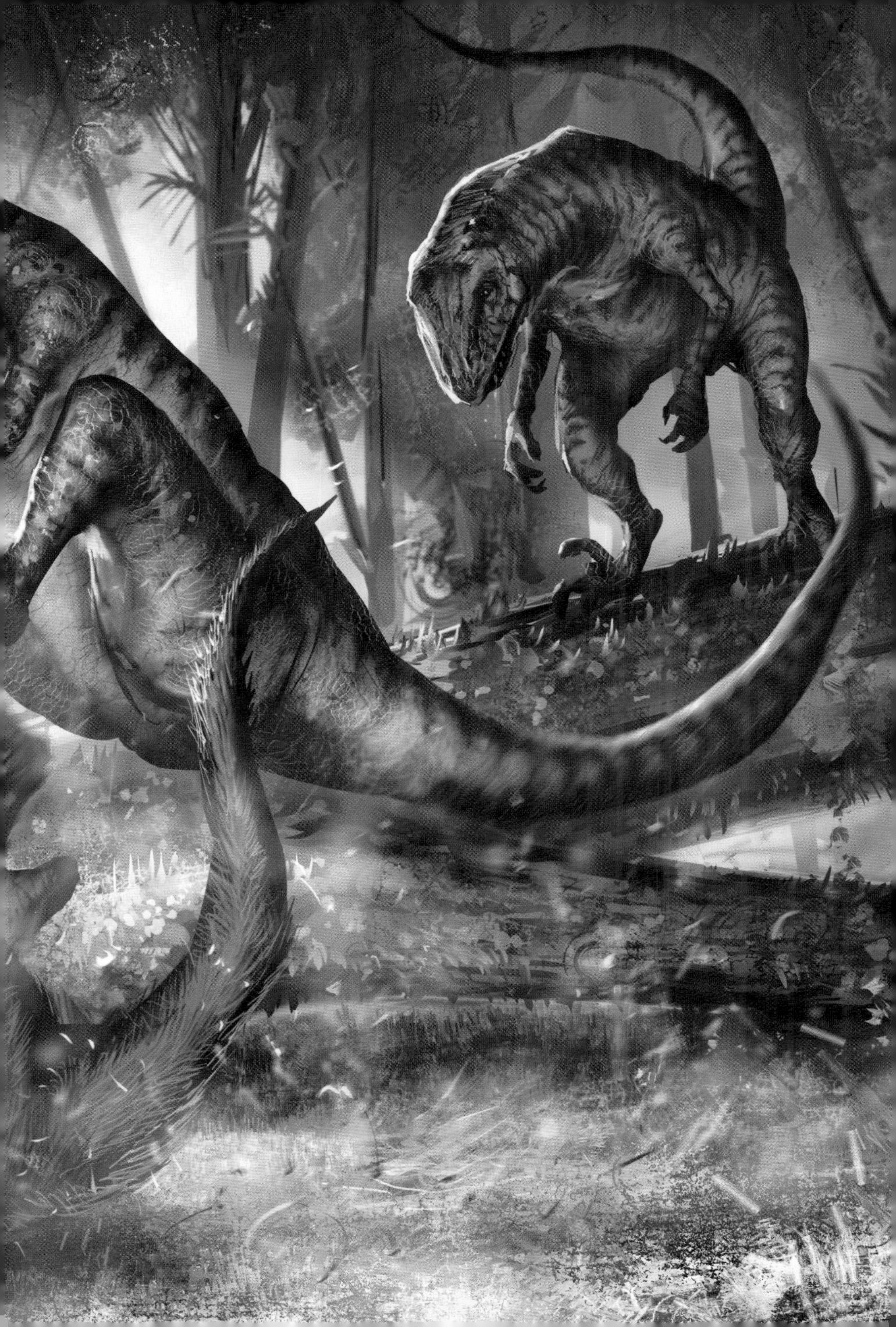

## CAPTURING THE CRETACEOUS!

### Beipiaosaurus

Its name comes from the city of Beipiao in Liaoning Province, China. It is among the largest feathered dinosaurs discovered to date, and a member of the superfamily Therizinosauroidea. Unlike other avetheropods, it had a second set of longer feathers and was more lightweight. Paleontologists believe this second set helped differentiate Beipiaosaurus subspecies.

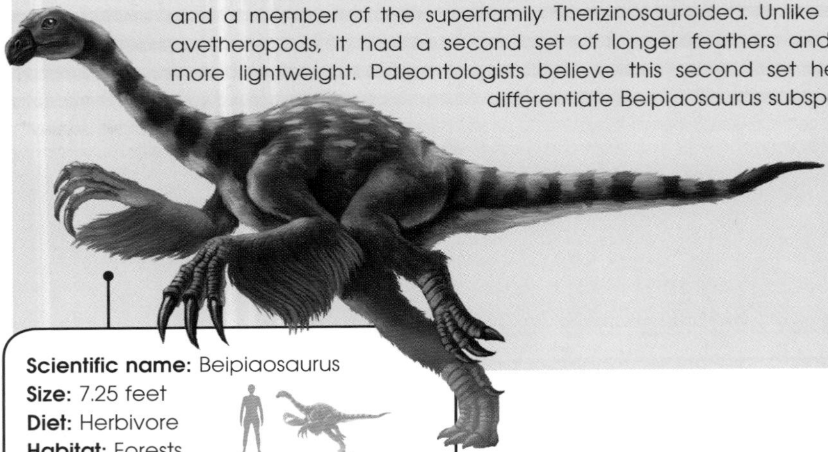

**Scientific name:** Beipiaosaurus
**Size:** 7.25 feet
**Diet:** Herbivore
**Habitat:** Forests
**Discovered:** Liaoning Province, China
**Period:** Early Cretaceous

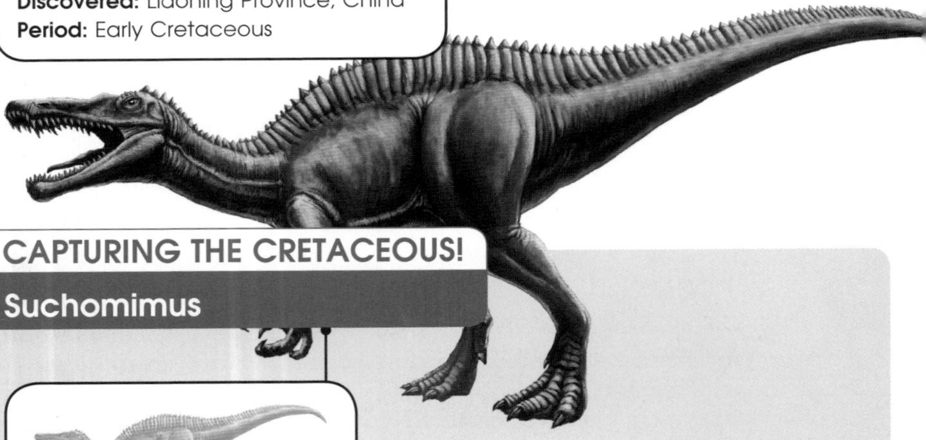

## CAPTURING THE CRETACEOUS!

### Suchomimus

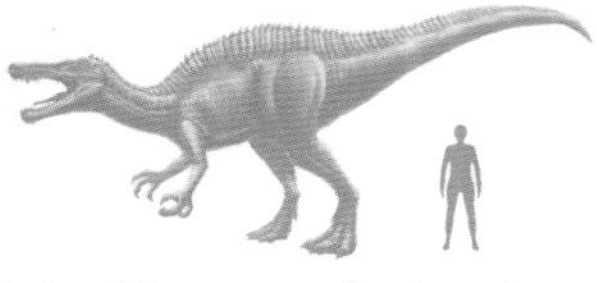

**Scientific name:** Suchomimus
**Size:** Around 36 feet
**Diet:** Carnivore
**Habitat:** Near rivers
**Discovered:** Africa
**Period:** Early Cretaceous

Suchomimus was a large spinosaurid dinosaur, notable for its crocodilian jaws which were full of up to 100 blunt, bent teeth. Its arms were long and hook-clawed to facilitate fishing, given that physical evidence indicated that small aquatic life were its preferred prey.

CHAPTER 4
# UP THE CREEK

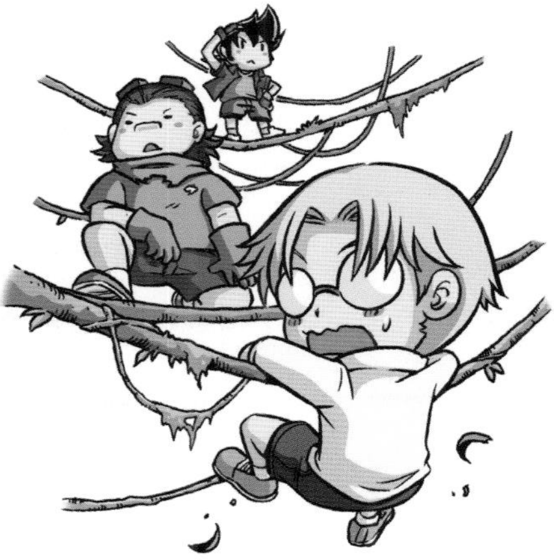

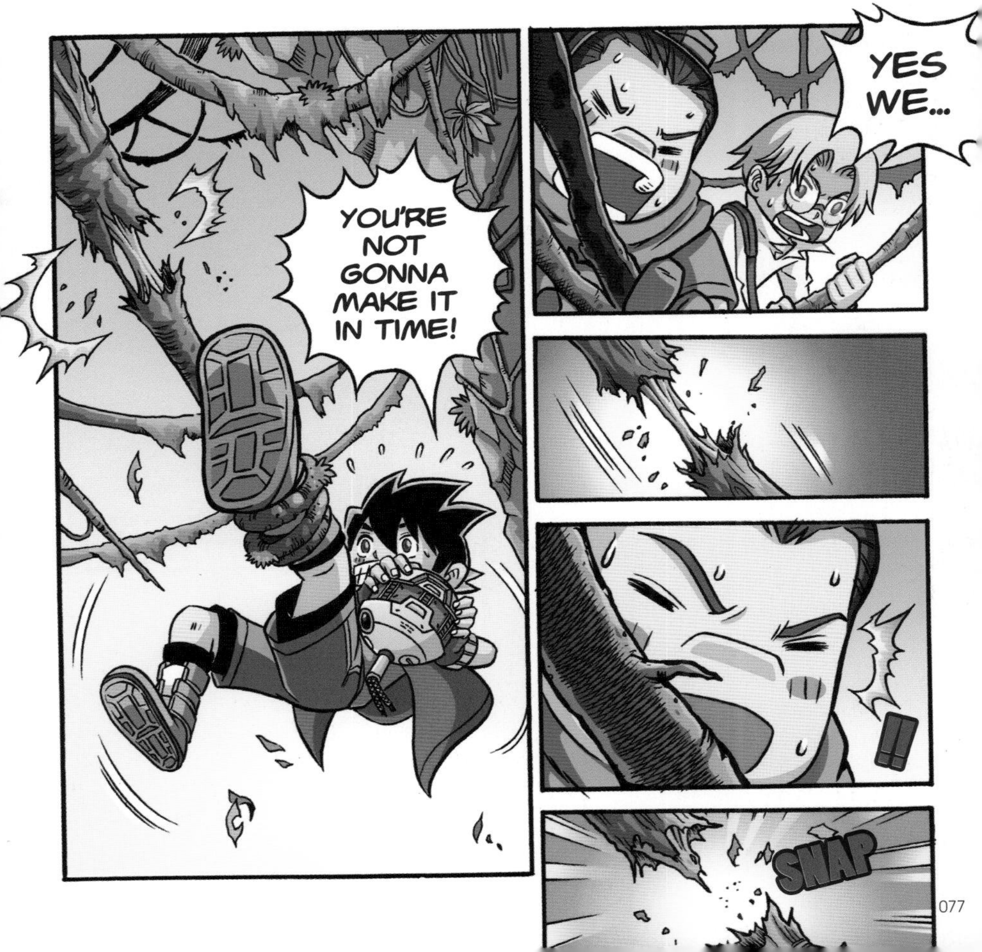
YOU'RE NOT GONNA MAKE IT IN TIME!
YES WE...
!!
SNAP

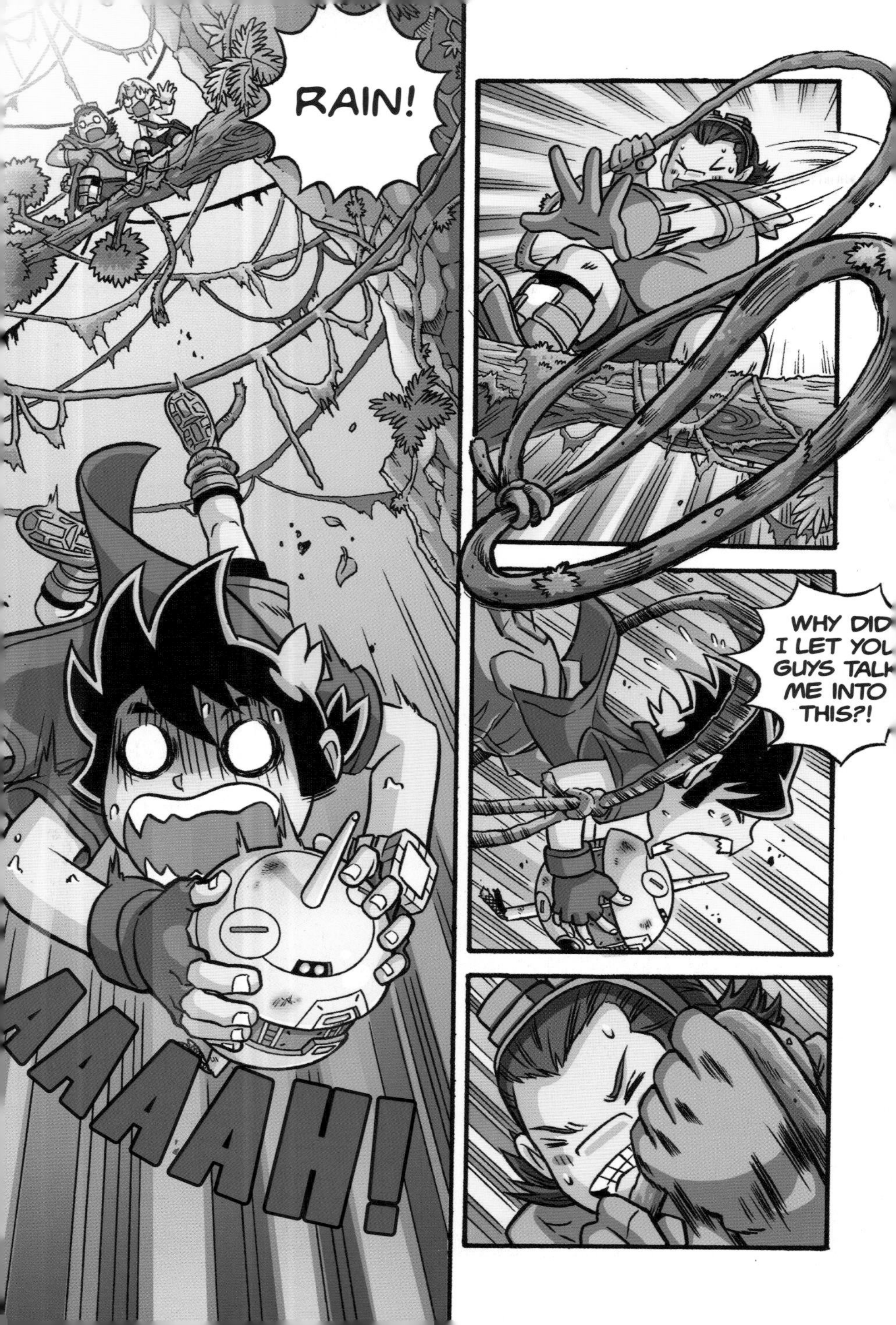
RAIN!
AAAAAAH!
WHY DID I LET YOU GUYS TALK ME INTO THIS?!

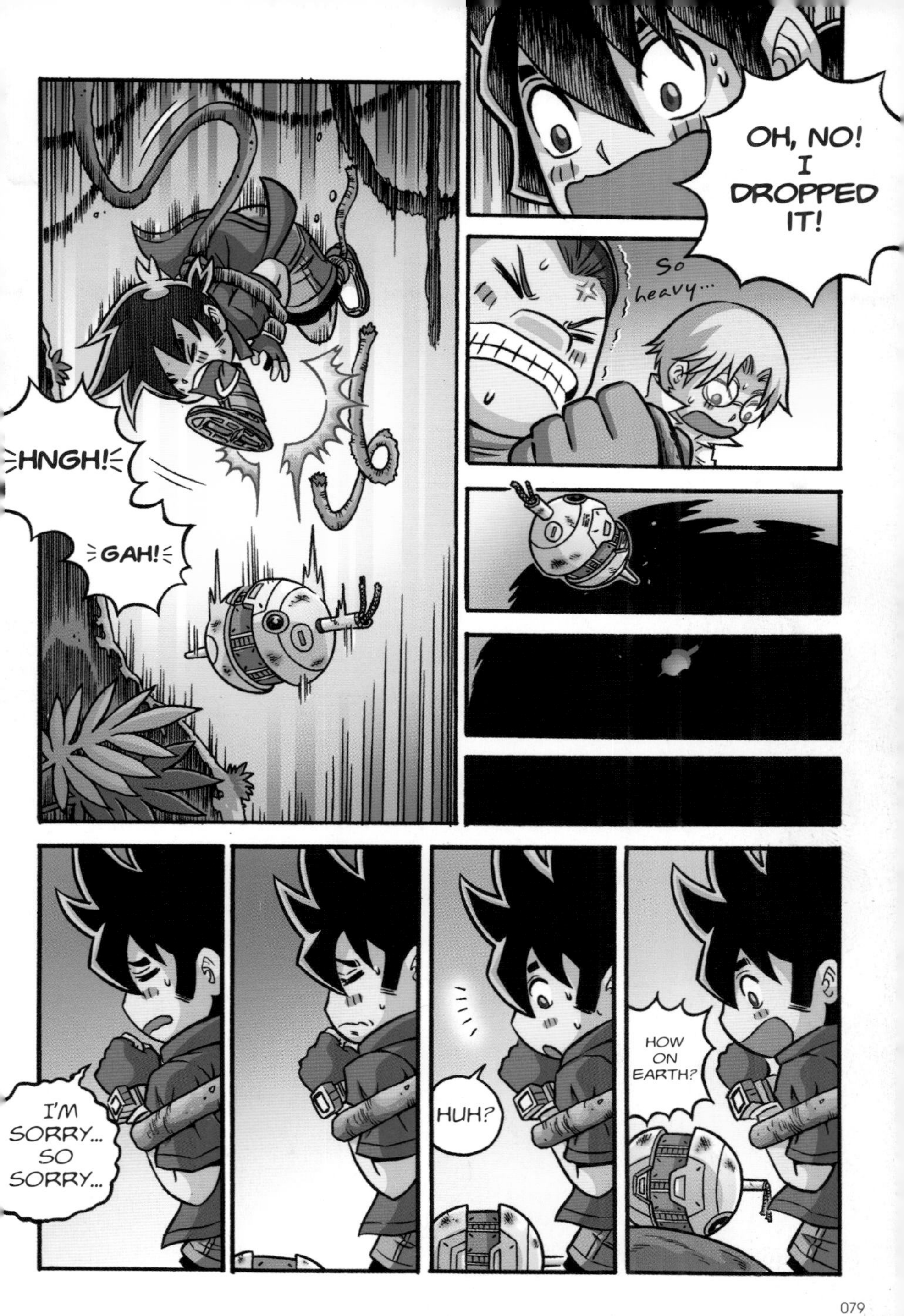
HNGH!
GAH!
OH, NO! I DROPPED IT!
So heavy...
I'M SORRY... SO SORRY...
HUH?
HOW ON EARTH?

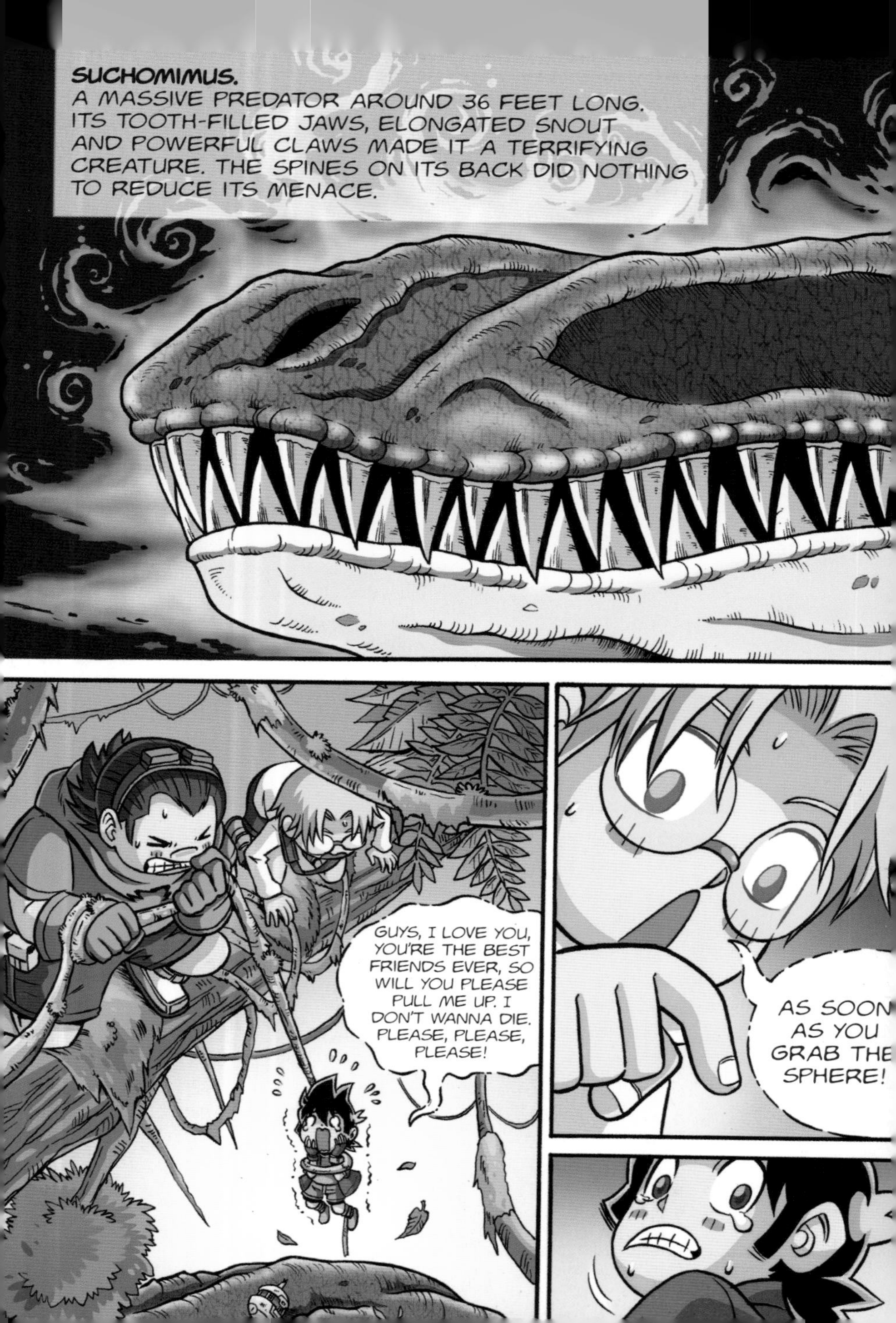
SUCHOMIMUS.
A MASSIVE PREDATOR AROUND 36 FEET LONG. ITS TOOTH-FILLED JAWS, ELONGATED SNOUT AND POWERFUL CLAWS MADE IT A TERRIFYING CREATURE. THE SPINES ON ITS BACK DID NOTHING TO REDUCE ITS MENACE.
GUYS, I LOVE YOU, YOU'RE THE BEST FRIENDS EVER, SO WILL YOU PLEASE PULL ME UP. I DON'T WANNA DIE. PLEASE, PLEASE, PLEASE!
AS SOON AS YOU GRAB THE SPHERE!

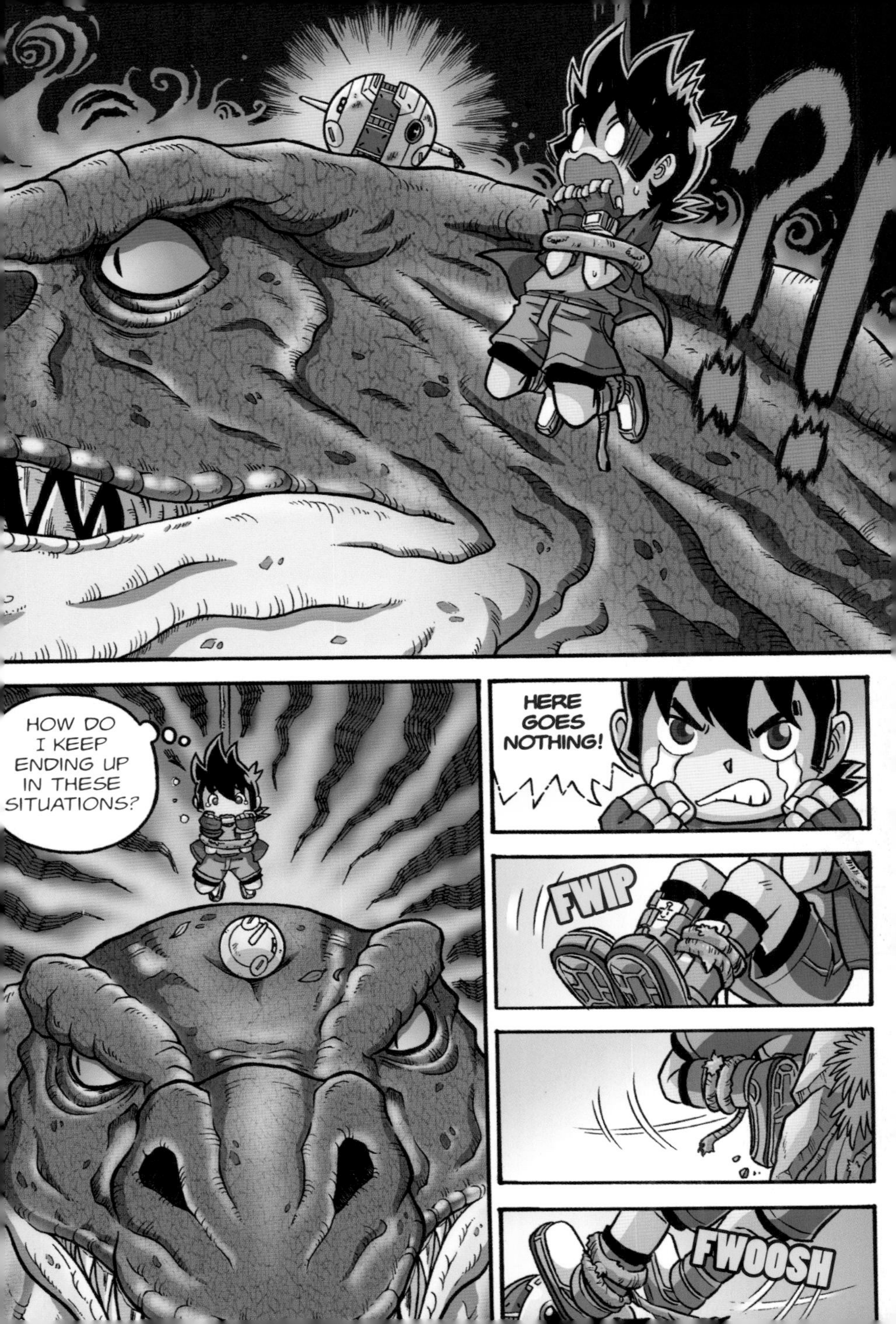
HOW DO I KEEP ENDING UP IN THESE SITUATIONS?
HERE GOES NOTHING!
FWIP
FWOOSH

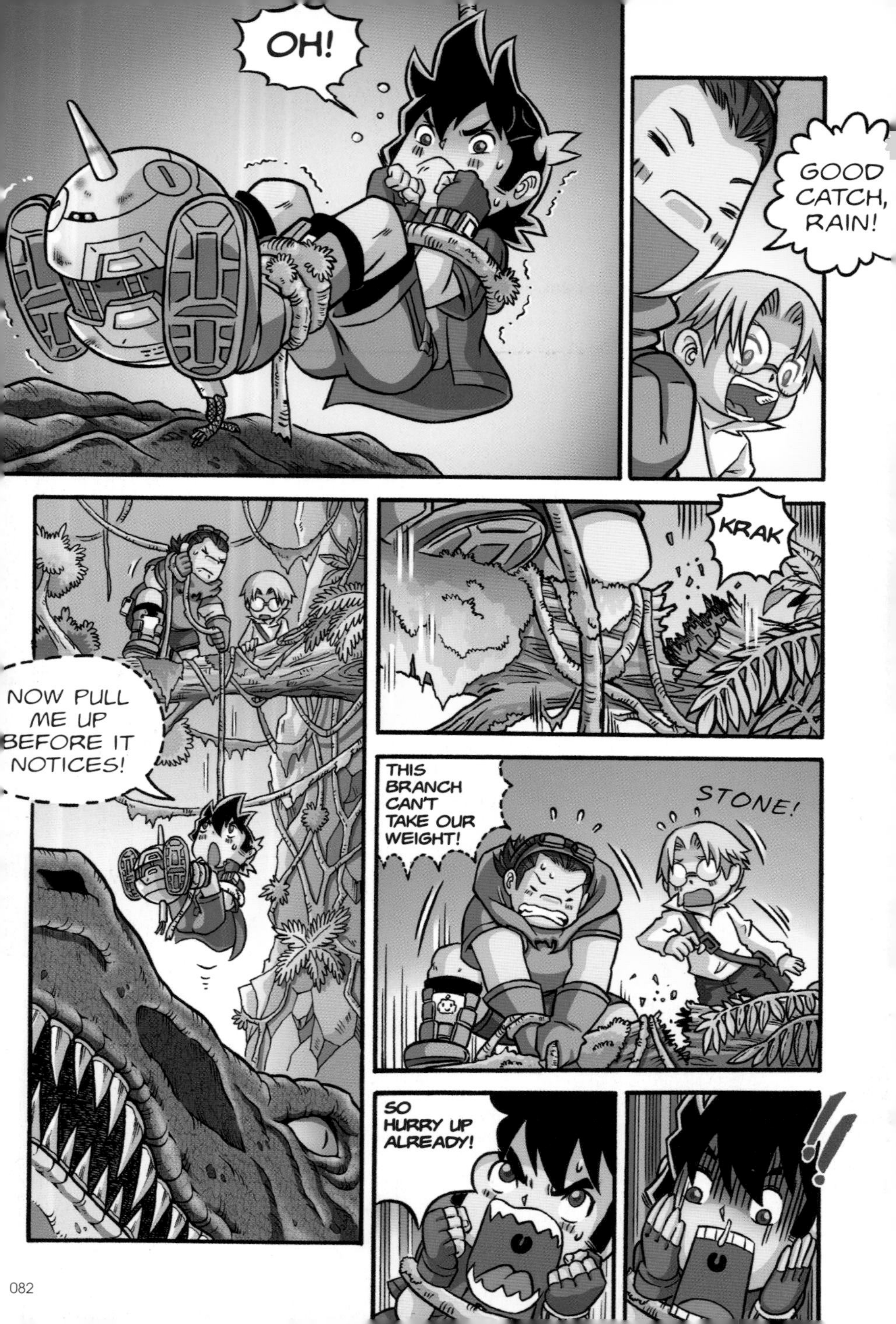
OH!
GOOD CATCH, RAIN!
NOW PULL ME UP BEFORE IT NOTICES!
KRAK
THIS BRANCH CAN'T TAKE OUR WEIGHT!
STONE!
SO HURRY UP ALREADY!
!!

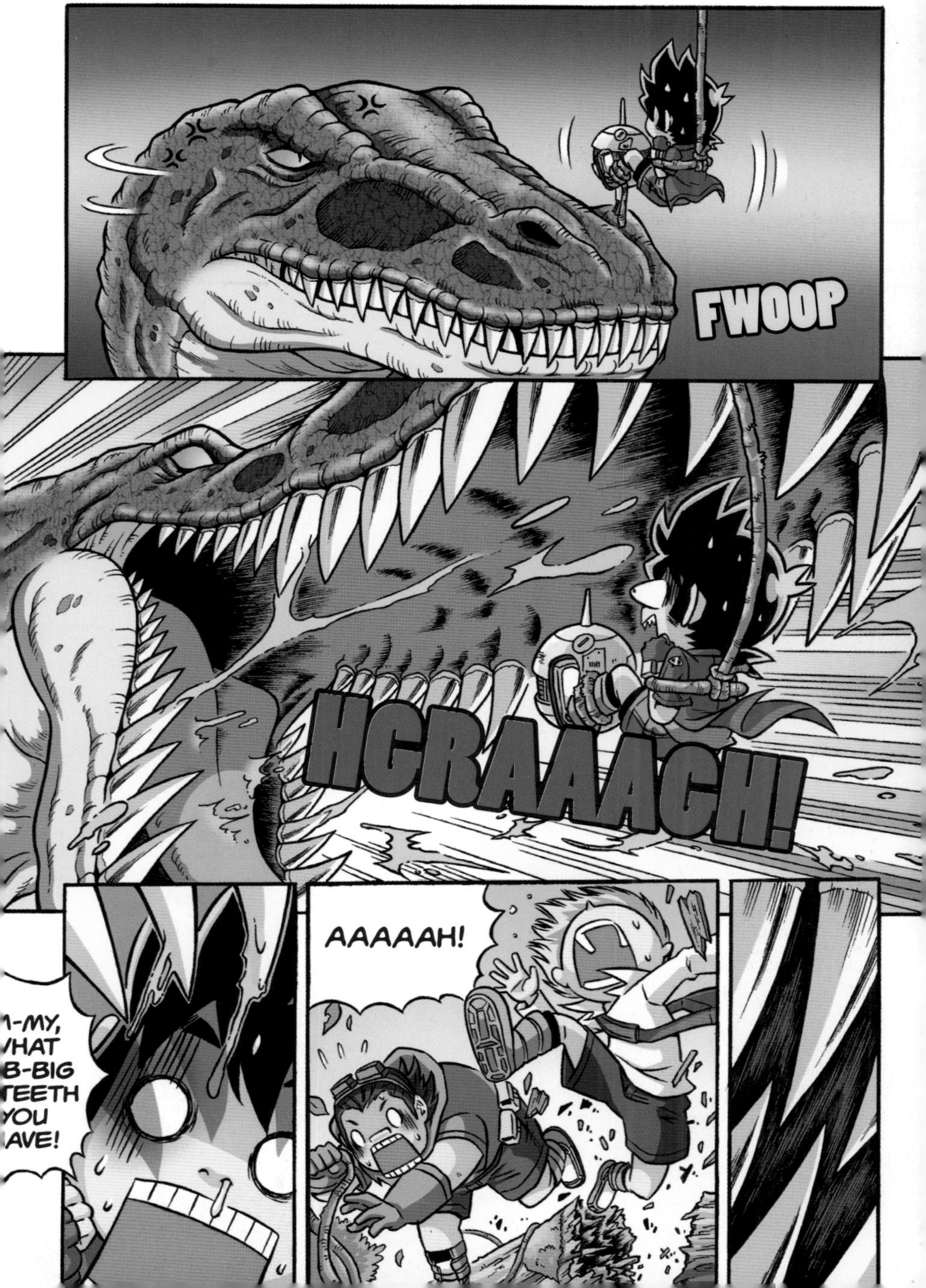
FWOOP
HCRAAACH!
M-MY, WHAT B-BIG TEETH YOU HAVE!
AAAAAH!

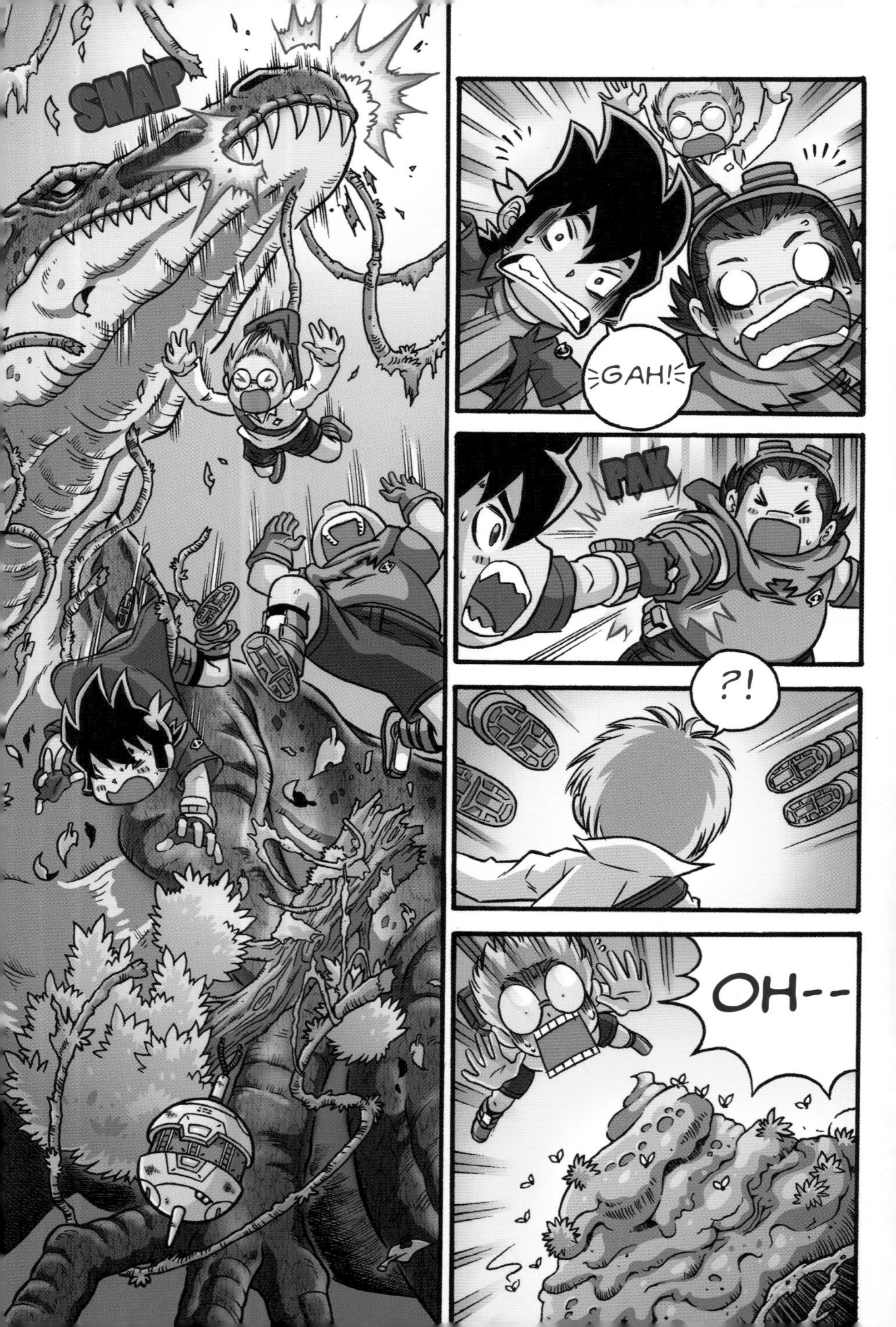
SNAP
GAH!
PAK
?!
OH--

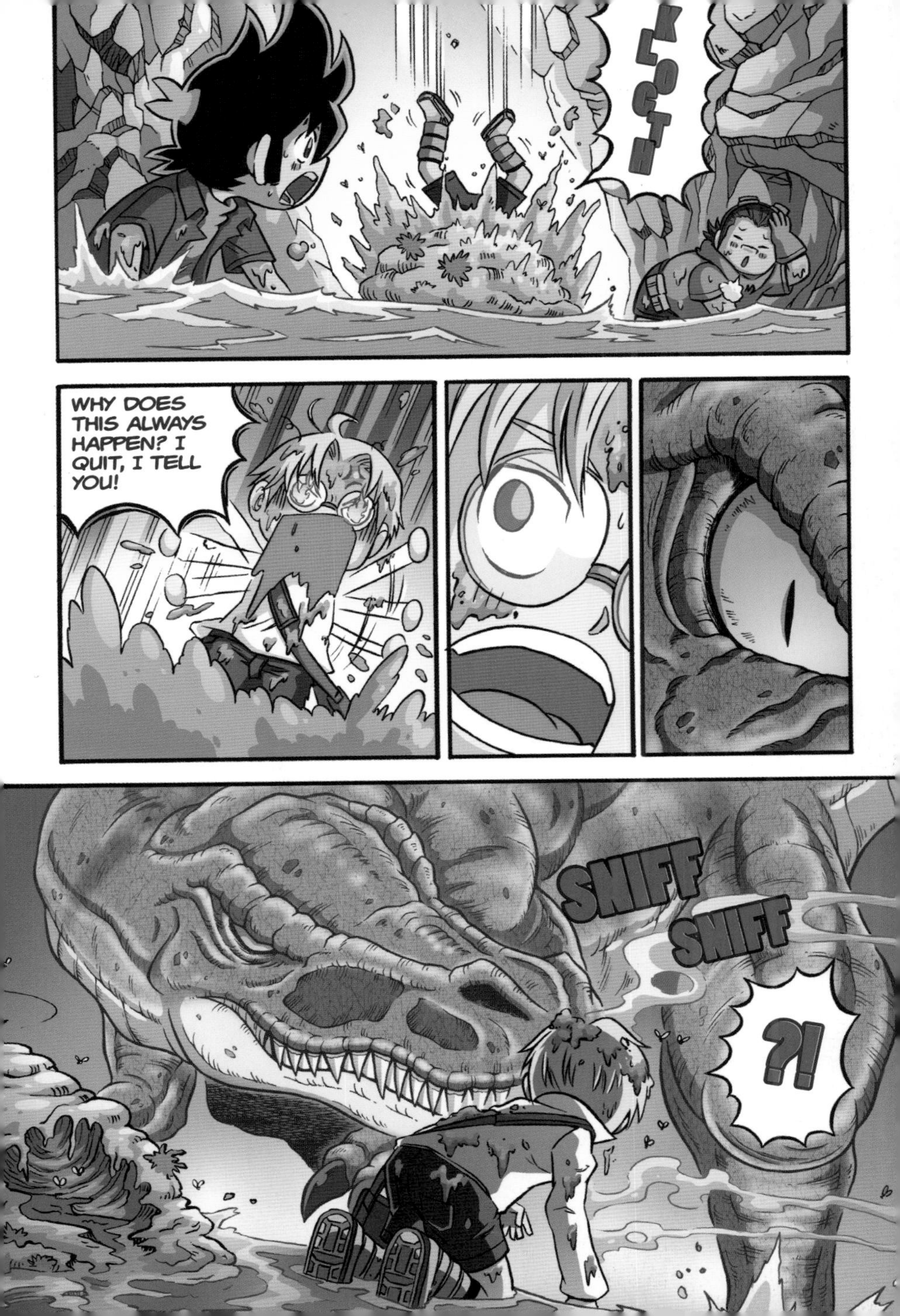
KLOCTH
WHY DOES THIS ALWAYS HAPPEN? I QUIT, I TELL YOU!
SNIFF
SNIFF
?!

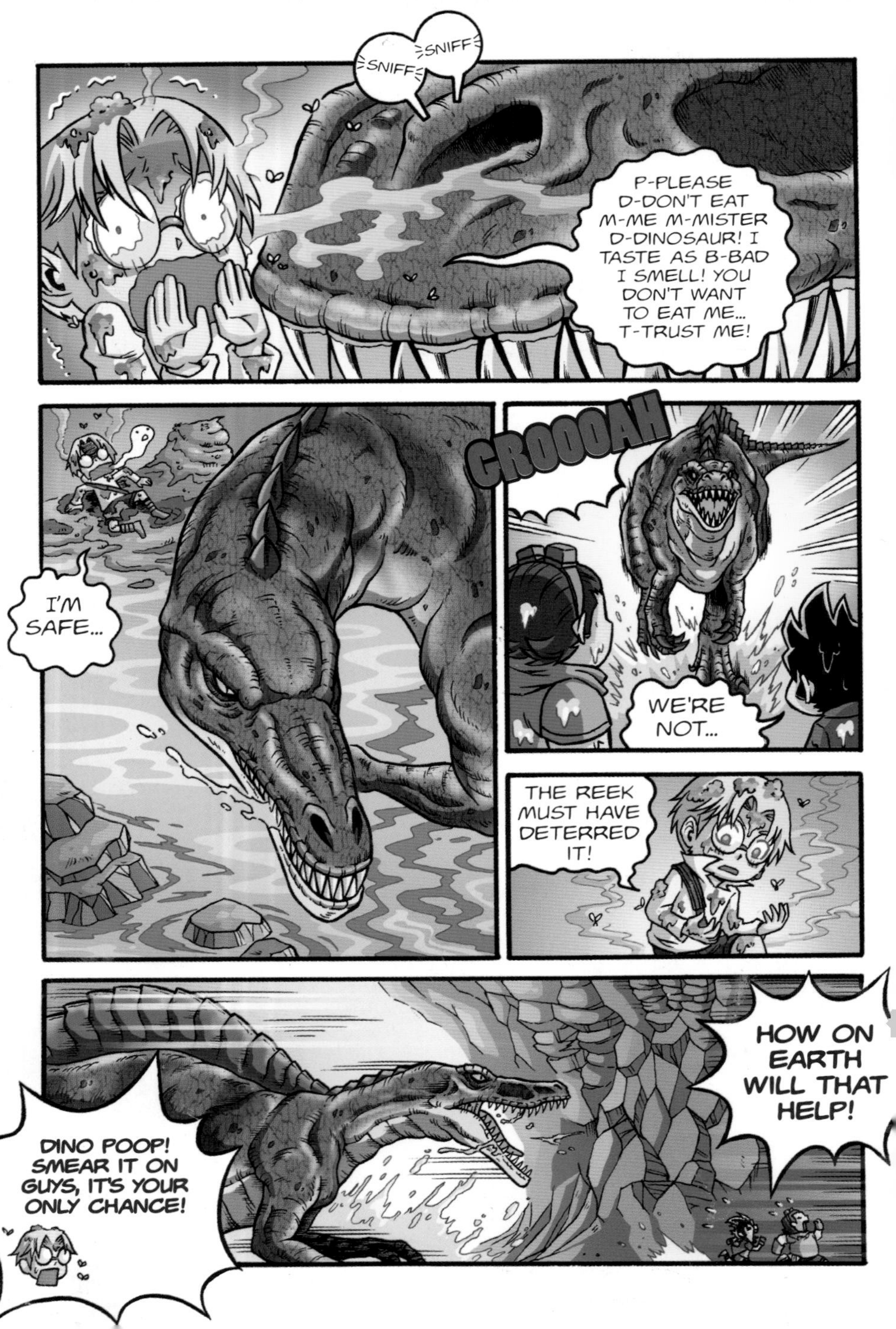
SNIFF SNIFF
P-PLEASE D-DON'T EAT M-ME M-MISTER D-DINOSAUR! I TASTE AS B-BAD I SMELL! YOU DON'T WANT TO EAT ME... T-TRUST ME!
I'M SAFE...
GROOOAH
WE'RE NOT...
THE REEK MUST HAVE DETERRED IT!
HOW ON EARTH WILL THAT HELP!
DINO POOP! SMEAR IT ON GUYS, IT'S YOUR ONLY CHANCE!

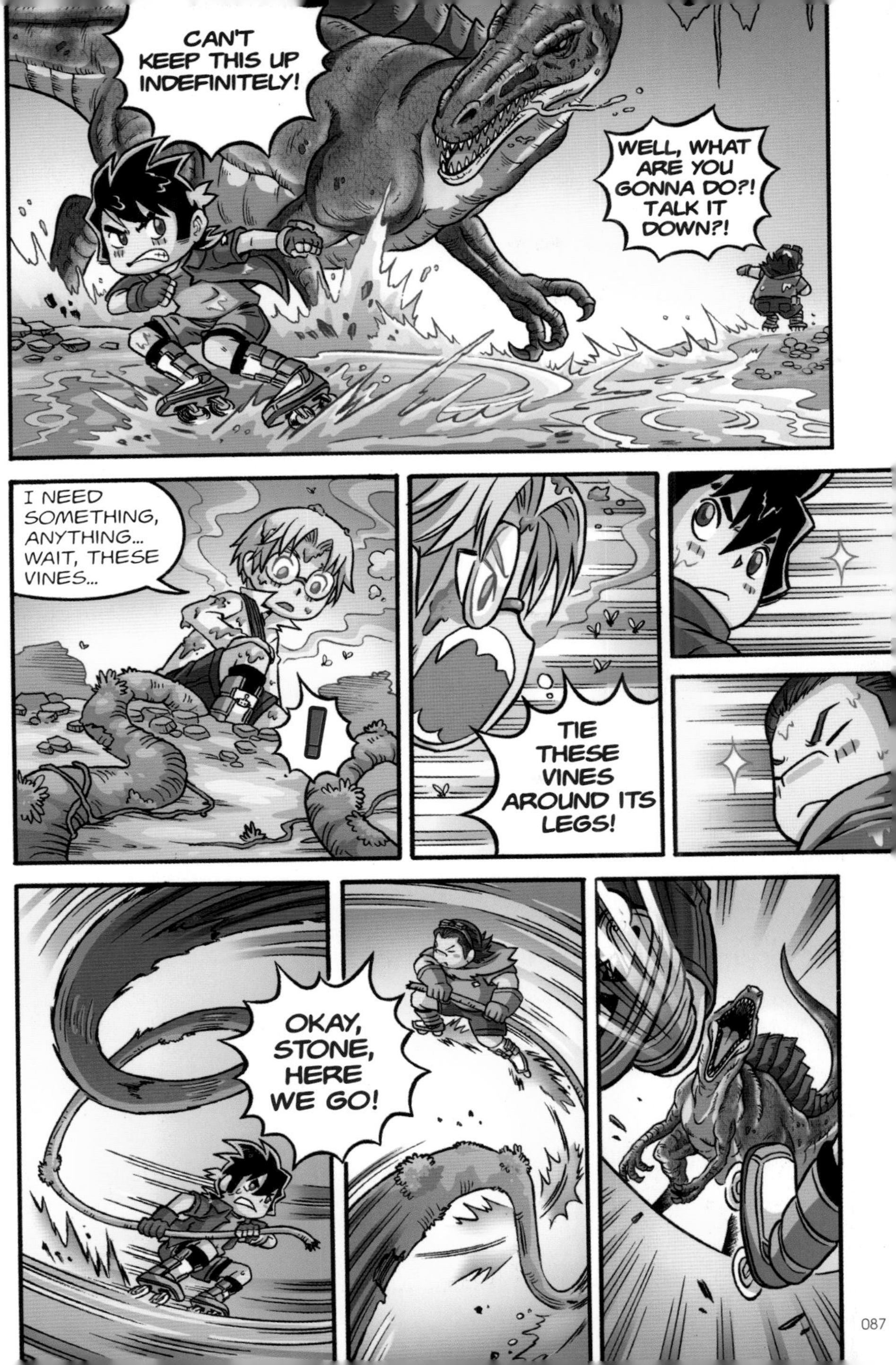

CAN'T KEEP THIS UP INDEFINITELY!
WELL, WHAT ARE YOU GONNA DO?! TALK IT DOWN?!
I NEED SOMETHING, ANYTHING... WAIT, THESE VINES...
!
TIE THESE VINES AROUND ITS LEGS!
OKAY, STONE, HERE WE GO!

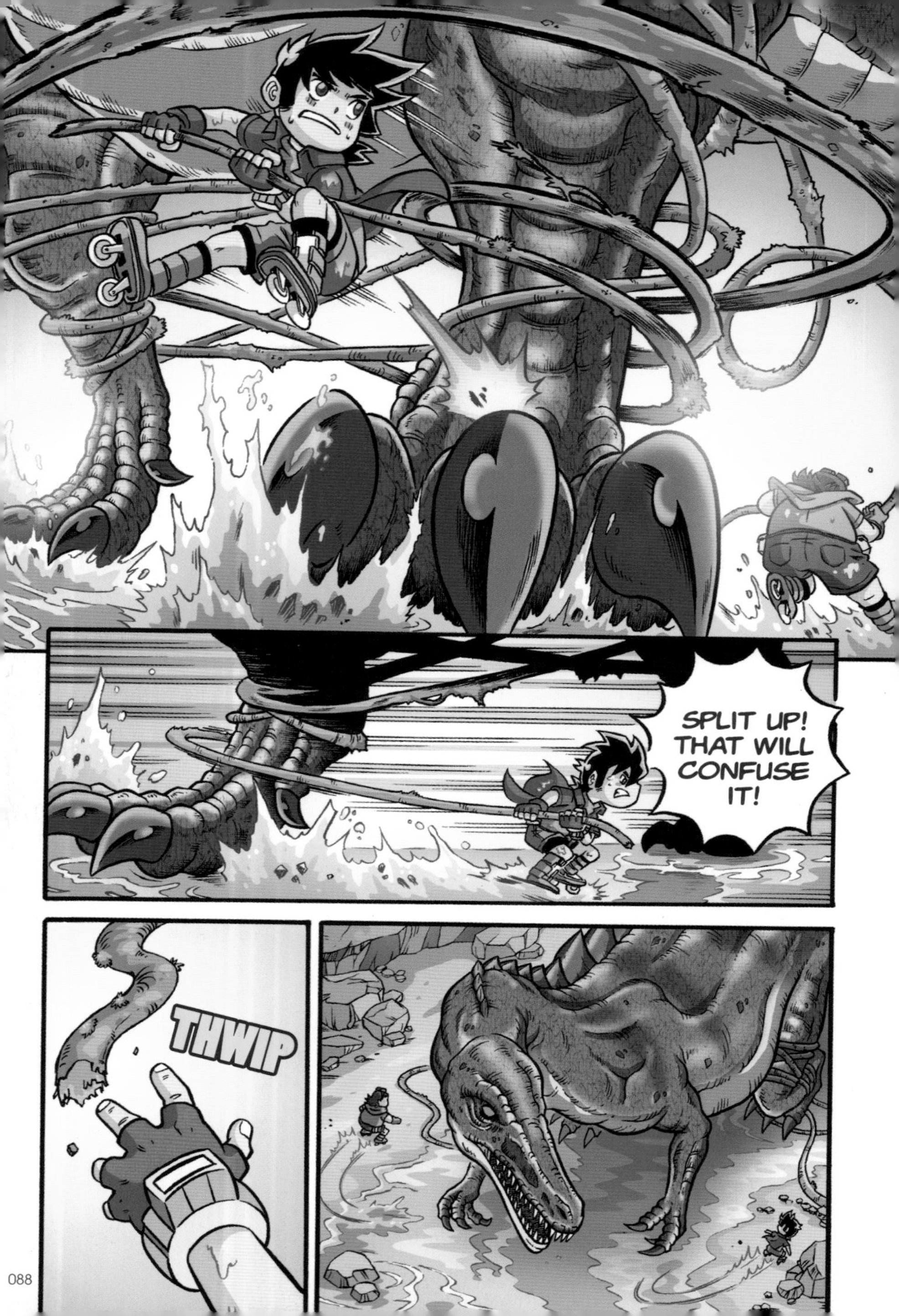
SPLIT UP! THAT WILL CONFUSE IT!
THWIP

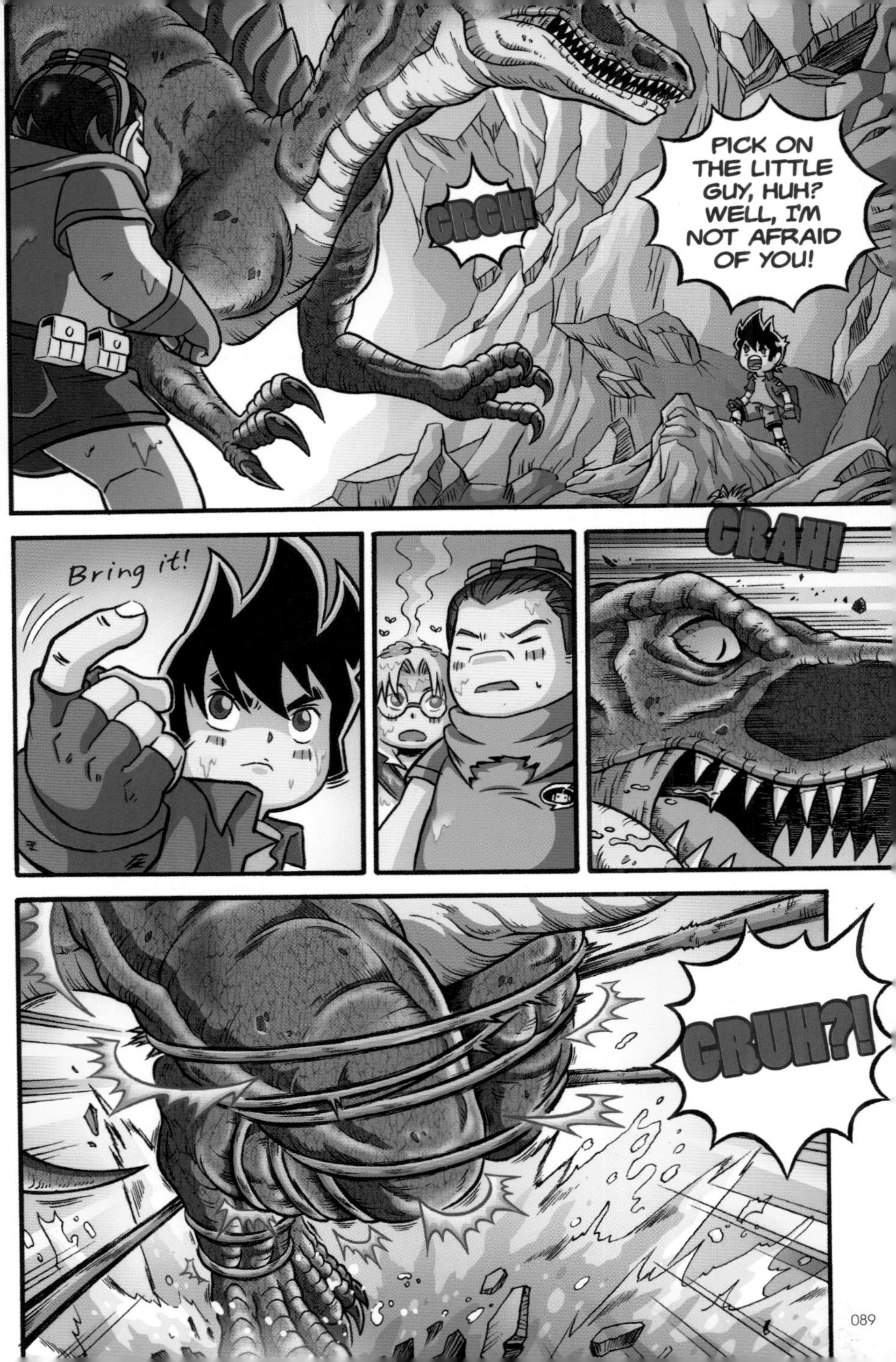
PICK ON THE LITTLE GUY, HUH? WELL, I'M NOT AFRAID OF YOU!
CRCH!
Bring it!
GRAH!
CRUH?!

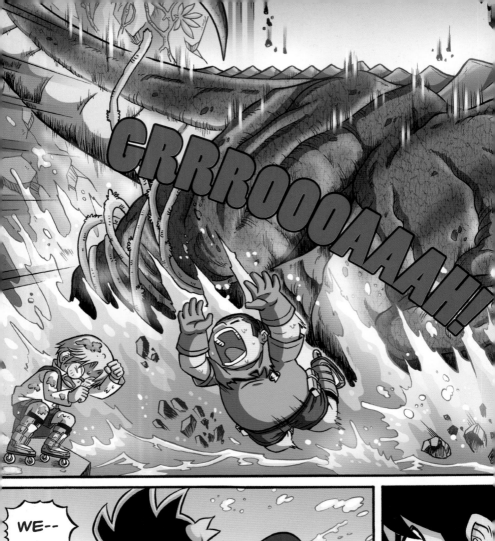

GRRROOOAAAH!

WE-- WE DID IT!

WE BEAT IT!

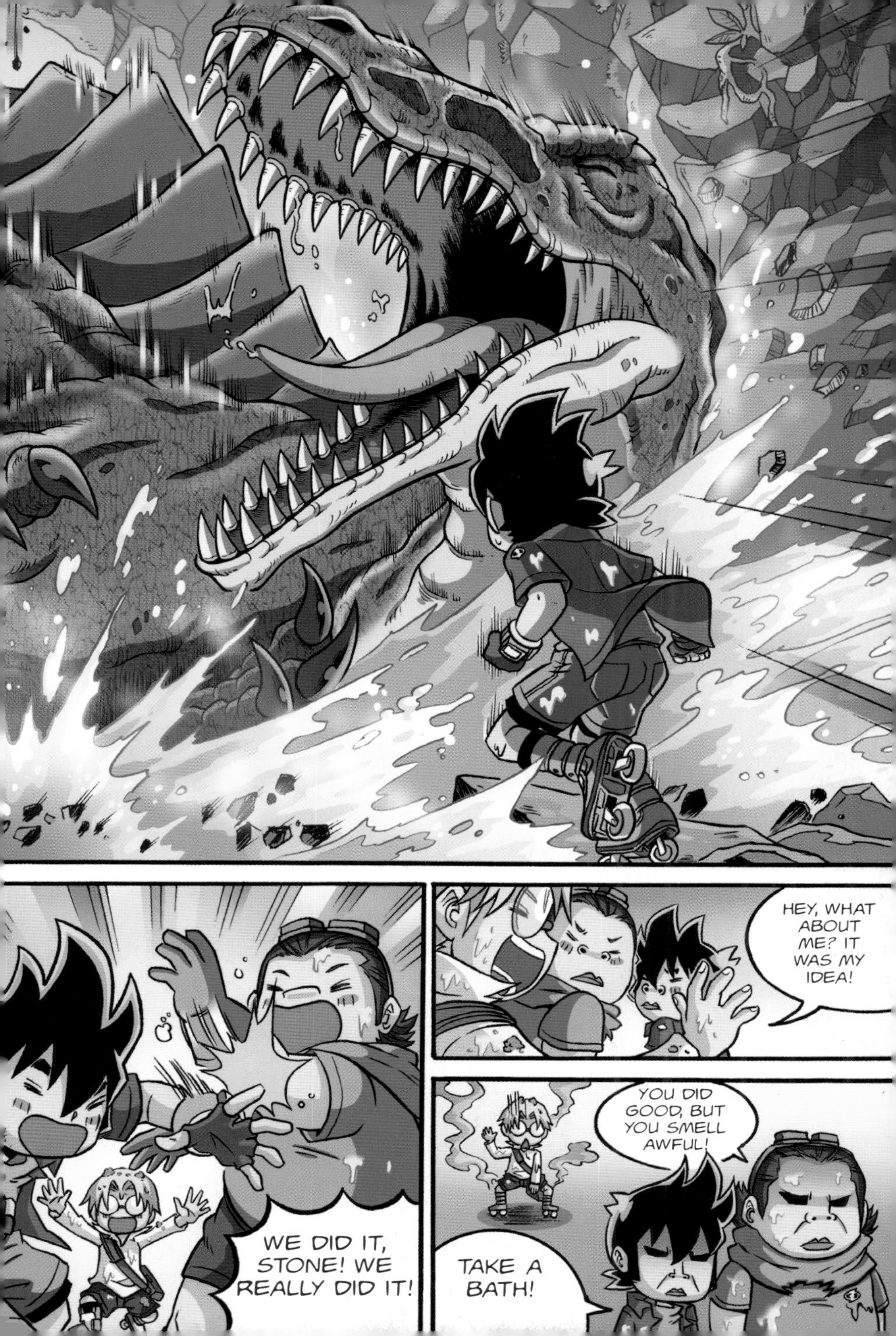
HEY, WHAT ABOUT ME? IT WAS MY IDEA!
WE DID IT, STONE! WE REALLY DID IT!
YOU DID GOOD, BUT YOU SMELL AWFUL!
TAKE A BATH!

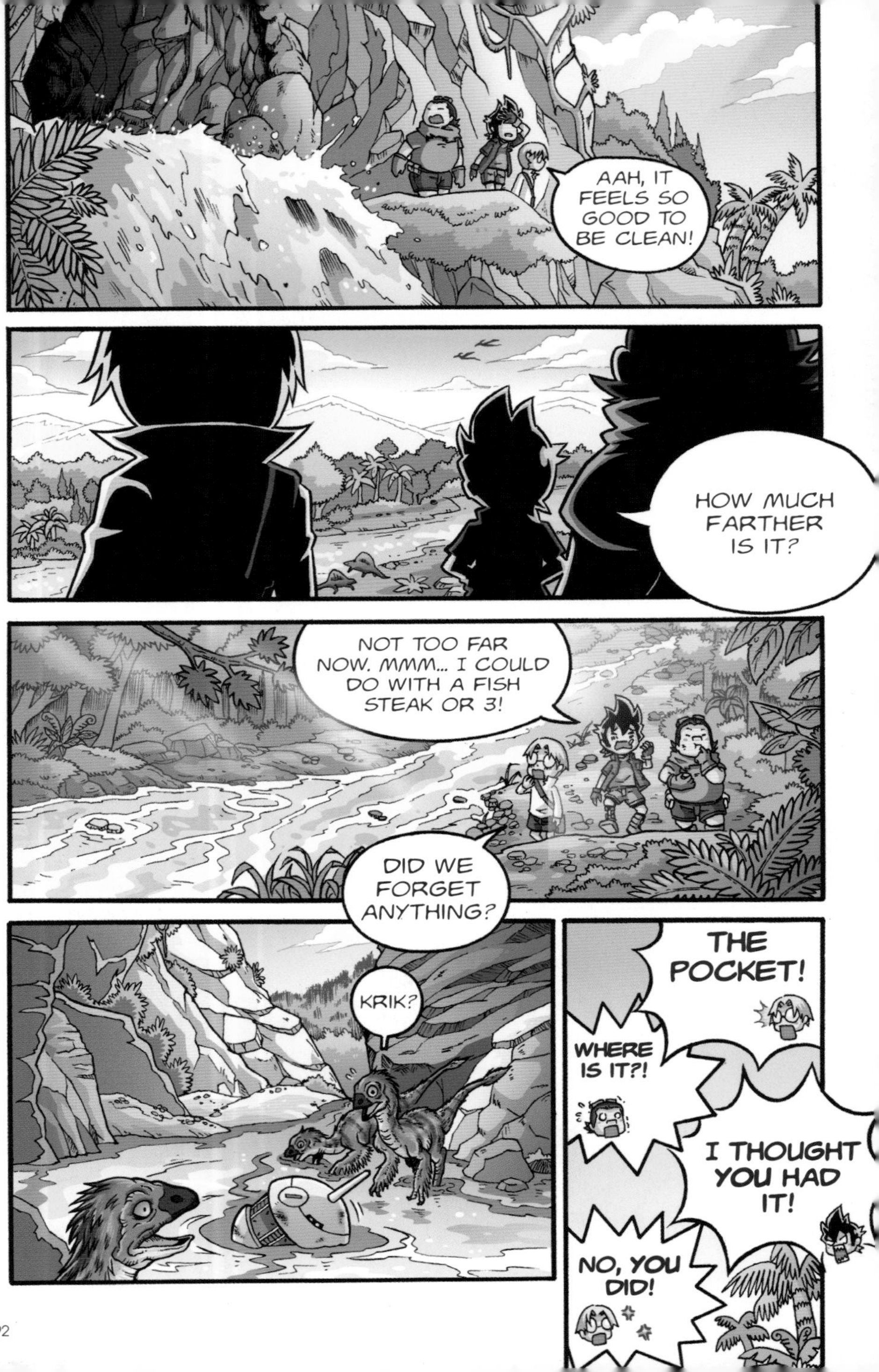
AAH, IT FEELS SO GOOD TO BE CLEAN!
HOW MUCH FARTHER IS IT?
NOT TOO FAR NOW. MMM... I COULD DO WITH A FISH STEAK OR 3!
DID WE FORGET ANYTHING?
KRIK?
THE POCKET!
WHERE IS IT?!
I THOUGHT YOU HAD IT!
NO, YOU DID!

# CAPTURING THE CRETACEOUS!

## Guanlong wucaii

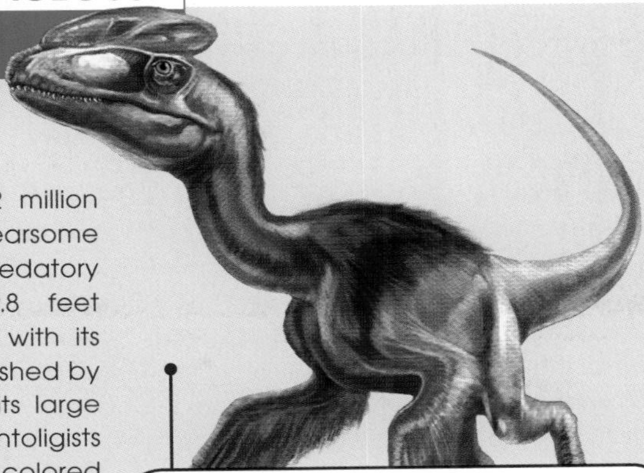

A proceratosaurid tyrannosauroid, Guanlong roamed the Late Jurassic, 92 million years before its famous and fearsome relative, the T-Rex. A light predatory theropod, it was about 9.8 feet long and shared many traits with its descendants, but was distinguished by some unusual ones, such as its large cranial crest, which paleontoligists think might have been brightly colored and used to attract mates. Unlike later tyrannosaurs, Guanlong had delicate three-fingered forelimbs, and crest aside, resembled its close relative Dilong, and like Dilong may have had a coat of primitive feathers.

**Scientific name:** Guanlong wucaii
**Size:** Approximately 9.8 feet
**Diet:** Carnivore
**Habitat:** Jungle
**Discovered:** China
**Period:** Late Jurassic

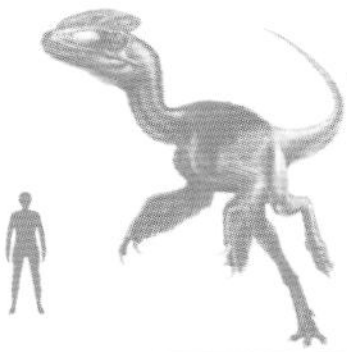

# CAPTURING THE CRETACEOUS!

## Rugops

The discovery of a Rugops skull found in Niger Africa in 2000, not only catapulted forward understanding of the evolution of avetheropods, but also proved that Africa was once part of Gondwana. With small, sharp teeth, it was considered to be a scavenger. There are also small depressions and pits on its skull, which might have formed horns or a bony "crown."

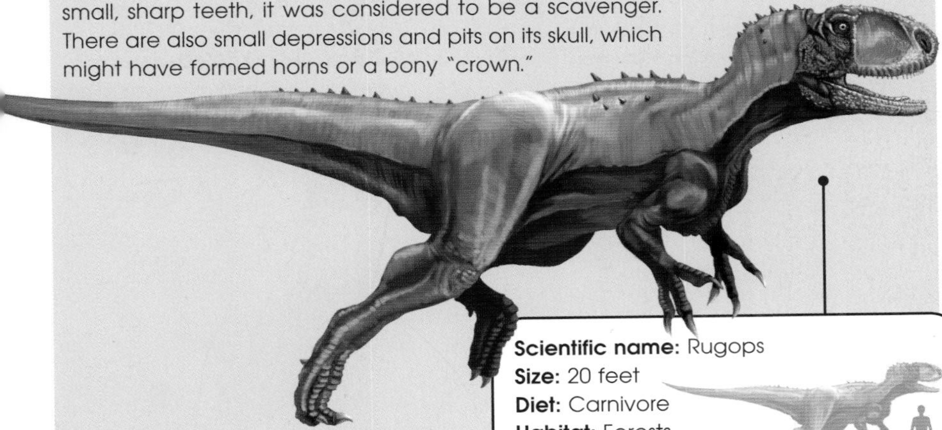

**Scientific name:** Rugops
**Size:** 20 feet
**Diet:** Carnivore
**Habitat:** Forests
**Discovered:** Africa
**Period:** Late Cretaceous

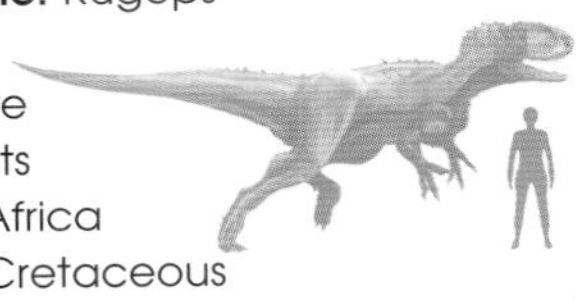

## How did dinosaurs communicate?
Sound mostly; if any dinosaur could have actually changed its skin color, that might have worked too.

## Did every dinosaur communicate through sound?
No. That said, of those that did, it is believed hadrosaurs used their peculiar head structures to amplify and/or create sounds to communicate over distances.

## Which dinosaurs could not 'speak'?
Research conducted on large sauropods namely Mamenchisaurus, Apatosaurus and Diplodocus showed that they would not have had complex vocal cords-making them all but mute.

Loudest dinosaur? The Parasaurolophus!

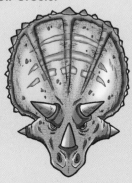

Hadrosaurs, such as this Lambeosaurus used their bizarre crests to produce a range of vocalizations.

The limited confines of a Pachycephalosaurus' mouth might have made for some odd sounds.

### Ceratopsids might have communicated via colorful "signals" on their crests.

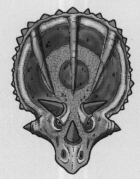

Eyelike patterns might have scared off predators.

Bright colors could have attracted mates.

## Diagram of the Parasaurolophus crest

Of all the hadrosaurs, the tubular crest of Parasaurolophus is the most dramatic. When it breathed, the movement of air within the crest created sounds. The curving shape of the crest could possibly have helped to modify tone and volume. This would have helped Parasaurolophus to communicate to a much higher degree than most other dinosaurs.

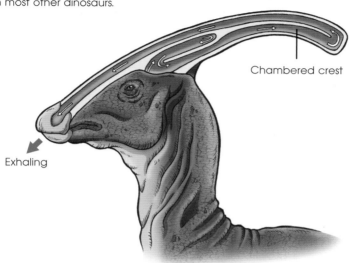

Chambered crest

Exhaling

## Saurolophus sound sending

The hadrosaur Saurolophus lacked a hollow crest; instead, it used a small, fleshy sac-like structure upon its forehead to contain and channel air. The shape and color of this sac could have also played a visual role in communication.

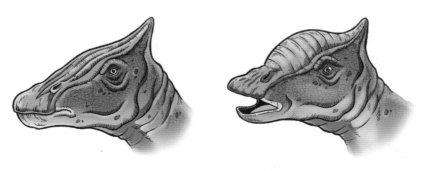

Empty air sac                    Full air sac

## CAPTURING THE CRETACEOUS!

### Baryonyx

Baryonyx is classified as part of family Spinosauridae and was named for its fearsome 9.85 inch "thumb" claws. Its elongated crocodilian jaws held 96 teeth, twice as many as T-Rex had, and combined with gaff-hook-like claws, Baryonyx' physical adaptations indicated it to be one of the few "piscivorous" (fish-eating) dinosaurs.

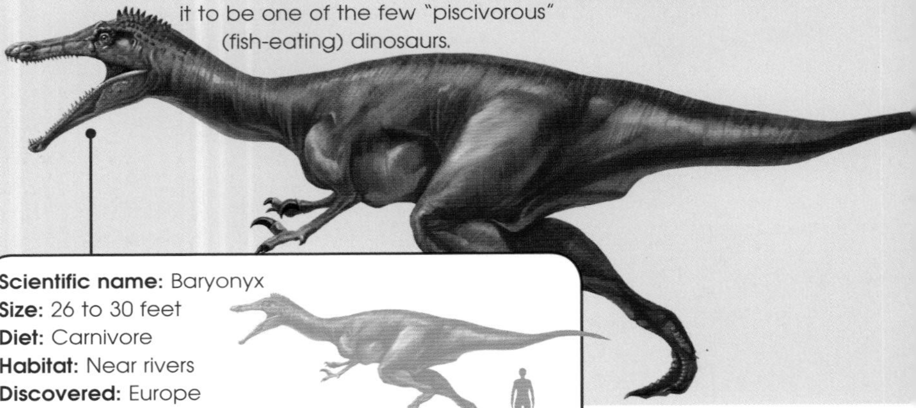

**Scientific name:** Baryonyx
**Size:** 26 to 30 feet
**Diet:** Carnivore
**Habitat:** Near rivers
**Discovered:** Europe
**Period:** Early Cretaceous

## CAPTURING THE CRETACEOUS!

### Deinonychus

Deinonychus, meaning "terrible claw" was a carnivorous dromaesaurid dinosaur. It is theorized that Deinonychus would have leapt upon prey and ripped it apart with its scythe-like second toes, aided by powerful jaws lined with around 70 curved blade-like teeth. It also had a relatively large brain for its size, which might have hinted at significant intelligence – perhaps enough to hunt in packs. With its large eyes and well-balanced tail, Deinonychus was perhaps one of the Cretaceous' most dangerous predators.

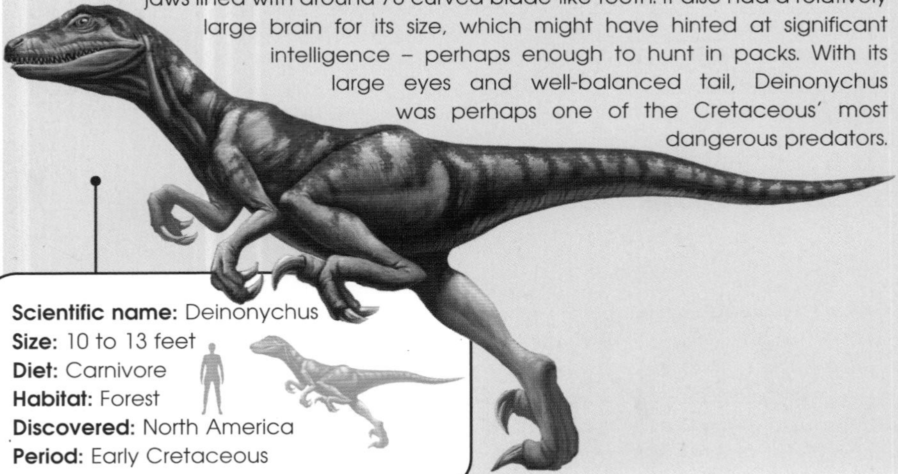

**Scientific name:** Deinonychus
**Size:** 10 to 13 feet
**Diet:** Carnivore
**Habitat:** Forest
**Discovered:** North America
**Period:** Early Cretaceous

CHAPTER 5

# SANDY BREACHES

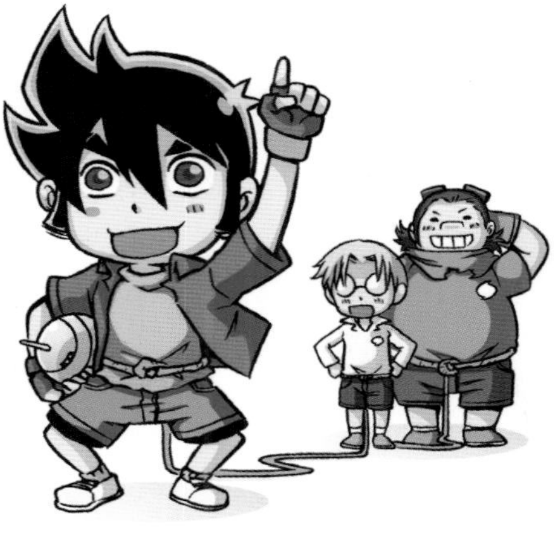

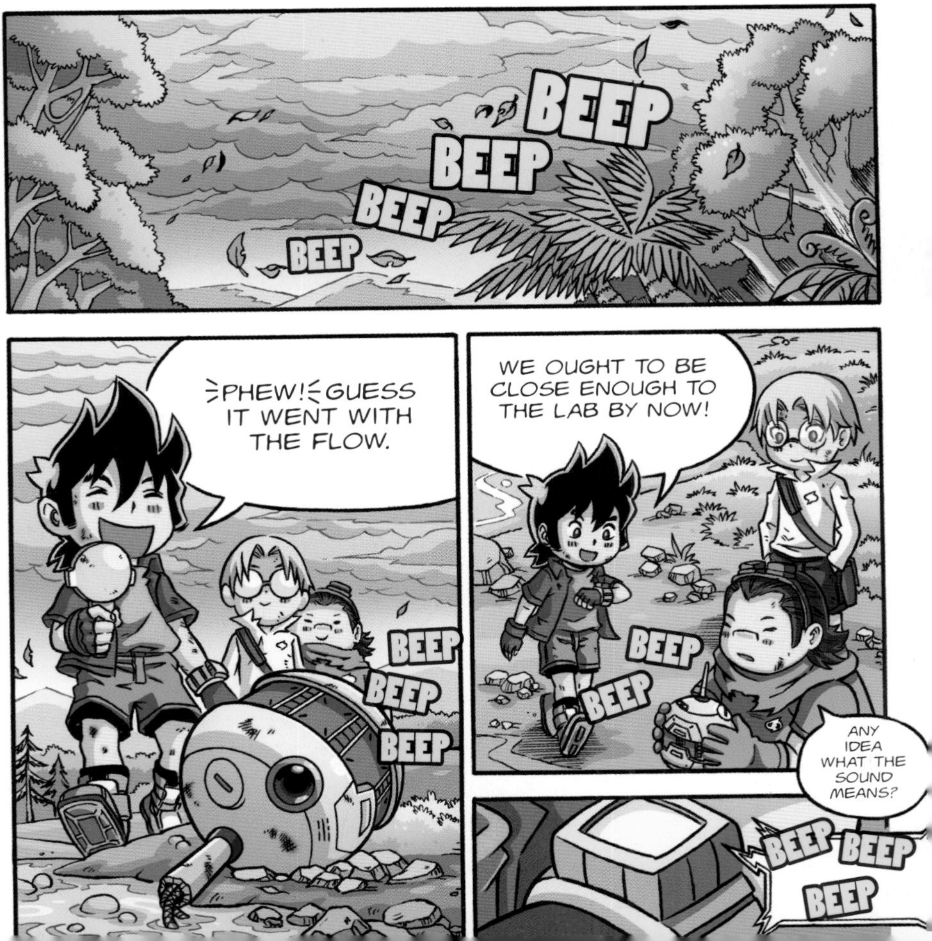
BEEP
BEEP
BEEP
BEEP
PHEW! GUESS IT WENT WITH THE FLOW.
BEEP
BEEP
BEEP
WE OUGHT TO BE CLOSE ENOUGH TO THE LAB BY NOW!
BEEP
BEEP
ANY IDEA WHAT THE SOUND MEANS?
BEEP
BEEP
BEEP

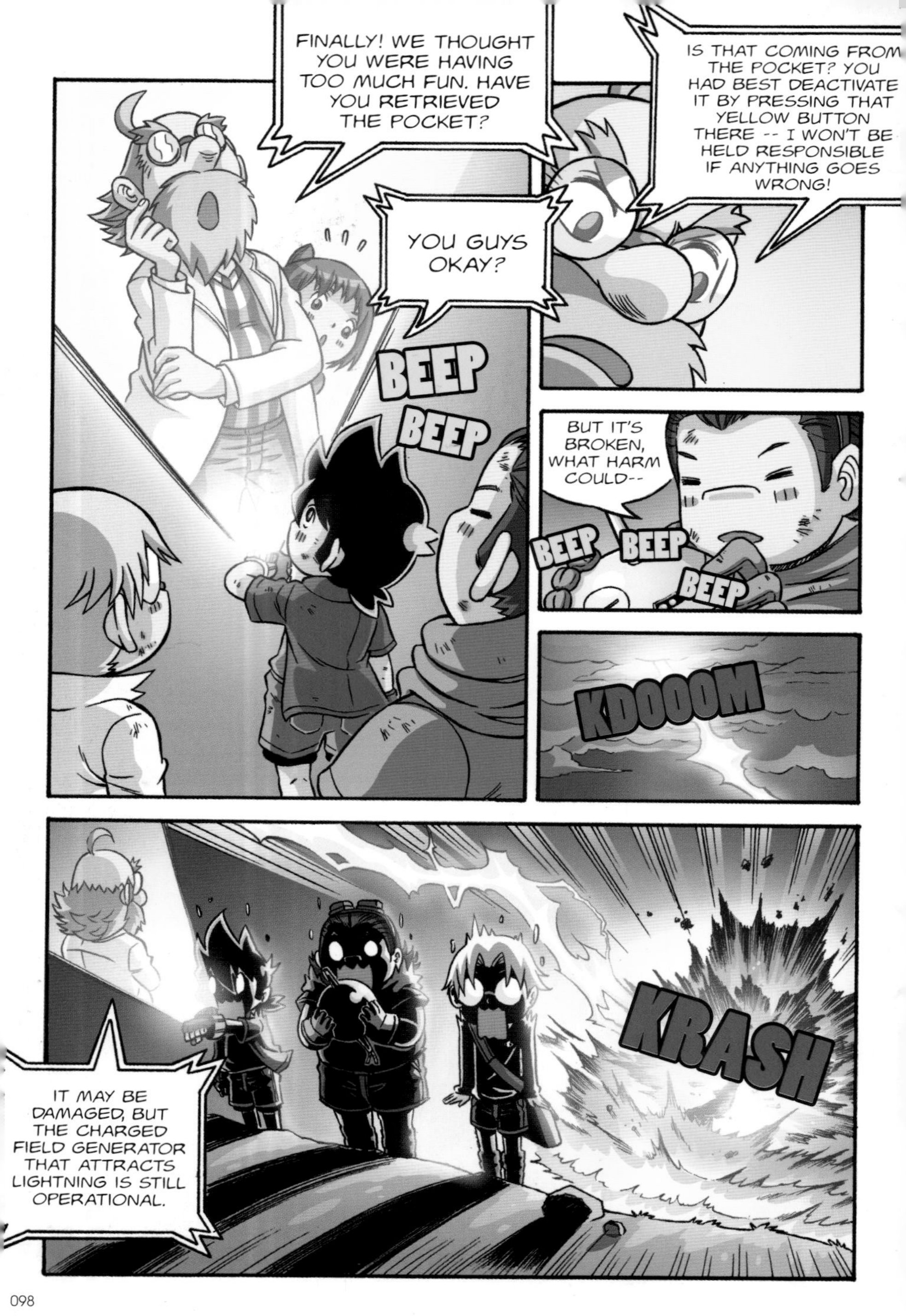
FINALLY! WE THOUGHT YOU WERE HAVING TOO MUCH FUN. HAVE YOU RETRIEVED THE POCKET?
YOU GUYS OKAY?
BEEP
BEEP
IS THAT COMING FROM THE POCKET? YOU HAD BEST DEACTIVATE IT BY PRESSING THAT YELLOW BUTTON THERE -- I WON'T BE HELD RESPONSIBLE IF ANYTHING GOES WRONG!
BUT IT'S BROKEN, WHAT HARM COULD--
BEEP
BEEP
BEEP
KDOOOM
KRASH
IT MAY BE DAMAGED, BUT THE CHARGED FIELD GENERATOR THAT ATTRACTS LIGHTNING IS STILL OPERATIONAL.

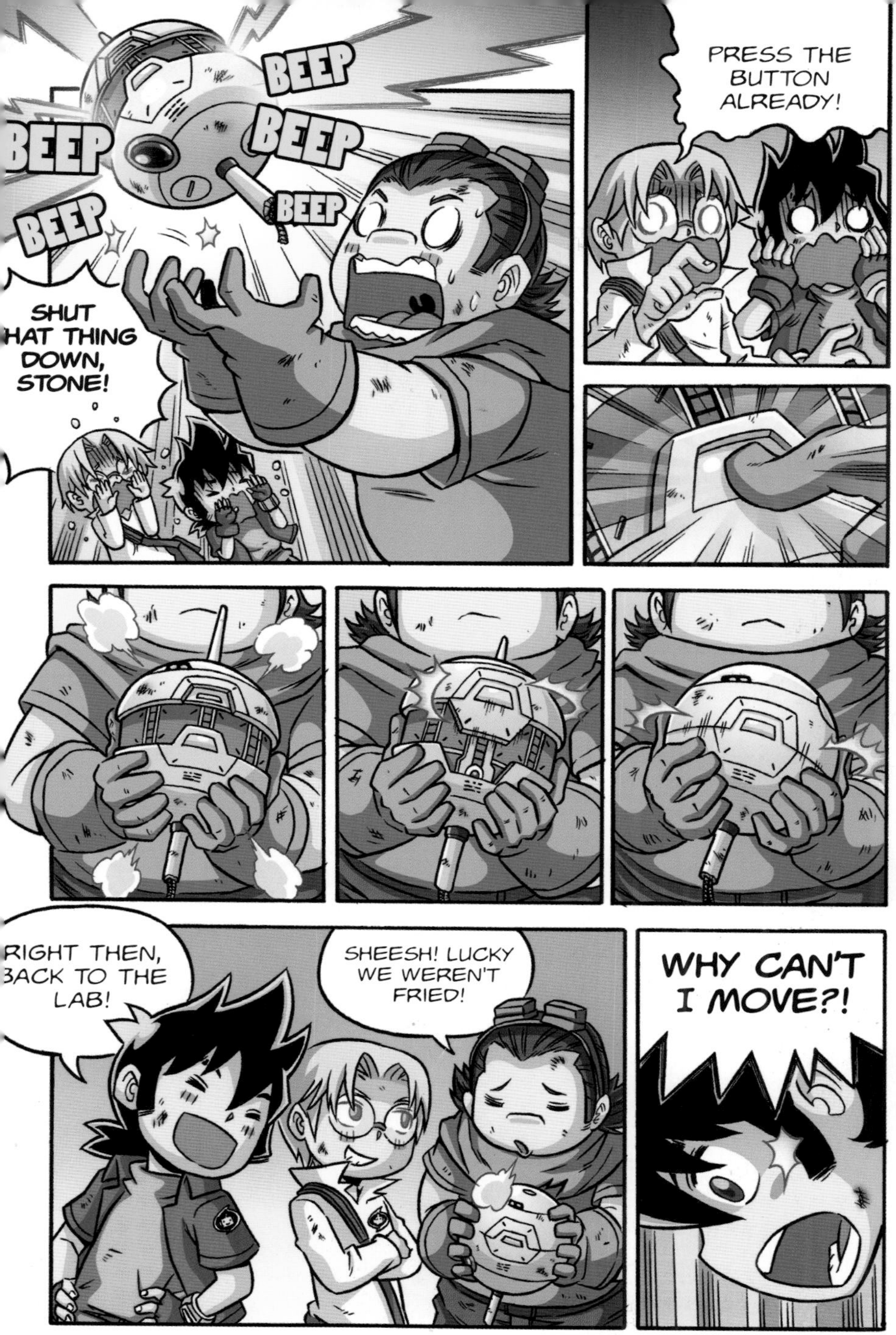
BEEP
BEEP
BEEP
BEEP
BEEP
SHUT
HAT THING
DOWN,
STONE!
PRESS THE
BUTTON
ALREADY!
RIGHT THEN,
BACK TO THE
LAB!
SHEESH! LUCKY
WE WEREN'T
FRIED!
WHY CAN'T
I MOVE?!

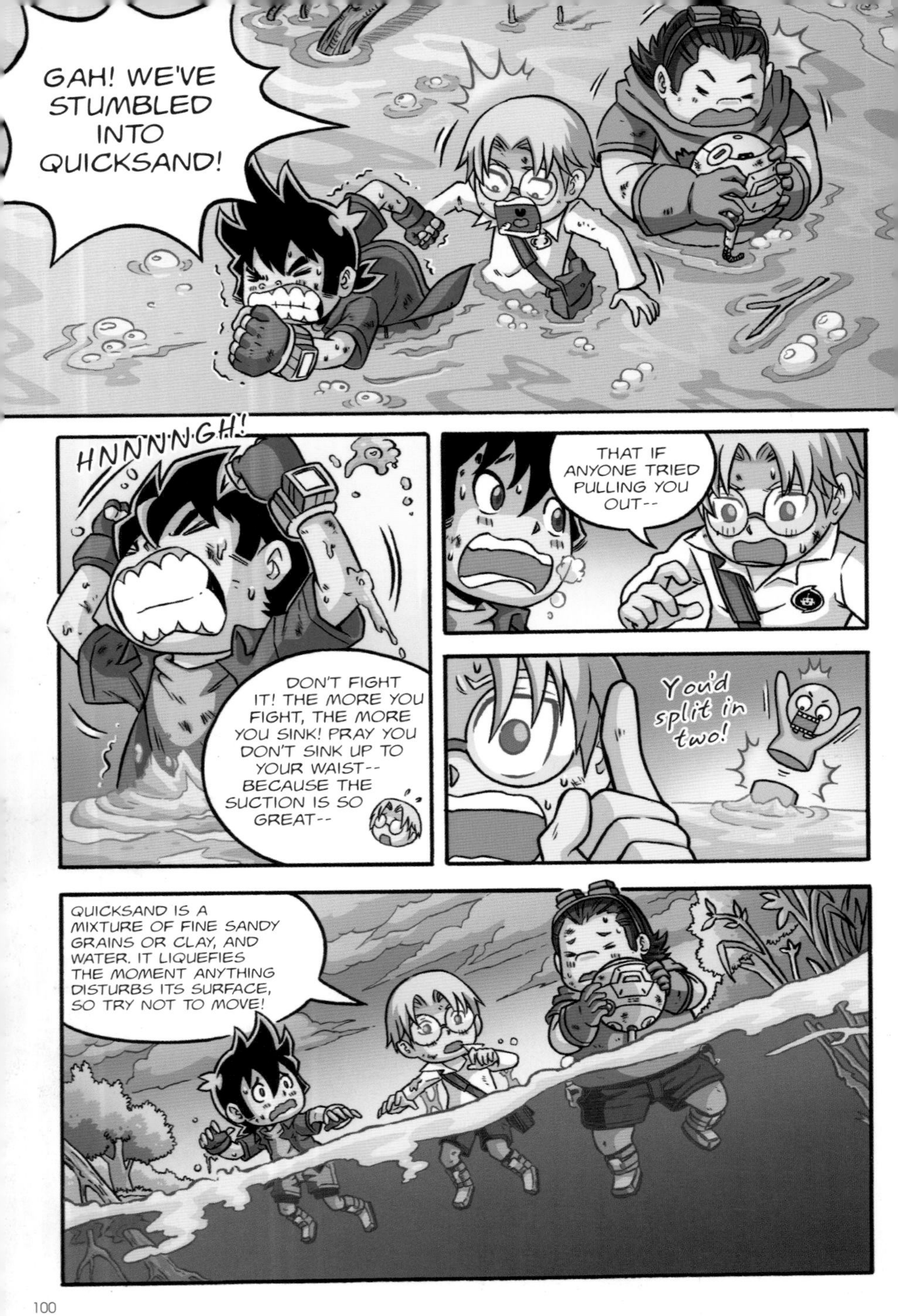
GAH! WE'VE STUMBLED INTO QUICKSAND!
HNNNNGH!
DON'T FIGHT IT! THE MORE YOU FIGHT, THE MORE YOU SINK! PRAY YOU DON'T SINK UP TO YOUR WAIST-- BECAUSE THE SUCTION IS SO GREAT--
THAT IF ANYONE TRIED PULLING YOU OUT--
You'd split in two!
QUICKSAND IS A MIXTURE OF FINE SANDY GRAINS OR CLAY, AND WATER. IT LIQUEFIES THE MOMENT ANYTHING DISTURBS ITS SURFACE, SO TRY NOT TO MOVE!

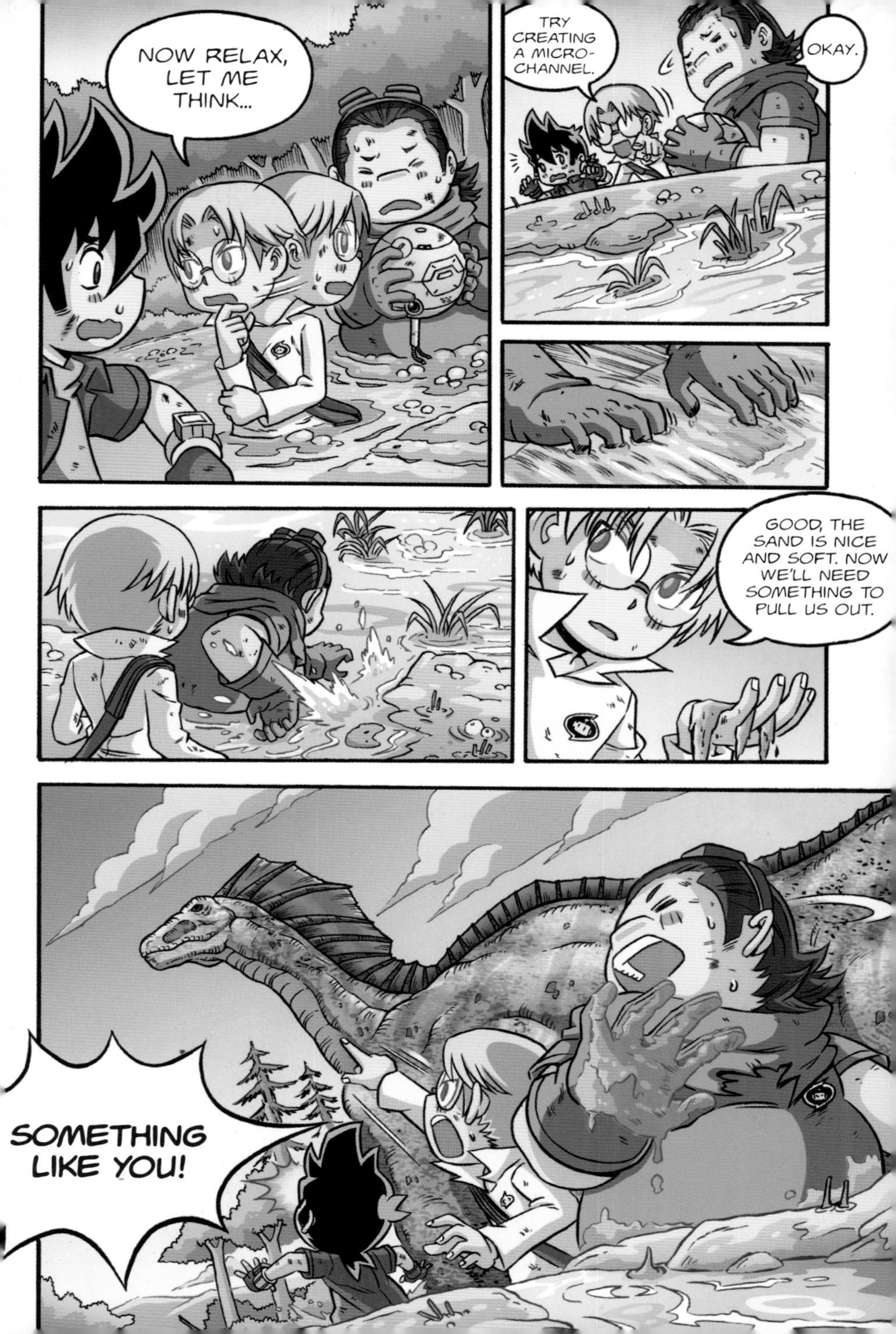

NOW RELAX, LET ME THINK...
TRY CREATING A MICRO-CHANNEL.
OKAY.
GOOD, THE SAND IS NICE AND SOFT. NOW WE'LL NEED SOMETHING TO PULL US OUT.
SOMETHING LIKE YOU!

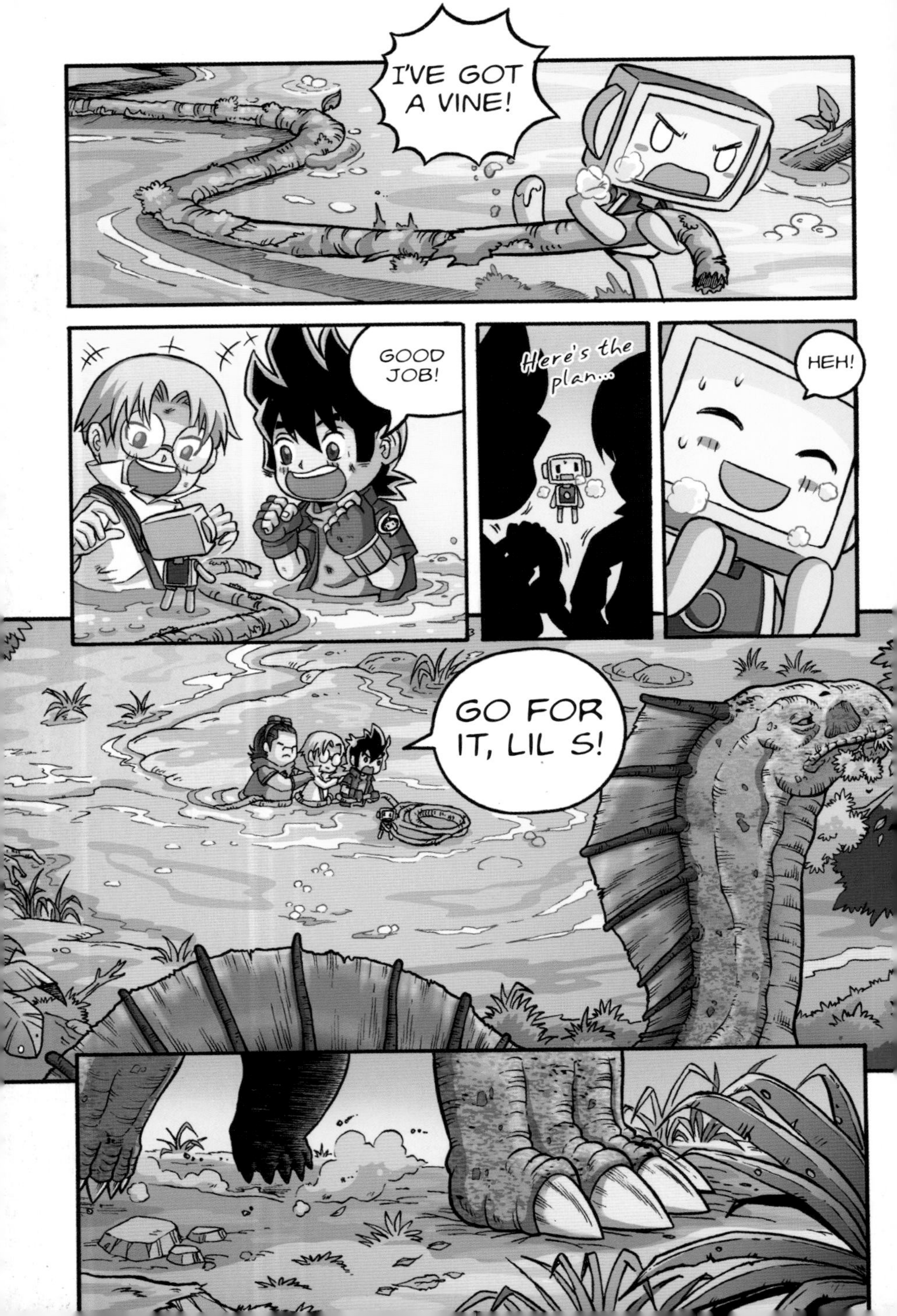
I'VE GOT A VINE!
GOOD JOB!
Here's the plan...
HEH!
GO FOR IT, LIL S!

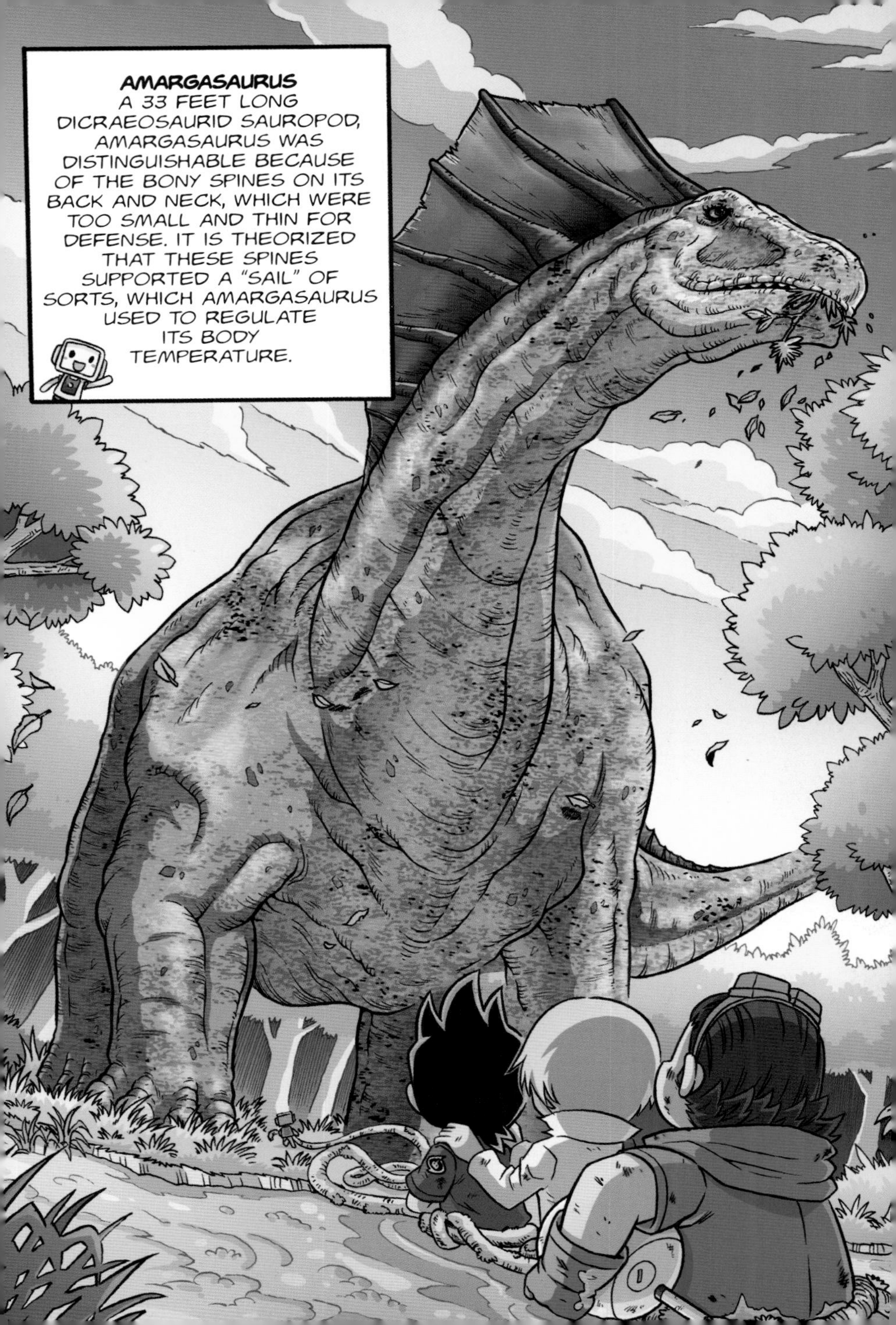
AMARGASAURUS
A 33 FEET LONG DICRAEOSAURID SAUROPOD, AMARGASAURUS WAS DISTINGUISHABLE BECAUSE OF THE BONY SPINES ON ITS BACK AND NECK, WHICH WERE TOO SMALL AND THIN FOR DEFENSE. IT IS THEORIZED THAT THESE SPINES SUPPORTED A "SAIL" OF SORTS, WHICH AMARGASAURUS USED TO REGULATE ITS BODY TEMPERATURE.

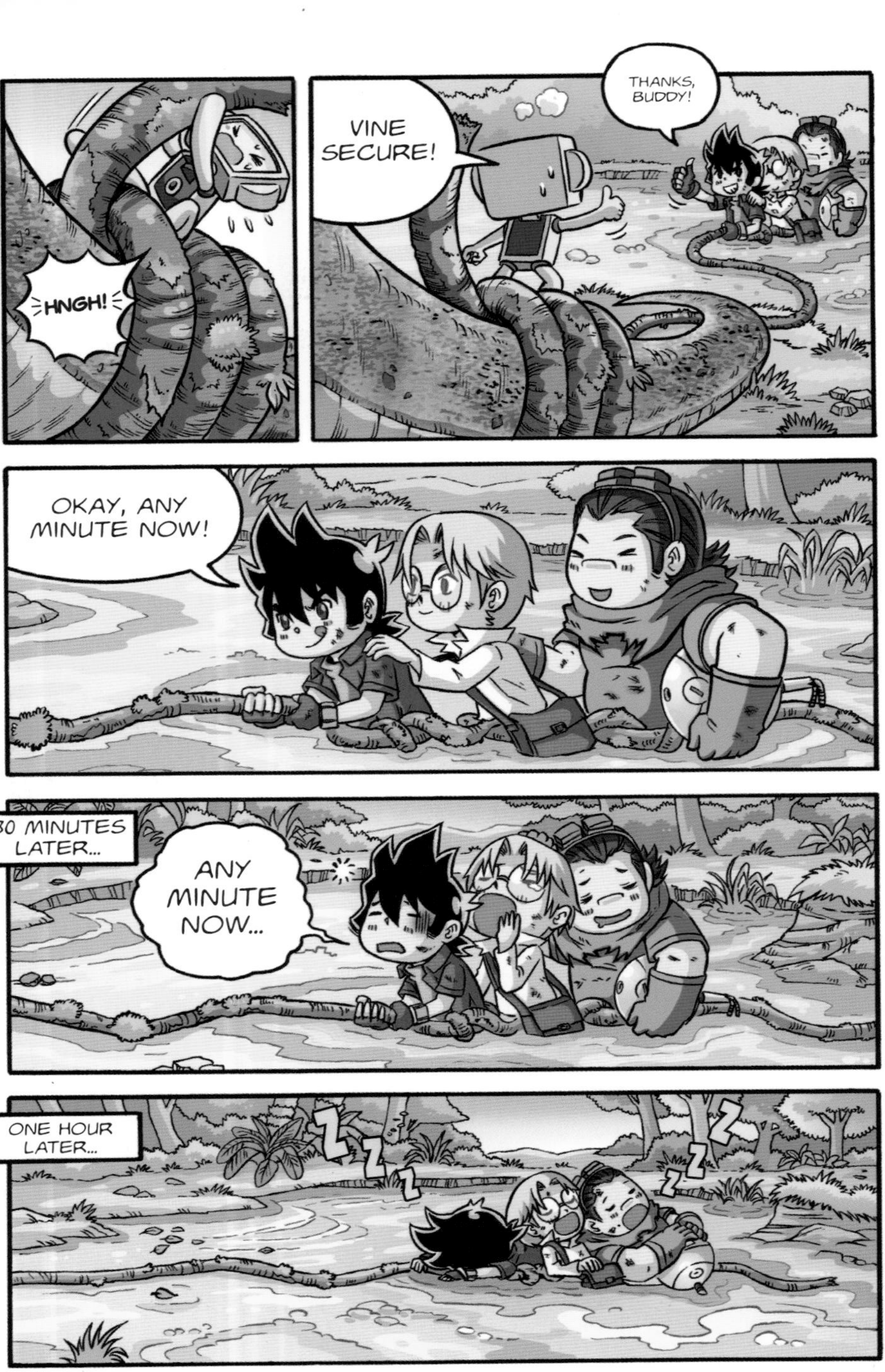
HNGH!
VINE SECURE!
THANKS, BUDDY!
OKAY, ANY MINUTE NOW!
30 MINUTES LATER...
ANY MINUTE NOW...
ONE HOUR LATER...
Z Z Z
Z Z Z

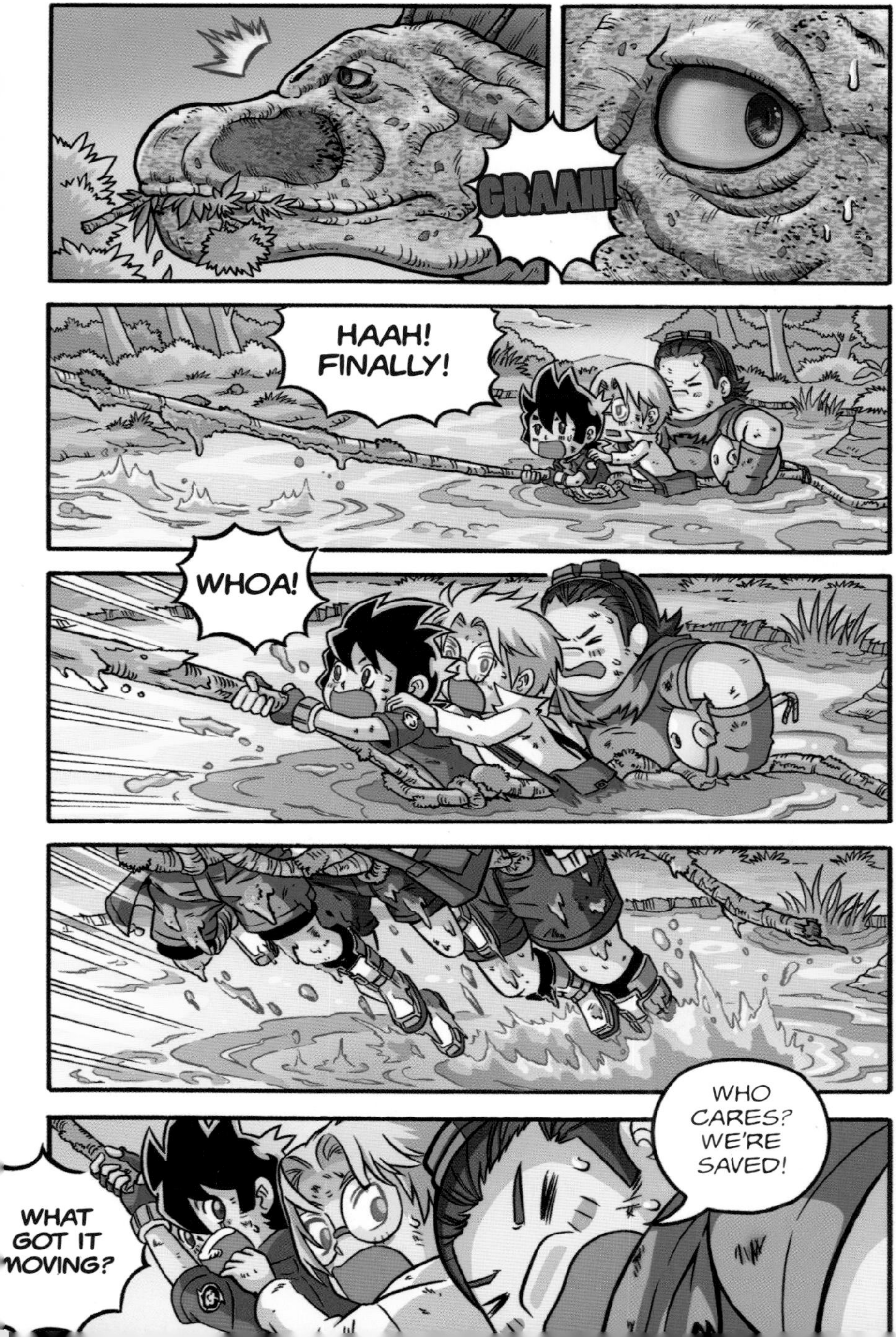
GRAAH!
HAAH! FINALLY!
WHOA!
WHO CARES? WE'RE SAVED!
WHAT GOT IT MOVING?

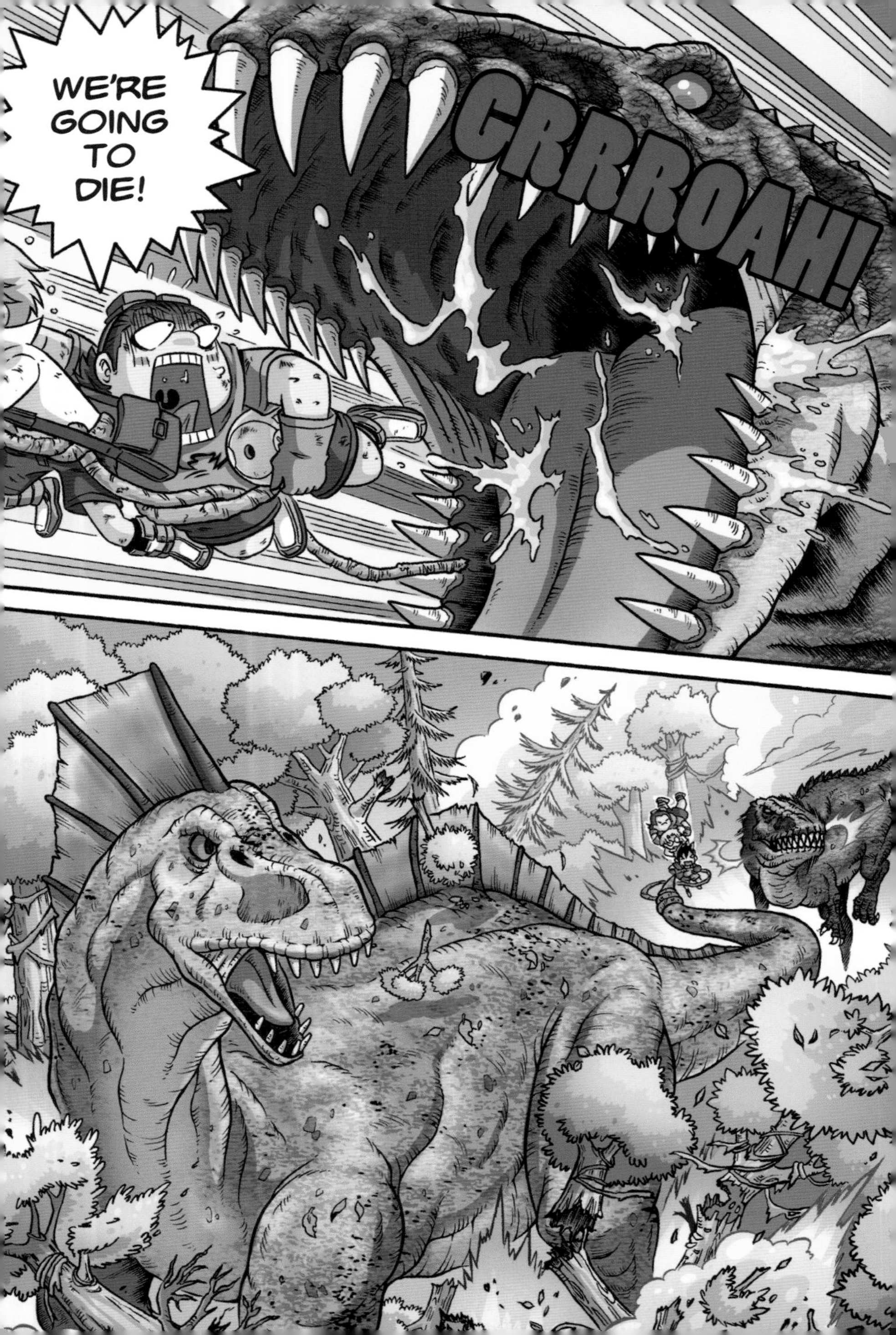
WE'RE GOING TO DIE!
GRRROAH!

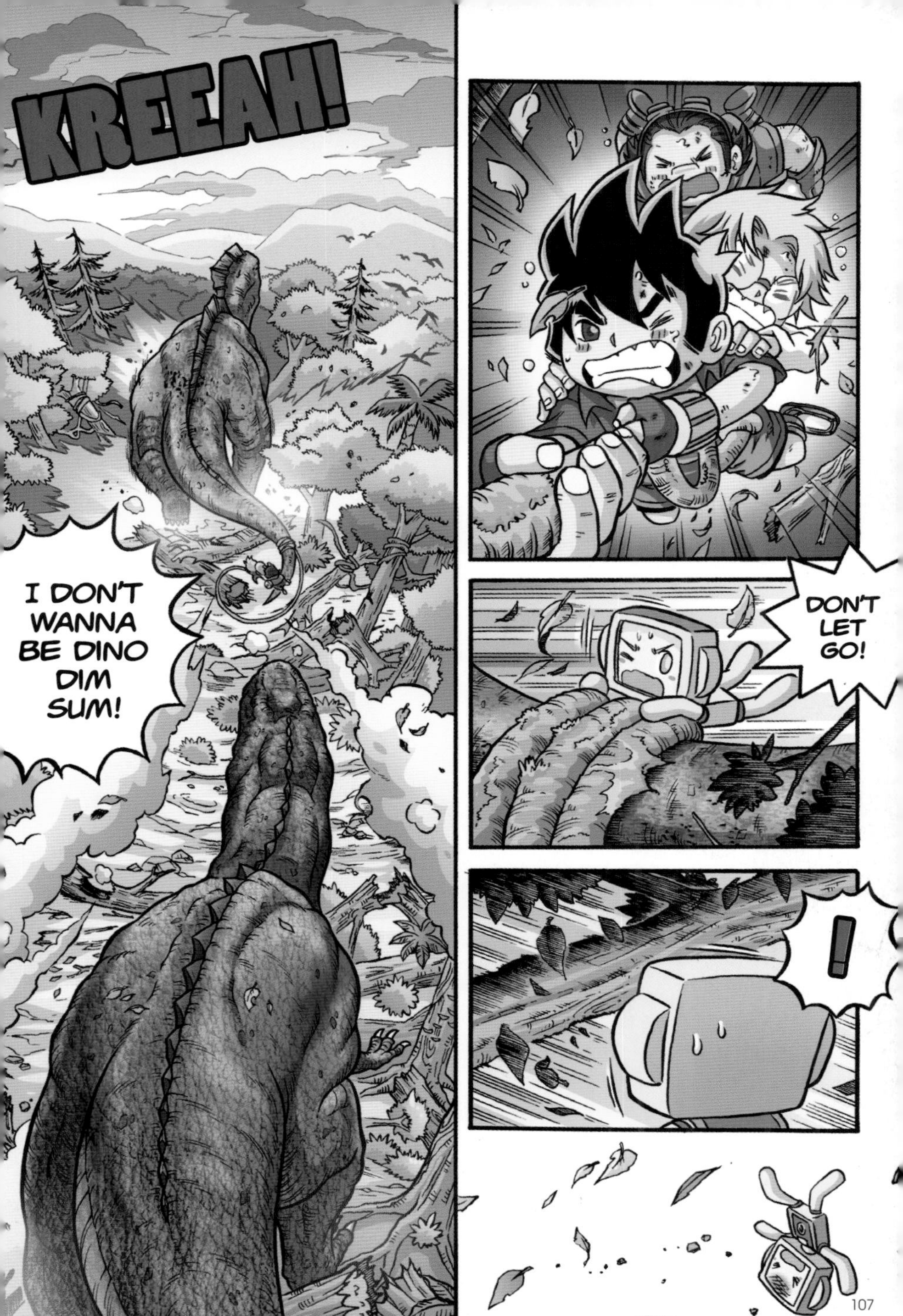
KREEAH!
I DON'T WANNA BE DINO DIM SUM!
DON'T LET GO!
!

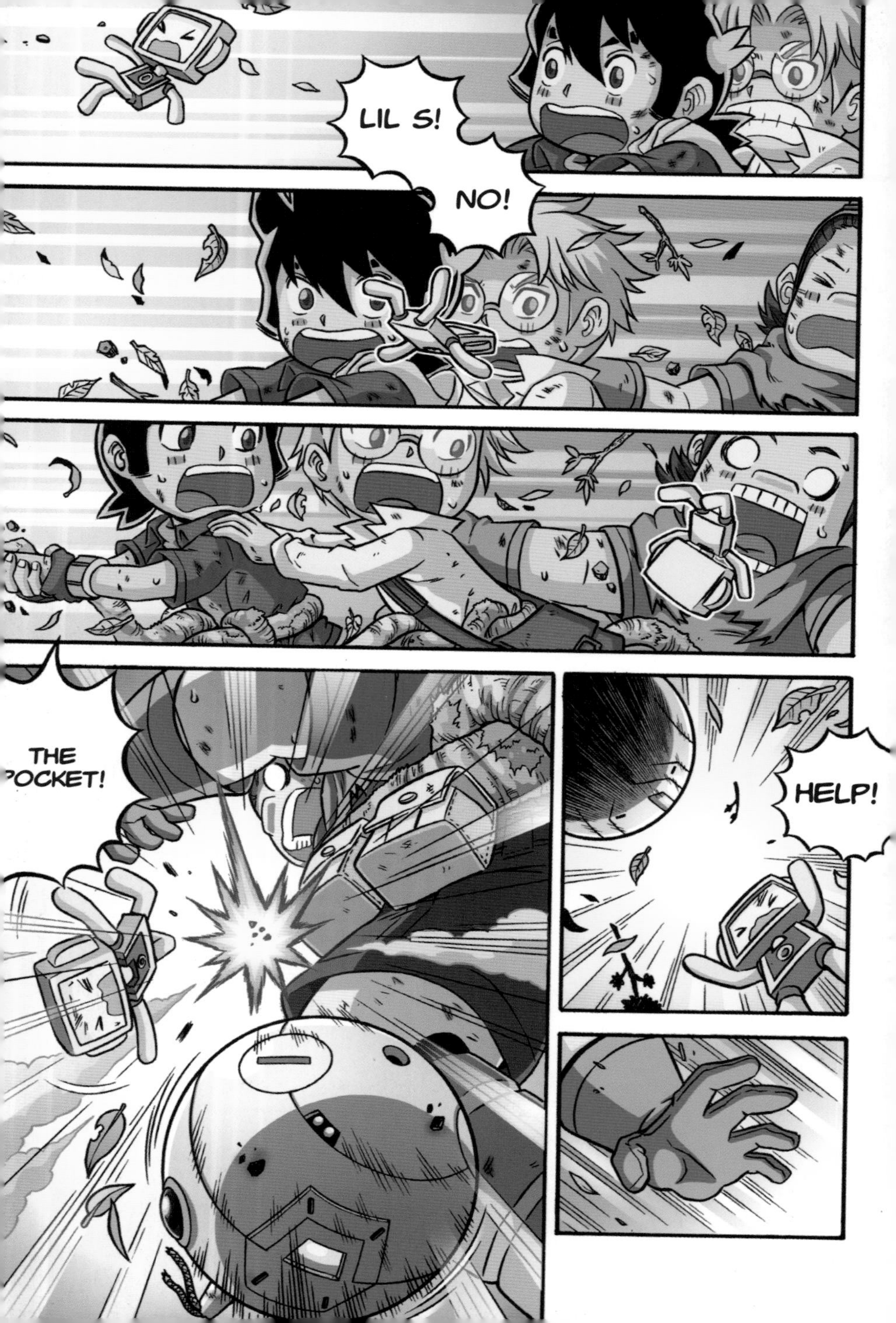
LIL S!
NO!
THE POCKET!
HELP!

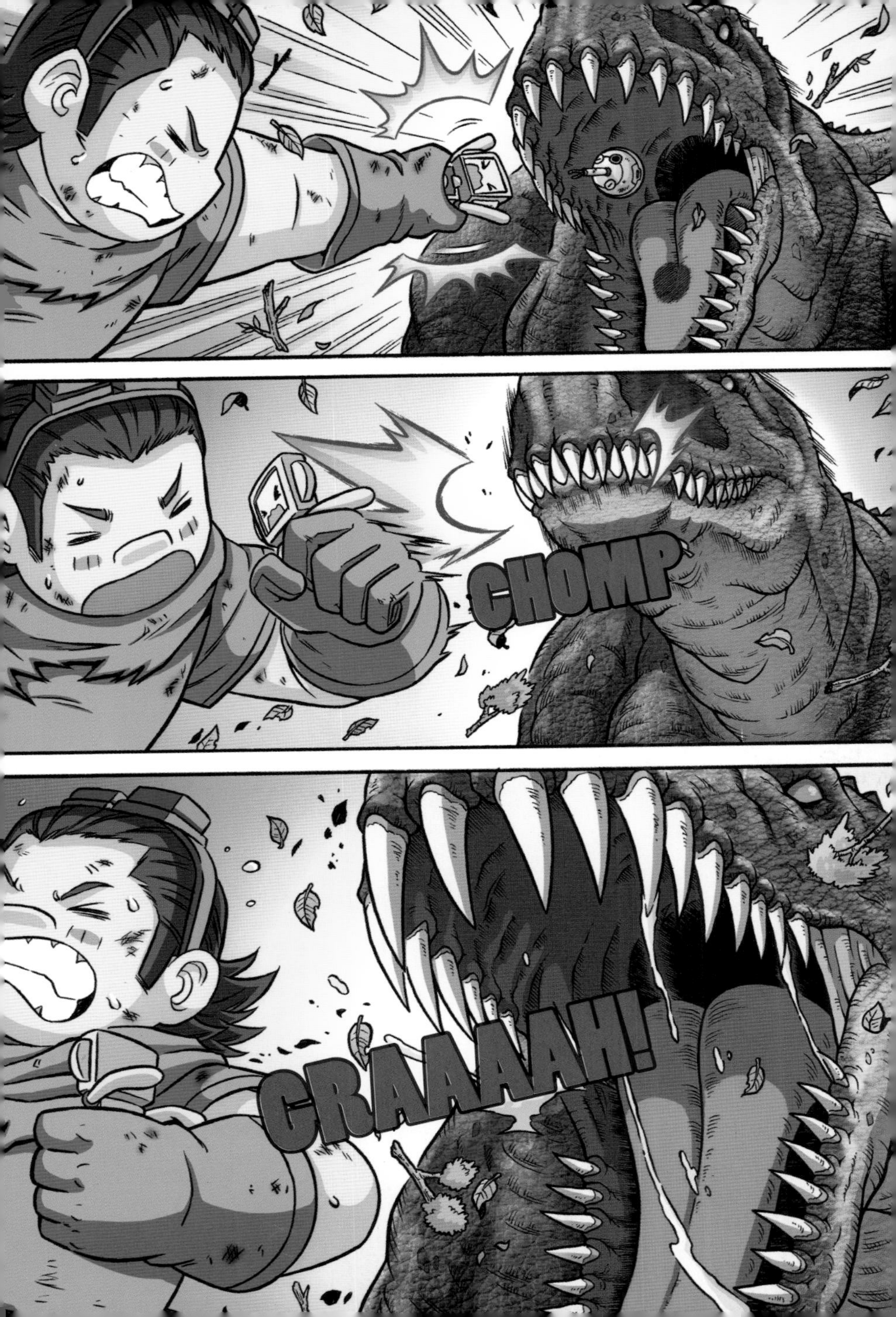

CHOMP
CRAAAAAH!

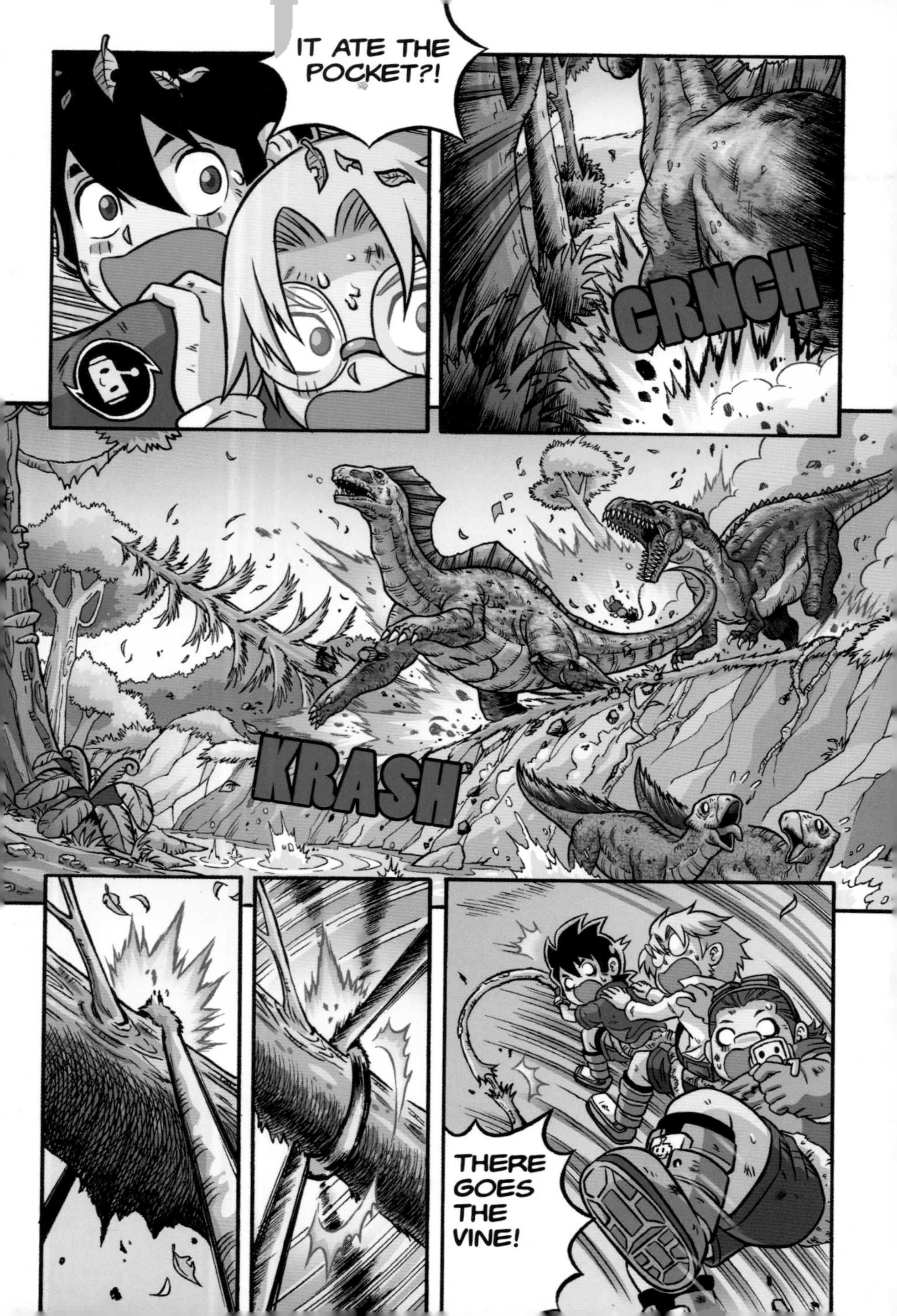

IT ATE THE POCKET?!
CRNCH
KRASH
THERE GOES THE VINE!

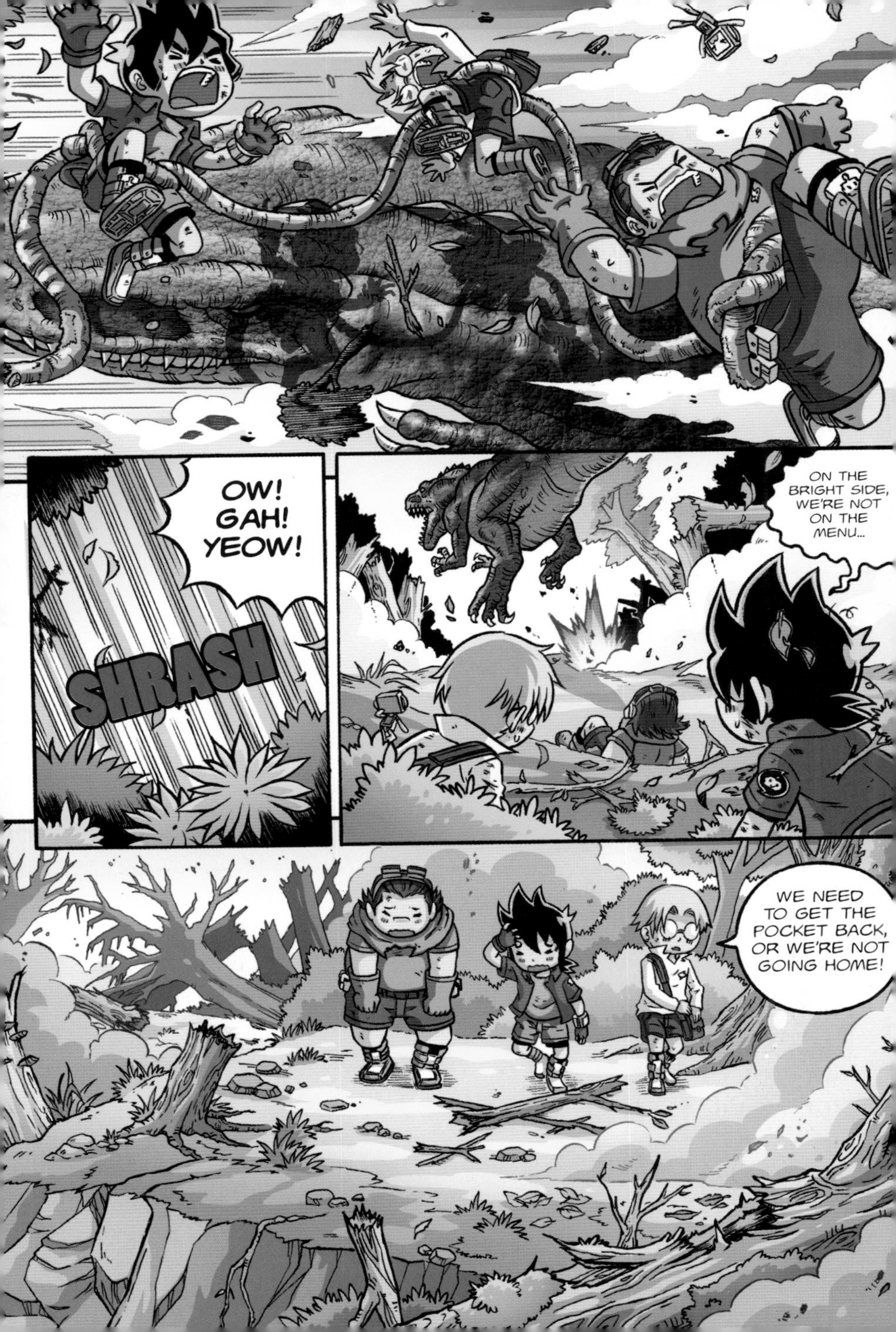
OW! GAH! YEOW!
SHRASH
ON THE BRIGHT SIDE, WE'RE NOT ON THE MENU...
WE NEED TO GET THE POCKET BACK, OR WE'RE NOT GOING HOME!

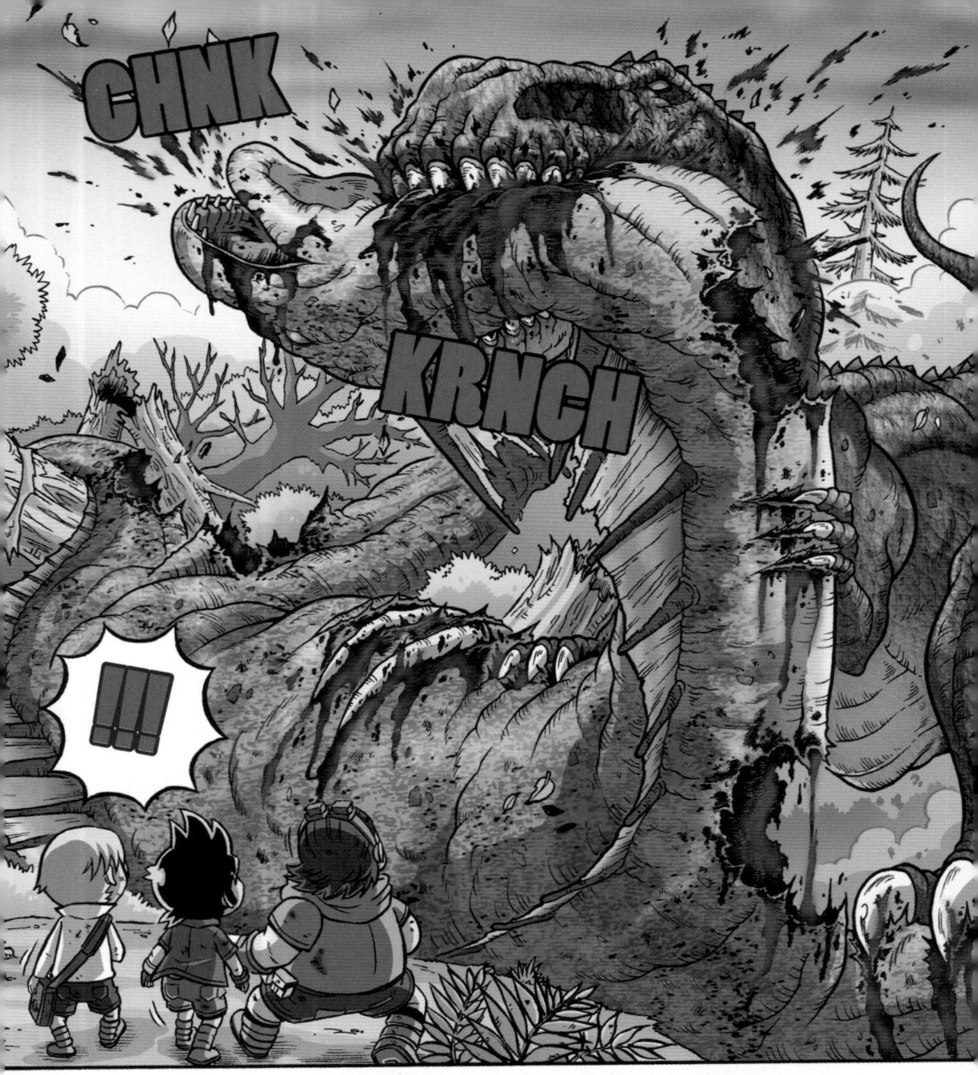
CHNK
KRNCH
!!!

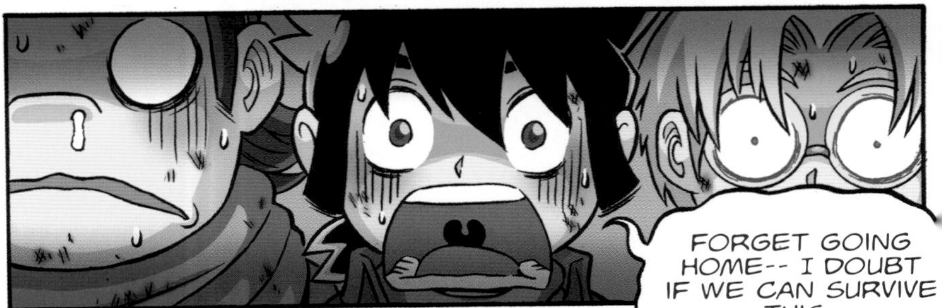
FORGET GOING HOME-- I DOUBT IF WE CAN SURVIVE THIS...

# CAPTURING THE CRETACEOUS!
## Sordes

Sordes ("scum" or "filth" in Latin) was named as a reference to evil spirits in local Kazakh folklore. Sordes belongs to suborder Rhamphorhynchoidea due to its small size. It might have had fur or feathers on its body, but not on its wings. Its thin, whip-like tail was almost as long as its body.

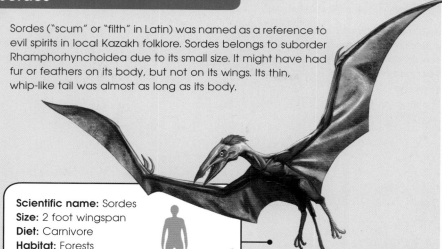

**Scientific name:** Sordes
**Size:** 2 foot wingspan
**Diet:** Carnivore
**Habitat:** Forests
**Discovered:** Kazakhstan
**Period:** Late Cretaceous

# CAPTURING THE CRETACEOUS!
## Pterodaustro

Pterodaustro was famous for its curved, elongated bristle-toothed lower jaw, which filtered out any water when it swooped down for fish. They were so finely spaced, they could even catch microscopic plankton. Its legs were very small; as such, it is theorized that Pterodaustro rarely spent time on land.

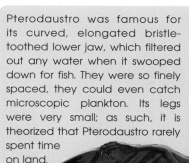

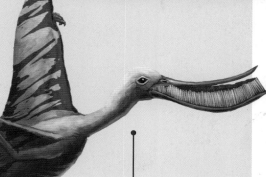

**Scientific name:** Pterodaustro
**Size:** 8 to 10 feet wingspan
**Diet:** Carnivore
**Habitat:** Lakes and seashores
**Discovered:** South America
**Period:** Early Cretaceous

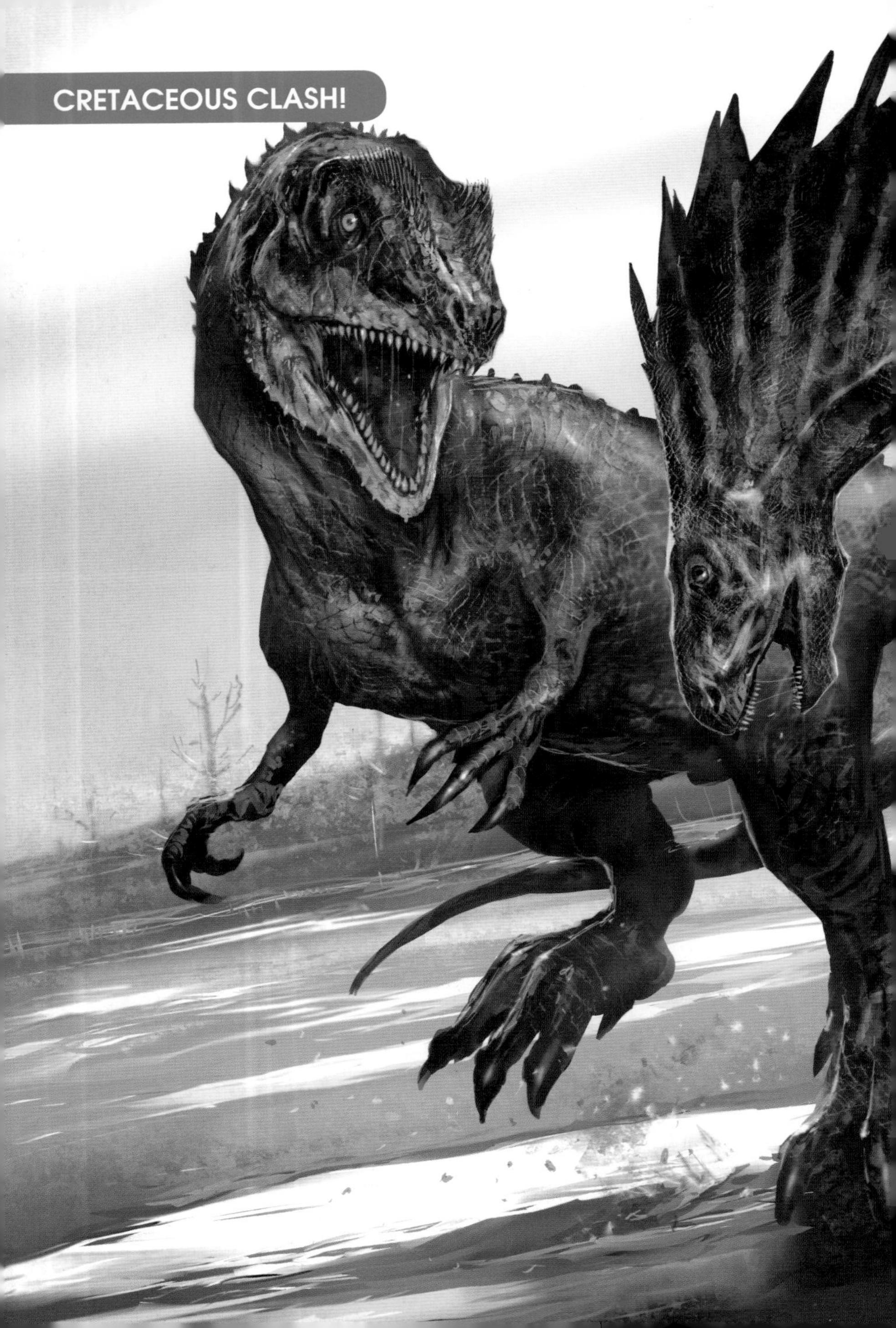

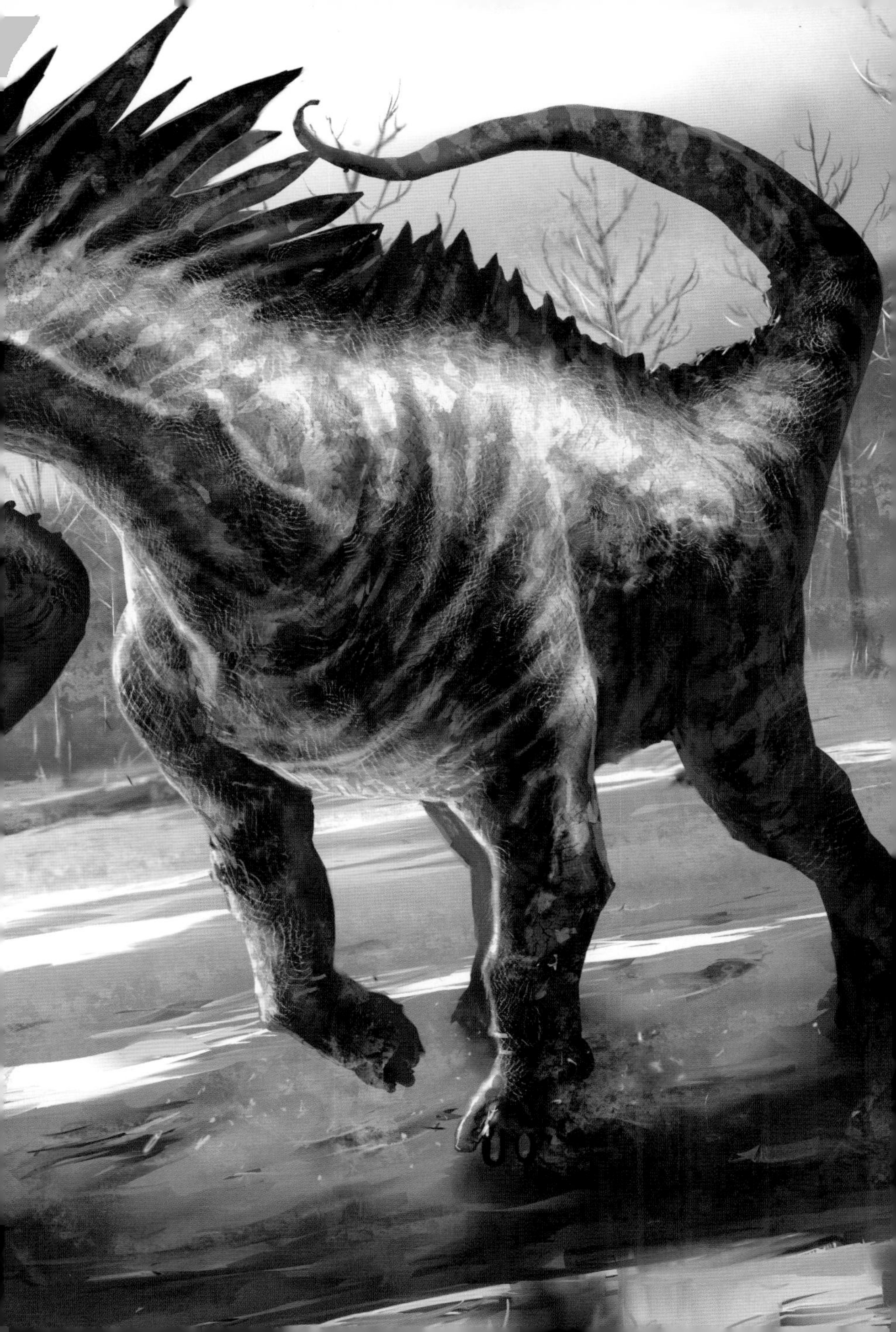

# CAPTURING THE CRETACEOUS!

## Amargasaurus

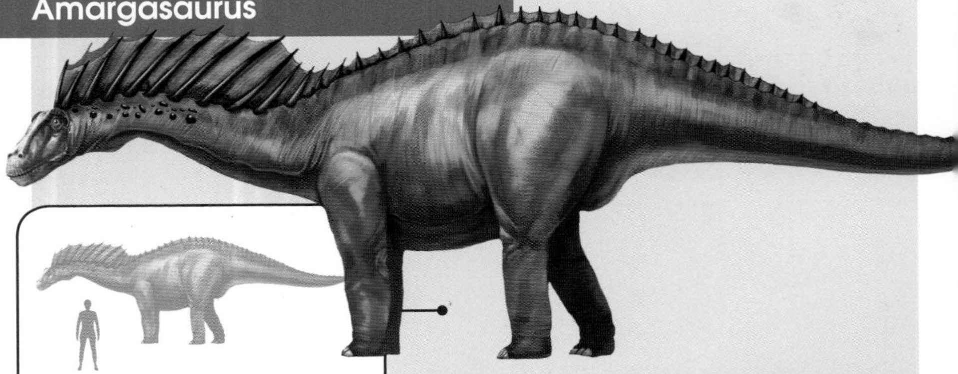

**Scientific name:** Amargasaurus
**Size:** 30 to 33 feet
**Diet:** Herbivore
**Habitat:** Near rivers
**Discovered:** Argentina
**Period:** Early Cretaceous

Classified as a sauropod, Amargasaurus was smaller than other members of the infraorder, reaching a mere 33 feet from snout to tail tip. Size aside, it is remarkable for the row of short, thin spines on its back. It is opined that these spines might have supported a small sail that helped control its temperature, but the debate goes on.

# CAPTURING THE CRETACEOUS!

## Muttaburrasaurus

Belonging to the same family as Iguanodon, Muttaburrasaurus was about 26 feet long, smaller and lighter than its more famous cousin. Its distinctive, hollow humped snout is believed to have been used to make various sounds for communication and attracting mates.

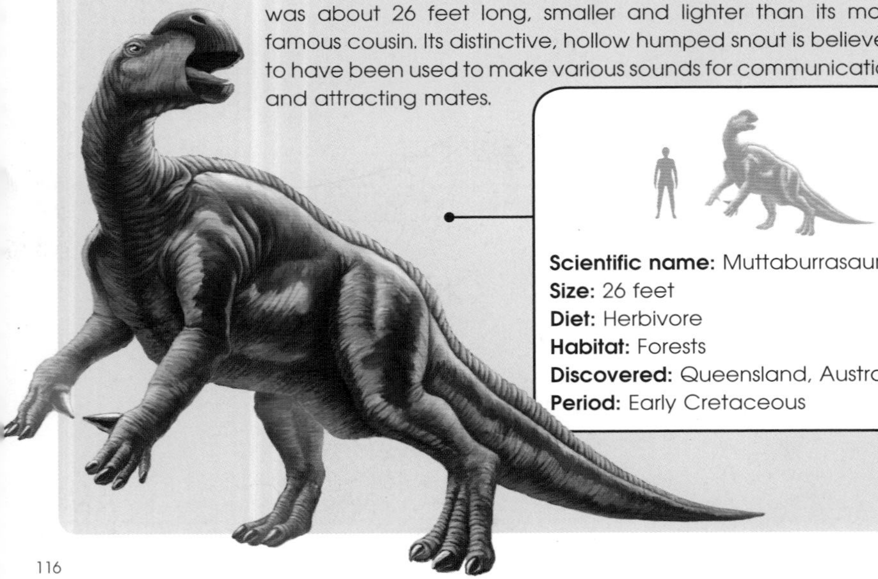

**Scientific name:** Muttaburrasaurus
**Size:** 26 feet
**Diet:** Herbivore
**Habitat:** Forests
**Discovered:** Queensland, Australia
**Period:** Early Cretaceous

CHAPTER 6

# A BITTER DRINK

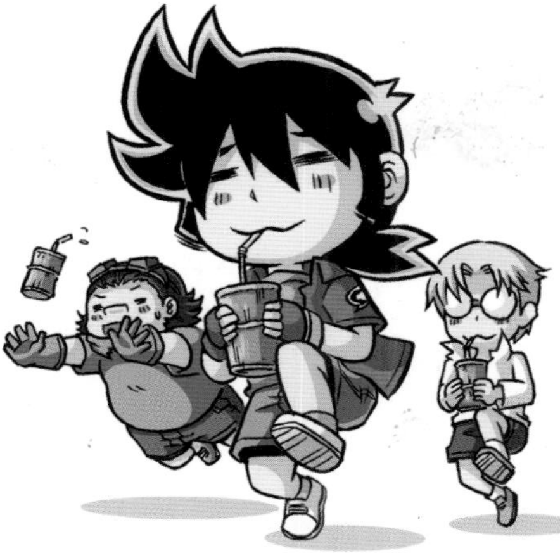

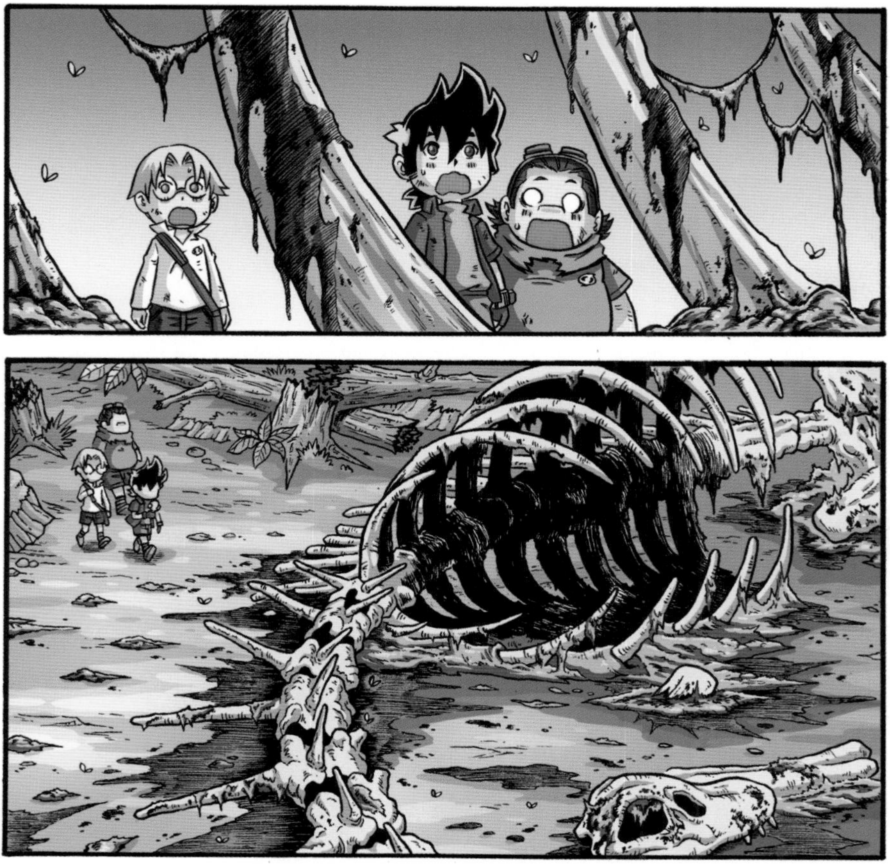

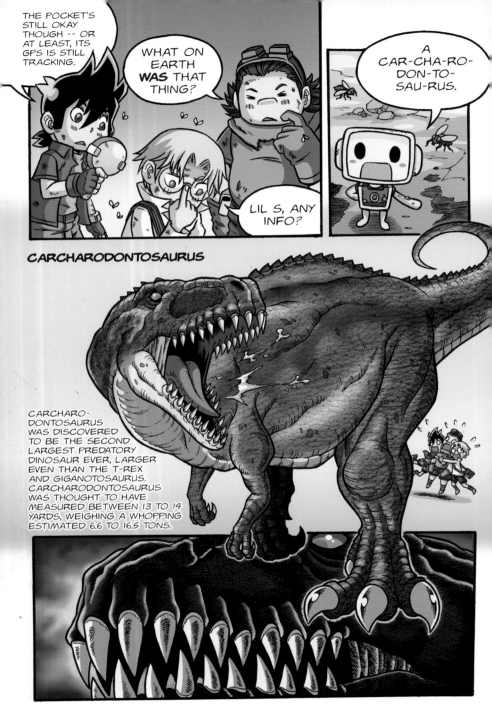

THE POCKET'S STILL OKAY THOUGH -- OR AT LEAST, ITS GPS IS STILL TRACKING.

WHAT ON EARTH **WAS** THAT THING?

LIL S, ANY INFO?

A CAR-CHA-RO-DON-TO-SAU-RUS.

CARCHARODONTOSAURUS

CARCHARO-DONTOSAURUS WAS DISCOVERED TO BE THE SECOND LARGEST PREDATORY DINOSAUR EVER, LARGER EVEN THAN THE T-REX AND GIGANOTOSAURUS. CARCHARODONTOSAURUS WAS THOUGHT TO HAVE MEASURED BETWEEN 13 TO 14 YARDS, WEIGHING A WHOPPING ESTIMATED 6.6 TO 16.5 TONS.

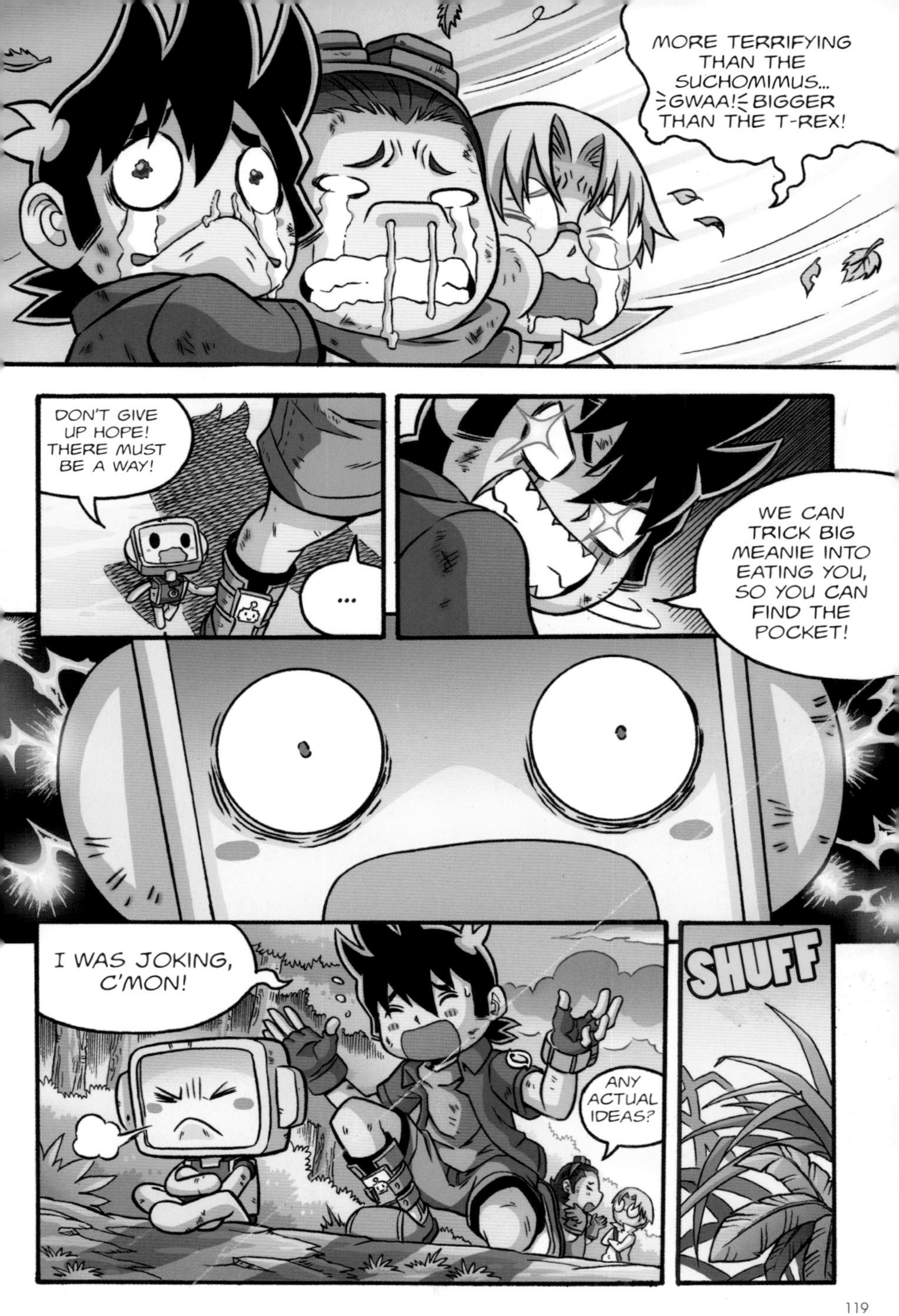
MORE TERRIFYING THAN THE SUCHOMIMUS... GWAA! BIGGER THAN THE T-REX!
DON'T GIVE UP HOPE! THERE MUST BE A WAY!
...
WE CAN TRICK BIG MEANIE INTO EATING YOU, SO YOU CAN FIND THE POCKET!
I WAS JOKING, C'MON!
ANY ACTUAL IDEAS?
SHUFF

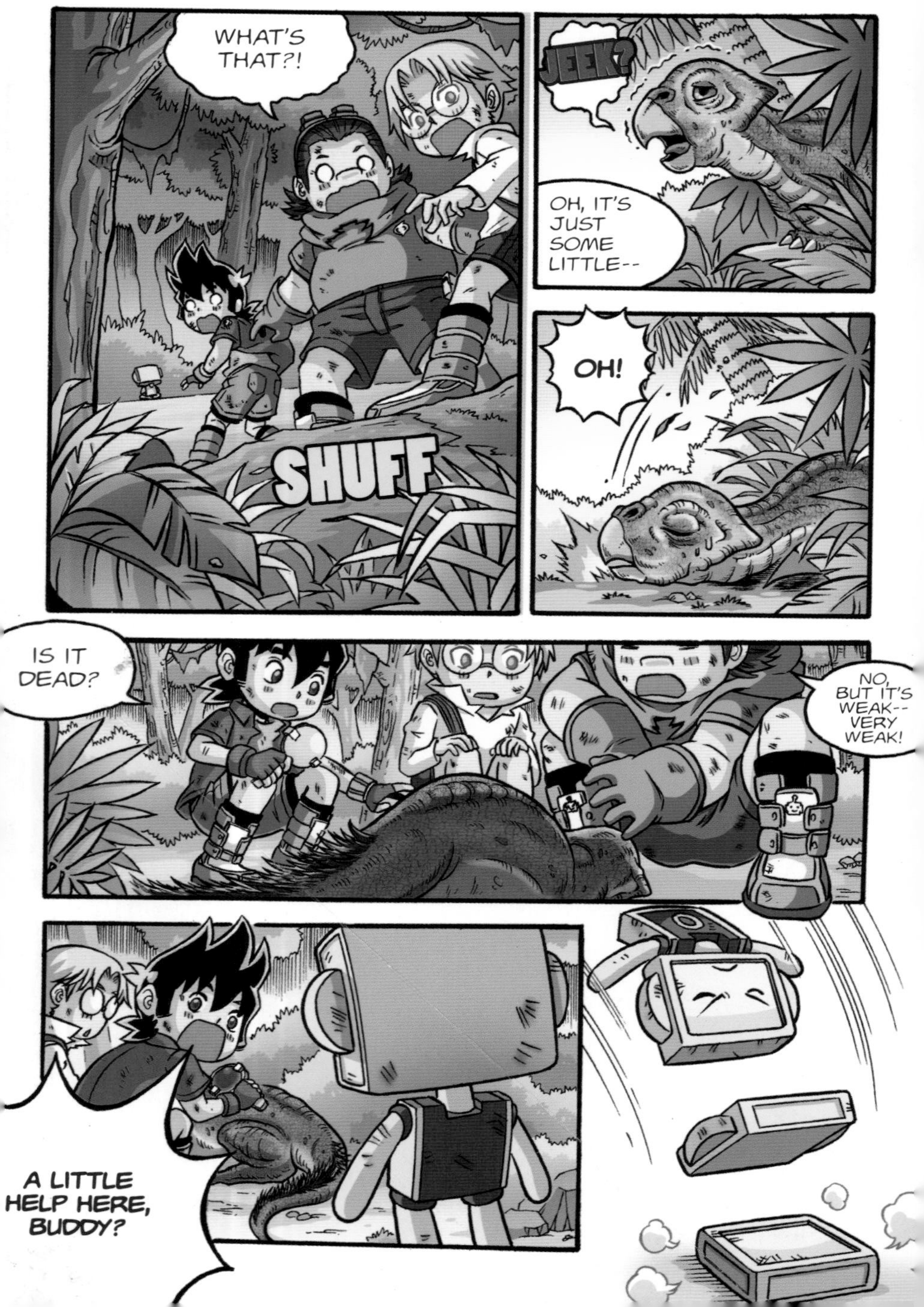
WHAT'S THAT?!
SHUFF
JEEK?
OH, IT'S JUST SOME LITTLE--
OH!
IS IT DEAD?
NO, BUT IT'S WEAK-- VERY WEAK!
A LITTLE HELP HERE, BUDDY?

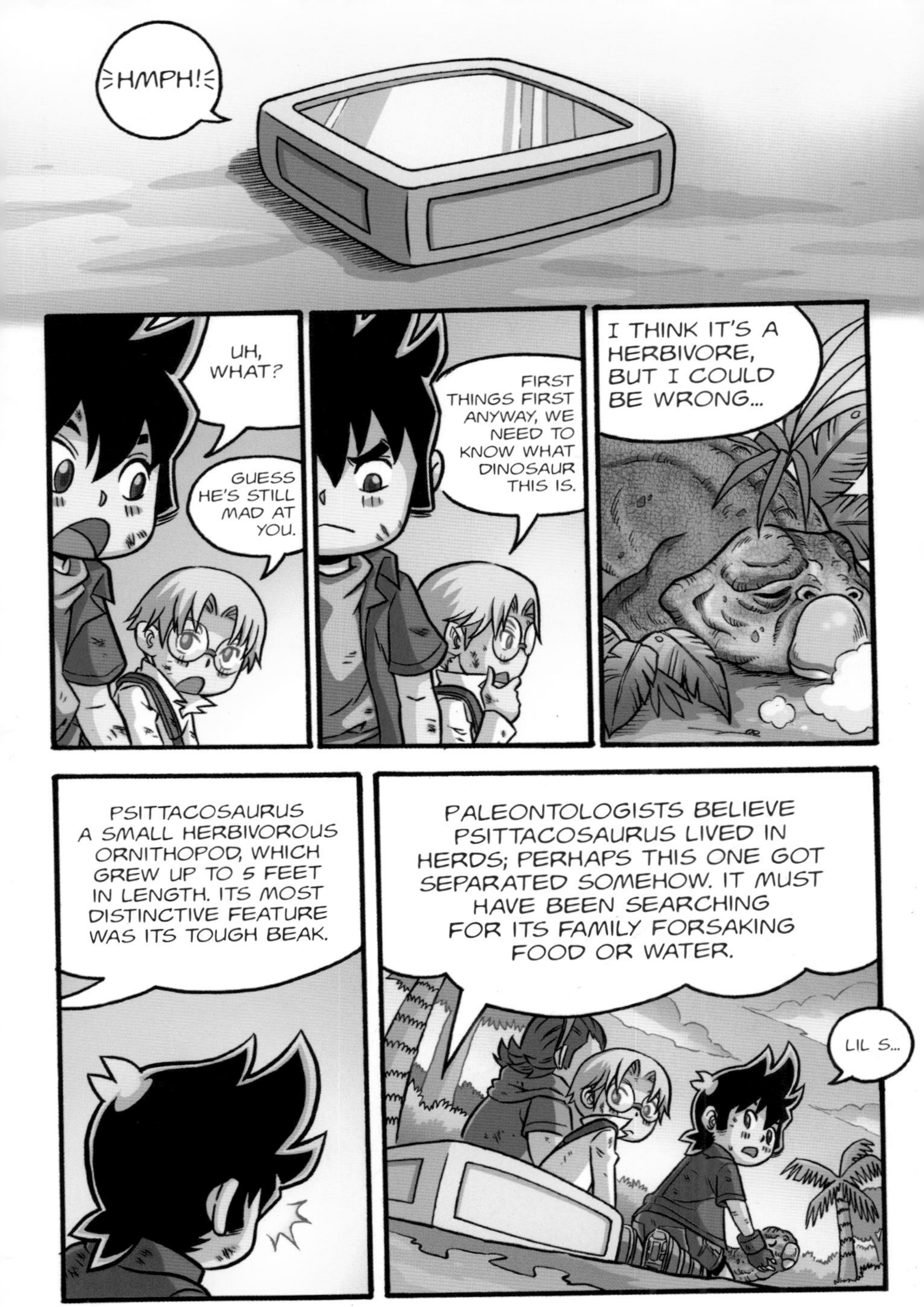
HMPH!
UH, WHAT?
GUESS HE'S STILL MAD AT YOU.
FIRST THINGS FIRST ANYWAY, WE NEED TO KNOW WHAT DINOSAUR THIS IS.
I THINK IT'S A HERBIVORE, BUT I COULD BE WRONG...
PSITTACOSAURUS A SMALL HERBIVOROUS ORNITHOPOD, WHICH GREW UP TO 5 FEET IN LENGTH. ITS MOST DISTINCTIVE FEATURE WAS ITS TOUGH BEAK.
PALEONTOLOGISTS BELIEVE PSITTACOSAURUS LIVED IN HERDS; PERHAPS THIS ONE GOT SEPARATED SOMEHOW. IT MUST HAVE BEEN SEARCHING FOR ITS FAMILY FORSAKING FOOD OR WATER.
LIL S...

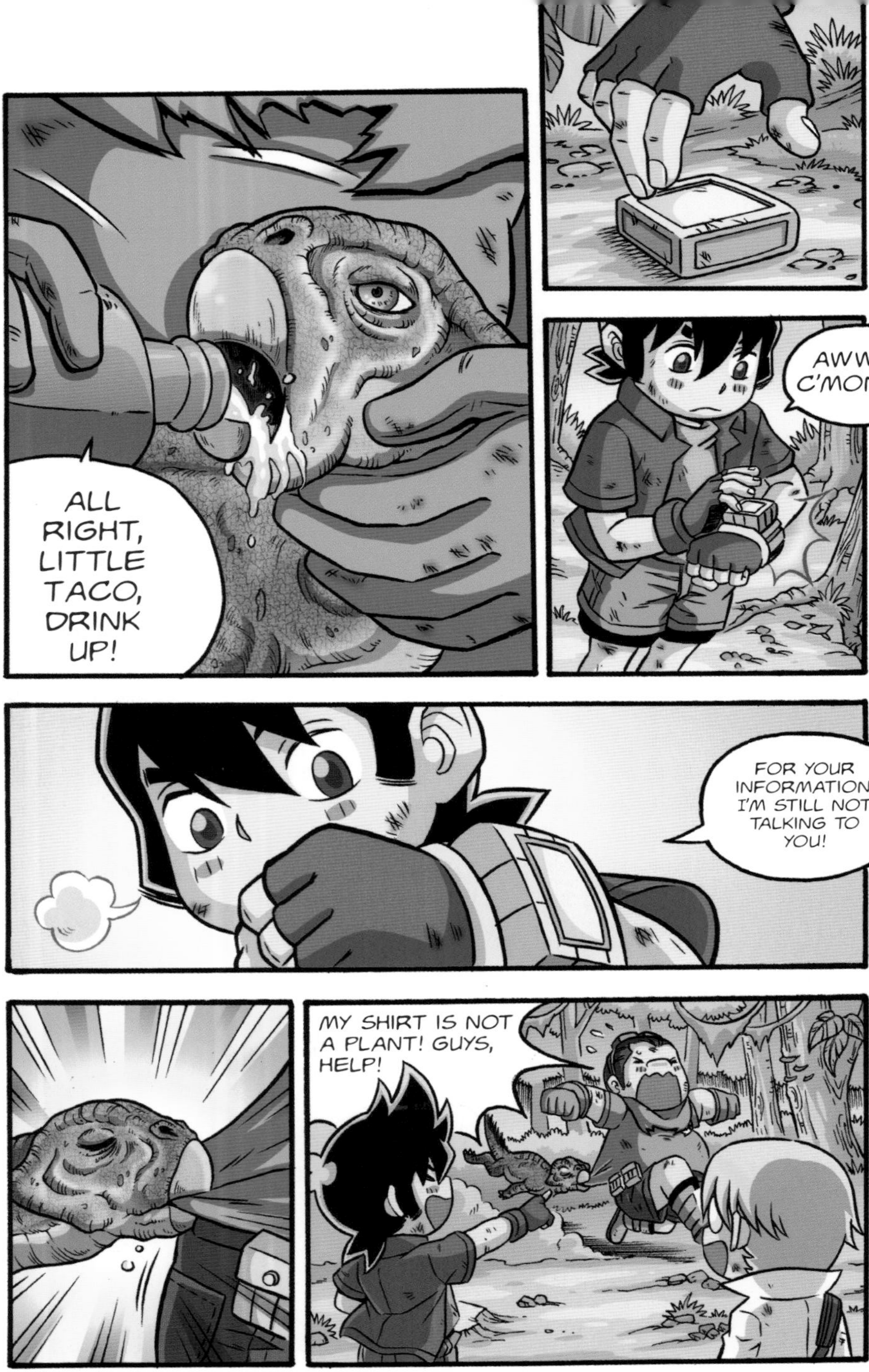
ALL RIGHT, LITTLE TACO, DRINK UP!
AWW, C'MON...
FOR YOUR INFORMATION, I'M STILL NOT TALKING TO YOU!
MY SHIRT IS NOT A PLANT! GUYS, HELP!

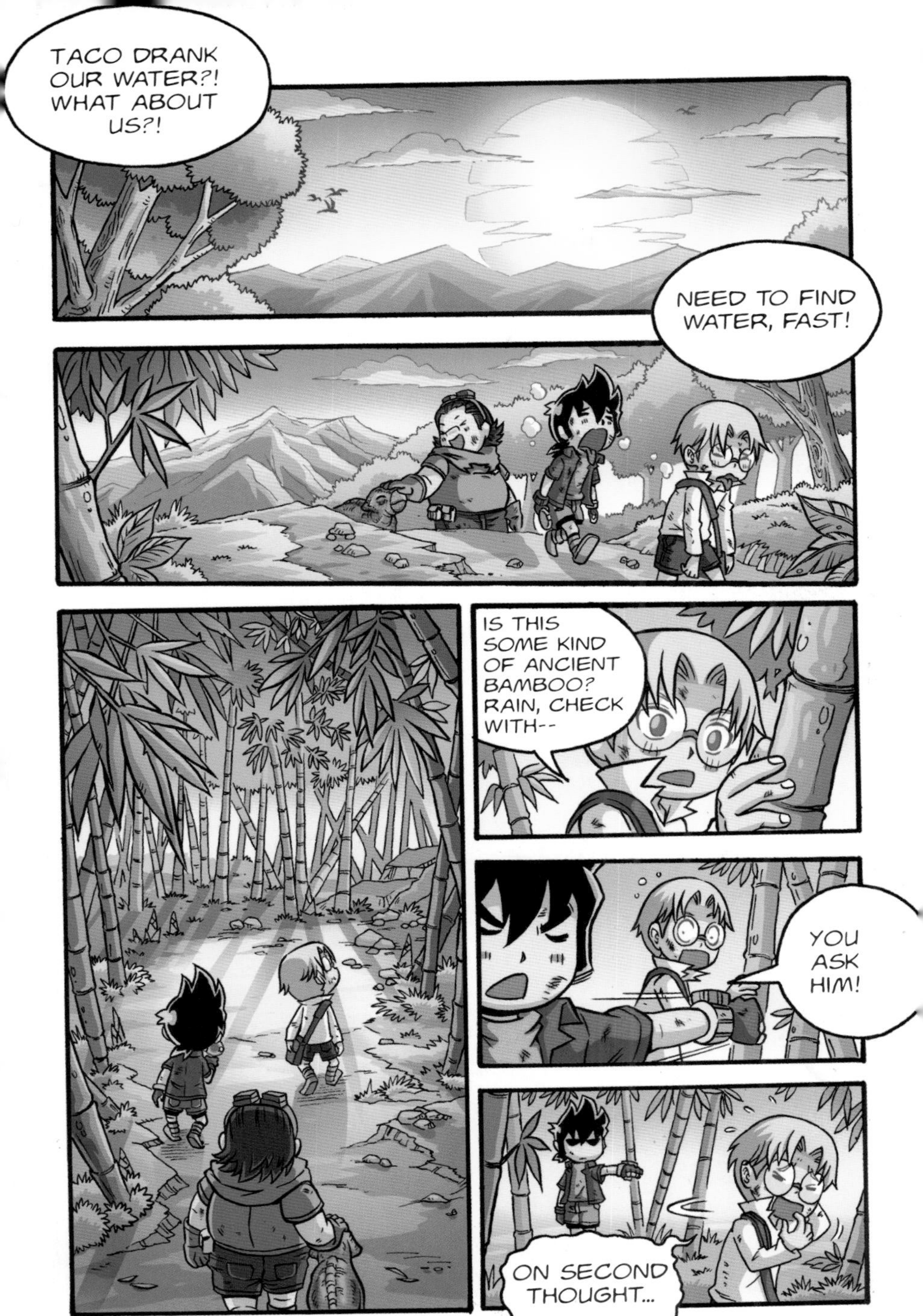
TACO DRANK OUR WATER?! WHAT ABOUT US?!
NEED TO FIND WATER, FAST!
IS THIS SOME KIND OF ANCIENT BAMBOO? RAIN, CHECK WITH--
YOU ASK HIM!
ON SECOND THOUGHT...

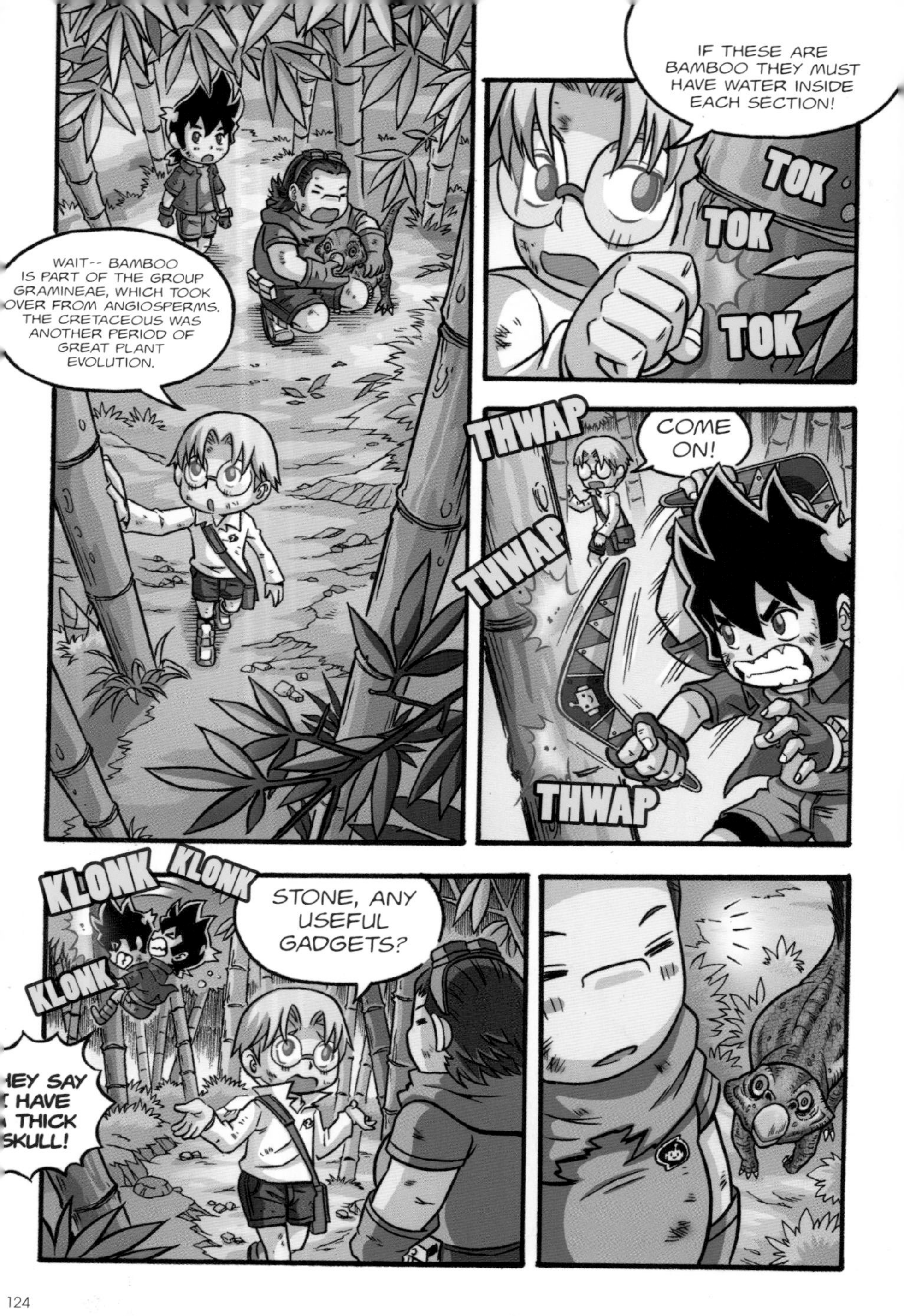
WAIT-- BAMBOO IS PART OF THE GROUP GRAMINEAE, WHICH TOOK OVER FROM ANGIOSPERMS. THE CRETACEOUS WAS ANOTHER PERIOD OF GREAT PLANT EVOLUTION.
IF THESE ARE BAMBOO THEY MUST HAVE WATER INSIDE EACH SECTION!
TOK
TOK
TOK
THWAP
COME ON!
THWAP
THWAP
KLONK
KLONK
KLONK
STONE, ANY USEFUL GADGETS?
EY SAY HAVE THICK SKULL!

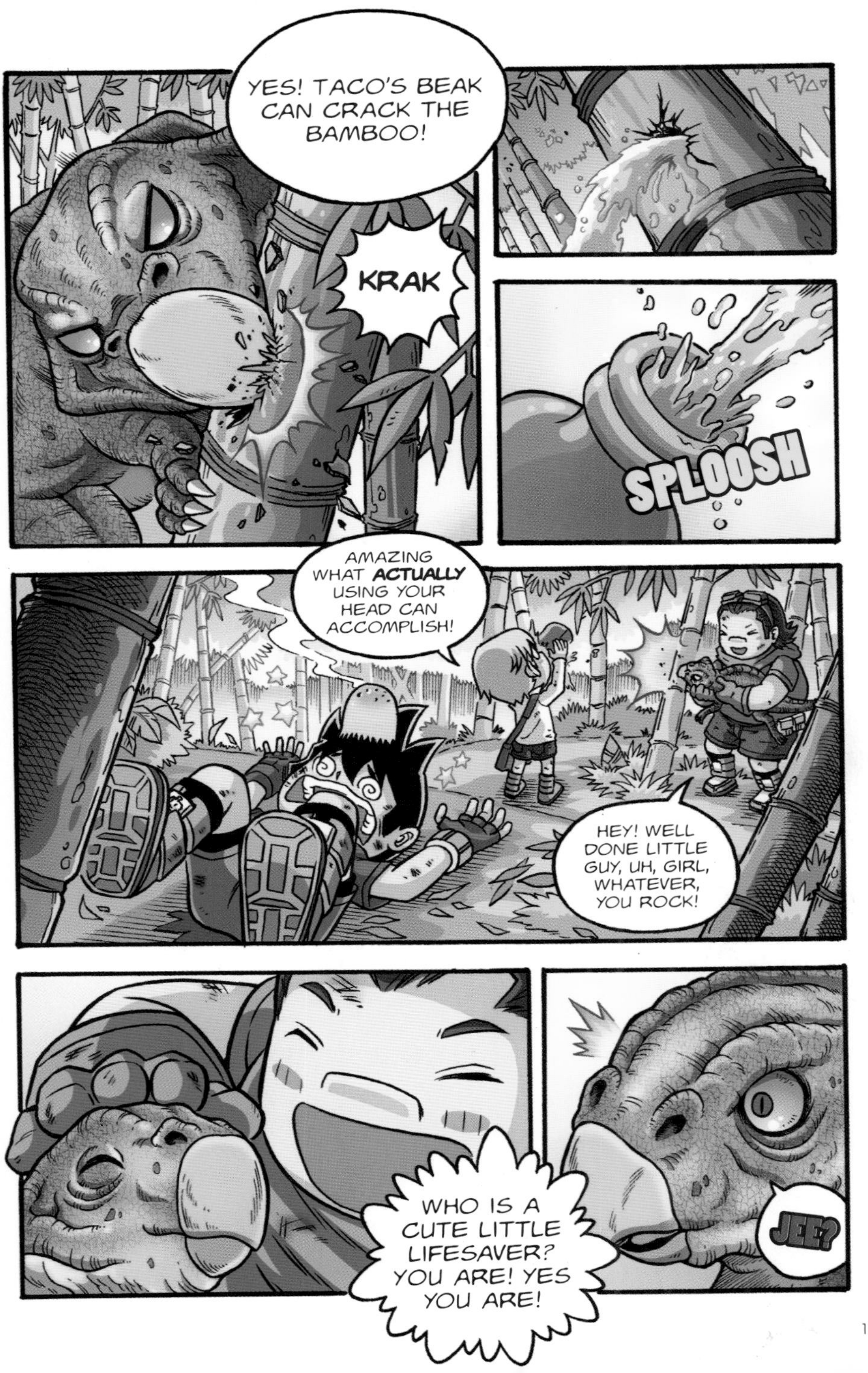
YES! TACO'S BEAK CAN CRACK THE BAMBOO!
KRAK
SPLOOSH
AMAZING WHAT **ACTUALLY** USING YOUR HEAD CAN ACCOMPLISH!
HEY! WELL DONE LITTLE GUY, UH, GIRL, WHATEVER, YOU ROCK!
WHO IS A CUTE LITTLE LIFESAVER? YOU ARE! YES YOU ARE!
JEE?

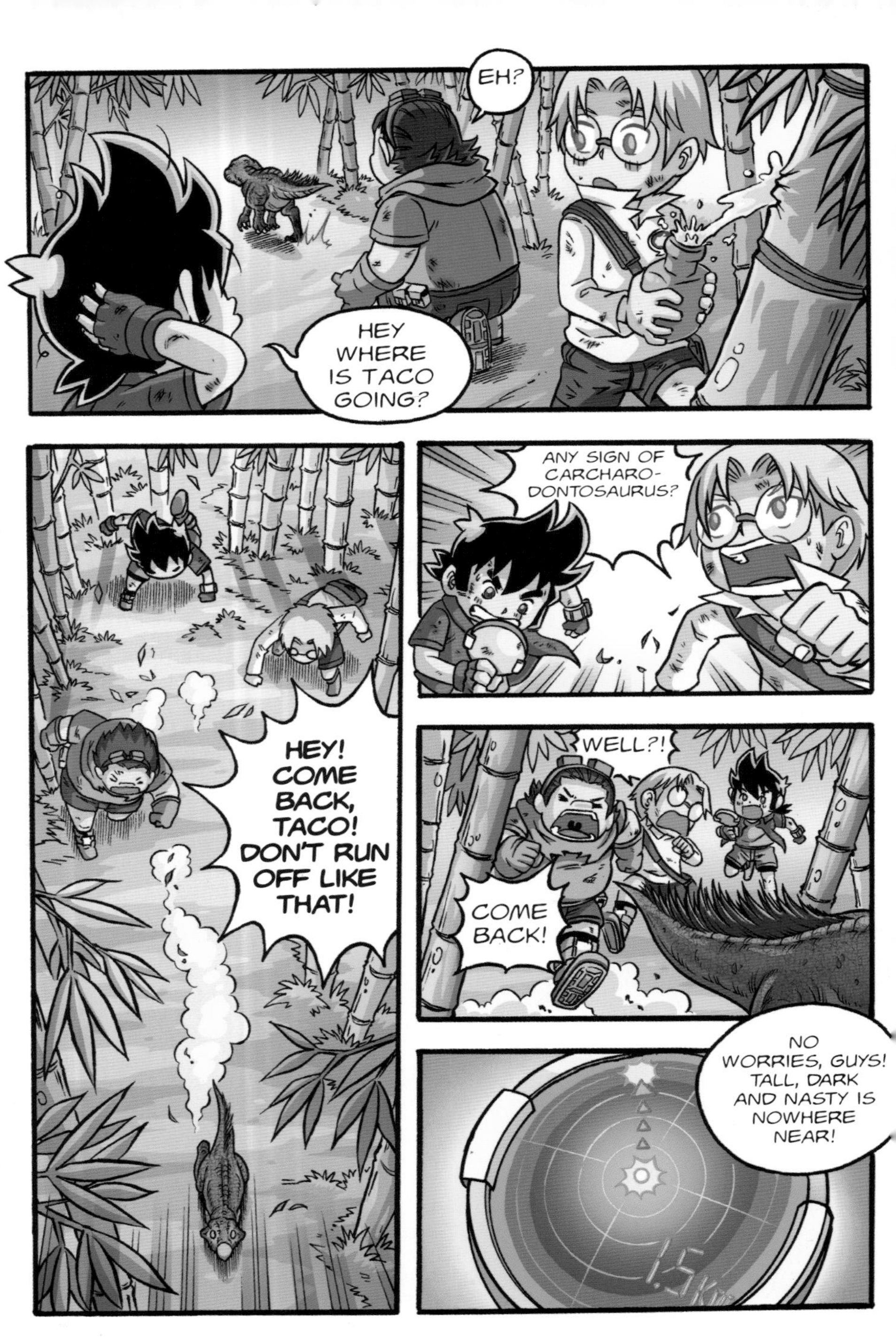
EH?
HEY WHERE IS TACO GOING?
HEY! COME BACK, TACO! DON'T RUN OFF LIKE THAT!
ANY SIGN OF CARCHARO-DONTOSAURUS?
WELL?!
COME BACK!
NO WORRIES, GUYS! TALL, DARK AND NASTY IS NOWHERE NEAR!
1.5Km

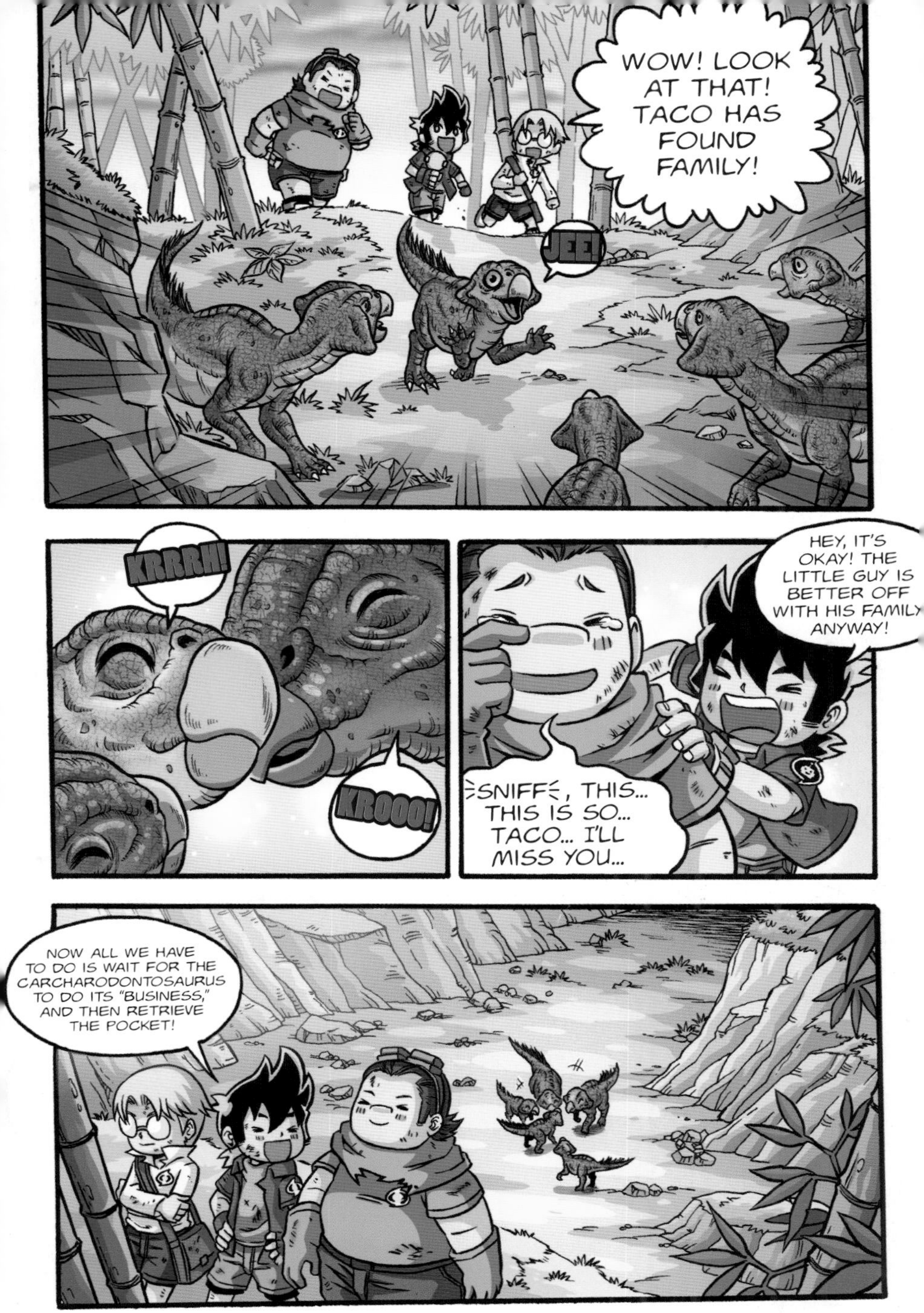
WOW! LOOK AT THAT! TACO HAS FOUND FAMILY!
JEE!
KRRRH!
KROOO!
HEY, IT'S OKAY! THE LITTLE GUY IS BETTER OFF WITH HIS FAMILY ANYWAY!
SNIFF, THIS... THIS IS SO... TACO... I'LL MISS YOU...
NOW ALL WE HAVE TO DO IS WAIT FOR THE CARCHARODONTOSAURUS TO DO ITS "BUSINESS," AND THEN RETRIEVE THE POCKET!

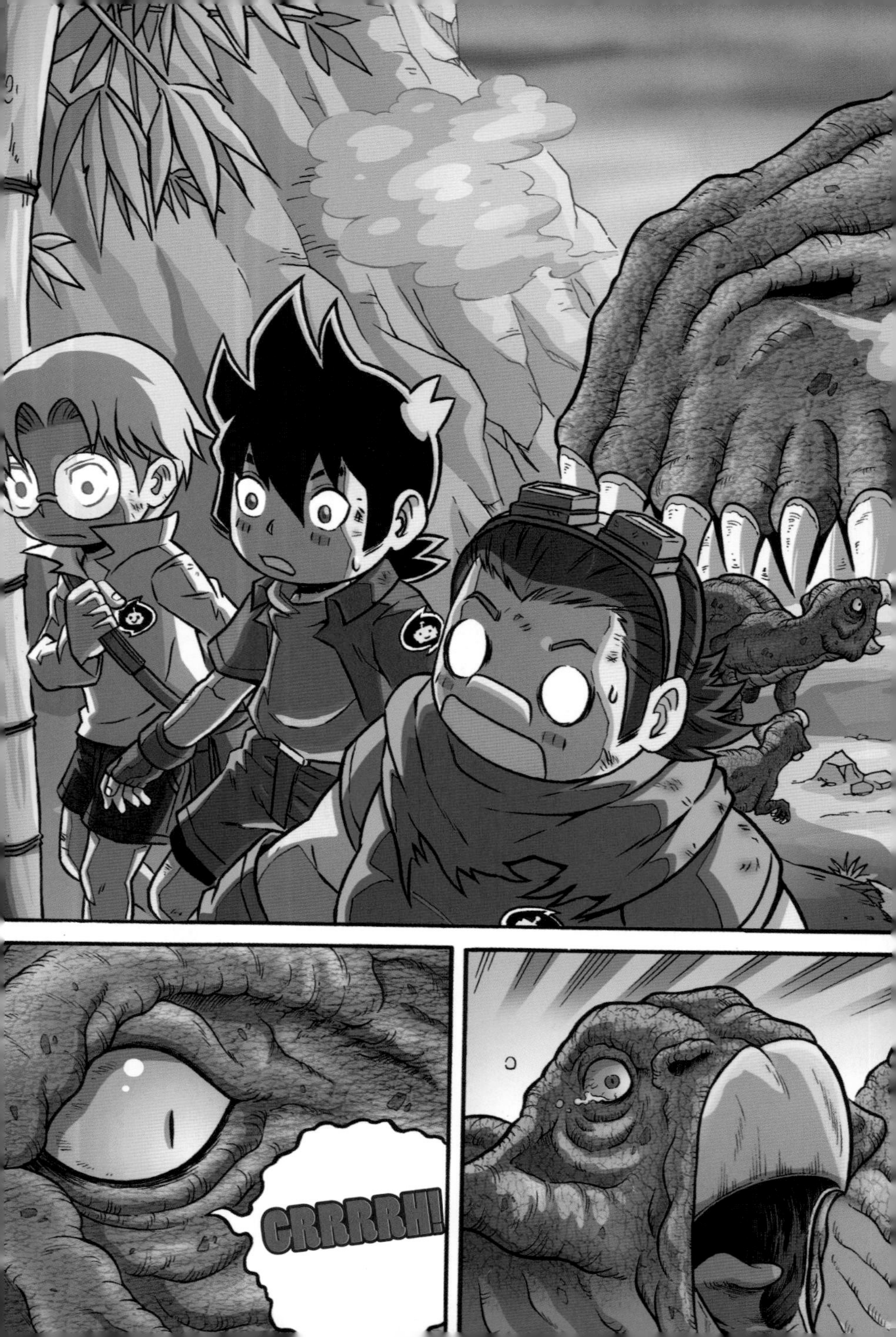
CRRRRH!

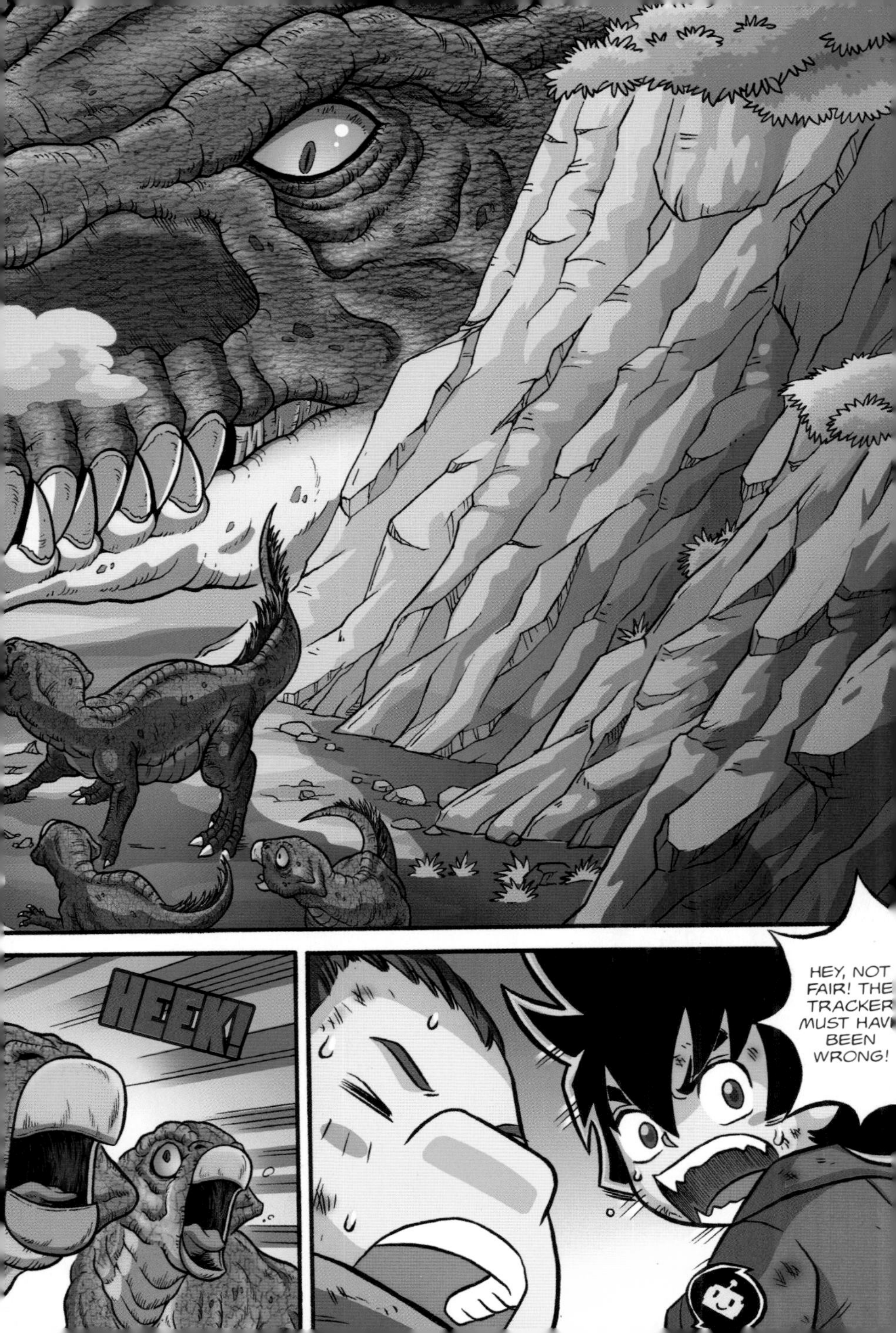
HEEK!
HEY, NOT FAIR! THE TRACKER MUST HAVE BEEN WRONG!

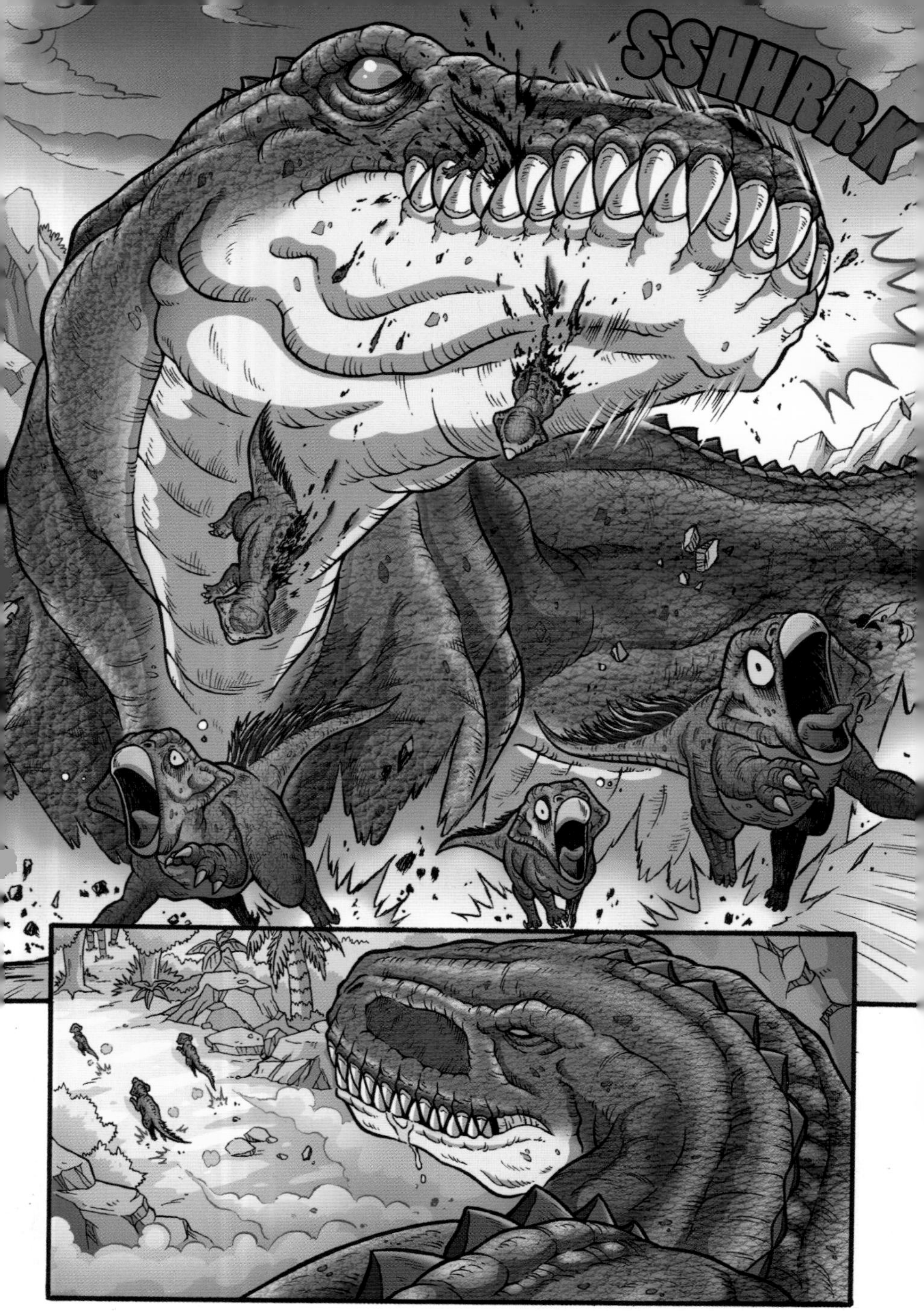
SSHHRRRK

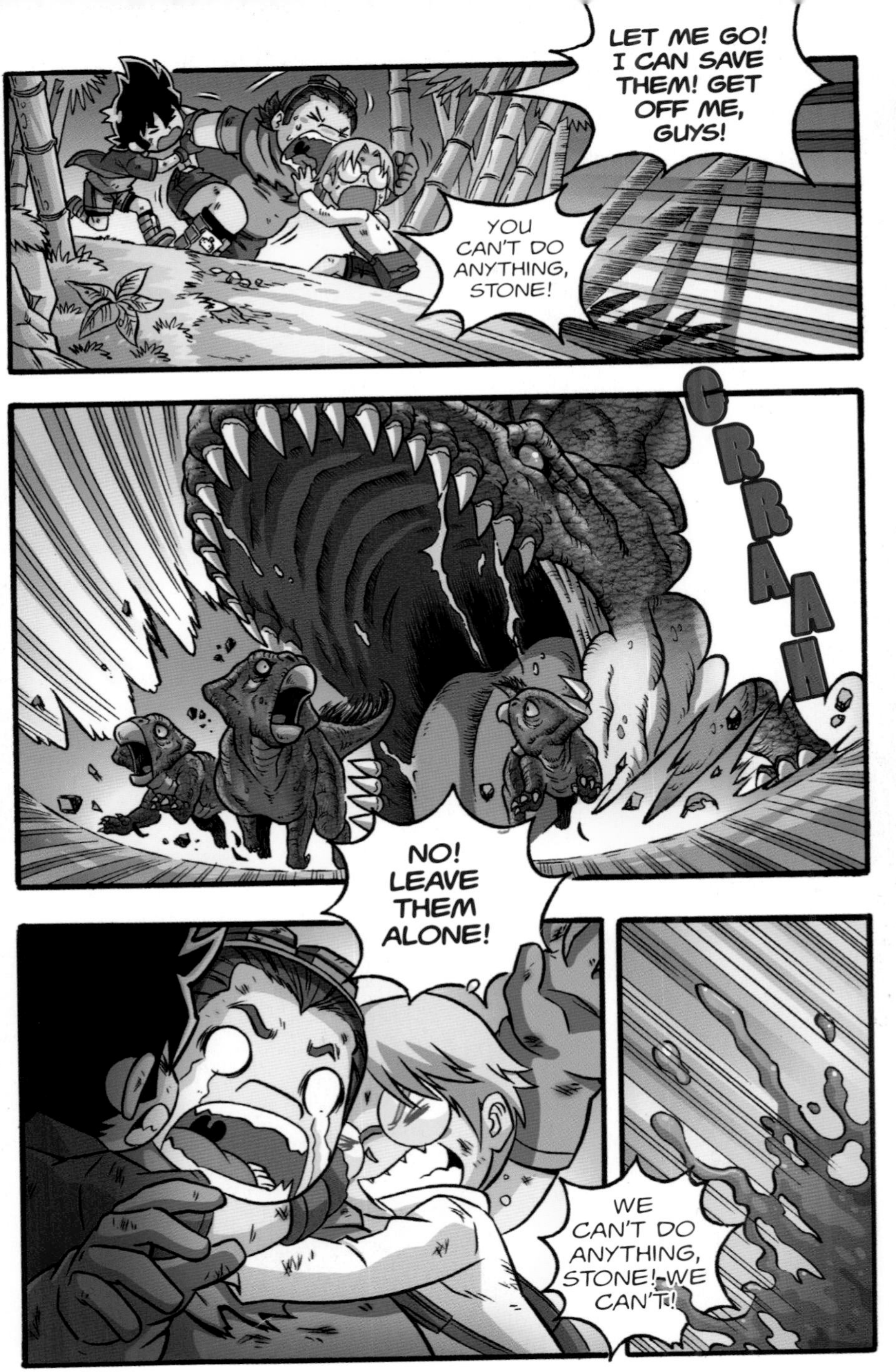
LET ME GO! I CAN SAVE THEM! GET OFF ME, GUYS!
YOU CAN'T DO ANYTHING, STONE!
GRRAAAH
NO! LEAVE THEM ALONE!
WE CAN'T DO ANYTHING, STONE! WE CAN'T!

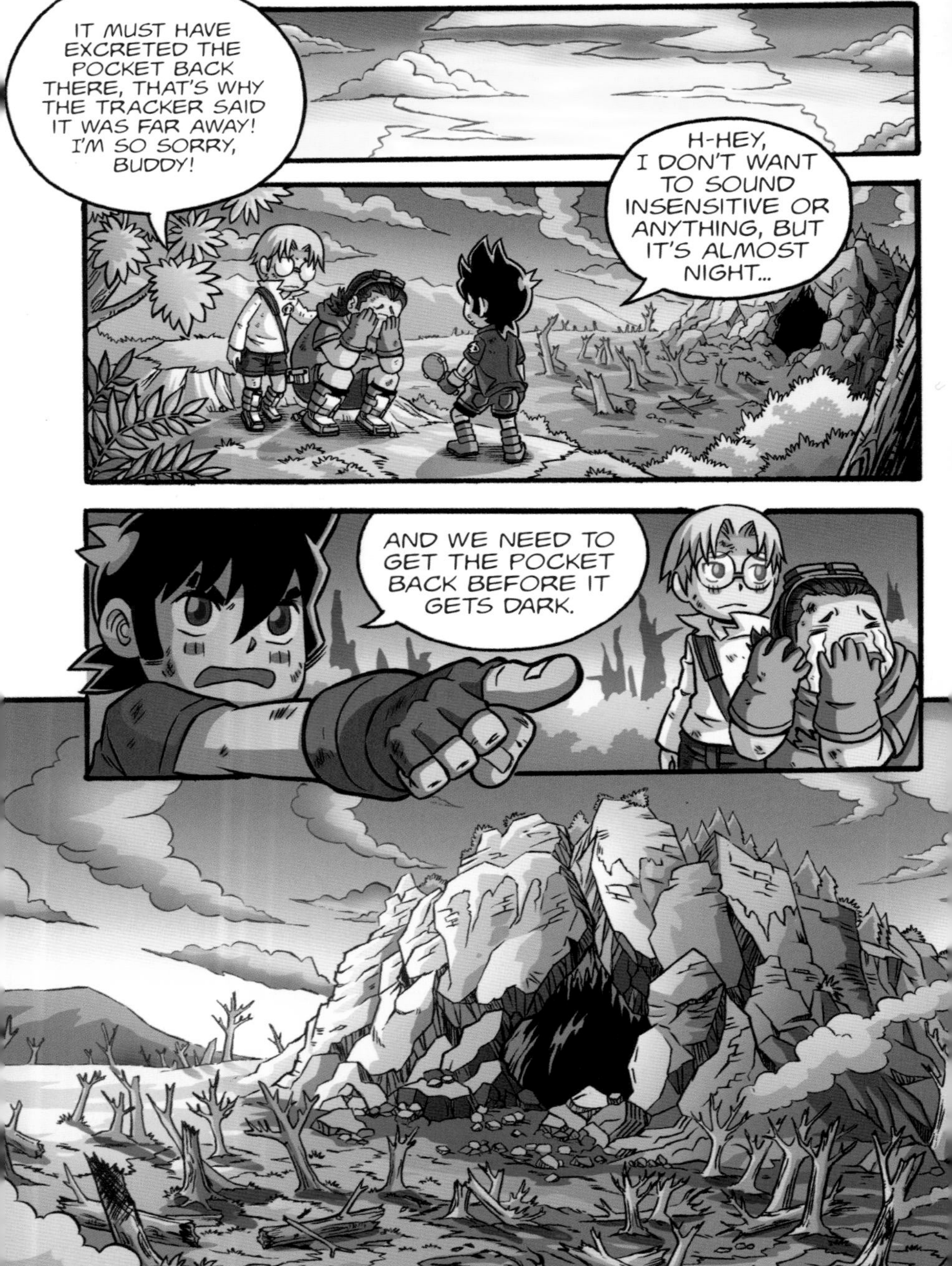
IT MUST HAVE EXCRETED THE POCKET BACK THERE, THAT'S WHY THE TRACKER SAID IT WAS FAR AWAY! I'M SO SORRY, BUDDY!
H-HEY, I DON'T WANT TO SOUND INSENSITIVE OR ANYTHING, BUT IT'S ALMOST NIGHT...
AND WE NEED TO GET THE POCKET BACK BEFORE IT GETS DARK.

## CAPTURING THE CRETACEOUS!

### Psittacosaurus

6.5 feet long Psittacosaurus weighed over 44 pounds, and several features (such as its beak) identify it as a ceratopsid from the early Cretaceous. Psittacosaurus had teeth to slice tough plants, not for chewing food, so it swallowed stones to help with digestion.

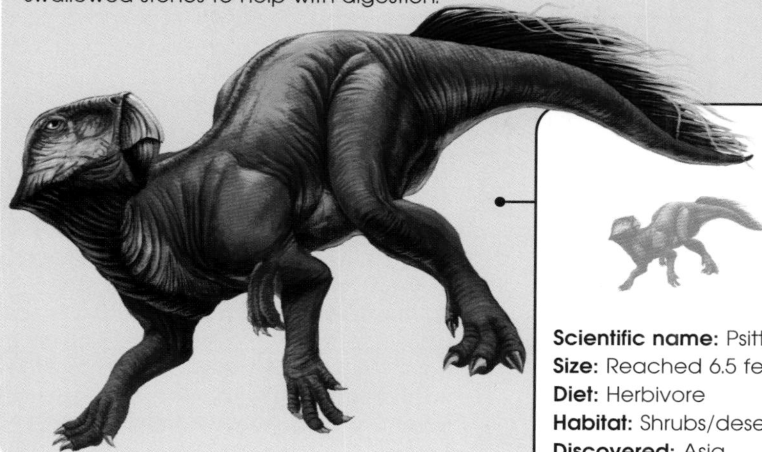

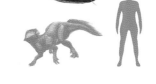

**Scientific name:** Psittacosaurus
**Size:** Reached 6.5 feet
**Diet:** Herbivore
**Habitat:** Shrubs/deserts
**Discovered:** Asia
**Period:** Early Cretaceous

## CAPTURING THE CRETACEOUS!

### Deltadromeus

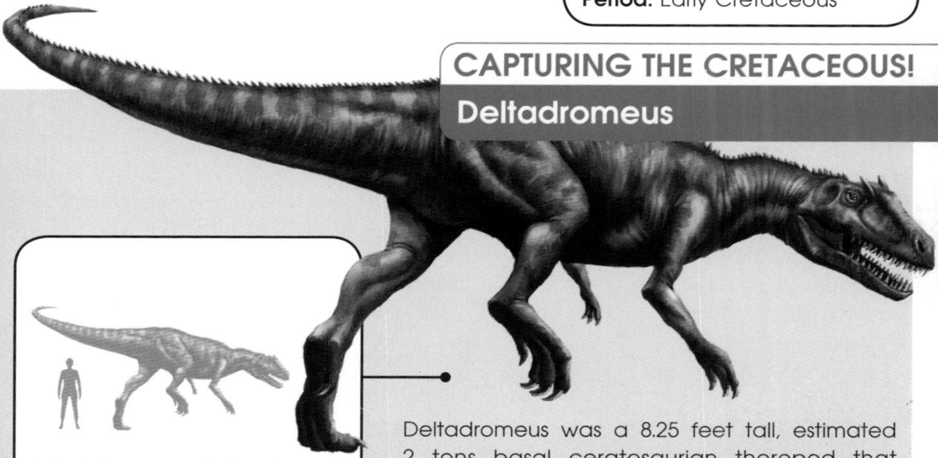

**Scientific name:** Deltadromeus
**Size:** 26 feet
**Diet:** Carnivore
**Habitat:** Flatlands
**Discovered:** Morocco, Africa
**Period:** Late Cretaceous

Deltadromeus was a 8.25 feet tall, estimated 2 tons basal ceratosaurian theropod that terrorized the Late Cretaceous. Unusually slender hind limbs for its size implies it was a swift runner. Deltadromeus skeletons have been found with those of Carcharodontosaurus and Spinosaurus, which did not bode well for herbivores of that time period!

## CAPTURING THE CRETACEOUS!

### Minmi

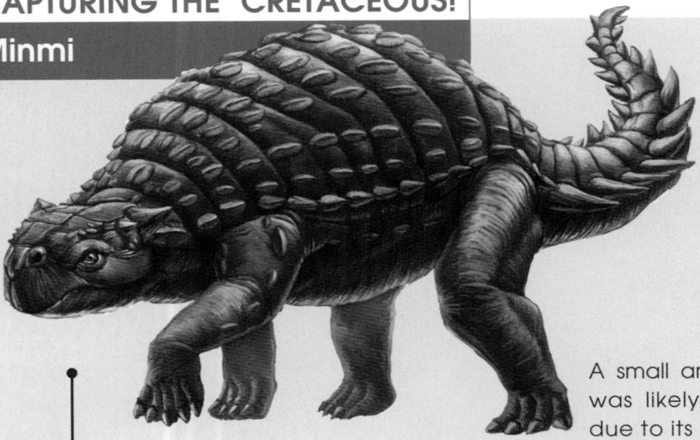

A small ankylosaur, Minmi was likely a slow mover due to its hind legs being longer than its front legs. It had a short neck, a wide head and a tiny brain. Uniquely, the arrangement of its armor differed from other ankylosaurs, with spikes pointing backwards. It was also discovered to have had proper teeth to chew its food as evinced by food remnants found in its gut, which indicated the absence of gastroliths.

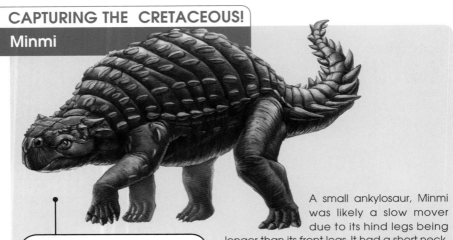

**Scientific name:** Minmi
**Size:** 9.8 feet
**Diet:** Herbivore
**Habitat:** Forests
**Discovered:** Australia
**Period:** Early Cretaceous

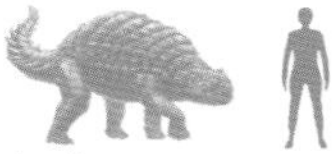

## CARRY ON, CRETACEOUS!

### Gastonia

Gastonia was a nodosaur that lived about 125 million years ago and was closely related to Polacanthus. Its spiked defences were formidable; its sacral shield and large shoulder spikes, provided Gastonia with ample defences against such threats as Utahraptor, the largest known dromaeosaurid.

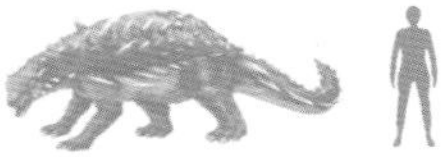

**Scientific name:** Gastonia
**Size:** 16.4 feet
**Diet:** Herbivore
**Habitat:** Forests
**Discovered:** United States
**Period:** Early Cretaceous

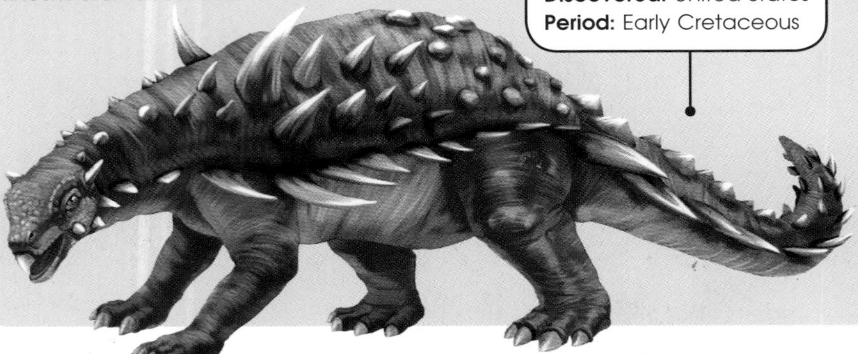

CHAPTER 7

# IN DEEP

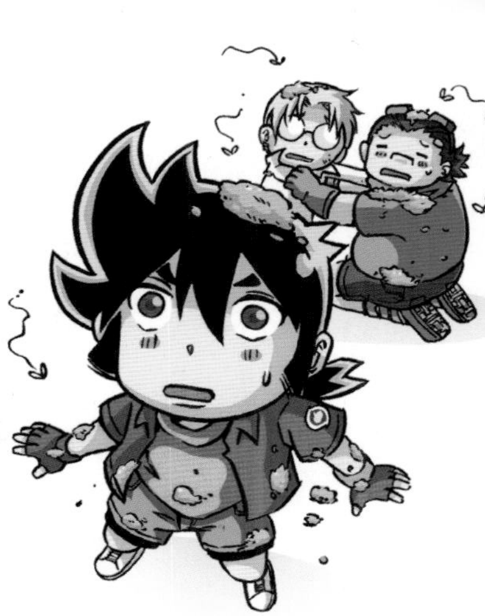

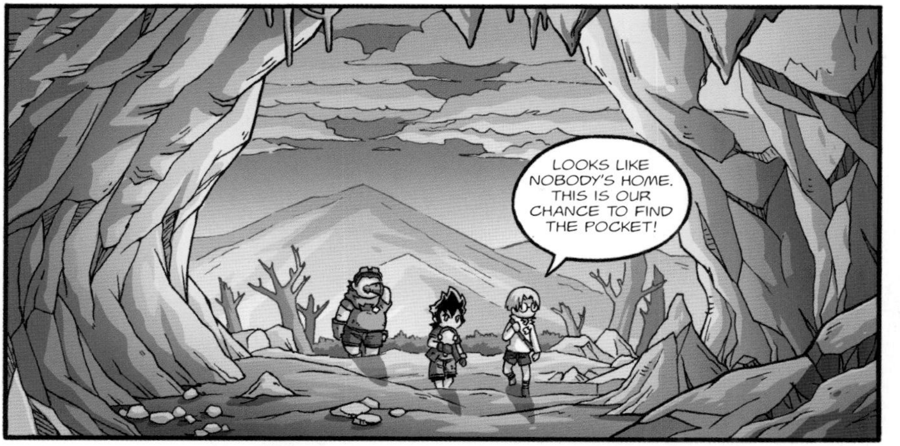
LOOKS LIKE NOBODY'S HOME. THIS IS OUR CHANCE TO FIND THE POCKET!

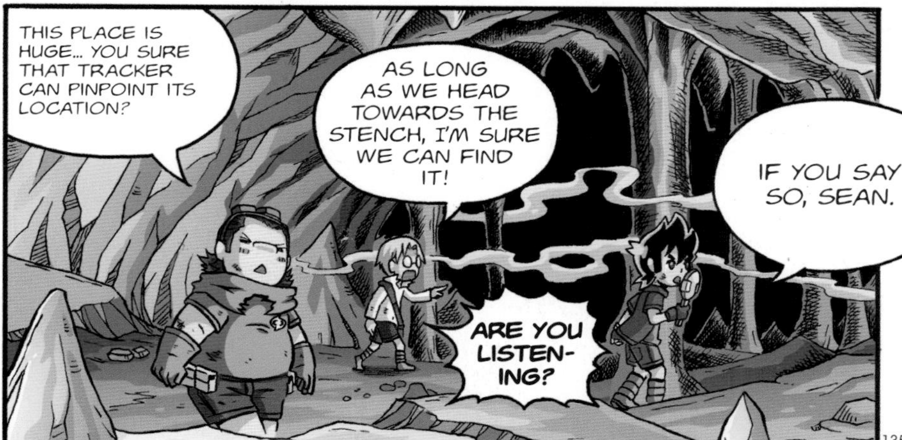
THIS PLACE IS HUGE... YOU SURE THAT TRACKER CAN PINPOINT ITS LOCATION?
AS LONG AS WE HEAD TOWARDS THE STENCH, I'M SURE WE CAN FIND IT!
ARE YOU LISTEN-ING?
IF YOU SAY SO, SEAN.

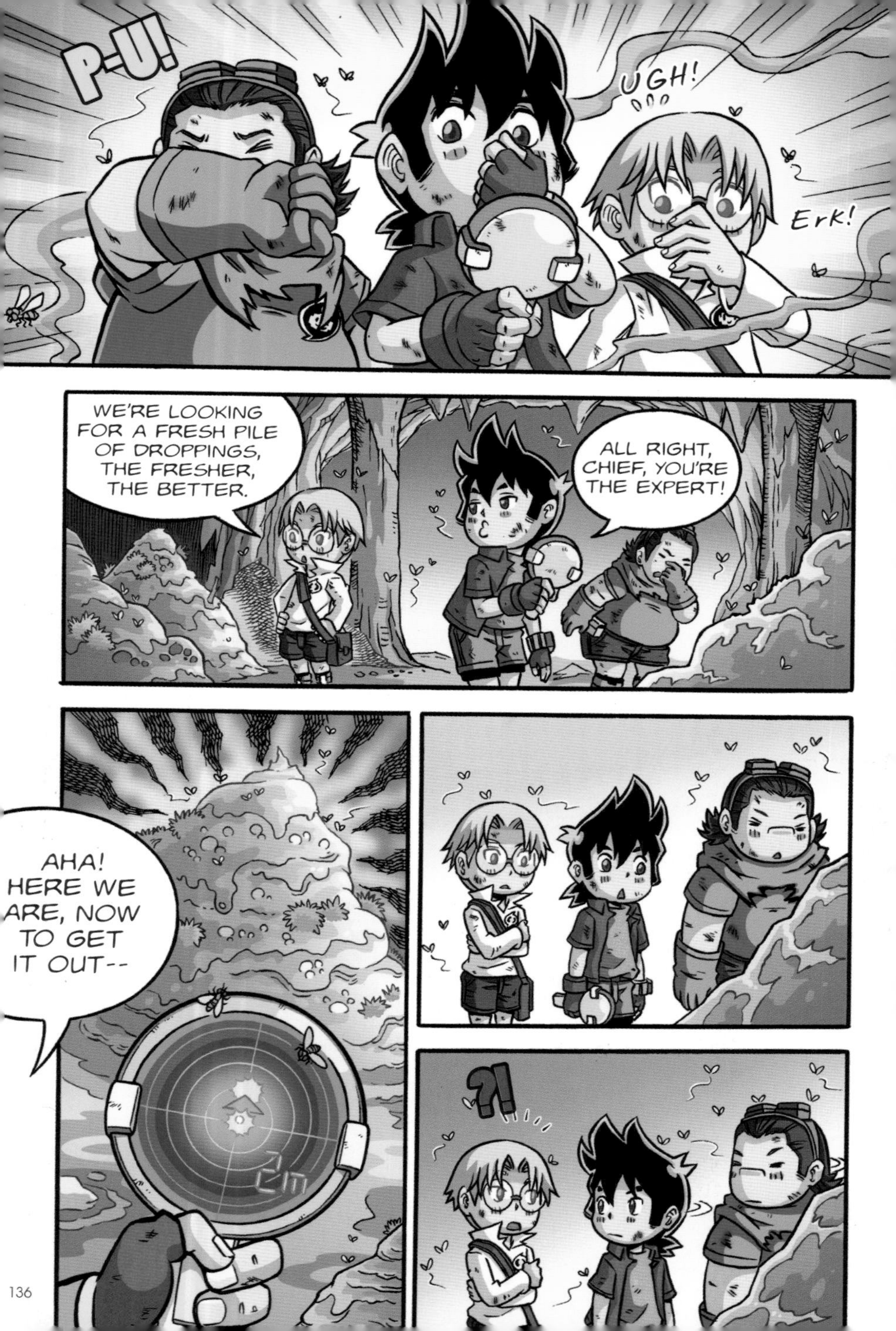

P-U!
UGH!
Erk!
WE'RE LOOKING FOR A FRESH PILE OF DROPPINGS, THE FRESHER, THE BETTER.
ALL RIGHT, CHIEF, YOU'RE THE EXPERT!
AHA! HERE WE ARE, NOW TO GET IT OUT--
?!

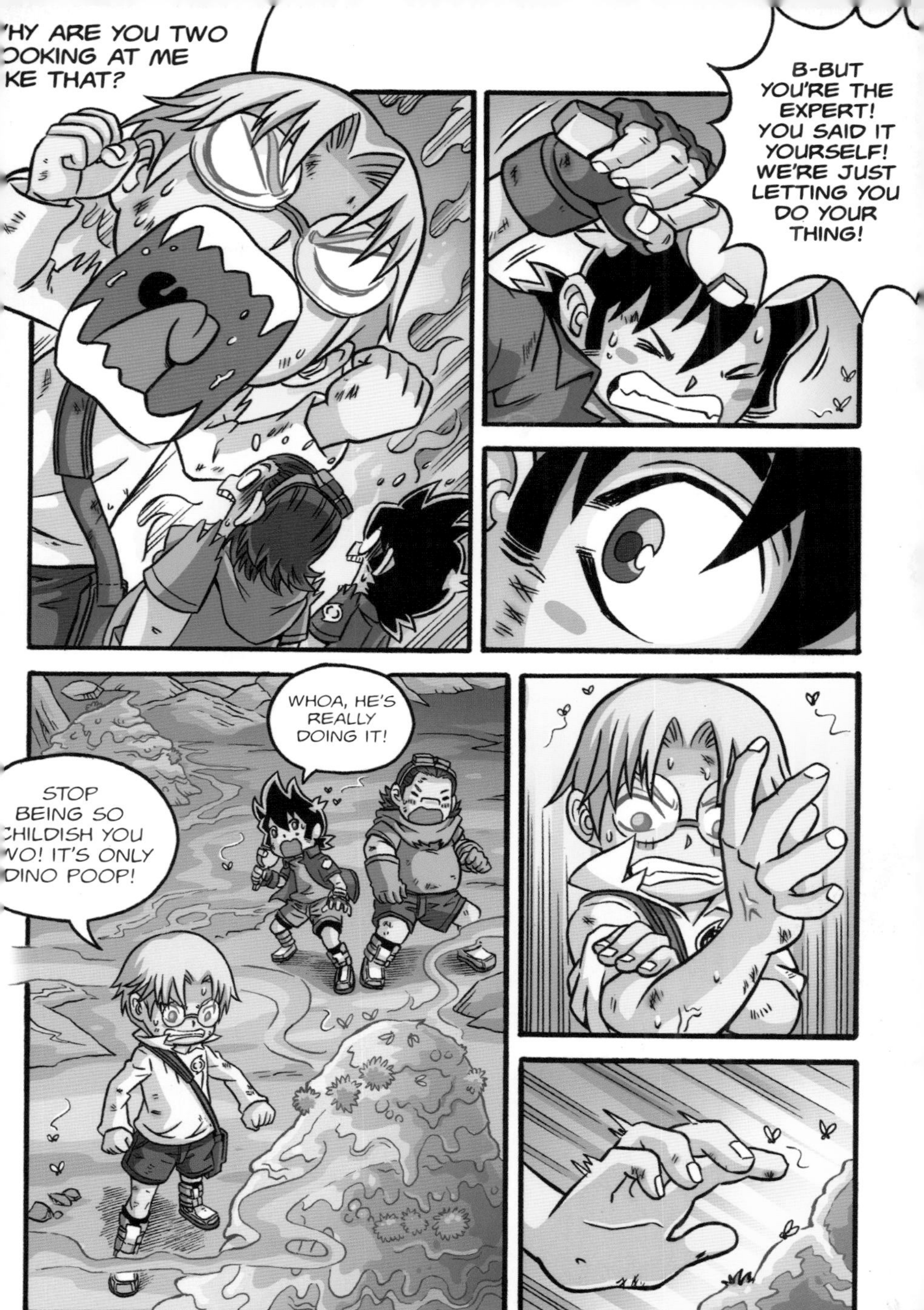
'HY ARE YOU TWO
OOKING AT ME
KE THAT?
B-BUT YOU'RE THE EXPERT! YOU SAID IT YOURSELF! WE'RE JUST LETTING YOU DO YOUR THING!
WHOA, HE'S REALLY DOING IT!
STOP BEING SO
CHILDISH YOU
VO! IT'S ONLY
DINO POOP!

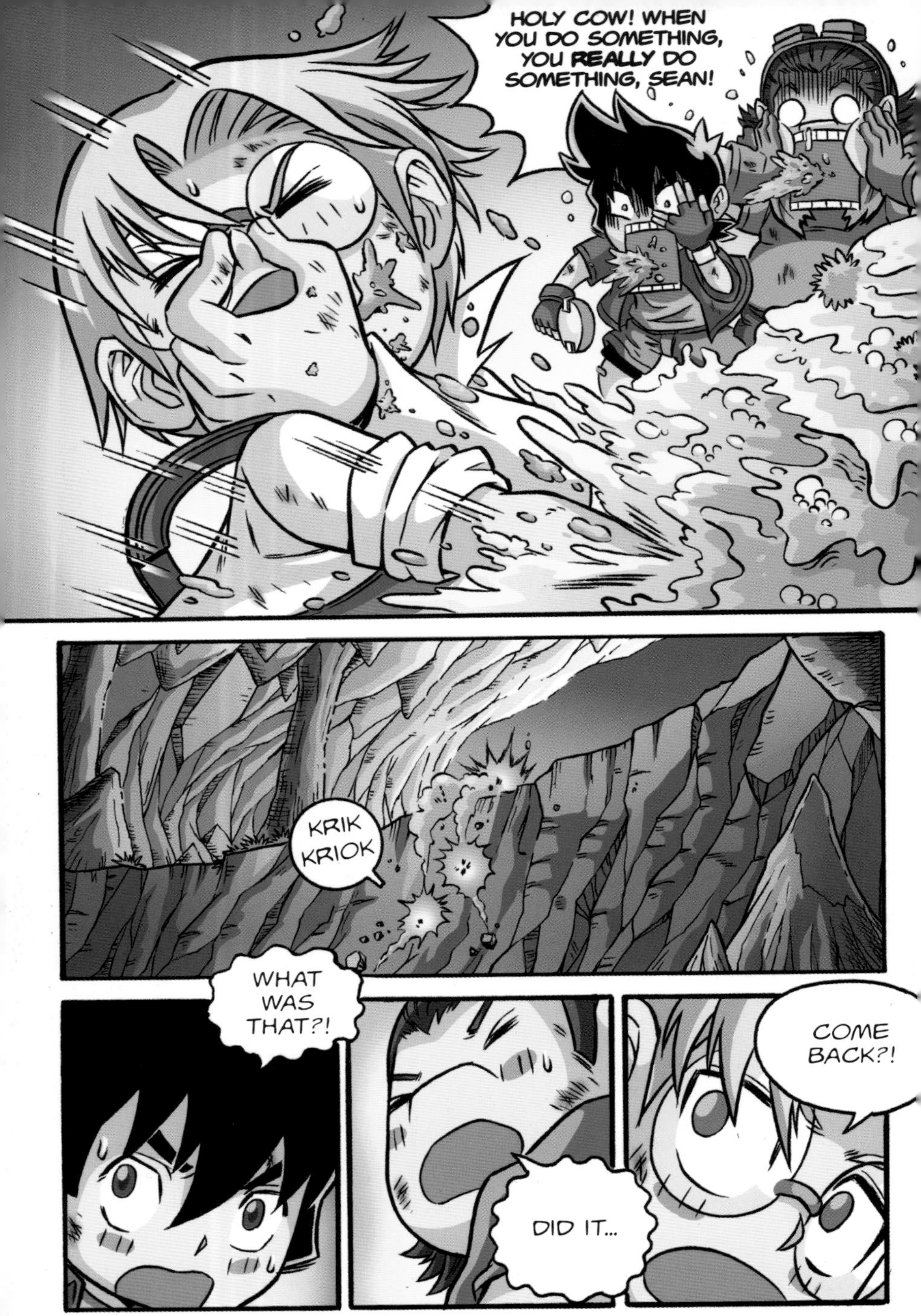
HOLY COW! WHEN YOU DO SOMETHING, YOU **REALLY** DO SOMETHING, SEAN!
KRIK KRIOK
WHAT WAS THAT?!
DID IT...
COME BACK?!

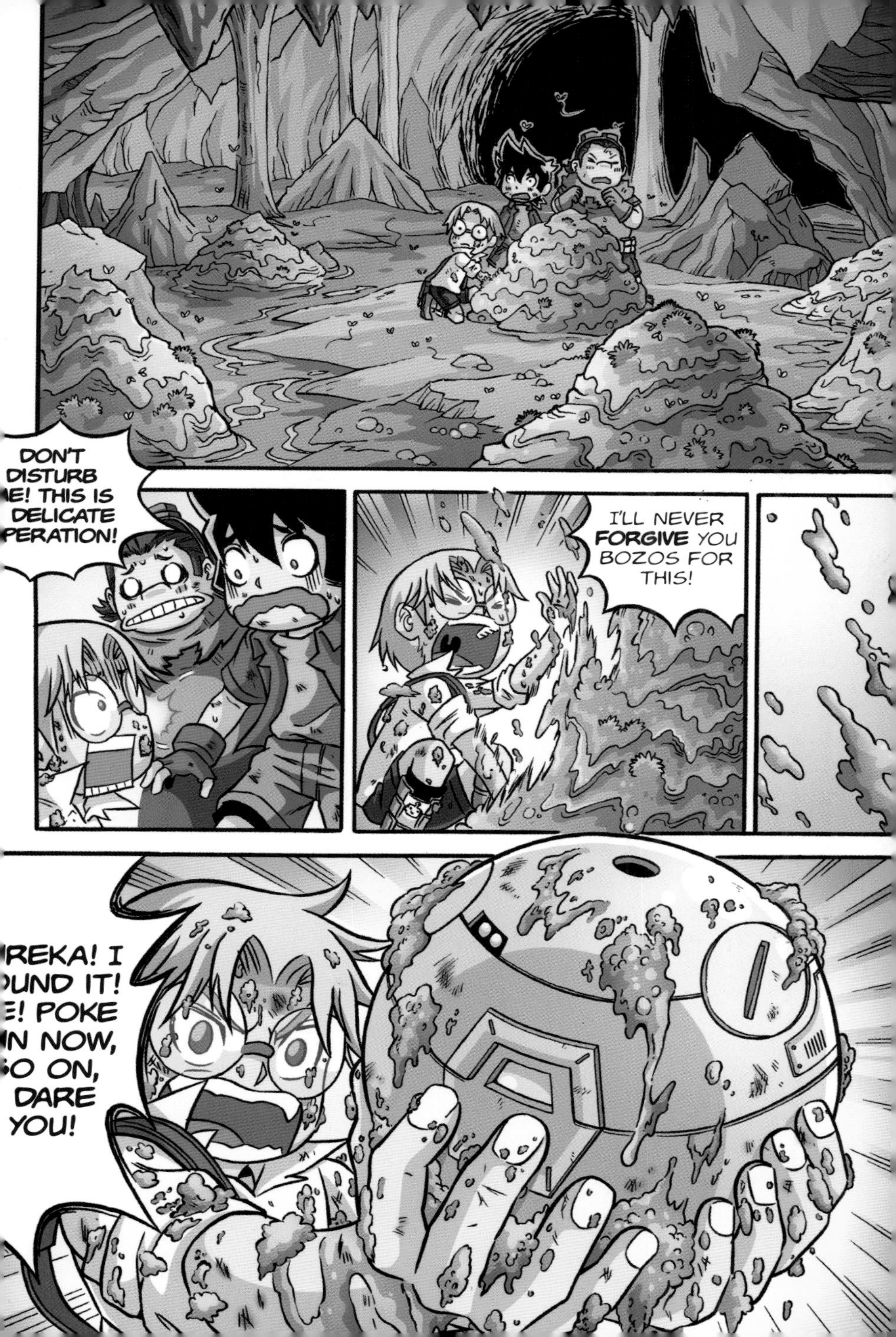
DON'T DISTURB E! THIS IS DELICATE PERATION!
I'LL NEVER FORGIVE YOU BOZOS FOR THIS!
REKA! I UND IT! E! POKE N NOW, O ON, DARE YOU!

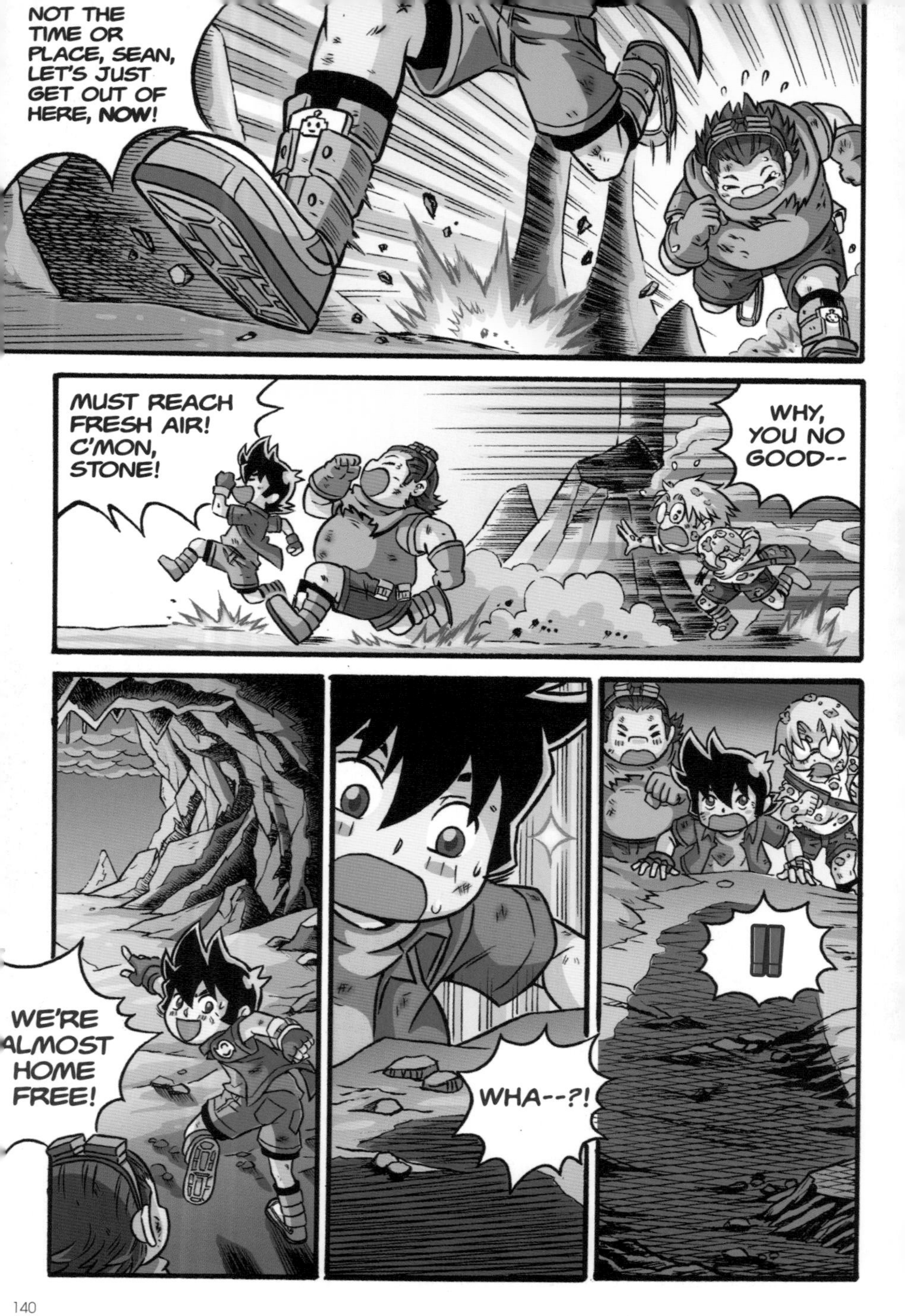
NOT THE TIME OR PLACE, SEAN, LET'S JUST GET OUT OF HERE, NOW!
MUST REACH FRESH AIR! C'MON, STONE!
WHY, YOU NO GOOD--
WE'RE ALMOST HOME FREE!
WHA--?!
!!

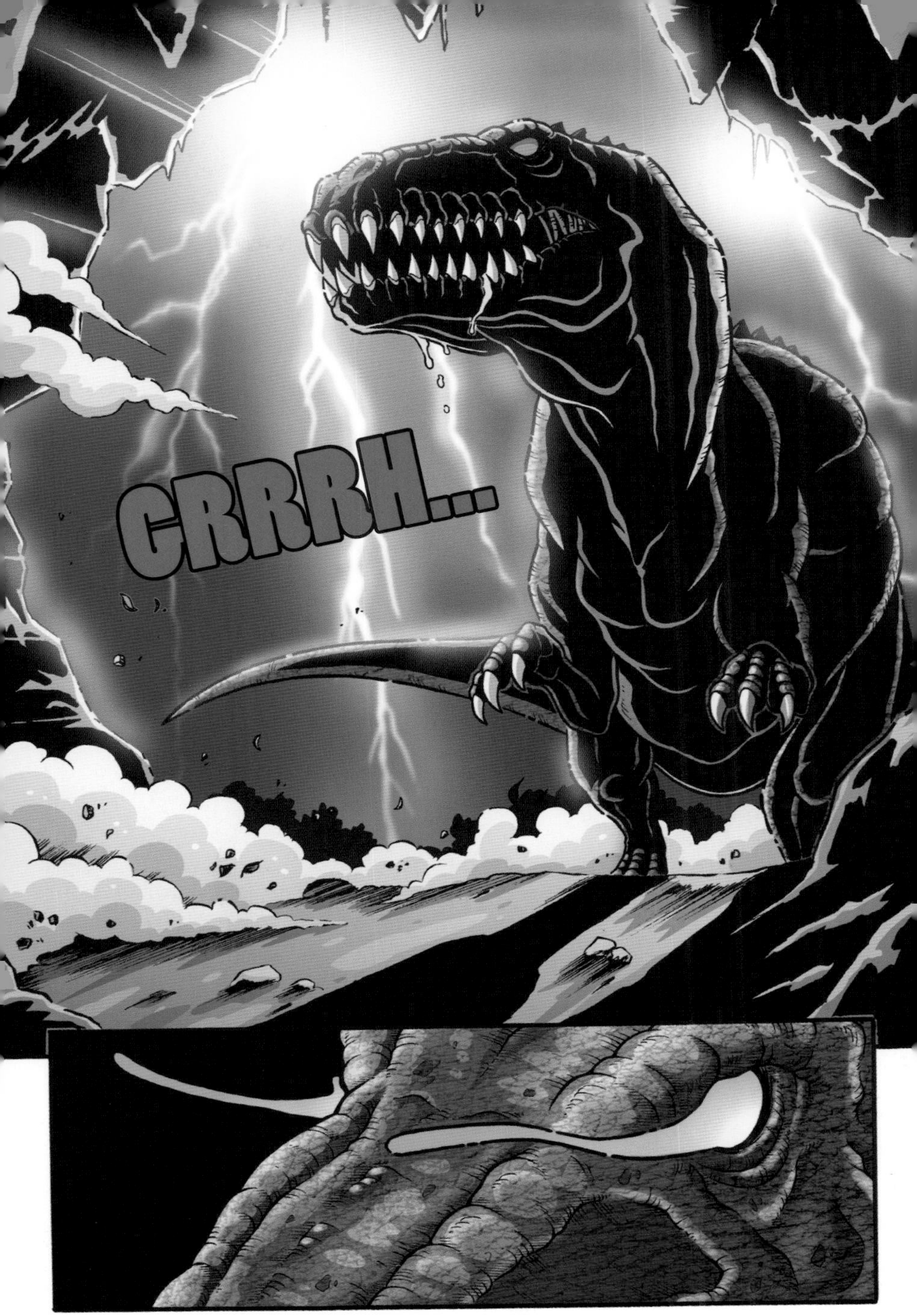
CRRRH...

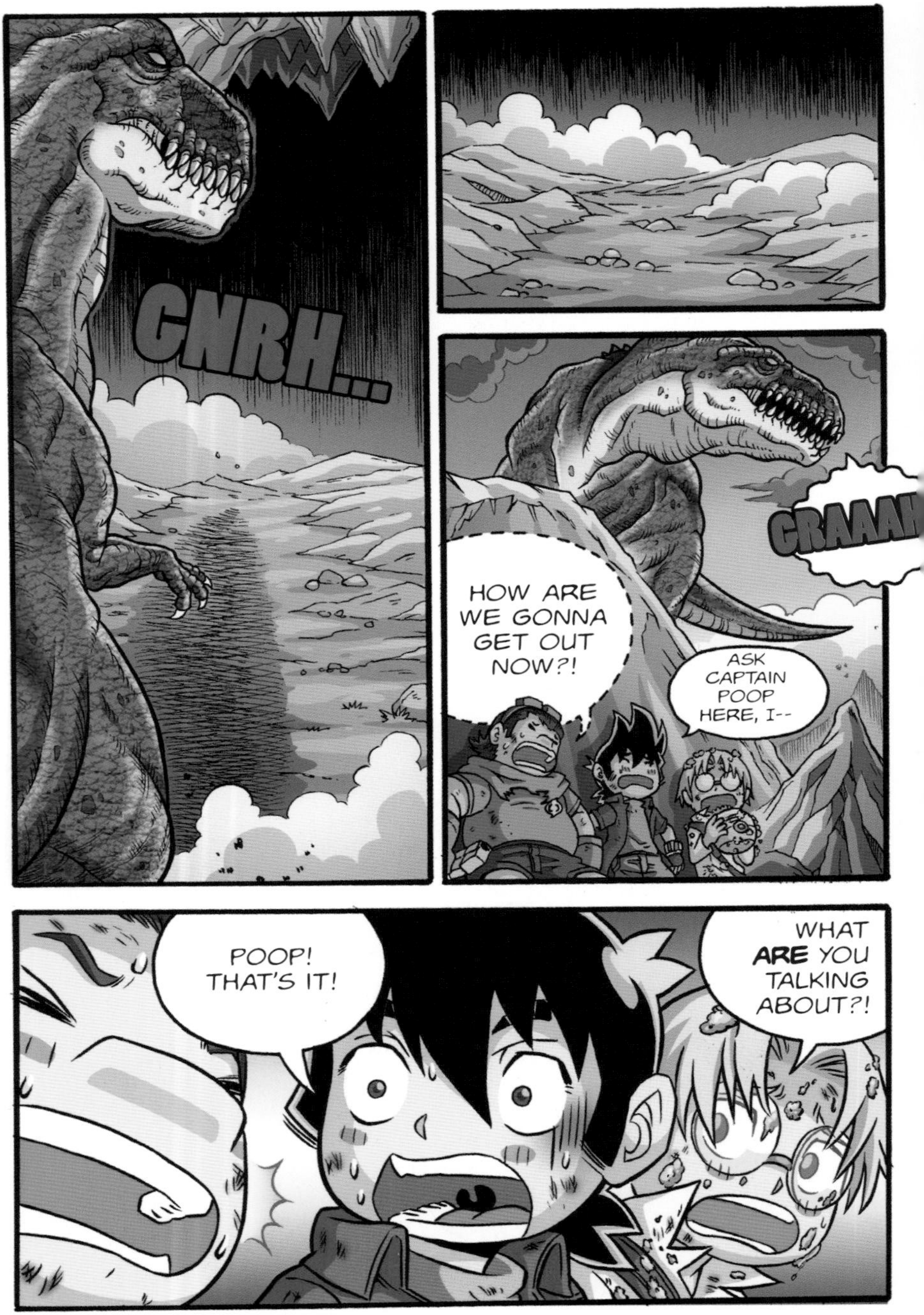

GNRH...
CRAAAH
HOW ARE WE GONNA GET OUT NOW?!
ASK CAPTAIN POOP HERE, I--
POOP! THAT'S IT!
WHAT **ARE** YOU TALKING ABOUT?!

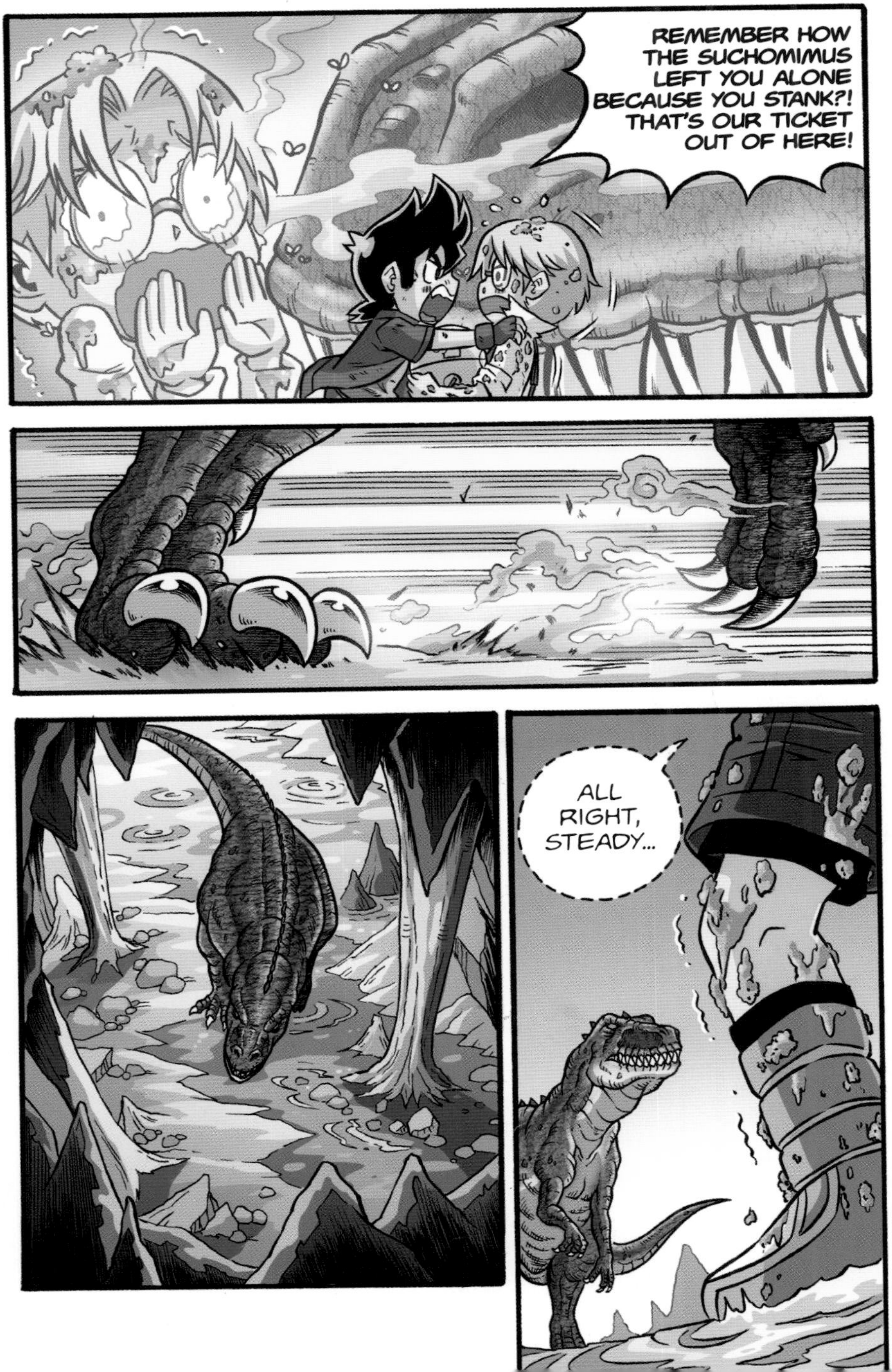
REMEMBER HOW THE SUCHOMIMUS LEFT YOU ALONE BECAUSE YOU STANK?! THAT'S OUR TICKET OUT OF HERE!
ALL RIGHT, STEADY...

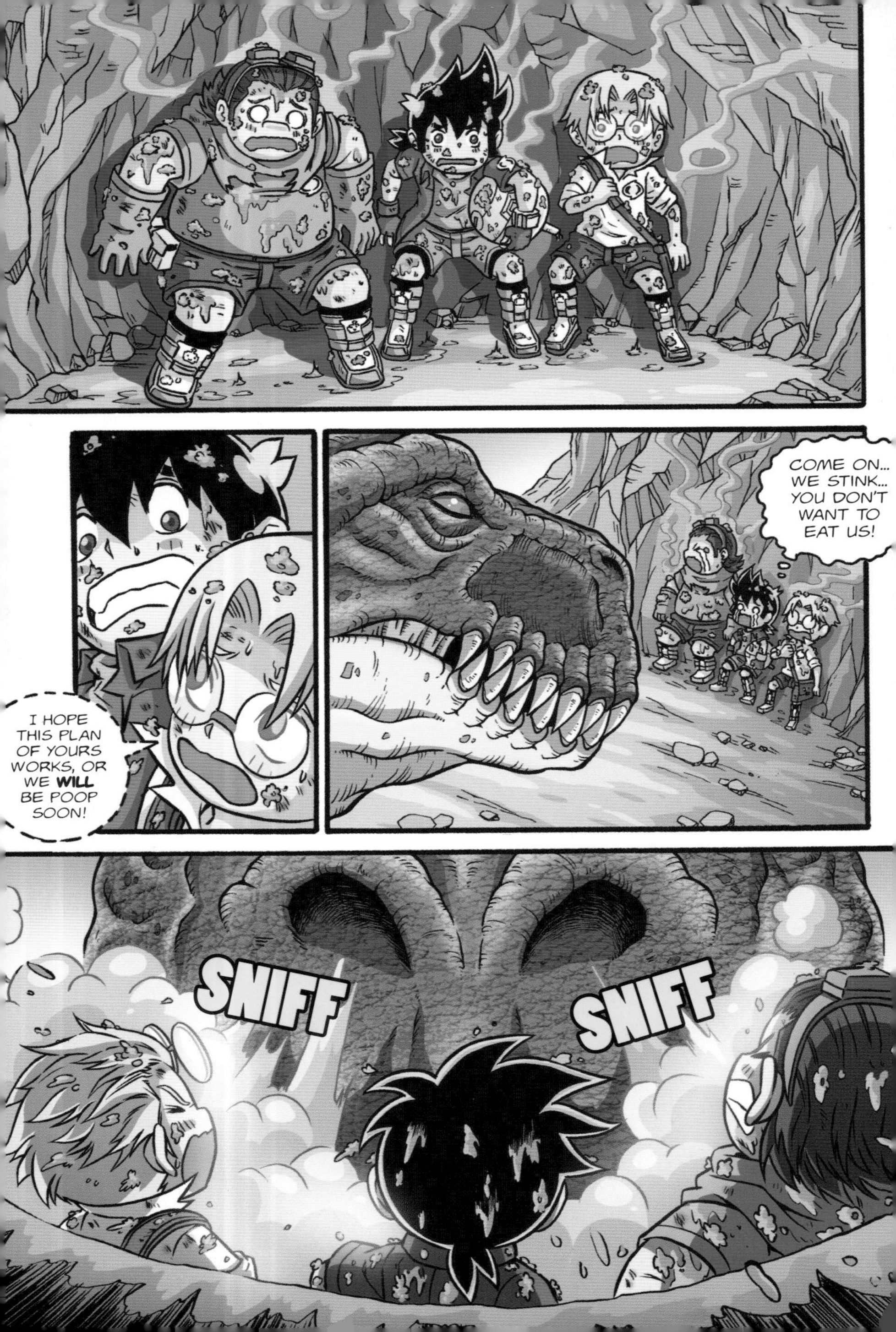

COME ON... WE STINK... YOU DON'T WANT TO EAT US!
I HOPE THIS PLAN OF YOURS WORKS, OR WE **WILL** BE POOP SOON!
SNIFF
SNIFF

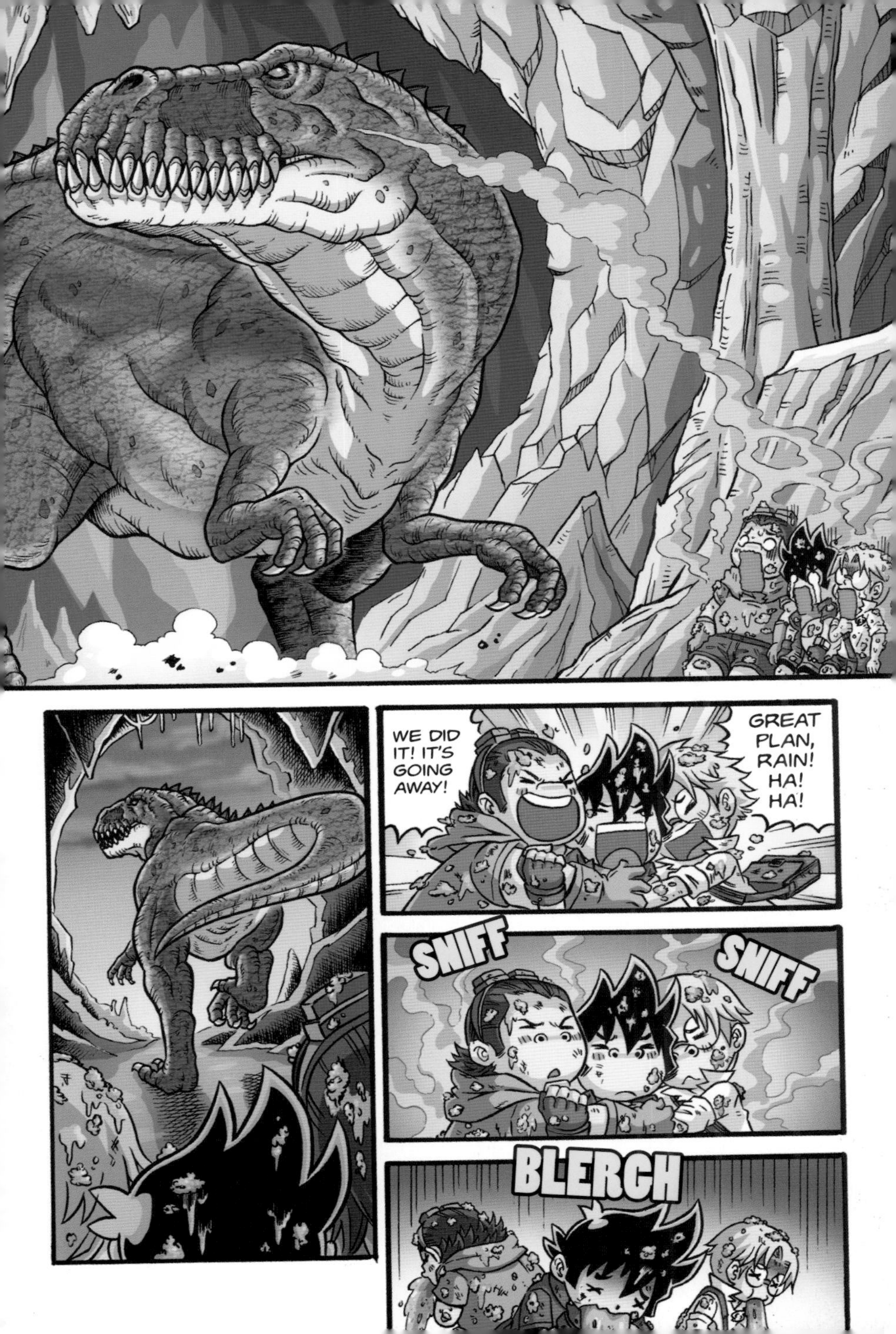
WE DID IT! IT'S GOING AWAY!
GREAT PLAN, RAIN! HA! HA!
SNIFF
SNIFF
BLERCH

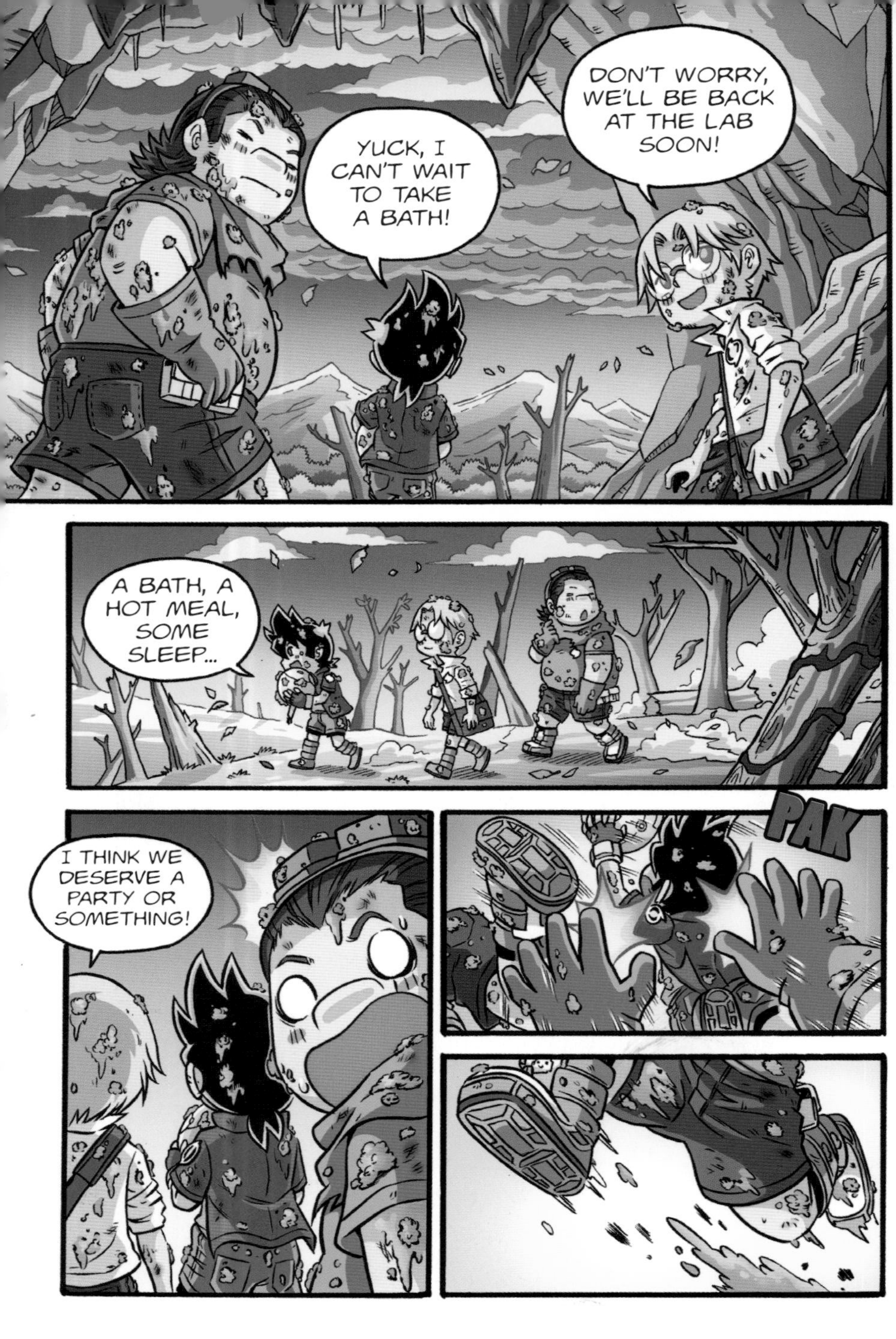
YUCK, I CAN'T WAIT TO TAKE A BATH!
DON'T WORRY, WE'LL BE BACK AT THE LAB SOON!
A BATH, A HOT MEAL, SOME SLEEP...
I THINK WE DESERVE A PARTY OR SOMETHING!
PAK

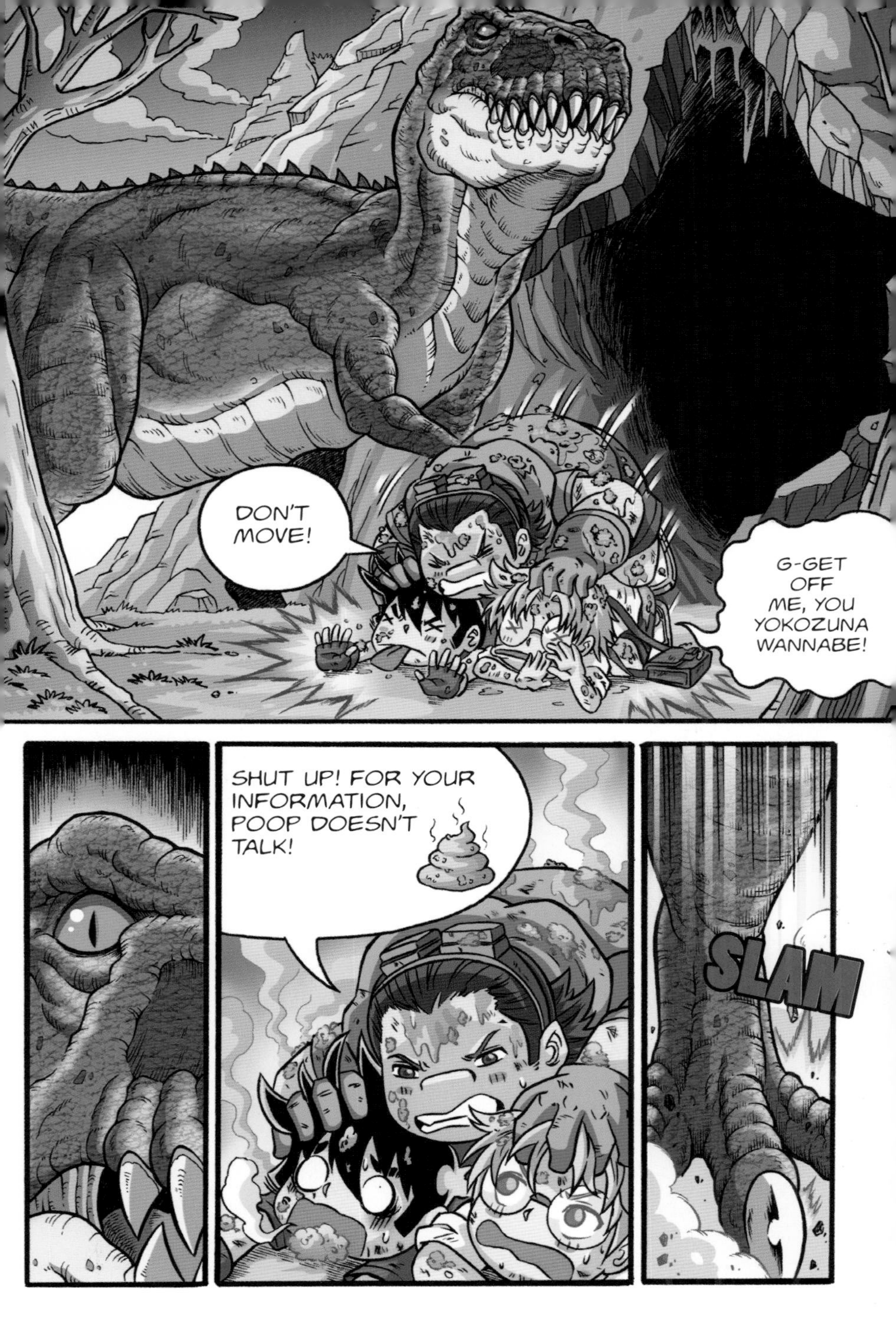
DON'T MOVE!
G-GET OFF ME, YOU YOKOZUNA WANNABE!
SHUT UP! FOR YOUR INFORMATION, POOP DOESN'T TALK!
SLAM

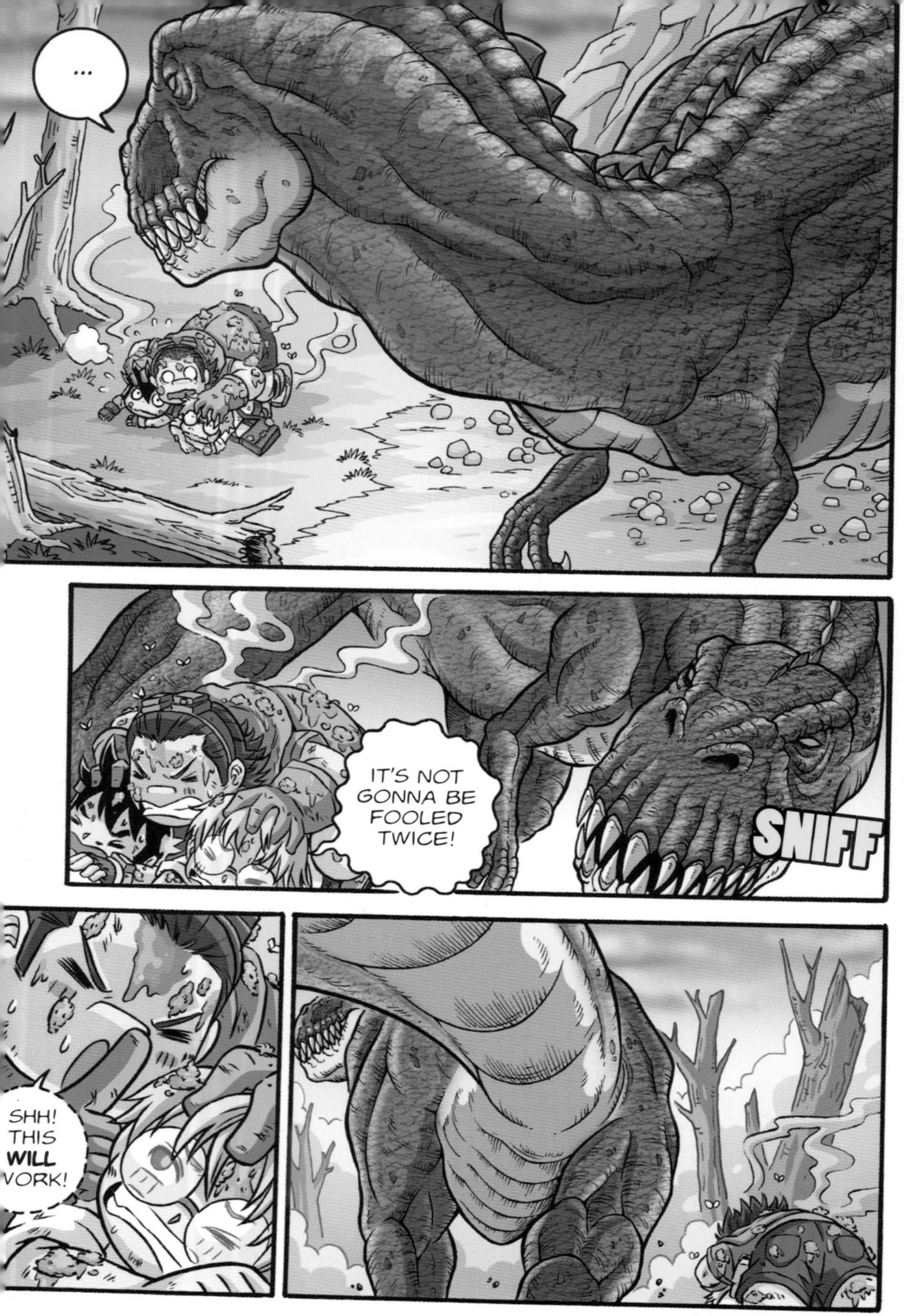
...
IT'S NOT GONNA BE FOOLED TWICE!
SNIFF
SHH! THIS **WILL** VORK!

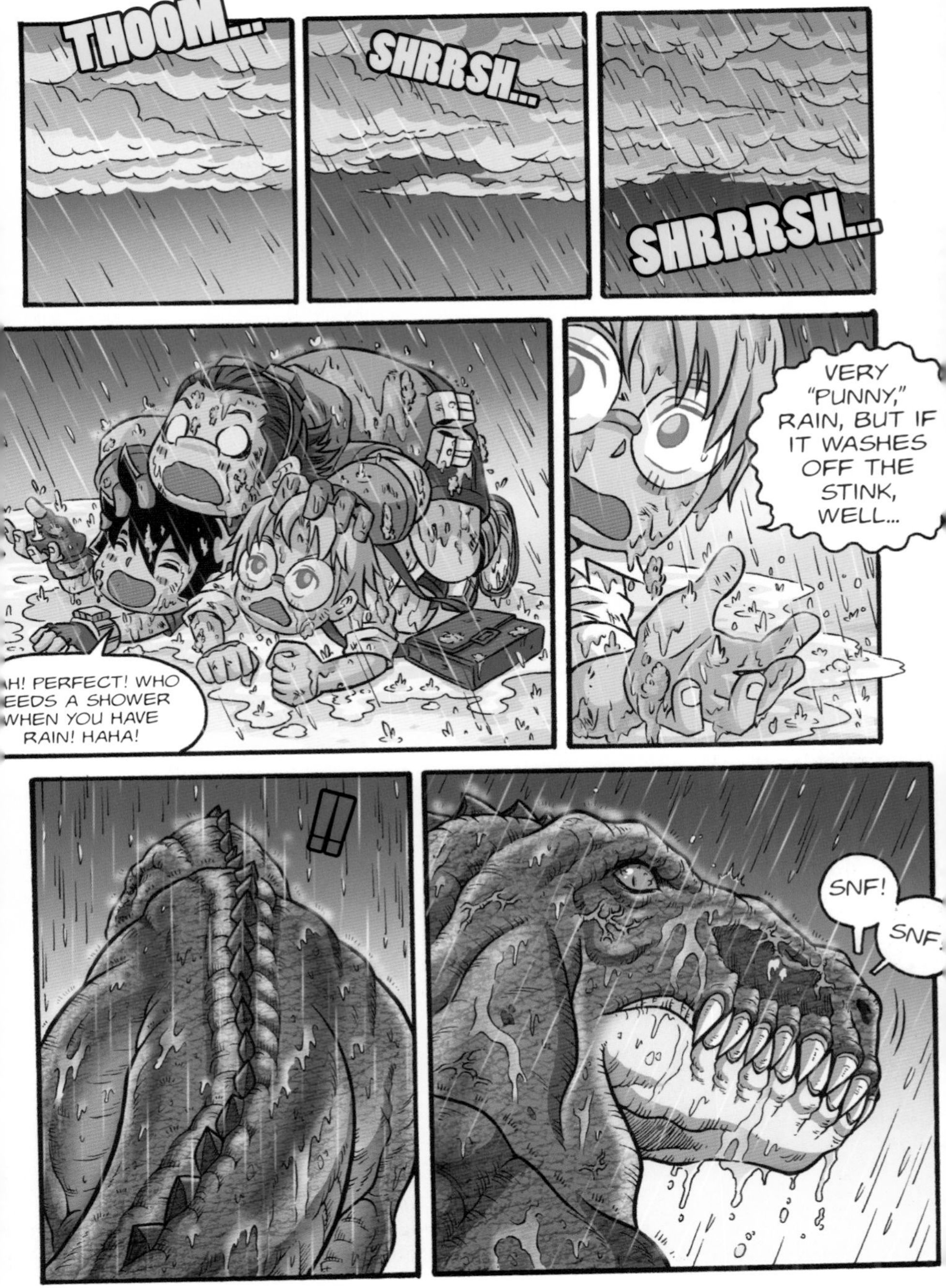
THOOM...
SHRRSH...
SHRRRSH...
H! PERFECT! WHO EEDS A SHOWER WHEN YOU HAVE RAIN! HAHA!
VERY "PUNNY," RAIN, BUT IF IT WASHES OFF THE STINK, WELL...
!!
SNF!
SNF

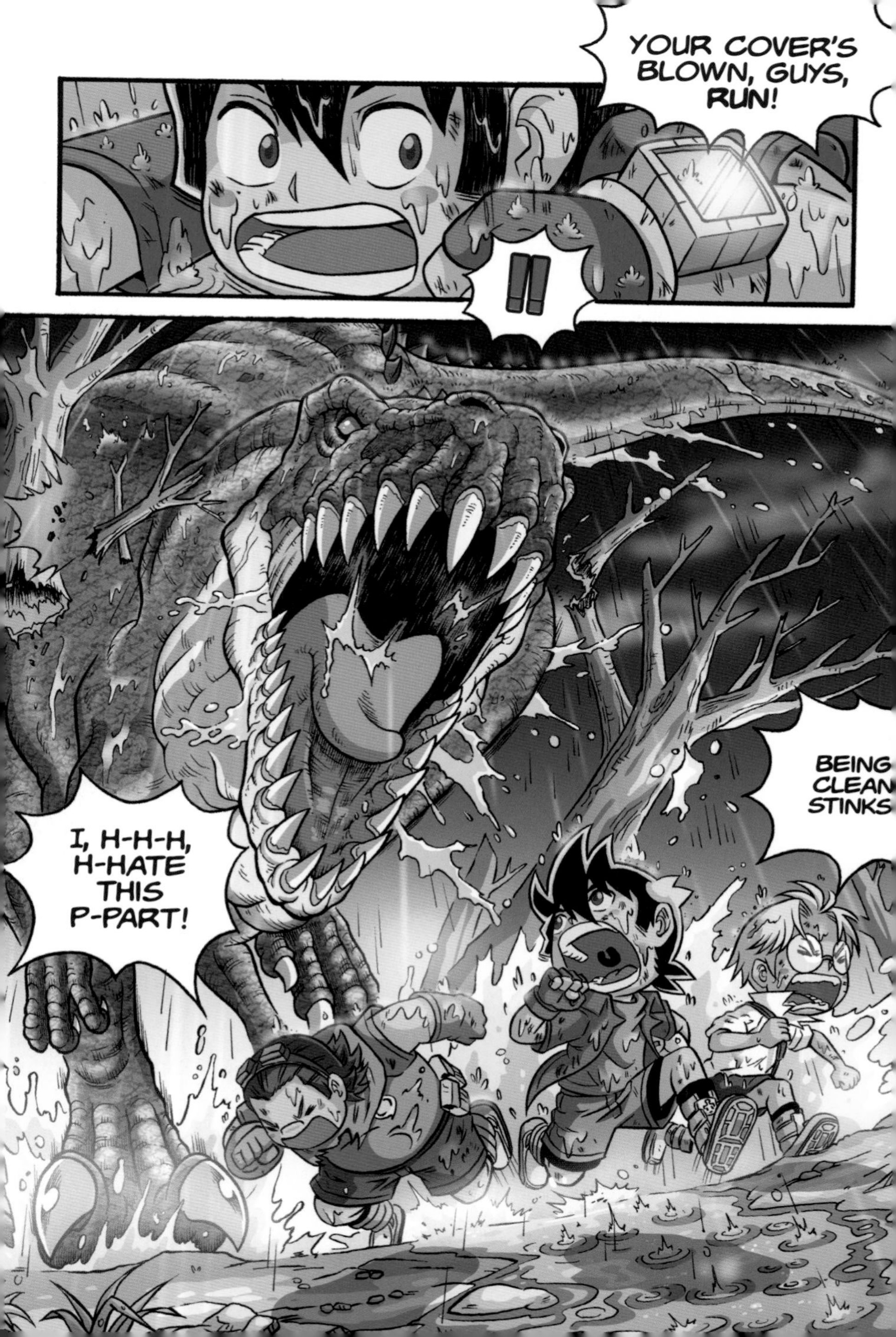

YOUR COVER'S BLOWN, GUYS, RUN!
!!
I, H-H-H, H-HATE THIS P-PART!
BEING CLEAN STINKS

## CAPTURING THE CRETACEOUS!

### Microraptor

Microraptor was one of the smallest known non-avian dinosaurs, with adults ranging between 30 to 36 inches. Though it was covered in feathers and even had winglike structures, Microraptor could not actually fly, but it has been theorized that it might have glided short distances. Because its legs were not really suited for land travel, it was thought to live in trees.

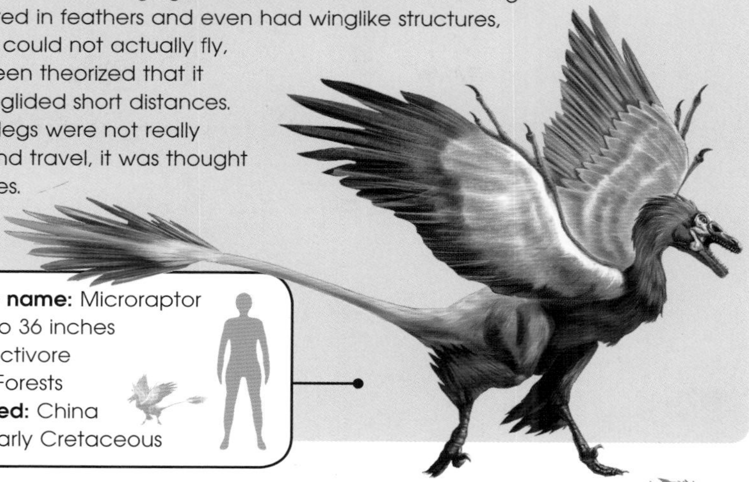

**Scientific name:** Microraptor
**Size:** 30 to 36 inches
**Diet:** Insectivore
**Habitat:** Forests
**Discovered:** China
**Period:** Early Cretaceous

## CAPTURING THE CRETACEOUS!

### Caudipteryx

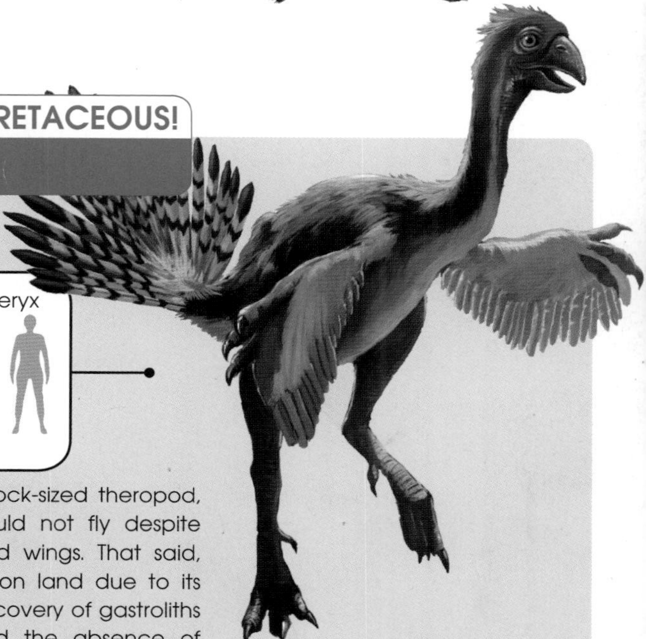

**Scientific name:** Caudipteryx
**Size:** 3 feet
**Diet:** Omnivore
**Habitat:** Lakes
**Discovered:** China
**Period:** Early Cretaceous

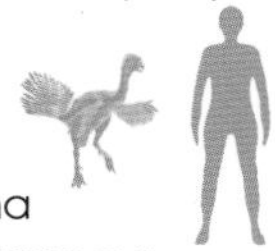

Caudipteryx was a peacock-sized theropod, that, like Microraptor could not fly despite having primitive feathered wings. That said, it was much more agile on land due to its powerful legs. With the discovery of gastroliths in Caudipteryx fossils and the absence of large tearing teeth, it was thought to have been omnivorous.

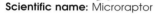

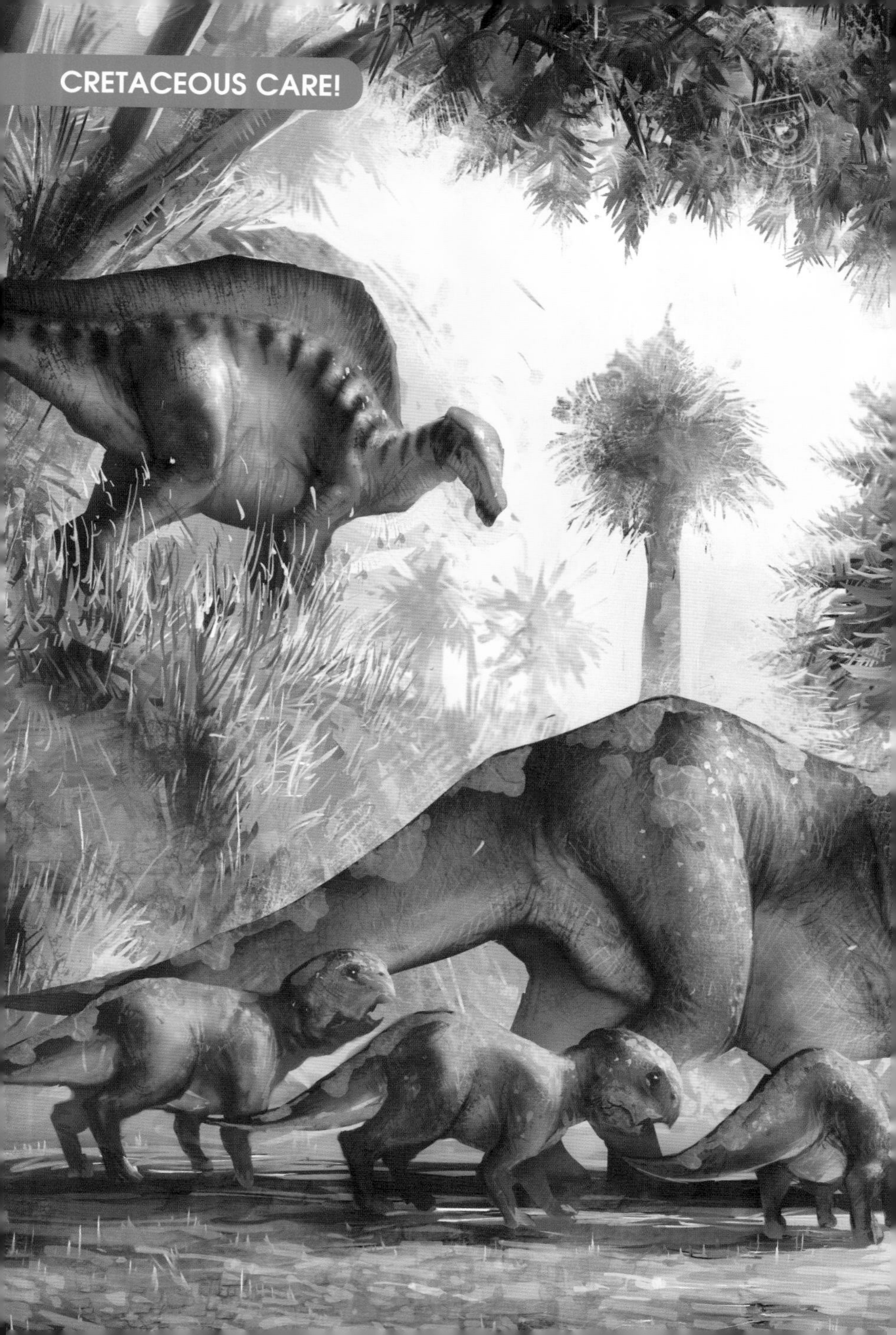

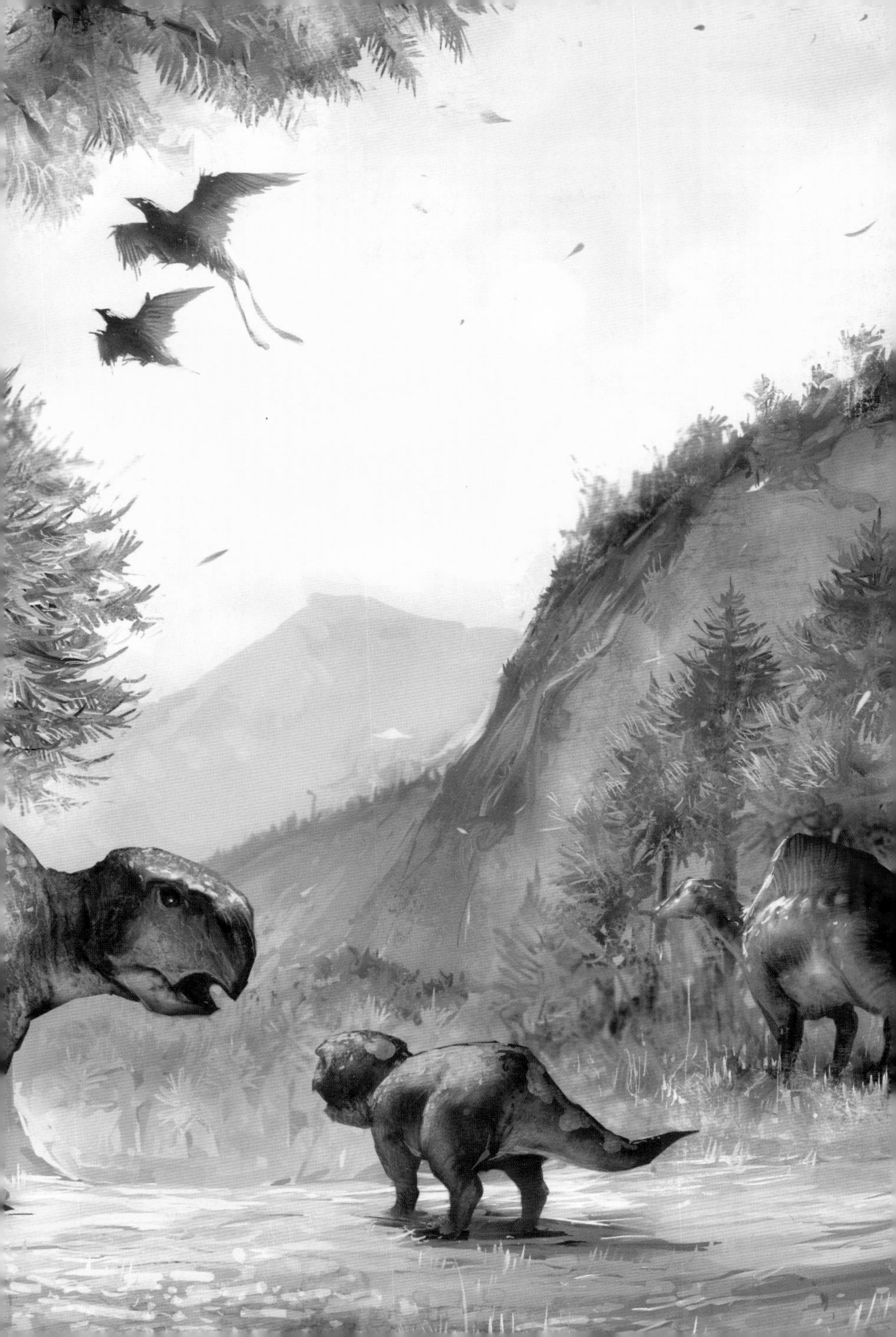

## CAPTURING THE CRETACEOUS!

### Incisivosaurus

**Scientific name:** Incisivosaurus
**Size:** 3 feet
**Diet:** Herbivore
**Habitat:** Forests
**Discovered:** China
**Period:** Early Cretaceous

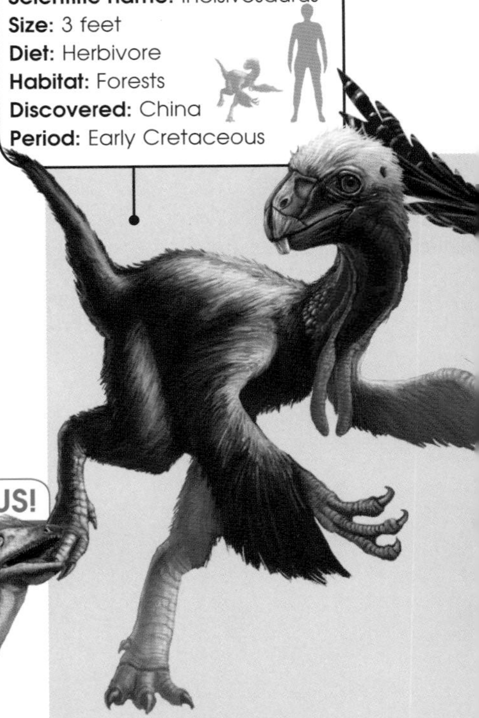

Incisivosaurus was a small, probably herbivorous maniraptoran theropod. Unique due to its apparent adoption of either a herbivorous or omnivorous lifestyle. It is thought to have had feathers, and bore great physiological similarity to Archaeopteryx.

## CAPTURING THE CRETACEOUS!

### Alxasaurus

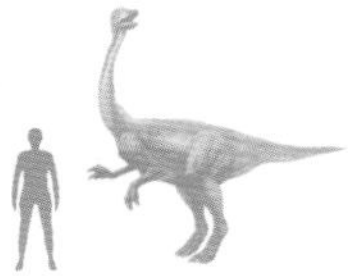

**Scientific name:** Alxasaurus
**Size:** 13 feet
**Diet:** Herbivore
**Habitat:** Forests
**Discovered:** China
**Period:** Mid-Cretaceous

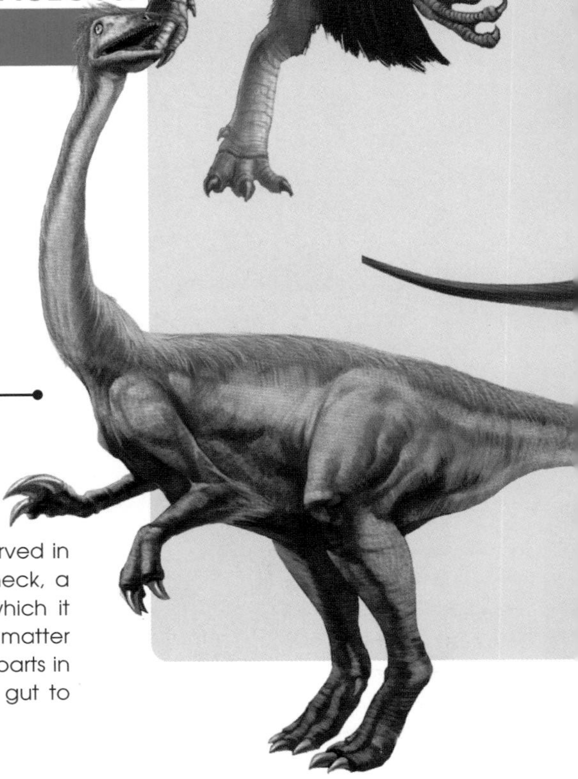

Alxasaurus displayed traits observed in later Therizinosauroids; a long neck, a short tail and dextrous arms, which it used to pluck and cut up plant matter before eating it. Like its counterparts in the superfamily, it had a large gut to process plant material.

## CAPTURING THE CRETACEOUS!

### Sinovenator

**Scientific name:** Sinovenator
**Size:** 3 feet
**Diet:** Carnivore
**Habitat:** Forests
**Discovered:** China
**Period:** Pre-Cretaceous

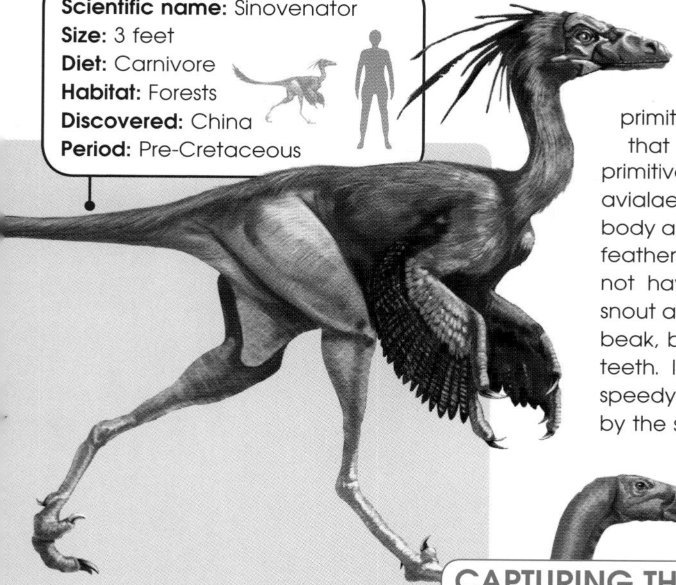

Sinovenator was a primitive troodontid dinosaur that shared many traits with primitive dromaeosaurids and avialae, such as a feathered body and long legs. It also had feathered wings, but could not have supported flight. Its snout also resembled an avian beak, but was filled with small teeth. It might have been a speedy predator as evinced by the sharp claws on its feet.

## CAPTURING THE CRETACEOUS!

### Segnosaurus

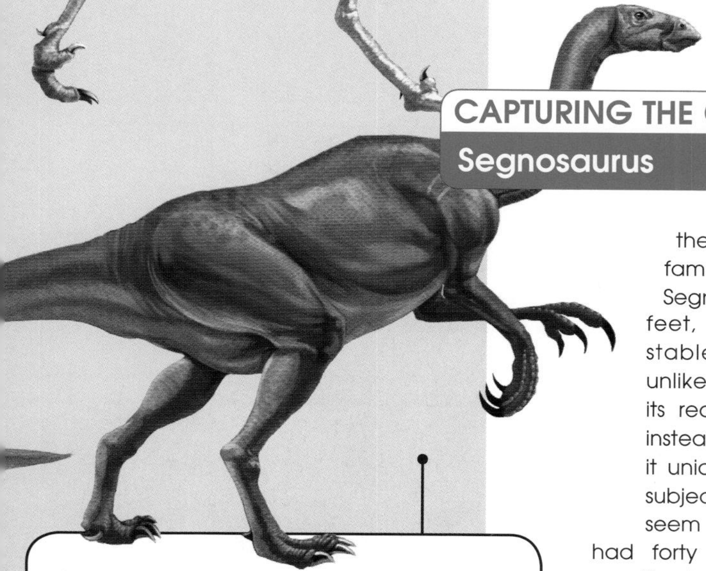

A herbivorous theropod belonging to family Therizinosauridae, Segnosaurus had stocky feet, which made it stable but slow and unlike other theropods, its rear feet had 4 toes instead of 3. What makes it unique is the debated subject of its diet; fossils seem to show that it had forty eight mandibular, peg-like teeth at the rear of its jaws, but a toothless beak. Its large stomach would have also been capable of holding a large intestine, unnecessary for carnivores and omnivores, but vital to herbivores.

**Scientific name:** Segnosaurus
**Size:** 19.7 feet
**Diet:** Herbivore (maybe)
**Habitat:** Forests
**Discovered:** China
**Period:** Late Cretaceous

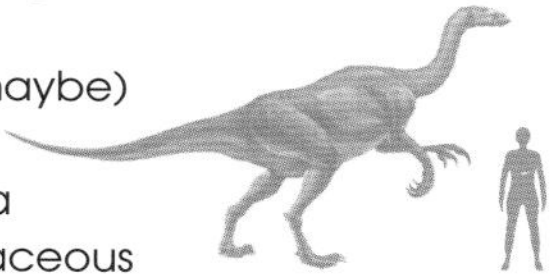

## CAPTURING THE CRETACEOUS!

### Giganotosaurus

Living up to its name, the largest Giganotosaurus' skull measured about 6 feet, as long as a tall man! It was slightly longer, but less-heavily built than the T-Rex. Its jaws were lined with serrated 3 inches long teeth, and bad news for Late Cretaceous sauropods, fossil remains indicate it might have hunted in packs.

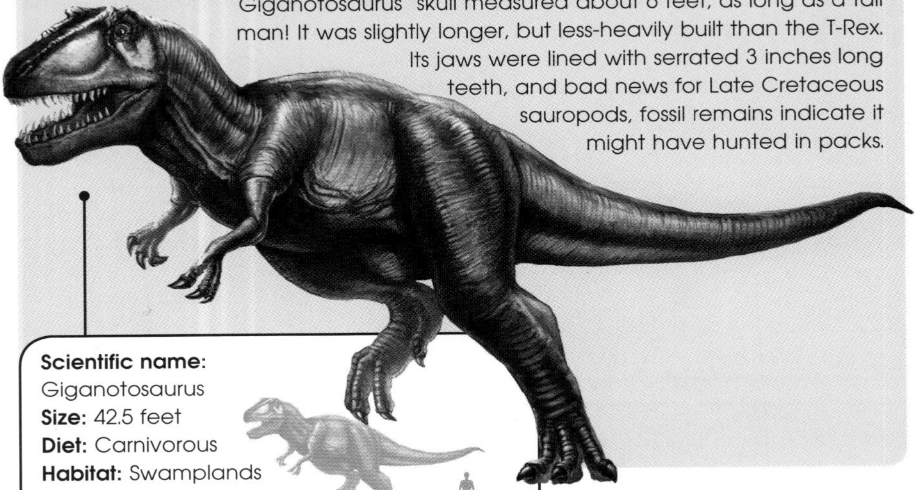

**Scientific name:** Giganotosaurus
**Size:** 42.5 feet
**Diet:** Carnivorous
**Habitat:** Swamplands
**Discovered:** Argentina
**Period:** Late Cretaceous

## CAPTURING THE CRETACEOUS!

### Kronosaurus

Kronosaurus is one of the largest known pliosaurs. Its skull alone comprised 25% of its total body length. It had 4 powerful flippers and a slim, streamlined body. Its triangular jaws were lined with large, conical teeth, ranging from 3 to 12 inches long, giving it one fatal bite.

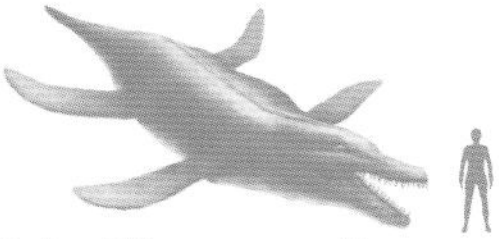

**Scientific name:** Kronosaurus
**Size:** 43 feet
**Diet:** Carnivore
**Habitat:** Oceans
**Discovered:** Queensland, Australia
**Period:** Mid-Cretaceous

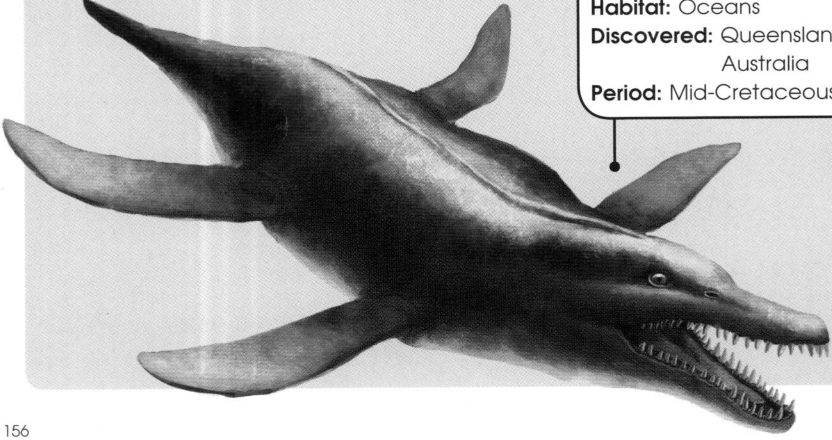

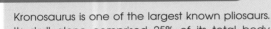

CHAPTER 8
# STRUCK DOWN!

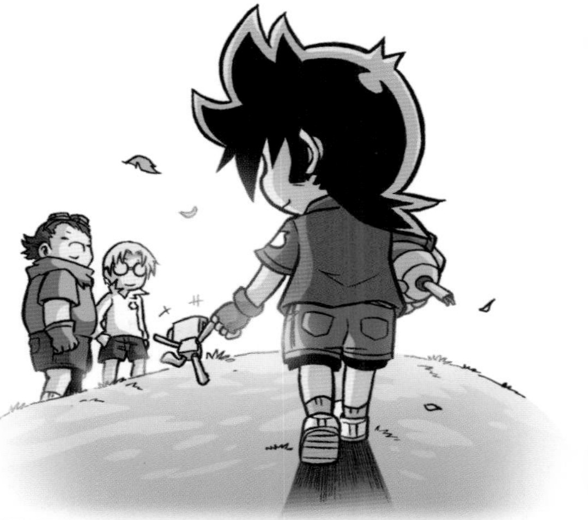

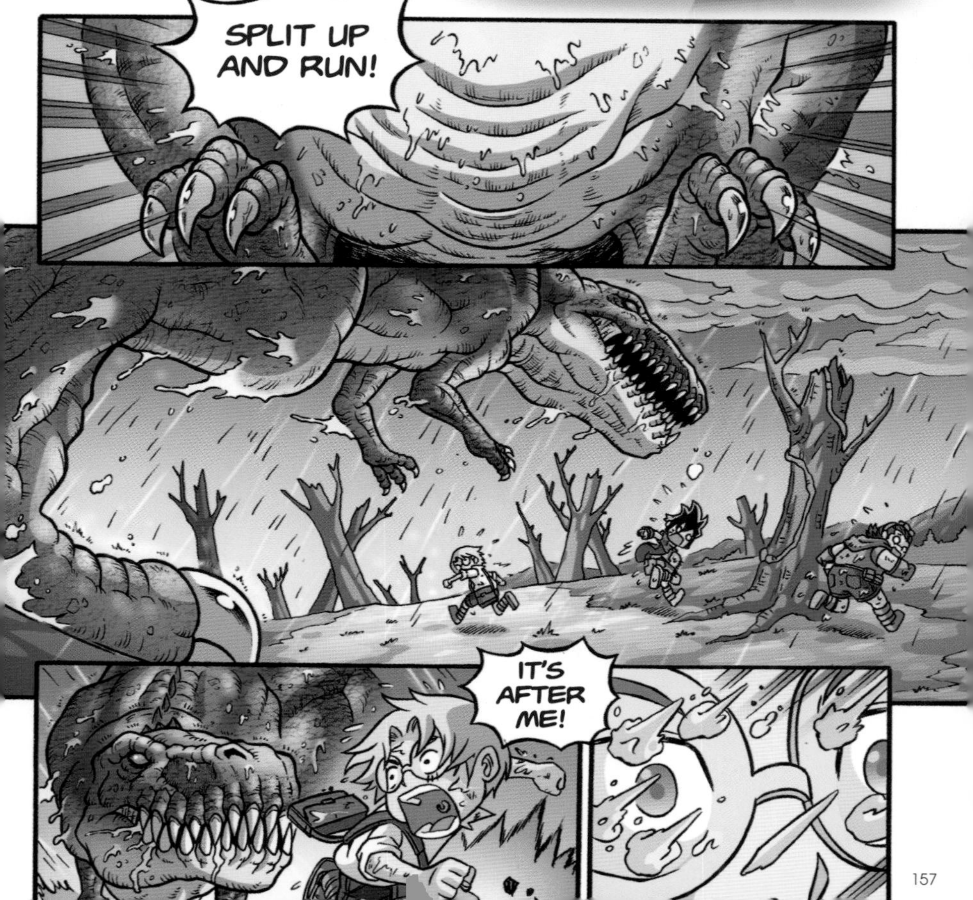

SPLIT UP AND RUN!
IT'S AFTER ME!

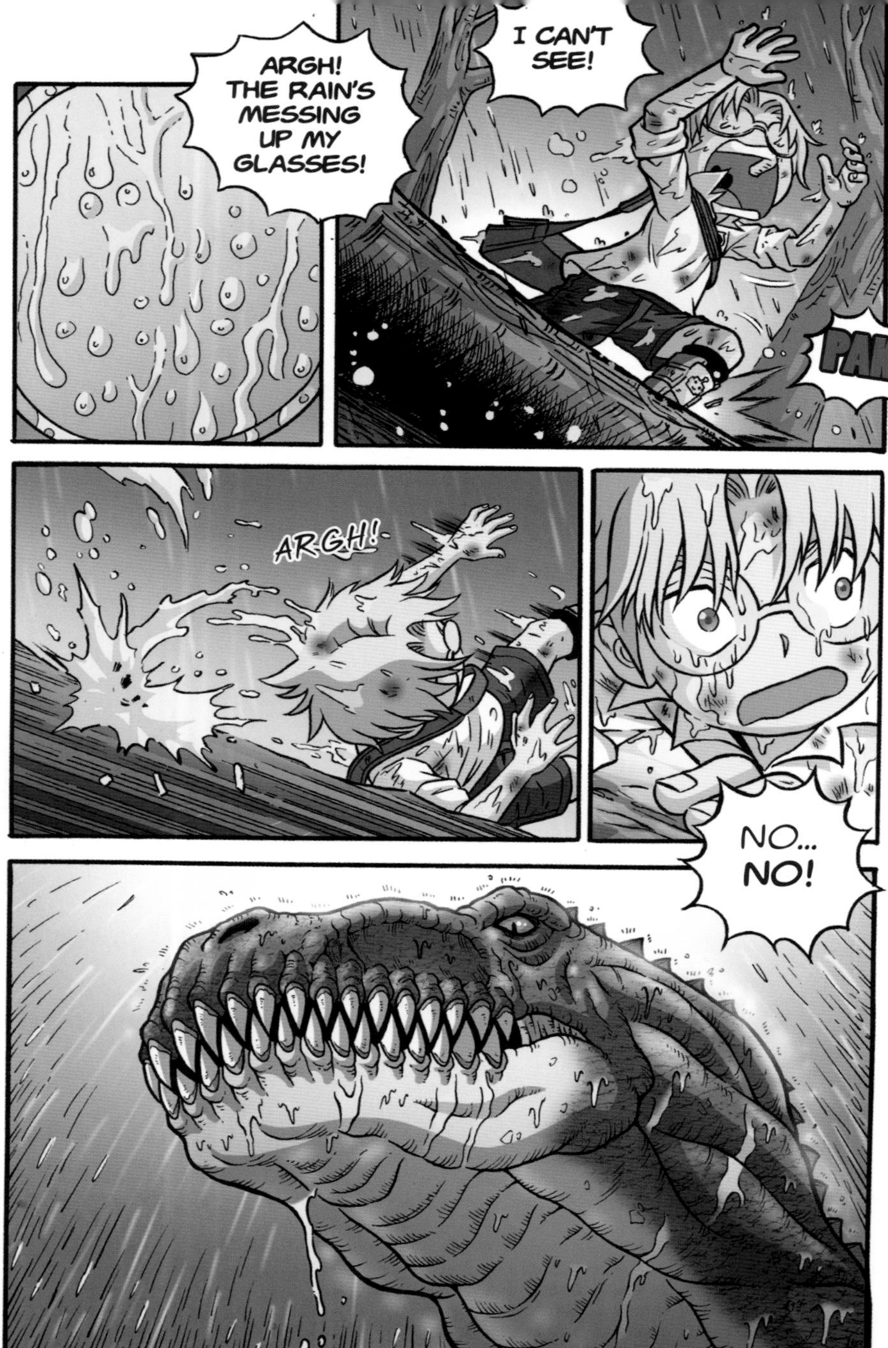
ARGH! THE RAIN'S MESSING UP MY GLASSES!
I CAN'T SEE!
PAK
ARGH!
NO... NO!

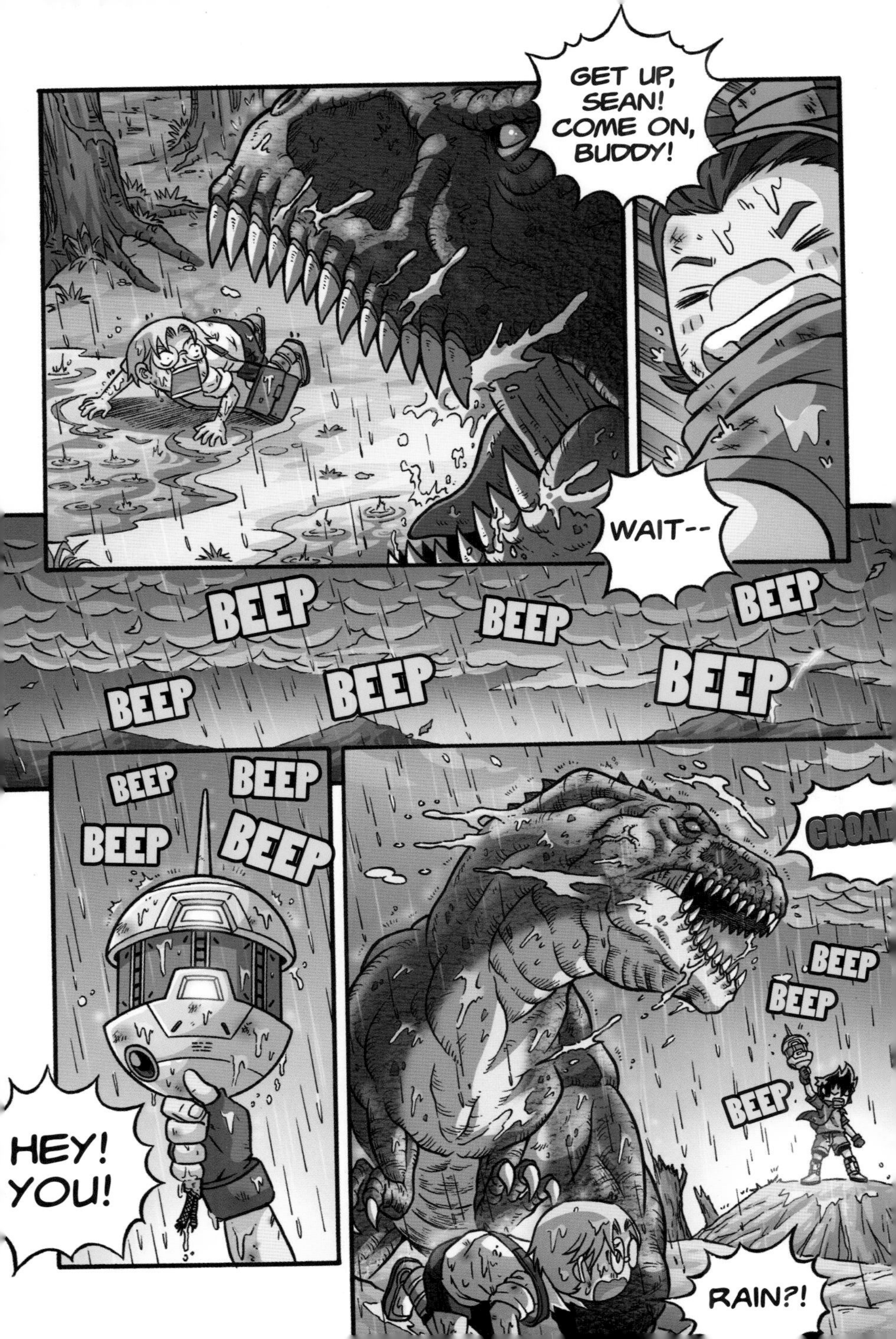
GET UP, SEAN! COME ON, BUDDY!
WAIT--
BEEP
BEEP
BEEP
BEEP
BEEP
BEEP
BEEP
BEEP
BEEP
BEEP
HEY! YOU!
GROAH
BEEP
BEEP
BEEP
RAIN?!

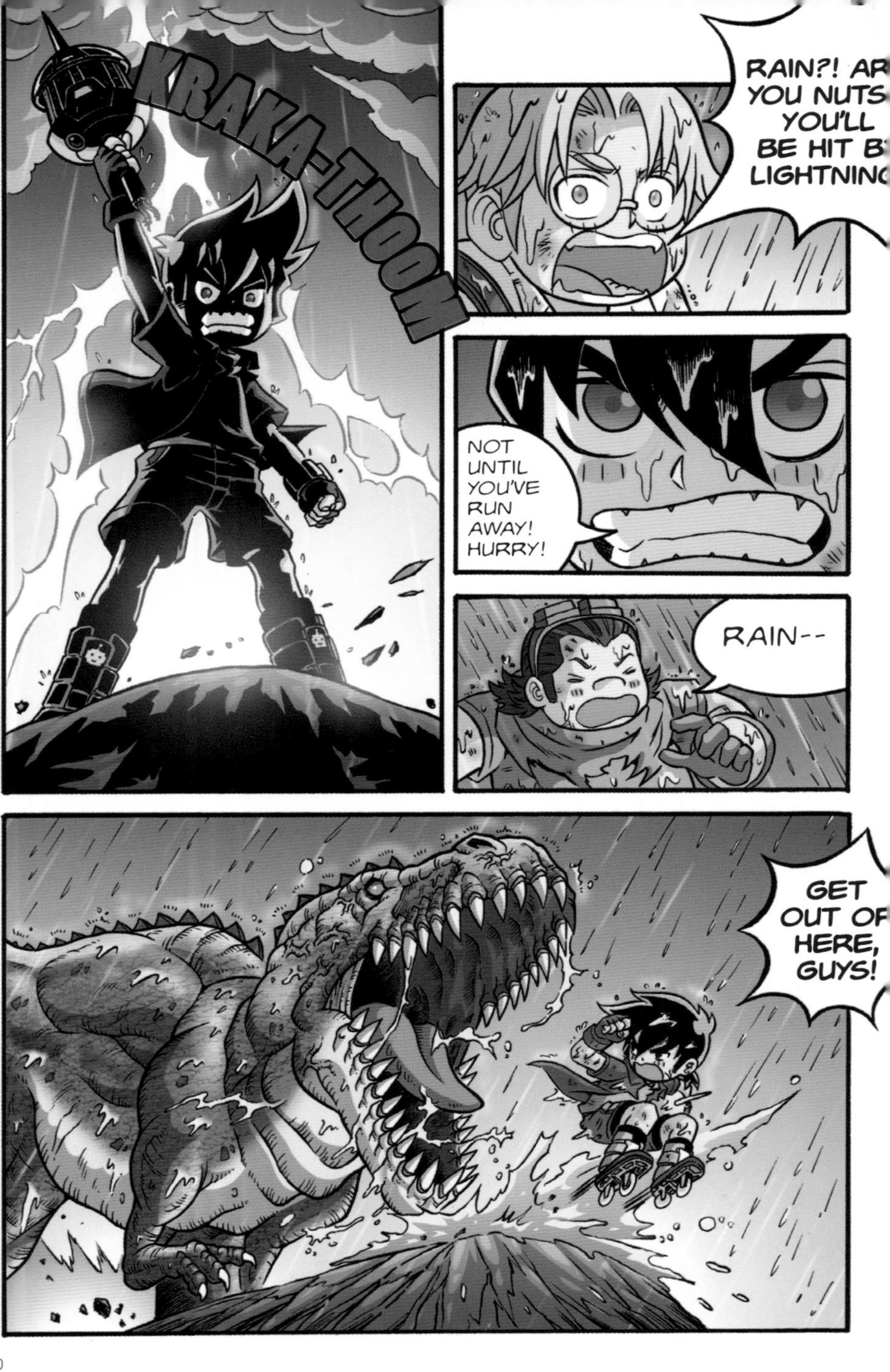
KRAKA-THOOM
RAIN?! AR
YOU NUTS
YOU'LL
BE HIT B
LIGHTNIN
NOT UNTIL YOU'VE RUN AWAY! HURRY!
RAIN--
GET OUT OF HERE, GUYS!

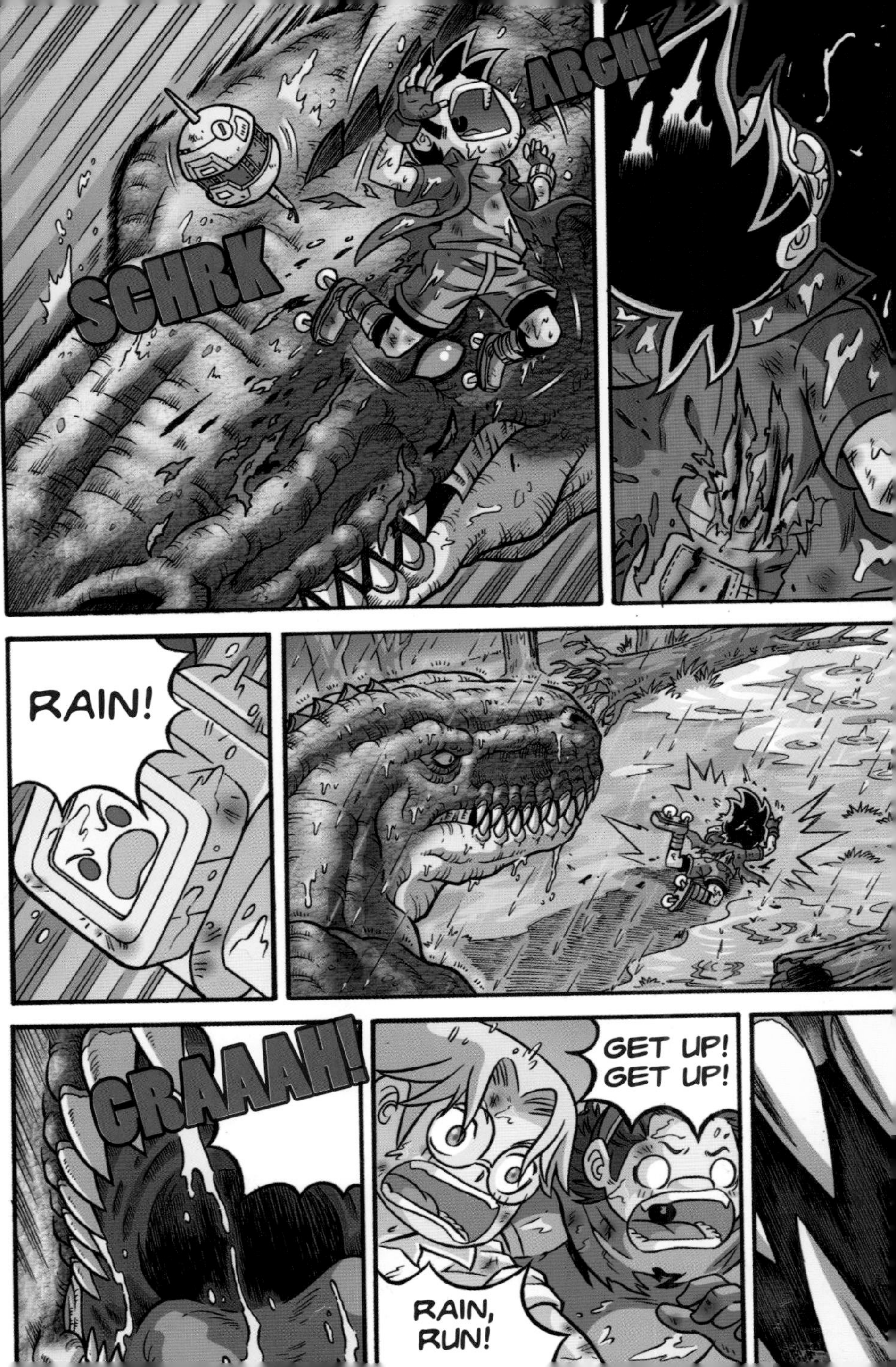
SCHRK
ARCH!
RAIN!
GRAAAH!
GET UP! GET UP!
RAIN, RUN!

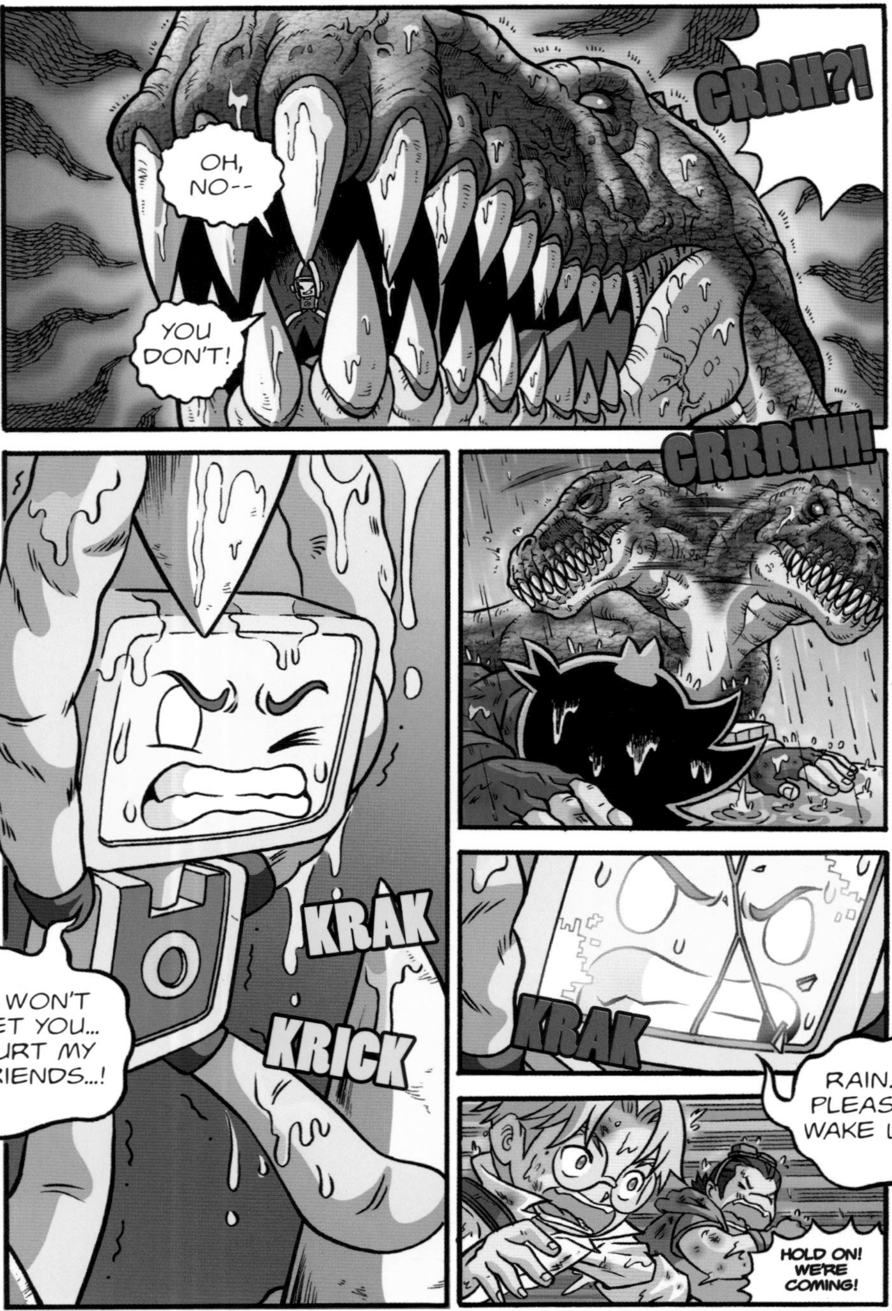
OH, NO--
CRRH?!
YOU DON'T!
CRRRNH!
KRAK
KRICK
I WON'T LET YOU... HURT MY FRIENDS...!
KRAK
RAIN... PLEASE WAKE U
HOLD ON! WE'RE COMING!

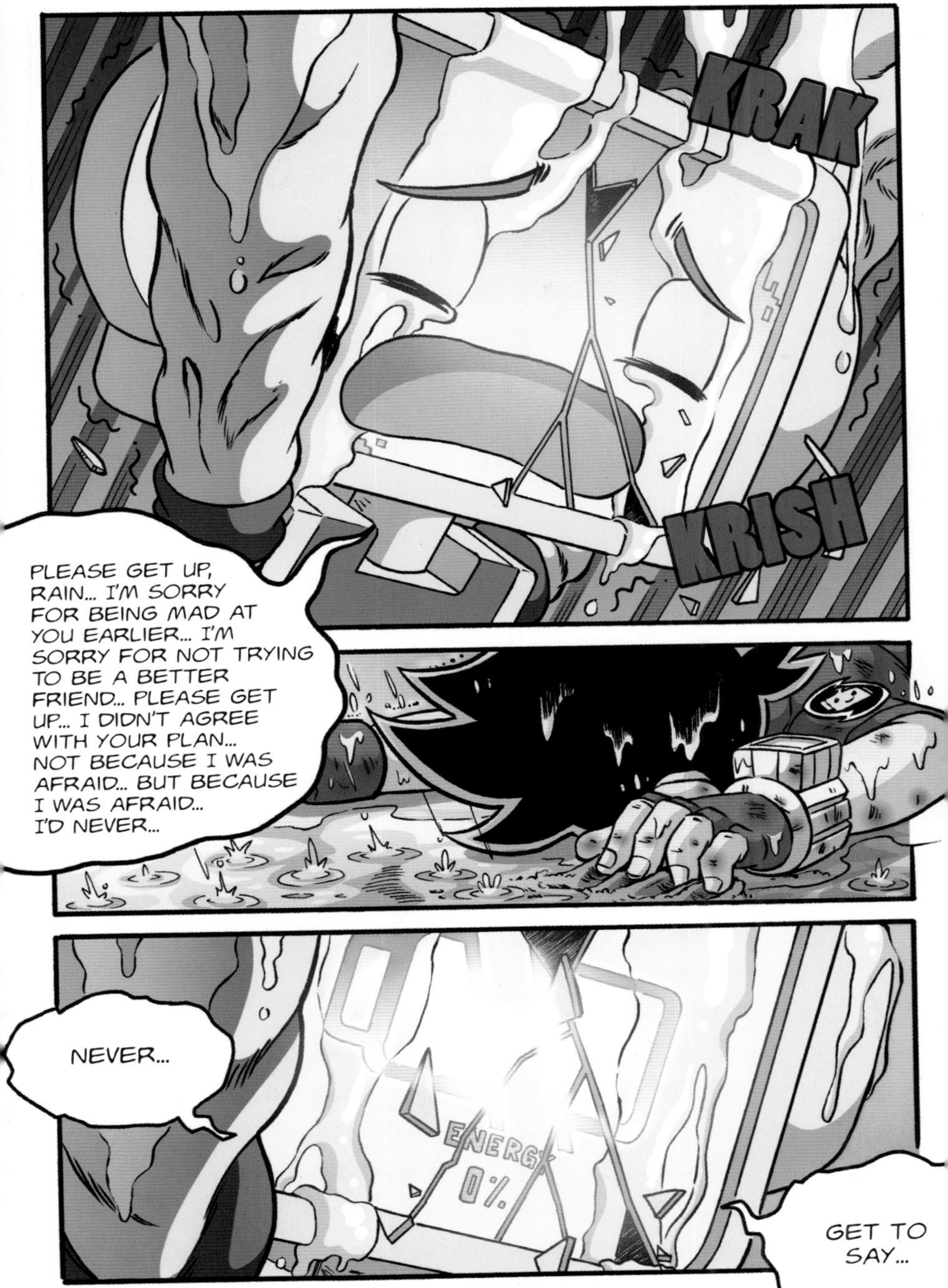
KRAK
KRISH
PLEASE GET UP, RAIN... I'M SORRY FOR BEING MAD AT YOU EARLIER... I'M SORRY FOR NOT TRYING TO BE A BETTER FRIEND... PLEASE GET UP... I DIDN'T AGREE WITH YOUR PLAN... NOT BECAUSE I WAS AFRAID... BUT BECAUSE I WAS AFRAID... I'D NEVER...
NEVER...
ENERGY 0%
GET TO SAY...

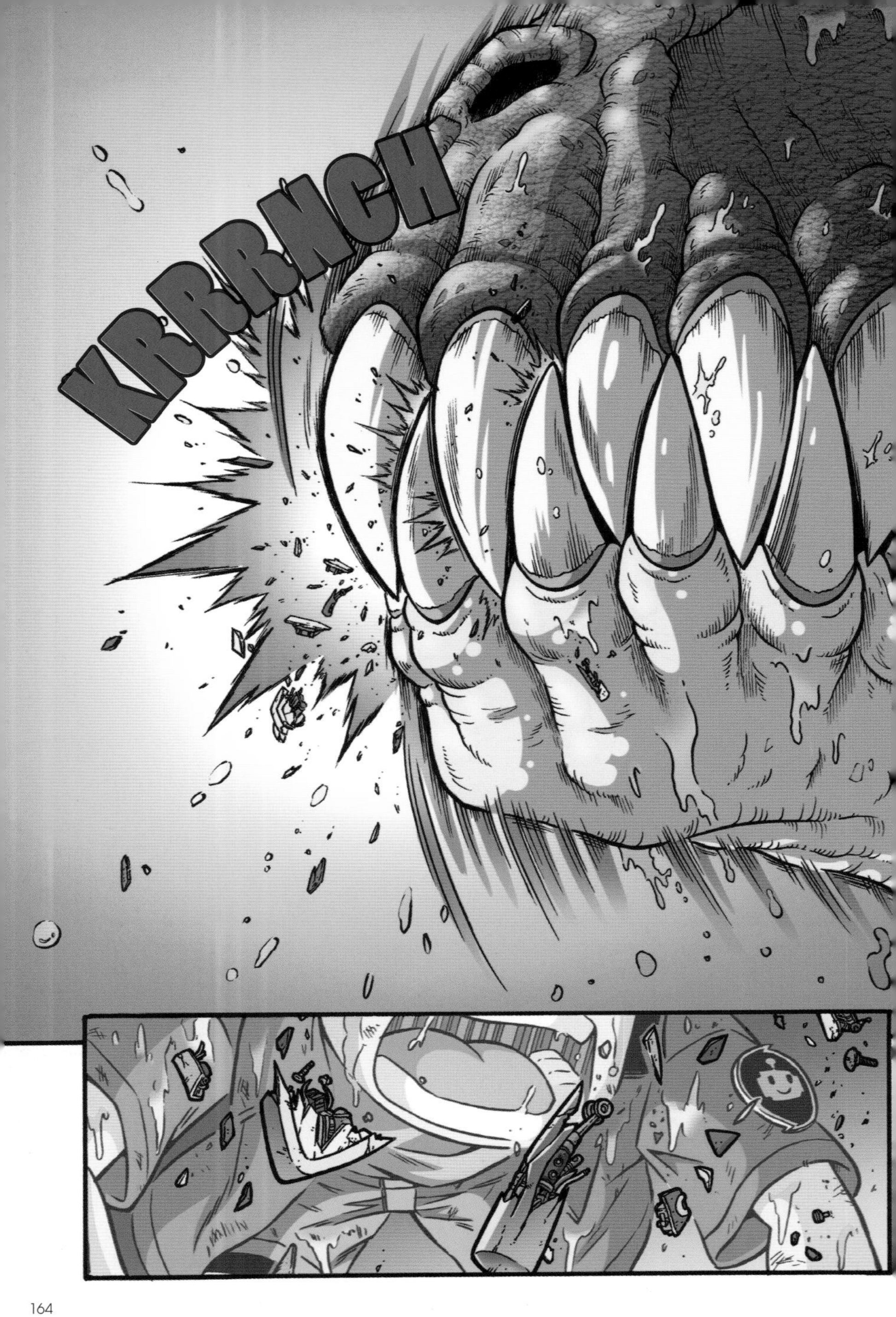
KRRRNCH

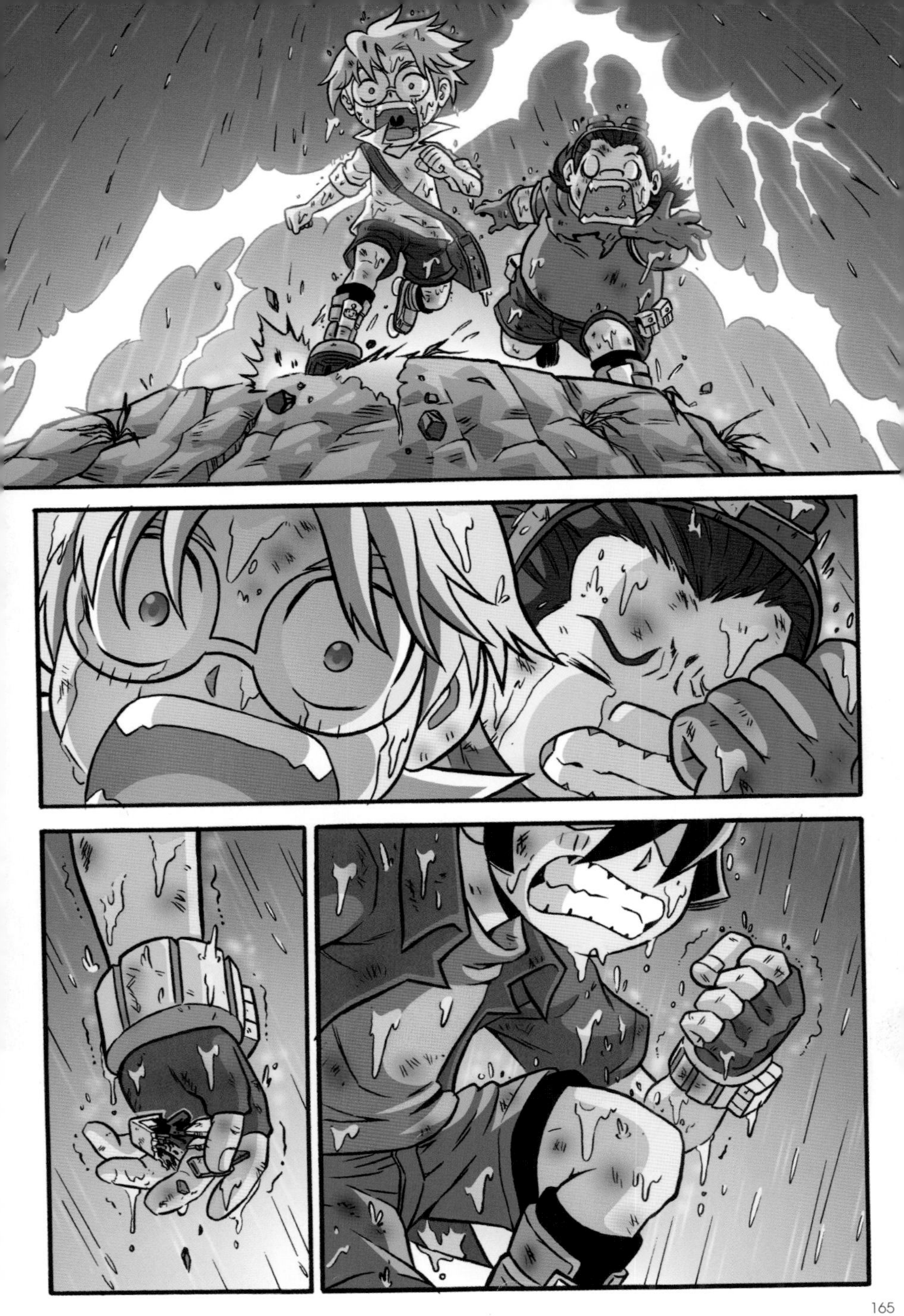

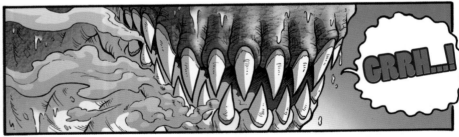

CRRH...!

?!

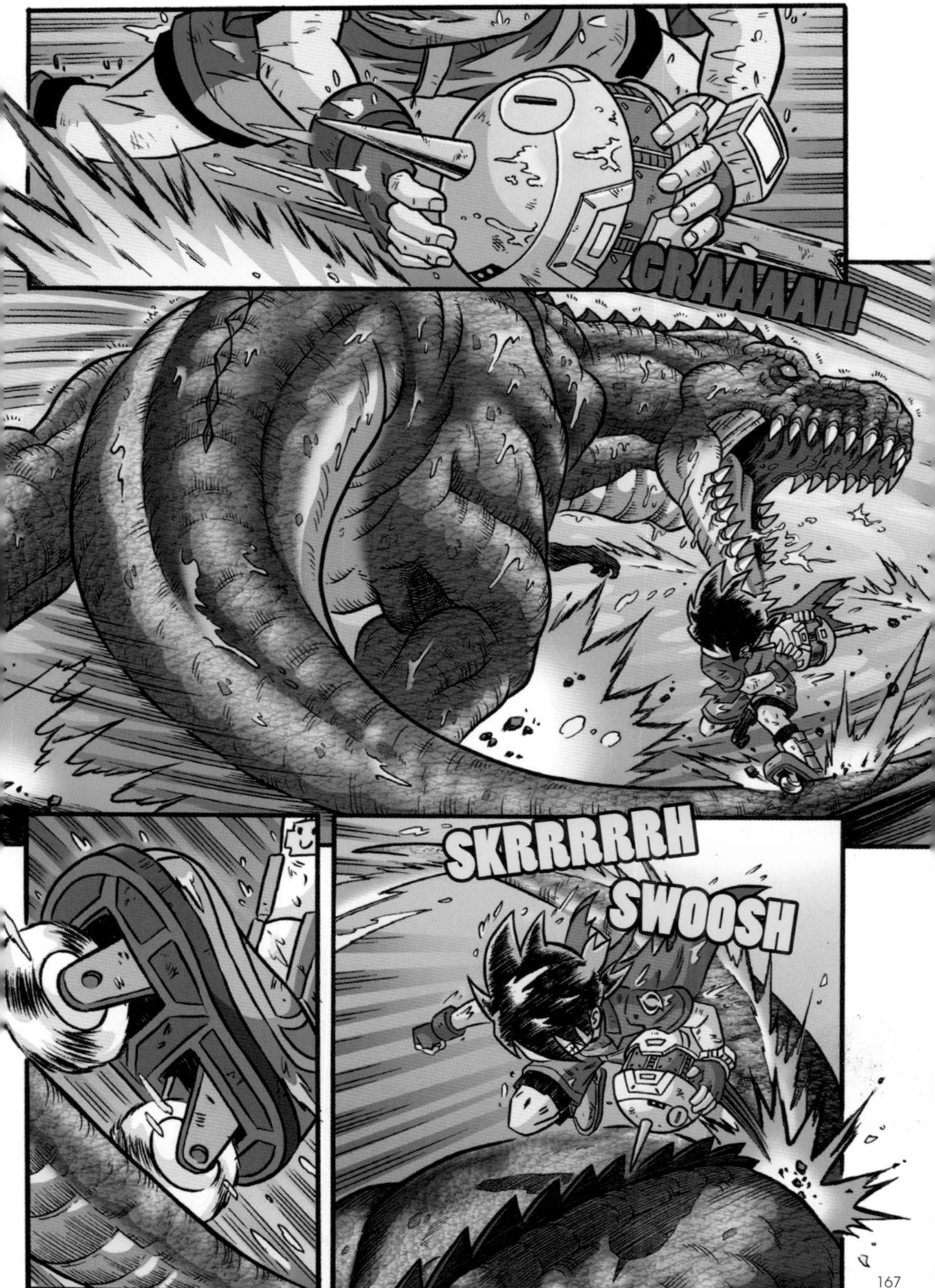
CRAAAAAH!
SKRRRRRRH
SWOOSH

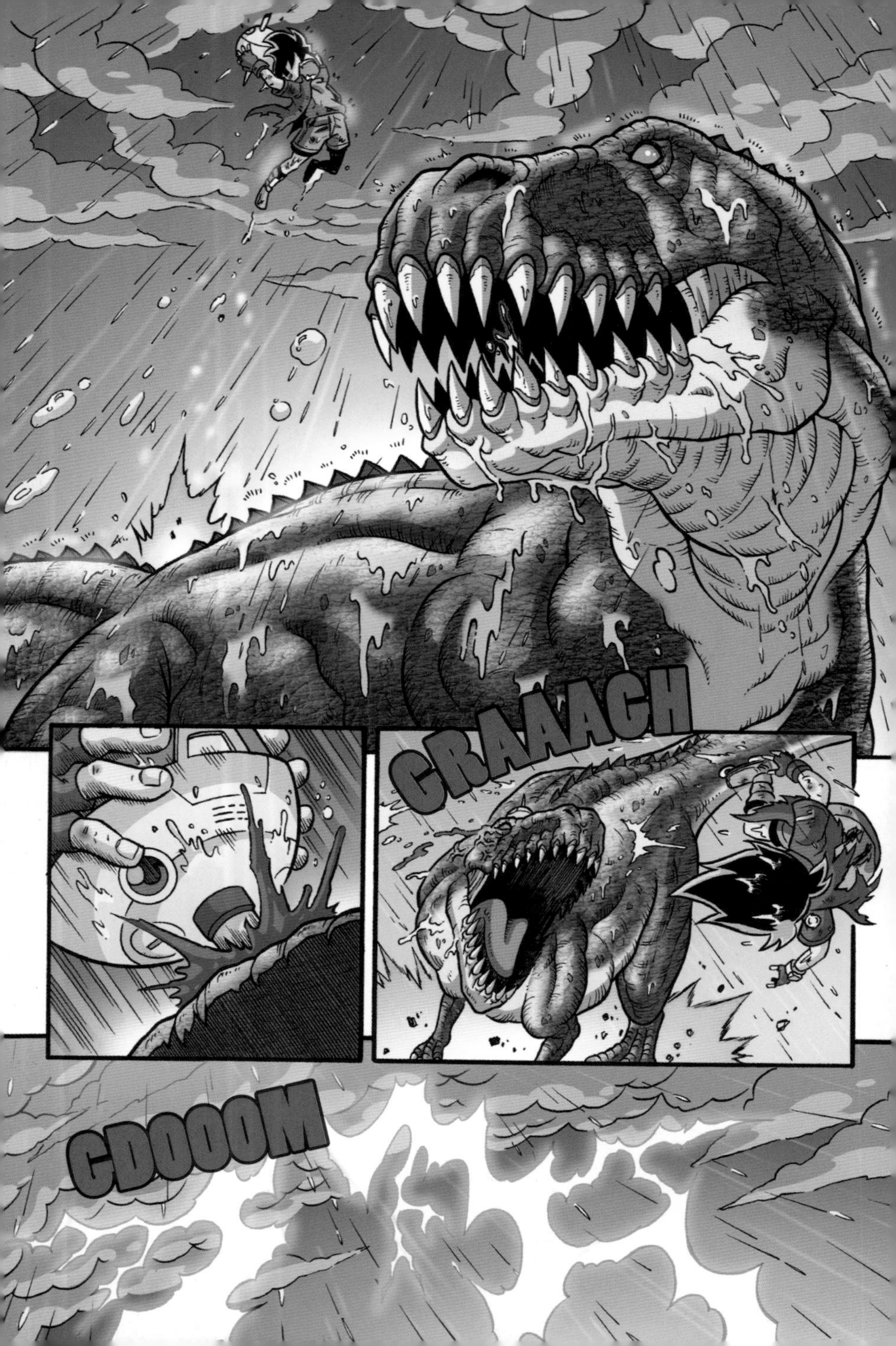
GRAAACH
CDOOOM

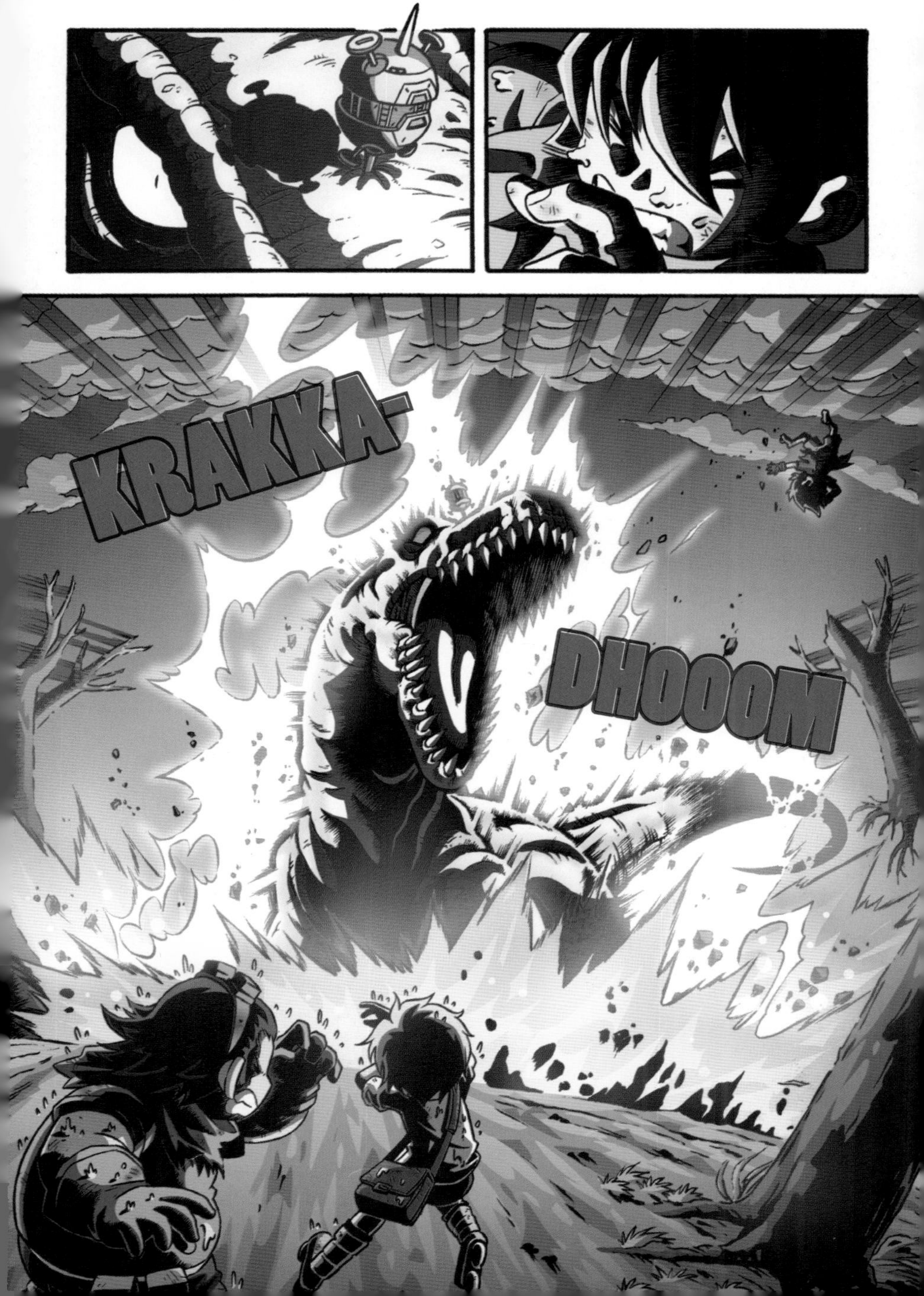
KRAKKA-
DHOOOM

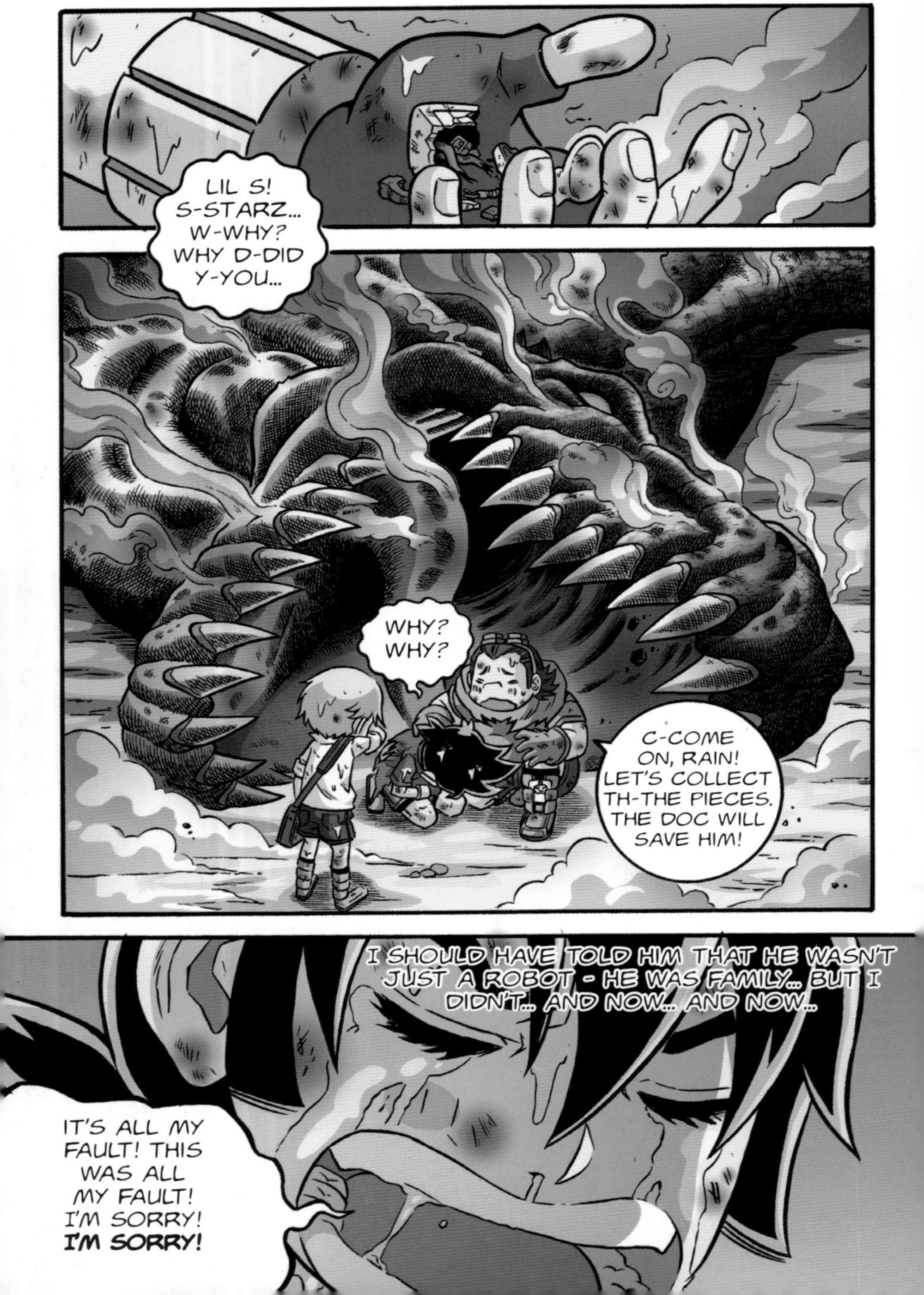

LIL S! S-STARZ... W-WHY? WHY D-DID Y-YOU...
WHY? WHY?
C-COME ON, RAIN! LET'S COLLECT TH-THE PIECES. THE DOC WILL SAVE HIM!
I SHOULD HAVE TOLD HIM THAT HE WASN'T JUST A ROBOT - HE WAS FAMILY... BUT I DIDN'T... AND NOW... AND NOW...
IT'S ALL MY FAULT! THIS WAS ALL MY FAULT! I'M SORRY! **I'M SORRY!**

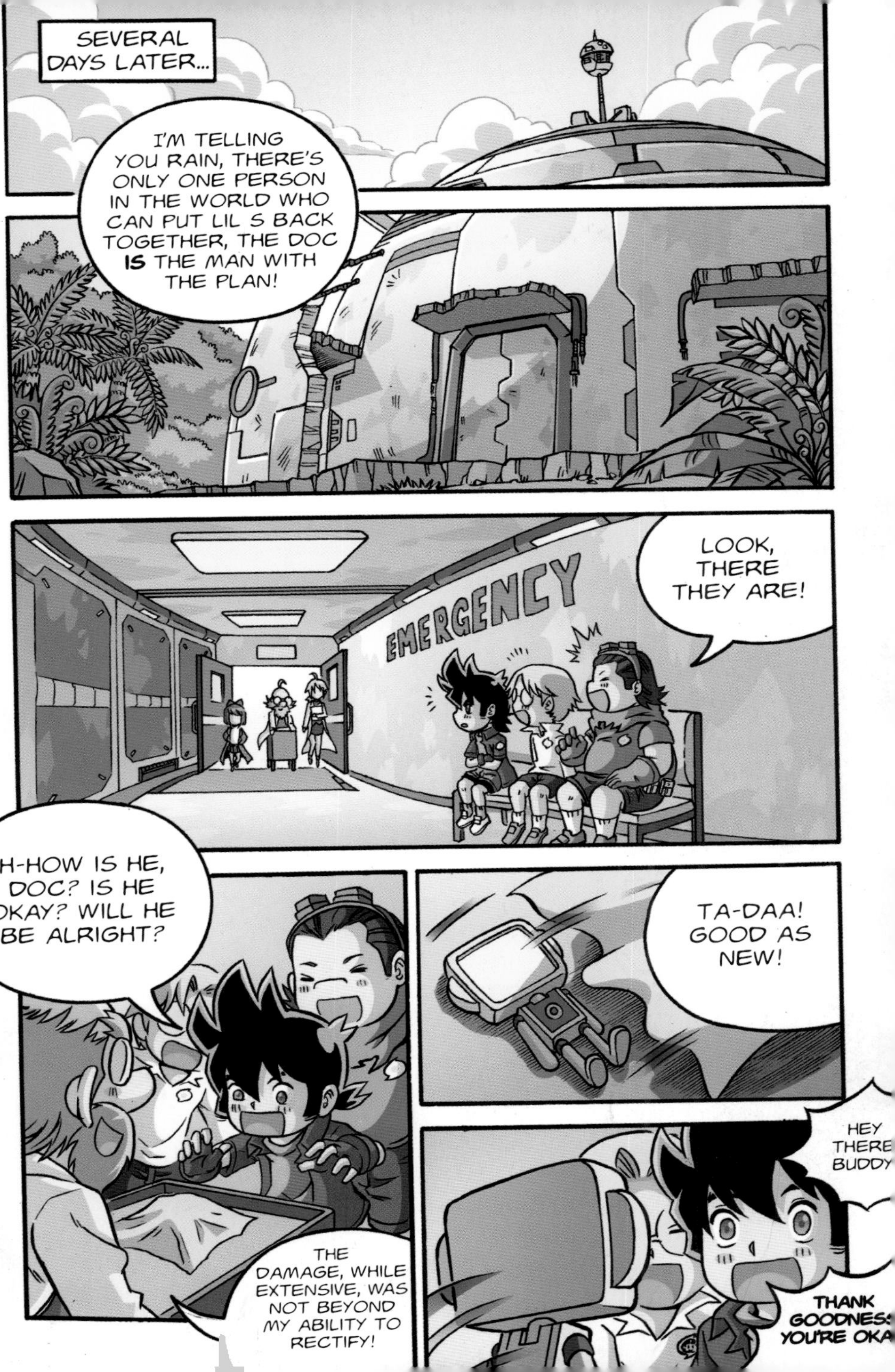

SEVERAL DAYS LATER...
I'M TELLING YOU RAIN, THERE'S ONLY ONE PERSON IN THE WORLD WHO CAN PUT LIL S BACK TOGETHER, THE DOC **IS** THE MAN WITH THE PLAN!
EMERGENCY
LOOK, THERE THEY ARE!
H-HOW IS HE, DOC? IS HE OKAY? WILL HE BE ALRIGHT?
THE DAMAGE, WHILE EXTENSIVE, WAS NOT BEYOND MY ABILITY TO RECTIFY!
TA-DAA! GOOD AS NEW!
HEY THERE BUDDY

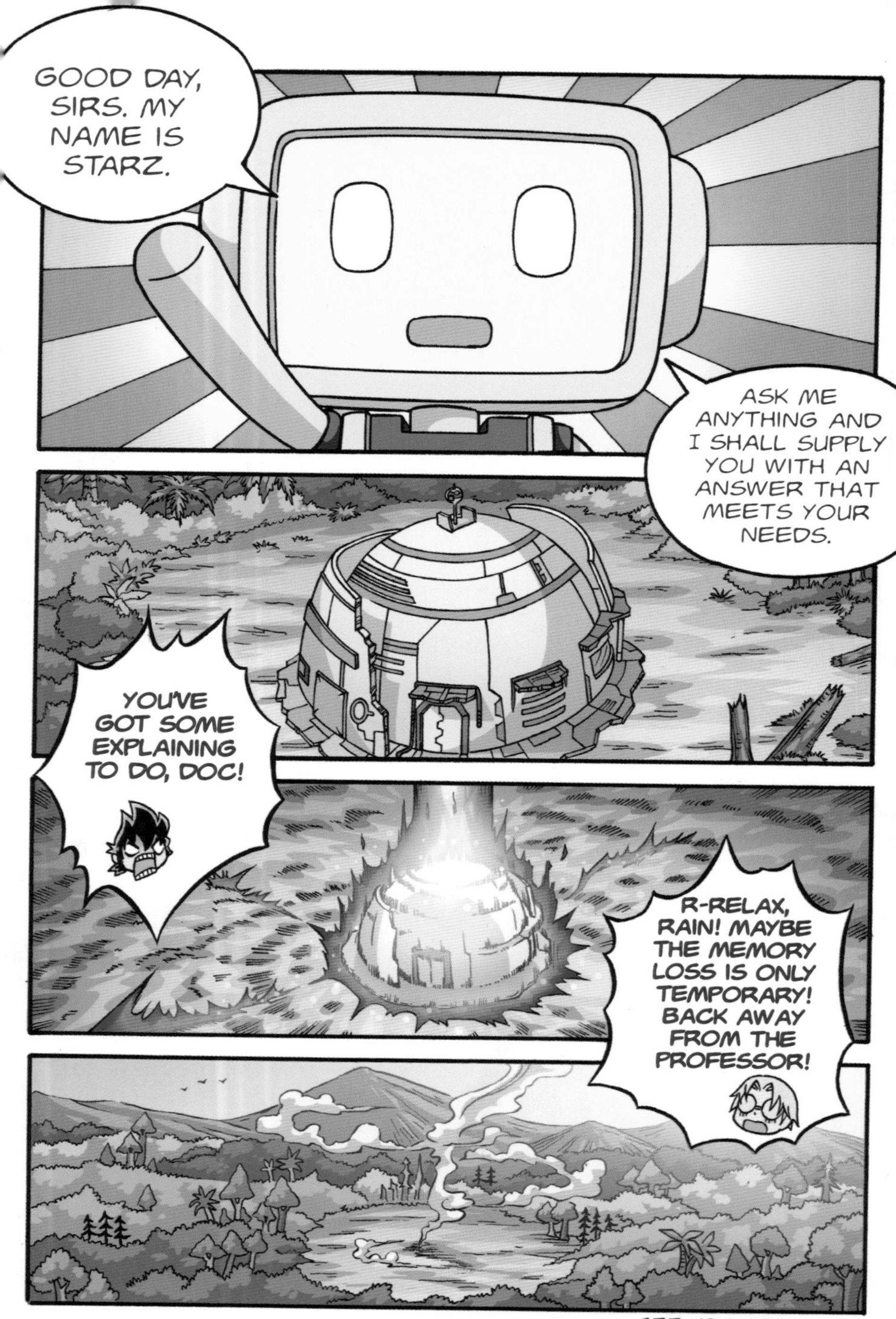
GOOD DAY, SIRS. MY NAME IS STARZ.
ASK ME ANYTHING AND I SHALL SUPPLY YOU WITH AN ANSWER THAT MEETS YOUR NEEDS.
YOU'VE GOT SOME EXPLAINING TO DO, DOC!
R-RELAX, RAIN! MAYBE THE MEMORY LOSS IS ONLY TEMPORARY! BACK AWAY FROM THE PROFESSOR!



SEE YOU NEXT TIME!

# CAPTURING THE CRETACEOUS!

## Carcharodontosaurus

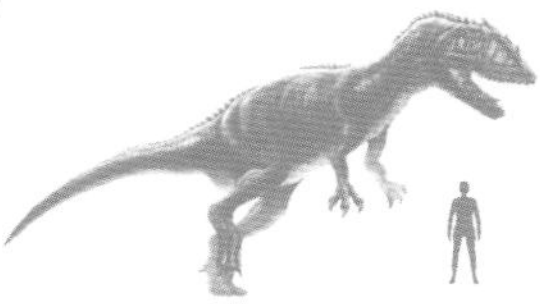

**Scientific name:** Carcharodontosaurus
**Size:** 46 feet
**Diet:** Carnivore
**Habitat:** Forests
**Discovered:** North Africa
**Period:** Mid-Cretaceous

Carcharodontosaurus was one of the largest predatory theropods ever, second only to Spinosaurus. Despite the fact it was larger than the T-Rex, its brain was only half the size. It was named after the shark genus Carcharodon, meaning "sharp/jagged teeth." It had the largest skull of any theropod, and its jaws housed serrated 8 inch teeth.

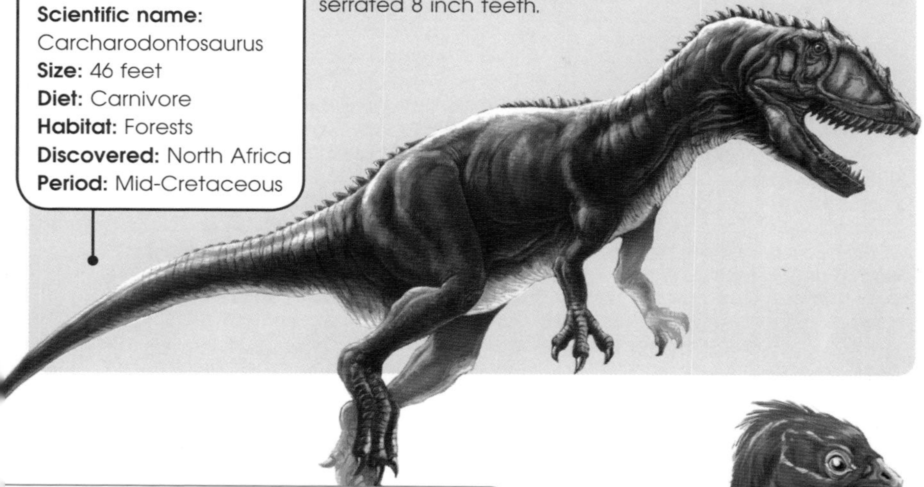

# CAPTURING THE CRETACEOUS!

## Mei

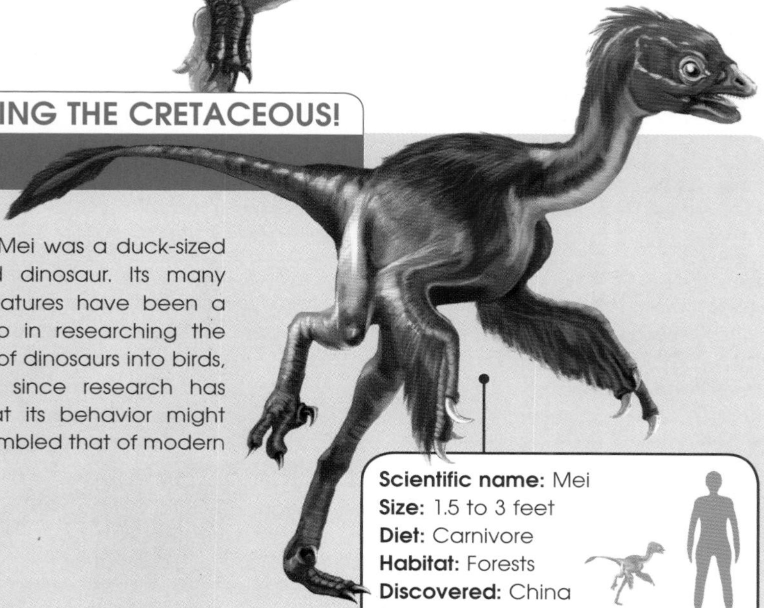

Miniscule Mei was a duck-sized troodontid dinosaur. Its many birdlike features have been a great help in researching the evolution of dinosaurs into birds, especially since research has found that its behavior might have resembled that of modern birds.

**Scientific name:** Mei
**Size:** 1.5 to 3 feet
**Diet:** Carnivore
**Habitat:** Forests
**Discovered:** China
**Period:** Early Cretaceous

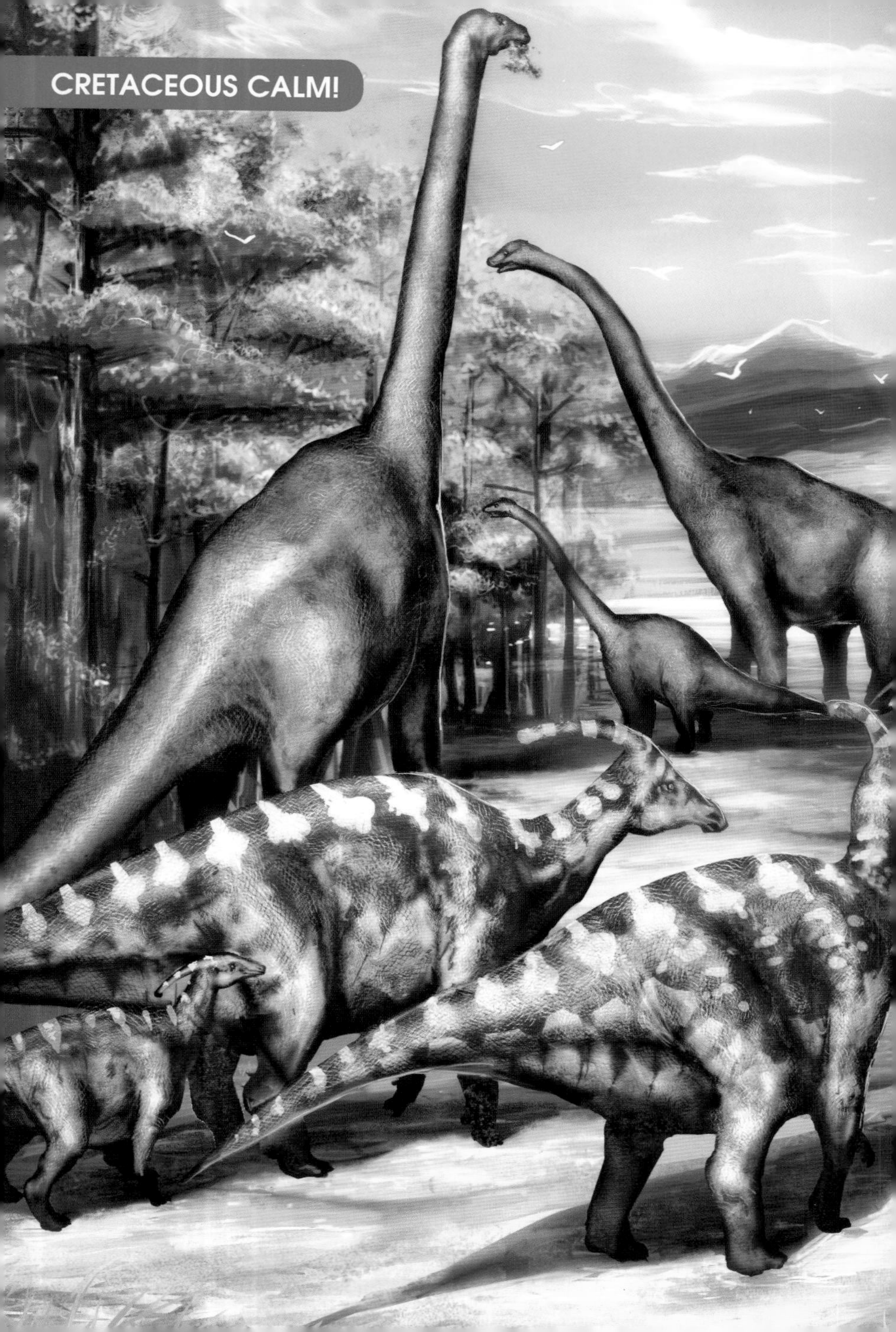
CRETACEOUS CALM!

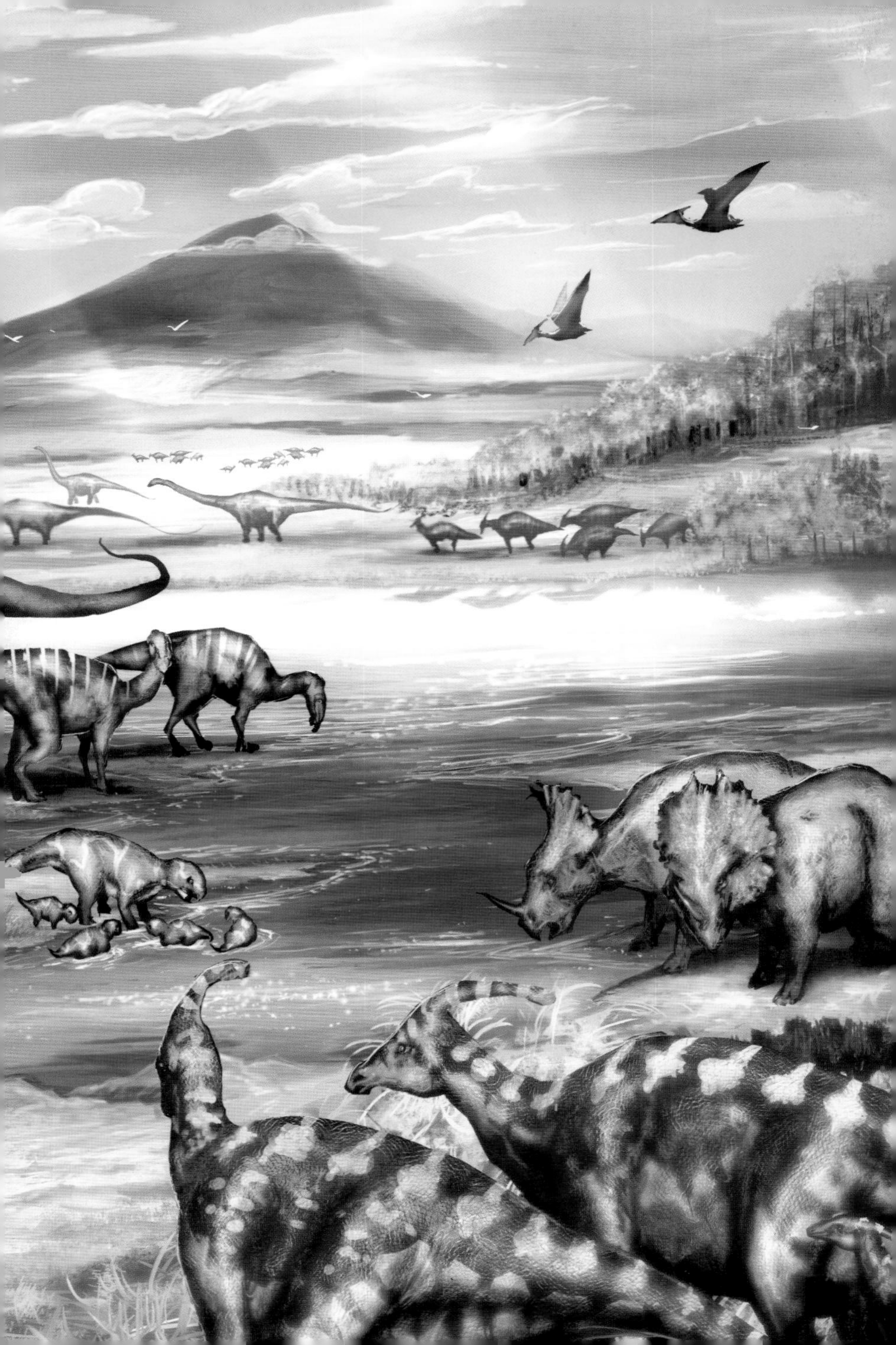

# WATCH OUT FOR PAPERCUTZ

Welcome to the shockingly suspenseful seventh DINOSAUR EXPLORERS graphic novel by Slaium and Albbie, writers, and Air Team, artists, from Papercutz, those Pandemic-avoiding people dedicated to publishing great graphic novels for all ages. I'm Jim Salicrup, Editor-in-Chief and mask-wearing survivor, here with some thoughts regarding DINOSAUR EXPLORERS and another Papercutz graphic novel that is sure to excite you...

In DINOSAUR EXPLORERS we follow Professor Da Vinci, Diana, Emily, Sean, Stone, Rain, and Starz as they interact with dinosaurs through the ages, having wild adventures that are based on the latest scientific knowledge regarding those awesome creatures. Papercutz has also recently published the premiere volume of series that is virtually the opposite of DINOSAUR EXPLORERS called THE MYTHICS. As the title implies, the series is based on mythology, not science. And although the lead characters are also modern kids, instead of having adventures back in the prehistoric past, they're having to confront great challenges that originated way back in the mythological past, right now in the present. In THE MYTHICS #1 "Heroes Reborn," we meet the modern-day ancestors of three ancient gods, who get handed down great powers. And we all know what happens when you get great powers, right? It all begins when...

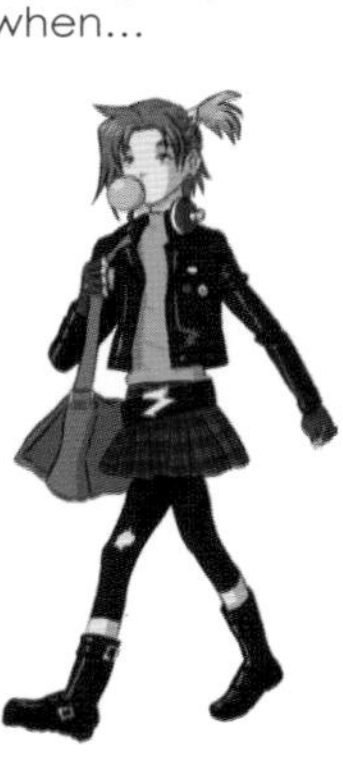

The god of lightning, Raijin, instills his powers in Yuko, a Japanese schoolgirl in a rock band. Yuko must learn to wield her newfound electrical powers to defeat Fuijin, the evil god of wind, before he destroys all of Japan.

Meanwhile, in Egypt, young Amir, a recently orphaned boy taking over his father's successful company and landholdings, encounters Horus, the Sun and Moon god. Horus and Amir must stop evil, in the form of Seth, from reanimating all the dead mummies and taking over the world.

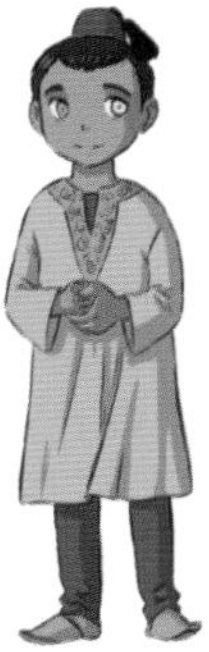

Lastly, a young opera hopeful, Abigail, must face a blizzard freezing all of Germany orchestrated by Loki, the evil god of mischief. Under the guidance of Freyja, the Norse god of beauty, Abigail must find her voice and her mythic weapon to stop evil in its tracks. And that's just the beginning, in THE MYTHICS #2 "Apocalypse Ahead," we'll meet three more ancestors of the old gods as they join the fight against ancient evil.

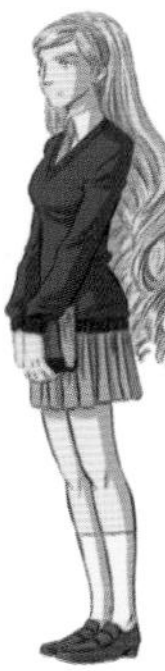

Meanwhile, we hope you enjoyed not only the Dinosaur Explorers' hair-raising adventure in this volume, but the fact-filled articles found between each chapter as well. And just to see if you're paying attention to all the dino-info in this volume, we have another little quiz for you on the following pages. Oh, and it's not like you're in school—you're allowed to look back into the book to find the answers. I'm sure I couldn't pass if I wasn't allowed to do that! And just to start you off, here's an easy P-Z (for Papercutz, of course!) question: What's coming soon that's sure to thrill, excite, and even educate you? Answer: DINOSAUR EXPLORERS #8 "The Lord of the Skies." You do not want to miss it!

Thanks,

Jim

**STAY IN TOUCH!**

EMAIL: salicrup@papercutz.com
WEB: www.papercutz.com
TWITTER: @papercutzgn
INSTAGRAM: @papercutzgn
FACEBOOK: PAPERCUTZGRAPHICNOVELS
FANMAIL: Papercutz, 160 Broadway, Suite 700, East Wing, New York, NY 10038

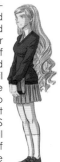

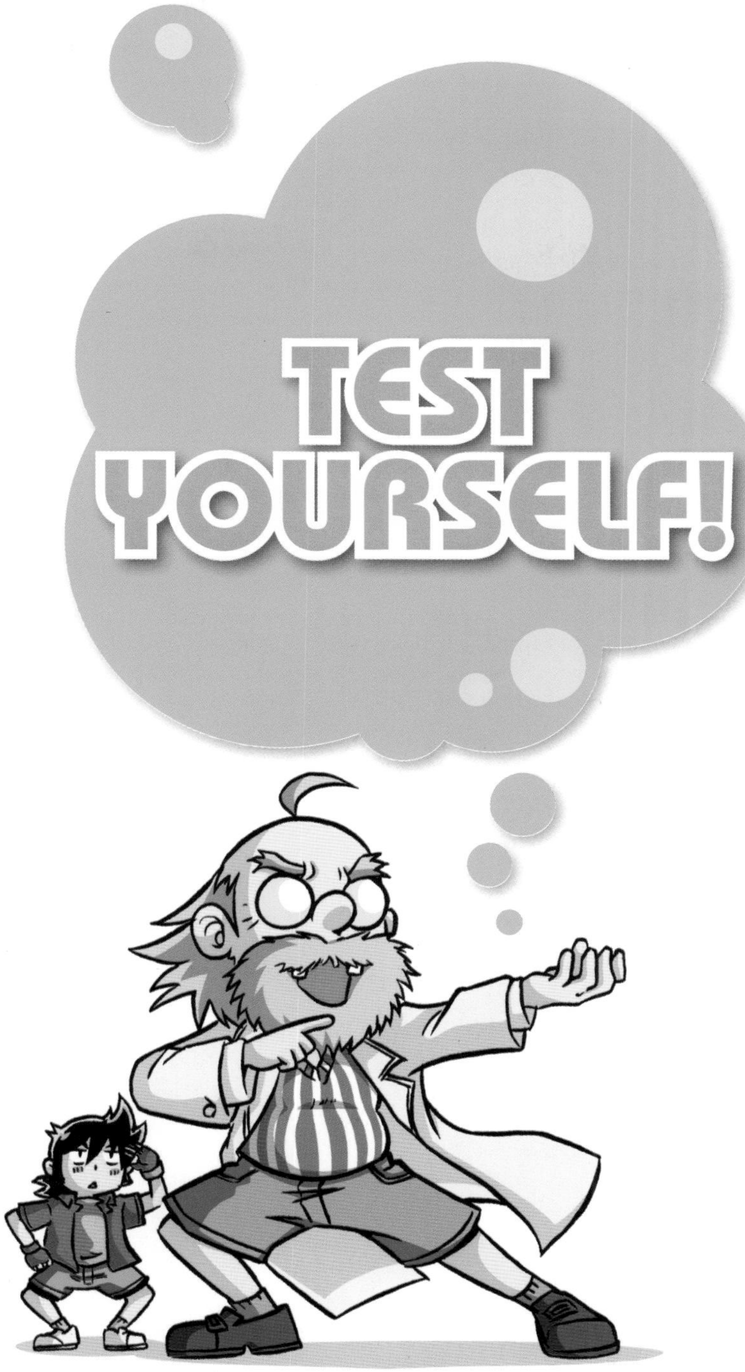
TEST YOURSELF!

# ABOUT THE CRETACEOUS...

**01** **What kind of dinosaur would have laid these eggs?**

**A** - Hadrosaurs

**B** - Maiasaurs

**C** - Small carnivores

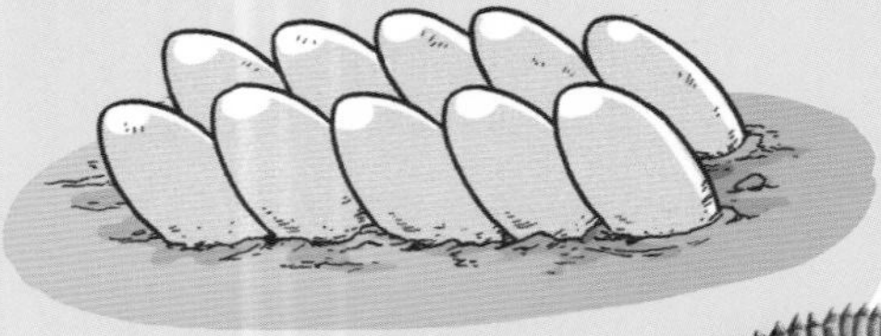

**02** **How long was the Cretaceous period?**

**A** - 50 to 60 million years

**B** - 60 to 70 million years

**C** - 70 to 80 million years

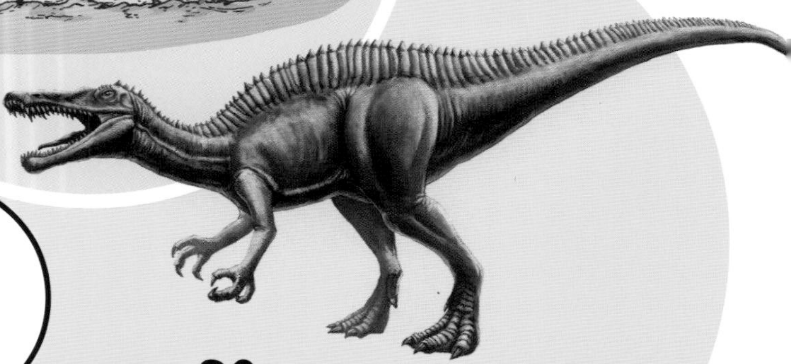

**03** **Where did this dinosaur live?**

**A** - Riverlands

**B** - Forests

**C** - Flatlands

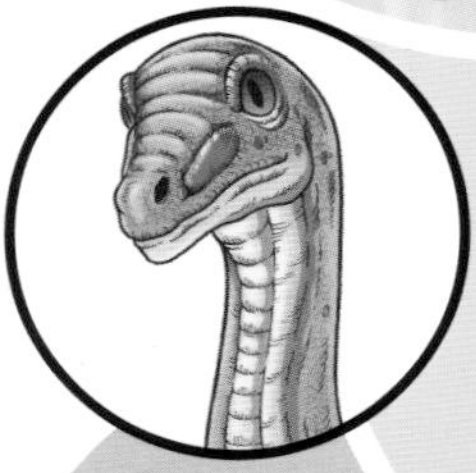

A Troodon

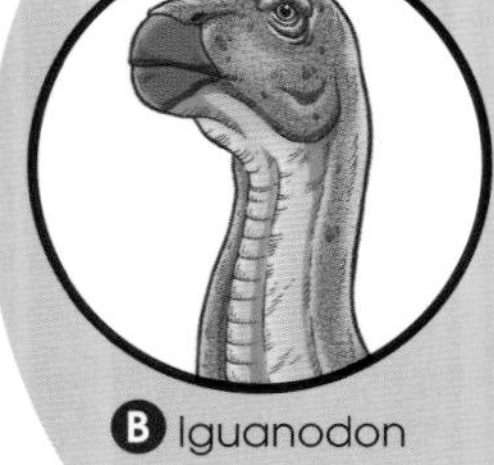

B Iguanodon

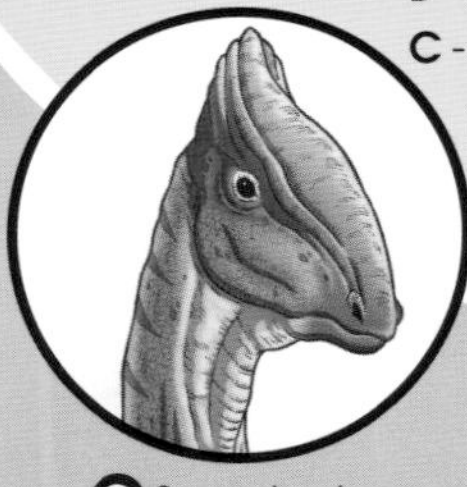

C Saurolophus

**04** **Which of these could amplify its voice?**

**05** **How did the Parasaurolophus create its weird sounds?**

**A** - Its head crest

**B** - Its skin

**C** - Its eyes

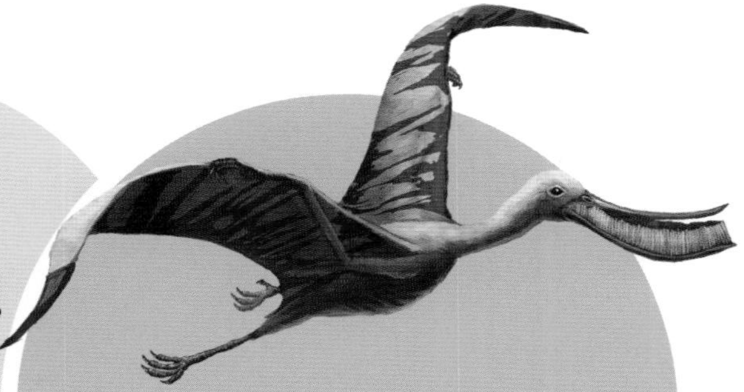

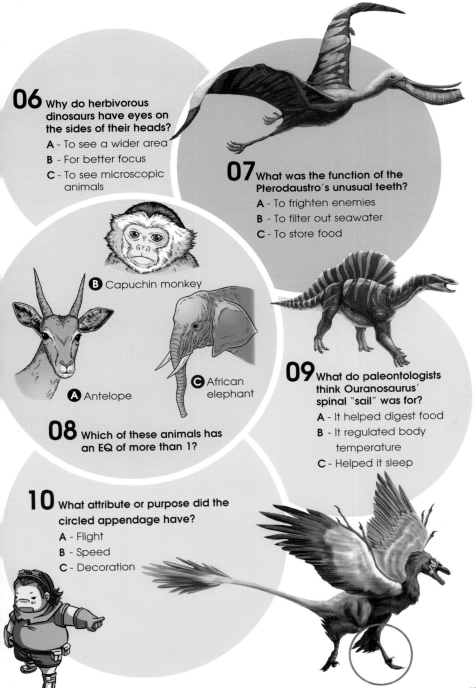

**06** **Why do herbivorous dinosaurs have eyes on the sides of their heads?**

**A** - To see a wider area

**B** - For better focus

**C** - To see microscopic animals

**07** **What was the function of the Pterodaustro's unusual teeth?**

**A** - To frighten enemies

**B** - To filter out seawater

**C** - To store food

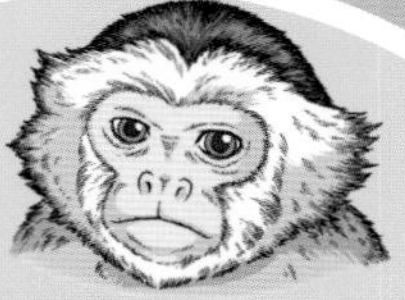

**B** Capuchin monkey

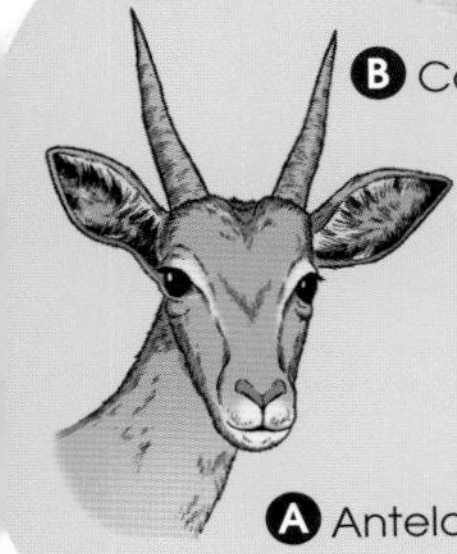

**A** Antelope

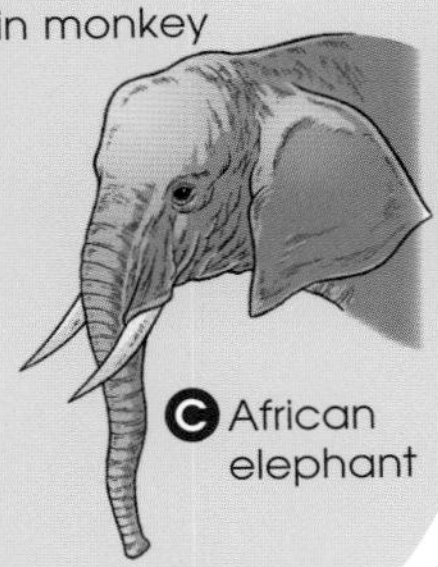

**C** African elephant

**08** **Which of these animals has an EQ of more than 1?**

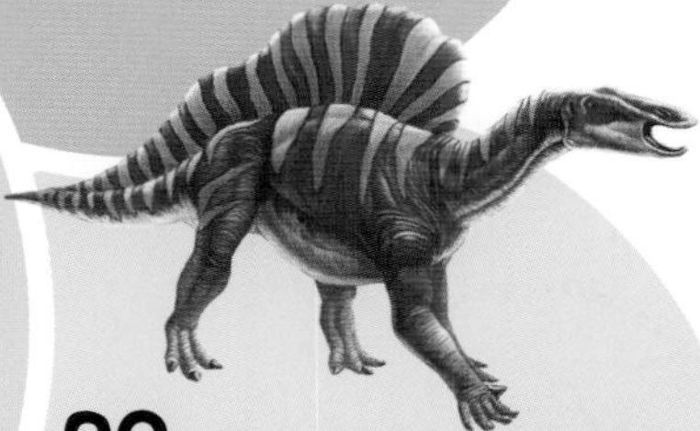

**09** **What do paleontologists think Ouranosaurus' spinal "sail" was for?**

**A** - It helped digest food

**B** - It regulated body temperature

**C** - Helped it sleep

**10** **What attribute or purpose did the circled appendage have?**

**A** - Flight

**B** - Speed

**C** - Decoration

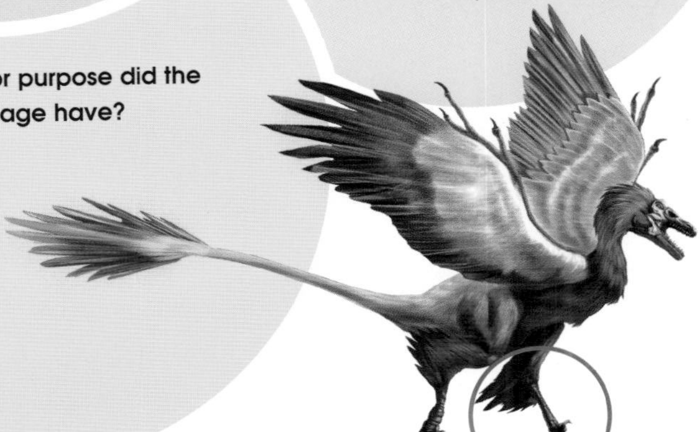

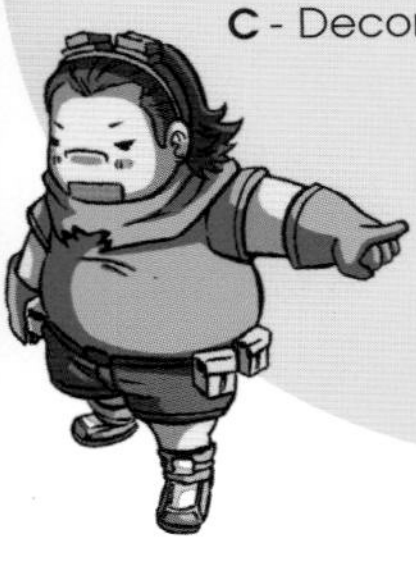

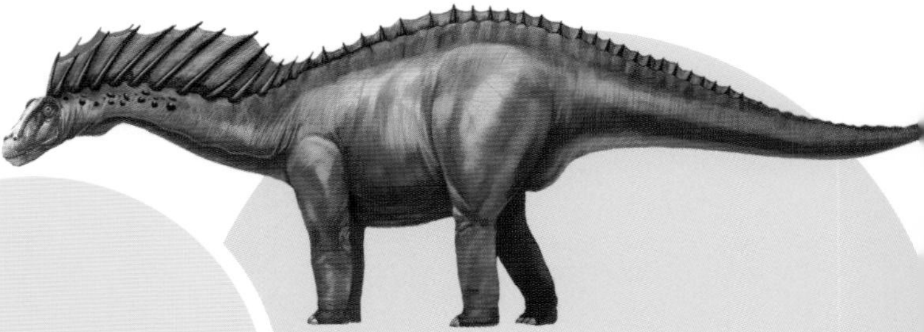

**11** **The T-Rex outdid the Carcharodontosaurus in one way – which one?**

**A** - Bigger body

**B** - Bigger brain

**C** - Bigger teeth

**12** **What is the name of the dinosaur above?**

**A** - Sordes

**B** - Muttaburrasaurus

**C** - Amargasaurus

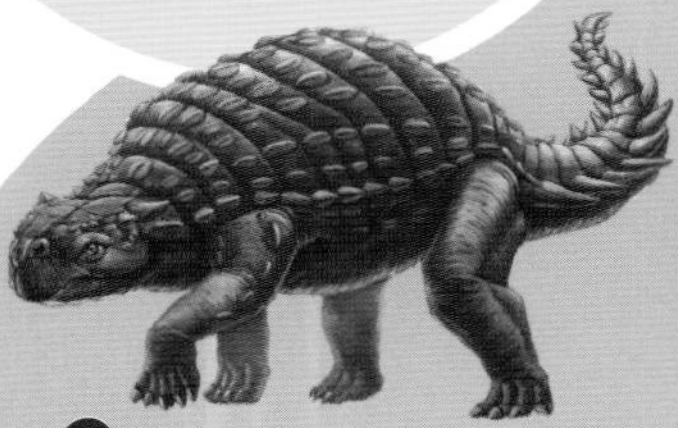

**A** Minmi

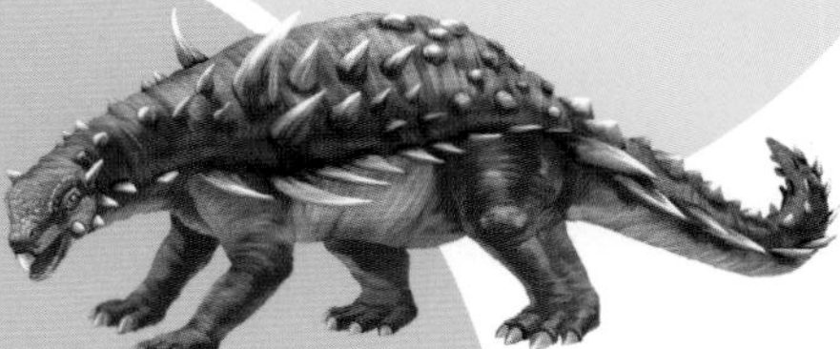

**B** Gastonia

**13** **Which of these was NOT a herbivore?**

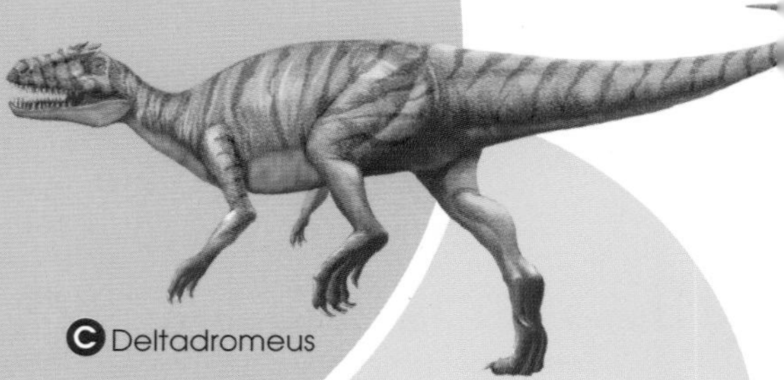

**C** Deltadromeus

**14** **Which of these helped Hypsilophodon to move rapidly?**

**A** - Short hip bone

**B** - Short tibia

**C** - Short tail

**15** **Which of these was a theropod that was even bigger than the T-Rex?**

**A** - Baryonyx

**B** - Deinonychus

**C** - Giganotosaurus

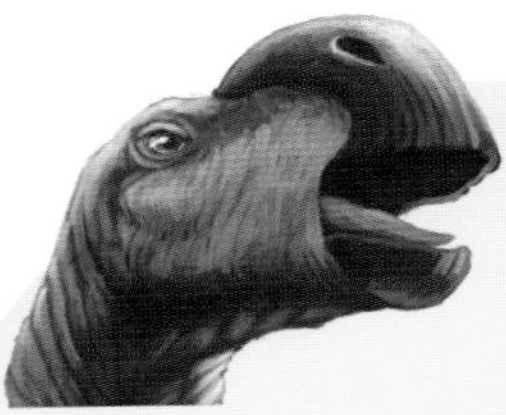

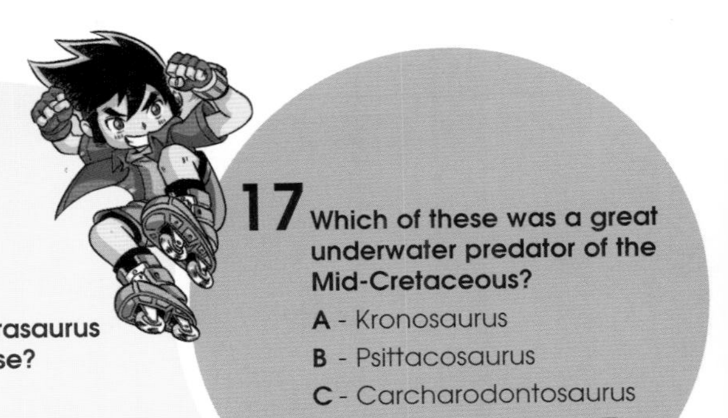

**16** **Why did the Muttaburrasaurus have such an odd nose?**

**A** - To help it smell

**B** - To make sounds to communicate and attract mates

**C** - To help it breathe

**17** **Which of these was a great underwater predator of the Mid-Cretaceous?**

**A** - Kronosaurus

**B** - Psittacosaurus

**C** - Carcharodontosaurus

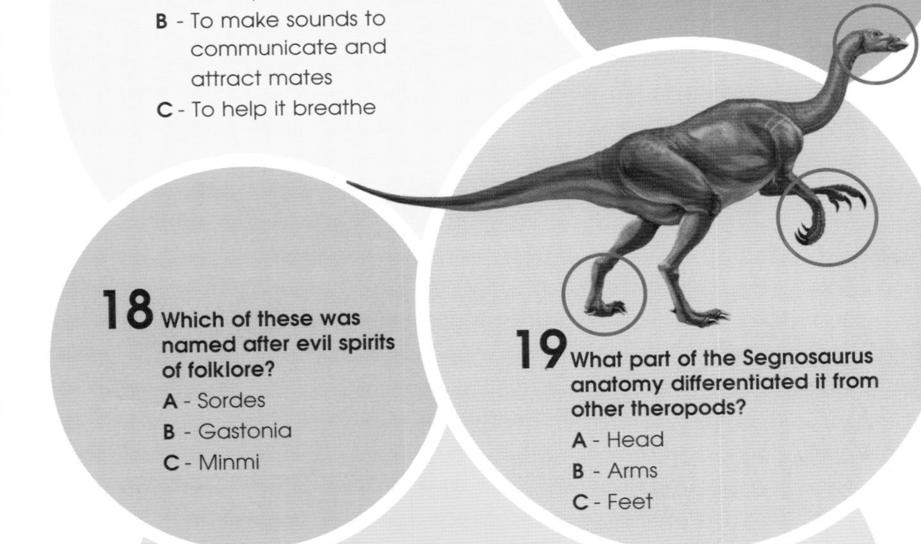

**18** **Which of these was named after evil spirits of folklore?**

**A** - Sordes

**B** - Gastonia

**C** - Minmi

**19** **What part of the Segnosaurus anatomy differentiated it from other theropods?**

**A** - Head

**B** - Arms

**C** - Feet

**B** Hylaeosaurus

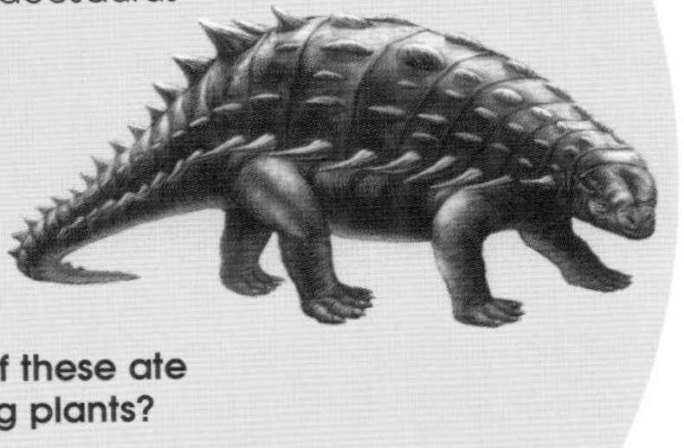

**A** Guanlong

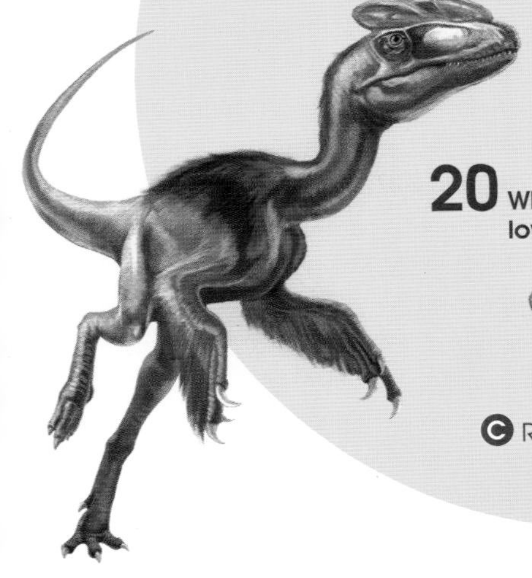

**20** **Which of these ate low-lying plants?**

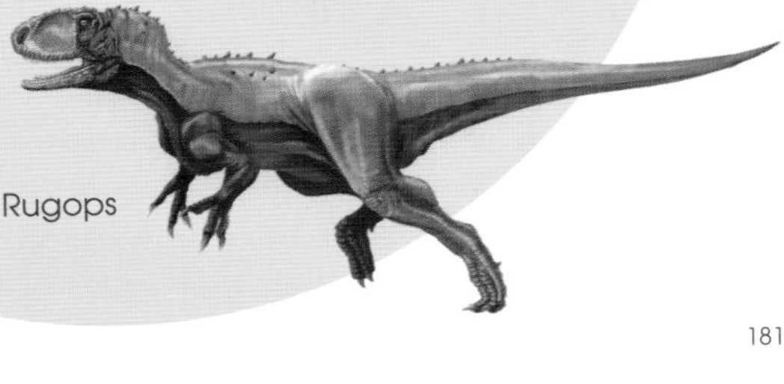

**C** Rugops

# ANSWERS

| | | | | |
|---|---|---|---|---|
| 01 C | 02 C | 03 A | 04 C | 05 A |
| 06 A | 07 B | 08 B | 09 B | 10 B |
| 11 B | 12 C | 13 C | 14 A | 15 C |
| 16 B | 17 A | 18 A | 19 C | 20 B |

**All correct?**
Congrats! You're as smart as I am! I think.

**16 – 19 correct?**
I'm actually smarter than the Doctor! Don't tell anyone!

**12 -15 correct?**
Don't just take in knowledge- apply it to real life!

**8 - 11 correct?**
What? You're smarter than me? Impossible!

**4 – 7 correct?**
Huh, looks like we both can use some work! Let's go to the library! Studying's better with friends!

**0 - 3 correct?**
Don't worry, you're as S-M-R-T smart as me!

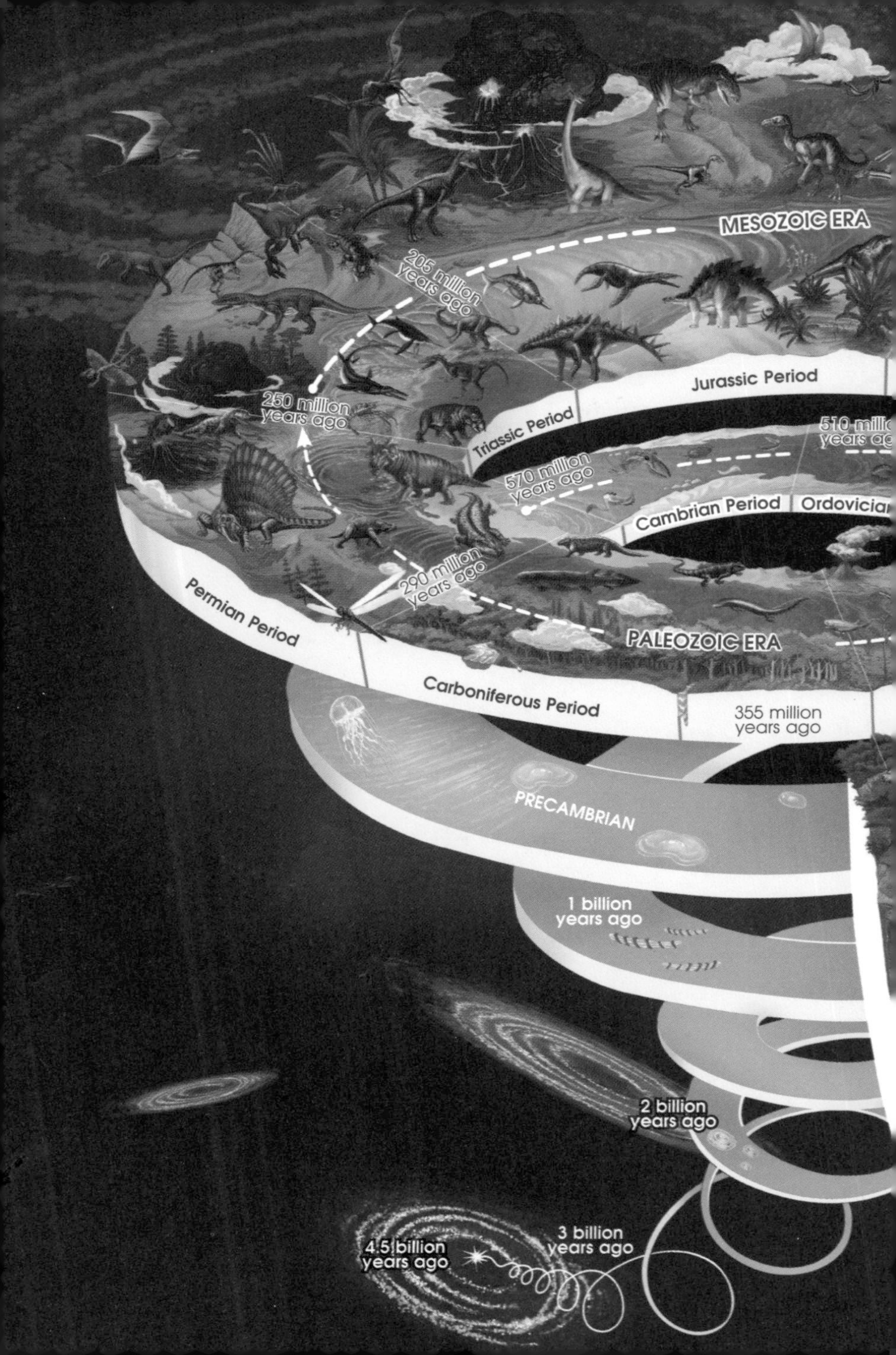
MESOZOIC ERA
205 million years ago
250 million years ago
Jurassic Period
Triassic Period
510 million years ago
570 million years ago
Cambrian Period
Ordovician
290 million years ago
Permian Period
PALEOZOIC ERA
Carboniferous Period
355 million years ago
PRECAMBRIAN
1 billion years ago
2 billion years ago
3 billion years ago
4.5 billion years ago